THE RIPPER WAS YOUNG

and the man was beautiful. There was a purity about the Ripper that was almost tangible, even though his image was blurred on the projection wall because the matrix didn't have the information to construct his true image.

A com-link rippled through the matrix. "Sir, you requested that I update you on the homicide department's latest suspect."

"Yes."

"He's not the man, sir."

"Do the police know this?"

"No, sir."

"Stay ahead of them. I believe Shay has something."

"Yes, sir." The com-link faded.

Crossing to the projection screen, he strove to reach through it and pull the Ripper into the room. He couldn't. Sparks of bright color flared. He rested his palms against the image. "I want you," he said in a hoarse voice. "And I WILL have you. . . . "

STALKER ANALOG

Mel Odom

A ROC BOOK

ROC
Published by the Penguin Group
Penguin Books USA Inc., 375 Hudson Street,
New York, New York 10014, U.S.A.
Penguin Books Ltd, 27 Wrights Lane,
London W8 5TZ, England
Penguin Books Australia Ltd, Ringwood,
Victoria, Australia
Penguin Books Canada Ltd, 10 Alcorn Avenue,
Toronto, Ontario, Canada M4V 3B2
Penguin Books (N.Z.) Ltd, 182-190 Wairau Road,
Auckland 10, New Zealand

Penguin Books Ltd, Registered Offices:
Harmondsworth, Middlesex, England

First published by Roc
an imprint of Dutton Signet,
a division of Penguin Books USA Inc.

First Printing, December, 1993
10 9 8 7 6 5 4 3 2 1

REGISTERED TRADEMARK—MARCA REGISTRADA

Printed in the United States of America

BOOKS ARE AVAILABLE AT QUANTITY DISCOUNTS WHEN USED TO PROMOTE PRODUCTS OR SERVICES. FOR INFORMATION PLEASE WRITE TO PREMIUM MARKETING DIVISION, PENGUIN BOOKS USA INC., 375 HUDSON STREET, NEW YORK, NEW YORK 10014.

For my mother, Imoneta Odom, who has always been there for me. She carried my dreams for me during those days I couldn't handle the weight.

Thanks, Mom.

ACKNOWLEDGMENTS

Picking up the pieces after a spouse leaves you is damn near impossible. There are a lot of people who stood by me during the times I didn't think I had legs, and who gave to me from their hearts when my own felt empty.

Feroze Mohammad and Cathy Haddad, who've always been more to me than editors and publishers, and who gave me not only my start, but my second wind as well.

Ethan Ellenberg, my agent, and a hell of a nice guy. Secret handshake and high sign, pal.

Joe Lansdale and Neal Barrett, Jr., brothers under the skin, who gave me advice and care straight from the heart of Texas, and who understand that country-boy mentality that still moves us.

Chris Schelling and Amy Stout, who helped me put this book into motion.

Nancy Berland and June Park, and the wonderful women of CORA who made me feel good about myself.

Marc Smith, private eye and good buddy, and the folks of ThunderCon and SoonerCon.

Pam Deck, a very special woman who taught me about Barney the Dinosaur. Her children, Carey, Kelly, and Tori. And sisters Tammy and Kim, who help make it all possible. "With a great big hug and a kiss from me to you."

My extended family: Maggie Ricks (who taught me everything I know about sex), Robert Lynn "Bob" MacDonald, Jack Roberts, Rick and Anne Means (parents of Eli and Jennie, and plumbers extraordinaire), Darrel Madden (Uncle Scummy), Keith and Karen Birdsong, Deborah Chester, and Sharon and Alan Burris (creator of the infamous pothole wizards).

As always in looking for a book title, I stumbled. Keith Birdsong, who did the fantastic cover, suggested *Necrobytes*. However, I believe Deborah Chester topped him with *Fried Green Circuits*.

To all of you I've named, and the ones that I forgot, I'm still standing because you believed in me. It don't get no better than that.

1

Bethany Shay pulled her seat belt tighter as the unmarked sedan slewed around the corner, slid off San Jacinto Street onto Isabella, and sped southeast. She thumbed the transmit button on the handset. "Dispatch, be advised that Blue Light Three is en route."

"Affirmative, Blue Light Three. Dispatch is advised," the male voice responded. "Do you need details?"

"Negative, Dispatch. We logged the squeal as it aired." Shay hung up the mike, dropped a hand into her windbreaker pocket, and found the rubber bands she kept there. She bound her shoulder-length auburn hair back, then tucked it inside the collar of the windbreaker. Maintaining her hold on the dashboard, she loosened the strap of the Glock 20 automatic riding high on her right hip.

"Two minutes, kid," her partner said, "and we'll be on top of it."

She was thirty-two years old and had ten active years in on the Houston Police Department. Detective Sergeant Tully Keever was the only officer who called her "kid." She wouldn't have let anyone else get away with it.

Reaching into the glove compartment, she took out the magnetic cherry and turned it on, rolled down her window, and slammed it onto the sedan's roof. The keening whine of the siren sliced along the battered sides of the street and echoed in the alleys.

To the northeast the Himeji Twins stood wreathed in the cloudy night where the old Rice Motel had once been. The buildings soared 121 stories tall, made of steel and glass and American labor paid in Japanese yen. It had been the last bit of big American construction done in Houston since Japanese businesses immigrated to Texas after Tokyo died in the big quake eight years ago.

Neon lights flickered up the sides of the buildings in golds and greens and reds and blues, carried product advertisements in English and Japanese and flashed product symbols that had become a language unto themselves. The flesh-and-blood workers might be gone from the Twins now that their twelve-hour day was finished, but the soul of advertising and selling lived on in neon tubing.

An old Mitsubishi van stuttered to a halt in front of the unmarked car. Keever didn't let off the accelerator. He pulled the steering wheel to the right, narrowly avoided one of the many unlighted streetlamps as the car jumped up onto the sidewalk, then pulled back onto the street. The sedan fishtailed, pinned a motorcycle in its lights for a moment, then slid back under Keever's smooth control. The oncoming traffic hurriedly pulled out of the way.

"Got to get their attention first," Keever said with a tight grin. "Then you get their respect." The roar of the engine grew louder.

"Yeah," Shay said. She let out a breath she hadn't known she was holding.

A bag lady of indeterminate age trundled her worldly possessions across the street in a wobbling wire shopping cart.

The pallid oval of a face slid by Shay's window only inches away. She had a momentary impression of black holes that were the thing's eyes, and the thumbtack-sized silver deckjacks at its temples.

"Christ," Keever said as he yanked the wheel hard left and skidded them out onto Ennis. "Fuckin' zoner. Didn't even see the son of a bitch till he was at my bumper."

"You missed him." A chill breathed down the back of Shay's neck. Although she was cybernetically augmented herself, zoners touched a primeval fear inside her. What they did to themselves was illegal, but by the time they were discovered, it was too late to help them. There was no rehabilitation from the endless loops of fantasies they programmed inside their own brains. Any contact with reality was sketchy for a zoner at best. They forgot things as the fantasies became the centerpiece of their lives, then filled it. Forgetting to keep jobs and pay rent put them out on the street. Forgetting to eat and find shelter when winter claimed the city made them prey for gypsy organ jackals looking to make a quick buck off parts too many hospitals wouldn't ask questions about. What was left afterward was burned in the municipal crematoriums.

"Poor bastard would have been better off if I'd hit him," Keever said.

Shay stared through the rainbow of neon cascading off the windshield. When she squinted, she could just make out the line of police cars blocking Palmer Street.

Keever applied the brake and killed the siren.

Accessing DataMain via the com-chip hardwired into her brain, Shay checked the time. It was 3:47 A.M. "Palmer's a dead end."

"Doesn't give the Scivally brothers much room, does it?" Keever stopped the car less than a yard from the rearmost police cruiser, then got out.

Hand on her weapon, Shay moved out on her side as well. She nudged the com-chip, slid it into the tach frequency they'd agreed to use, and listened to the ripple of men's voices fill her head.

"Moody!" Keever yelled through his cupped hands.

Six heads snapped around as the police officers squatted behind the open doors of their cars looked for him. The stream of conversation on the Tach frequency died.

Shay identified Moody by the officer's close-shorn gray hair. The sergeant held down a gunner's position at the driver's side of the vehicle fronting the triangle of cruisers. The whirling cherries colored his blunt features in alternating waves of red and blue. The other men looked young, the way night shift uniforms usually were. She remembered being one of them, and knew that tonight's action was probably the first for some of them.

"Here," Moody yelled back.

"Back with me," Keever ordered.

Moody fell back, hunkered down as he carried the Remington 870 pump in the ready position.

Shay scanned the neighborhood. A line of single-story houses were barely discernible in the darkness. Lights were on in a few of them. More winked into existence, creating yellow rectangles against windowshades, as sluggish home AIs responded to threatened security perimeters. Trees and underbrush broke up concrete squares and ribbons. The Fourth Ward was a combat zone where citizens fought outsiders and each other for survival.

"Goddammit," Moody said harshly as he squatted down behind Keever, "I told Dispatch we could handle this ourselves. You didn't need to be out here."

"And I distinctly remember giving the watch sergeant hard copy regarding Aaron Scivally and his crew," Keever growled back. A few inches over six feet, the big detective looked like he was built from railroad ties and held together with barbed wire. He wore glasses, too old-fashioned to go in for the microsurgery that could have corrected his vision. His mustache, dark brown with touches of gray like his hair, was a scraggly line over his hard mouth.

"Yes sir," Moody said. "But we don't know that this has anything to do with the Scivallys."

"Bullshit." Keever invaded Moody's personal space, made the other man flinch and lean back. "There have been two calls logged through nine-one-one identifying Aaron or Larry Scivally since this whole thing went down."

"Civilians," Moody sneered. But the expression didn't come off right. "The play wallscreens have been giving the Scivallys, it's a wonder people aren't seeing them in their closets and under their beds."

Reading the hostility in her partner's posture, Shay twisted slightly, readying herself for any move Keever might choose to make. Moody's street reputation wasn't all clean anymore. It hadn't been for years. Tonight she had to wonder how deep the tarnish ran, whether there was any metal left in his shield.

"You lyin' chickenshit bastard," Keever growled in a low voice that didn't reach any ears beyond Shay's.

"Fuck you," Moody said in an equally low voice. "I don't have to take any of this crap." He started to stand.

Keever knotted a big hand in the uniformed officer's shirt and dragged him back down. When Moody tried to buttstroke him with the shotgun, Keever slammed him into the side of the unmarked sedan.

Shay thumbed the safety off her pistol and ignored the flutter of nervous anticipation that tightened her stomach. The metallic click froze Moody in place with his hand inches from his sidearm. "No," she said in a cold voice. Her left hand rested lightly under her right. The muzzle settled without a waver directly between Moody's eyes.

2

"You fucking assholes don't know what you're doing," Moody said harshly. But his hand lifted from the holstered pistol.

Keever took the weapon from the man and kicked the Remington away. "You're under arrest. Stand up."

"For what?" Moody demanded. He didn't try to stand.

Whirling the man around and bringing him to his feet, Keever bounced Moody off the side of the sedan. "Keep him covered, Beth."

Shay nodded as she came to her feet and stayed well in the clear for her shot if necessary. Perspiration filmed her hands and the back of her neck despite the residual chill hanging in the night.

Metal grated when Keever snapped the cuffs on Moody's wrists. Arms behind his back, Moody was shoved into the rear of the sedan. The sergeant struggled to a sitting position, then batted his head angrily against the wire mesh separating the backseat from the front.

Turning, his .475 Wildey Magnum in his hand beside his leg, Keever addressed the astonished officers watching him. "Michaelmann."

"Yes sir."

Shay identified the man as Moody's partner.

"Internal affairs is going to be interested in talking to your buddy. You see any reason why they should want to talk to you?"

Michaelmann's face paled. "No sir."

"We still have a job to do."

"Yes sir."

"Then get your asses over here," Keever said, "and let's get it done."

The five men came slowly, then hunkered down around

the hood of the unmarked car as Keever spread a street map out. He weighted it down with the .475 Wildey.

Keeping her weapon out, Shay covered her partner's back and managed to scan the street map at the same time. Dirty cops weren't the rule, but with the money flowing through the streets from domestic crime and the new wave brought in with the Japanese Yakuza, the exceptions weren't as few as they used to be.

"I think the Scivallys' wrecking crew is in there," Keever said. "We've been blanketing the news and the crime shows with intel about these people for weeks. I'm ready to buy a civilian report at this point."

"What would interest the Scivallys about this area?" one of the young officers asked. "Everything I've seen on them or their people suggests that they're only after institutions. Banks, savings and loans, armored cars, and malls. That sort of thing."

"Sergeant Moody's been taking protection money from a gambling operation located here." Keever tapped the map with a forefinger. "Word on the street is that this place is turning over a million dollars every night they open for business. And tonight's one of the nights."

Two of the uniforms glanced at Shay. She kept her face impassive, not letting on that she hadn't known about the setup either.

Keever dropped a folded piece of paper on top of the map, then smoothed it out. It was crudely drawn, but details were clear. "Used to be a warehouse," the big detective said, glancing at the assembled men over his glasses. "Five, six years ago, Terrence Scroggins opened up shop running numbers and making a book."

"That long ago?" an officer asked. "Christ, you'd think we'd have been up on it before now."

"It was kept quiet," Keever said. "At first. A nice solid little operation that could generate a dependable income. About a year ago, Scroggins got greedy. Put in craps tables, blackjack dealers, a wheel, and some slots. Instead of playing monies through electronic accounts at the banks, he started going after the physical cash from the streets too. Dollars, yen. His people are set up to take it all." He tapped the penciled map. "Entrances and exits are here, here, here, here, and here. Bars cover the windows. There are hard guys, stunscreens, and tanglers on every door. Including the emergency exit on the second story. The whole system's ramrodded by an outlaw AI programmed to kill if necessary."

"Sounds like a goddam fortress."

"It is. Make no doubts about it. You do, you're dead."

"When did you get this information?" Michaelmann asked suspiciously.

Keever glanced at the man, features neutral. "Today."

Michaelmann shifted uncomfortably. "That's an awful lot of information to get at one time."

Keever nodded. "Amazing, isn't it?"

"How do you plan on getting through the AI's defenses?" another uniform asked.

"If the Scivallys are in the area," Keever said, "I'm betting they'll do it for us. Otherwise, we got no reason to go inside."

"Yes sir."

Keever took up his pistol, refolded the map and the paper, and tucked them inside the sedan. Moody was still and silent in the rear seat. "Rosemont, you're in charge of our prisoner here, and you're coordinating the mobile operations people when they arrive. Orders will be coming from myself or Detective Shay. Understood?"

"Yes sir."

"Pair up," Keever ordered. "Michaelmann, you're with me."

Shay started to object, then locked eyes with Keever and didn't. However it went down in the long run, the big man was determined to have it his way. She gave him a small, tight nod. Searching the three men left, she chose an officer named Deke Bonner. She was vaguely familiar with him. Young, black, and athletically built, Bonner had a reputation as a straight shooter who was cool under pressure.

Sheathing her sidearm, Shay reached under the sedan's seat, rolled out the sliding rack, and took a CAR-15 from it. Specially modified to fire silenced three-round bursts, it would almost put her on a par with the weapons the Scivallys were known to carry. Bonner returned to his squad car for a moment and came back with a SPAS 15 combat shotgun.

After checking the assault rifle's action, Shay retreated to the trunk of the sedan. She keyed it open with her thumbprint, then took out a Kevlar bulletproof vest and jammed six ammunition magazines into the pockets.

Keever shrugged into the other vest, then got out extra shells for the Mossberg military model 12-gauge shotgun he held. He winked at her when he closed the trunk.

Shay wiped her hands on her jeans-covered thighs and moved back toward Bonner. Her heart was pounding now. She could feel it. No matter how many times she'd found herself in situations like this, the effect was always the same. A familiar dryness touched the back of her throat. She pulled on a pair of fingerless black gloves from her back pocket. The com-chip brushed feathery soft inside her head when it was activated.

"Move out," Keever ordered. "Keep it tight once you get in close. If the Scivallys haven't taken over at this point and set out guards of their own, the casino people will have them. Don't hesitate to shoot first if it looks like they're going to make a play."

Shay took the lead, immediately dropped into the shadows surrounding the houses. The CAR-15 felt heavy and reassuring in her arms. Bonner was almost silent at her heels.

They crossed an open alley between houses, eased into the backyard of a vacant house, and skirted a rusting swingset that had chains but no seats. Despite the April chill still hanging in the air, a light mask of perspiration covered Shay's face. Accessing the com-chip, she buzzed Keever, then switched freqs to their private partnered line.

Keever joined her there a heartbeat later. "Yeah?"

"So give."

His laughter rang quietly inside her head. "I found out about Scroggins's operation a few weeks ago. Found out about Moody's connection to it at the same time. If I worked it through channels at the PD, I figured there'd be no case when we made the bust. Got me to thinking."

Shay pushed through brush, muttered a curse as the leaves scratched her cheek, then led the trot across a backyard. Dark shadows to her right caught her attention. It took a moment to make out the drainage ditch that ran behind the fenceline. She put a hand on the fence and vaulted over. Bonner followed.

"The kind of money the casino was pulling in," Keever went on, "I knew it would be something the Scivallys would be interested in."

"You *knew* they found out about it," Shay transmitted back. She talked low enough that the internal mike could pick it up without Bonner overhearing.

Keever didn't hesitate. "Yeah. Couldn't take Moody and Scroggins without internal affairs being involved, and couldn't get a line on the Scivallys. Figured maybe we could bag two birds with one stone tonight. One of the anonymous people that called nine-one-one tonight was a snitch I leaned on to watch the casino for the past few weeks. He called me first."

"You could have told me."

"Like hell, kid. There's times you still try to play too hard by the rules. I didn't have the time to sell you on a wild-card call like this."

The incline leading into the drainage ditch was steep and slick from the morning dew. Shay didn't try to remain on her feet. She dropped onto her side and slid down. Her tennis shoes crunched into the semifrozen rocky mud. Confident that she and Bonner couldn't be skylined now, she picked up the pace.

Shay's com-chip beeped for attention. She and Keever flickered out of their private circuit, dropped back into the tach freq. A pile of fallen brush and tree limbs blocked the ditch. Leaning into the incline, Shay took the vertical at a dead run, gained enough distance to clear the blockage, then let gravity pull her back on an even keel.

Bonner hadn't been quite as graceful. He'd caught a foot in a forked limb and came spilling down. He was on his feet in seconds.

Rosemont's voice came in clear and clean over the com-chip linkage. "I reached Dispatch, Detective Keever. They've got a MOP headed this way."

"What's the ETA?" Keever asked.

"Fifteen, twenty minutes."

"Unless something breaks out," Keever said, "I want them rolling silent on this. I'm guessing nobody's made the squad cars you have bunched up there yet."

"That's going to add time to their arrival."

"I know. Get it done."

"Yes sir." Rosemont rippled out of the circuitry.

Counting off the last house, she dug in her feet and pushed herself up the incline. Her breath came more rapidly now, burned her throat. Even with the spring chill surrounding her, the dark sweatshirt she wore under her windbreaker was damp. Her bra strap cut into her back and chafed.

At the top of the incline she lay down. Bonner fell in beside her, his breathing heavier than hers.

"Damn, you in some kind of shape, lady," the man said.

"I like to run," Shay said. "Keeps me from being built like one of those patrol-car seats."

Bonner nodded and continued wheezing.

The back door of the warehouse was less than fifty yards away. It stood two stories tall under a dark canopy of shadow-drenched trees. The windows must have had blackout film over them. Shay knew the people's vision inside wouldn't be hampered. Although it didn't look like it to the unprofessional eye, the grounds behind the warehouse had been chopped down to give a clear field of fire. The building itself was rectangular, ran two hundred feet back from Palmer's circular dead end, then a hundred feet across. There were no exterior signs or advertisements about what the warehouse had once been in the business of doing legitimately. An eight-foot fence topped with barbed-wire strands done in matte black enclosed the structure, left small parking areas on both sides and behind it. Less than a dozen vehicles were inside the fence.

Accessing her com-chip, Shay asked, "Where are the cars that belong to the casino guests?"

"Different places," Keever responded. "Scroggins has the players bused in at staggered times."

"No way we can tell how many people are inside?"

"I was told around a hundred most nights."

"We're moving in," Shay transmitted.

Keever hesitated. "You watch your ass, you hear me?"

"Roger." Screwing up her courage, Shay got to her feet and stayed low as she closed on the fence. The CAR-15 was tight in her fists. At the metal door with Bonner covering her, she slung the rifle over her shoulder, then slipped an electromagnetic lockpick kit free of her ankle. There were some rules she found easier to break than others, especially if her survival or the survival of another officer was at stake.

She accessed her com-chip, half-closed her eyes, and read the combination of tumblers from the neural maze that blossomed into life in her mind when she activated the L-mag picks. The lock clicked open in seconds. Well-oiled hinges let the door open silently.

Taking up the CAR-15 again, she ran across the intervening space to the rear of the warehouse. Rickety wooden steps led up to the back door. Once Bonner was in place beside her, she slipped her shield out, hung it from her belt where it would be visible, and went up the stairs.

The back door was partly open. Harsh voices echoed inside. Orders were being given. There was no response. The smells of cigarettes, reefer, and red satin coasted out on a rolling breeze of warm air that skimmed over Shay's face. Someone started to say something, then a shouted command overrode the voice. The light issuing from inside was pale fluorescence.

Shay accessed the com-chip. "They're inside."

"The Scivallys?" Keever asked.

"Yeah."

"The situation?"

"Seems to be under their control." Shay held her position at the door. Sliding her foot forward, she inched the toe of her tennis shoe inside. The door moved easily. She forcibly relaxed her grip on the rifle.

Unbidden, memories of the violence the Scivallys were capable of whispered through her mind. Seventeen people had died under the Scivally guns in the last eight months. They'd started out as robbery's problem, became homicide's project after they killed three people during a bank robbery in Pasadena, Texas, in late August.

The hollow pop of a large-caliber pistol launched a wave of screams. More shots followed.

Accessing the com-chip, Shay said, "You've got shots fired inside, Tully. Bonner and I are going in."

"Keep your head low. I'll be there soon as I can."

Maintaining the com-chip connection, Shay checked the time. It was 4:05 A.M. Eighteen minutes into the call and everything had already slid out of control. Her stomach turned sour, but she moved inside the door anyway. A rectangle of pale light framed another doorway ten feet farther on. Darkness covered the lobby.

Without warning, a hand dropped over Shay's wrist and closed in a warm, wet grip.

3

Almendariz studied her from his bus seat without letting her know he was looking.

The woman was plain, young yet looked old and faded. Short dishwater-blond hair showed traces of two different color rinses. Makeup would have helped cover the acne scars that tracked across her cheeks and the bridge of her nose, but she wore a too-dark rouge that only drew attention to them. Her arms were wrapped protectively around a small bag of groceries. The twisted neck of a bread loaf poked past the rim of the brown sack.

A tremor of disgust raced through Almendariz when he turned from watching her. He pulled his coat tighter around him. God, if it had to be anybody, why did it have to be this pathetic creature? What was it about her that could have ever have caught his unguarded attention? But then he had asked himself that about the other two as well. He had no answers.

Fear quickly followed the disgust.

He put the questions out of his mind. He knew what he had to do, and knew where he was going to do it.

"Hey, whitebread," the black man to Almendariz's left said in a rasping voice. "You ain't sick, are you?"

"No." Almendariz was shocked at the quaver in his voice. Usually it was so strong.

"Man, you over there shakin' and shit. Gives me the willies just lookin' at you." The man's ebony features pinched up as he studied Almendariz. "Don' want you to up an' be pukin' all over me."

"Must be something I ate," Almendariz said softly. He glanced over the man's shoulder to check the woman.

"At leas' you got to eat today." The black man shoved his hands deep in the pockets of his Army fatigue jacket.

"I'm sorry to hear about your misfortune, friend."

Almendariz reached into his coat pocket, avoided the shoehorn tucked there, and brought out the cash money he had.
Three dollar bills were crumpled in his fingers. He offered
them to the man. "Here. You can get yourself something to
eat tonight."

The man stared at him in disbelief. "This some kind of
joke?"

Almendariz glanced at the money, felt foolish and felt angry all at the same time. "No joke."

"That all you got?"

"Yes."

"And you're willing to give it to me because I said I
didn't eat today?"

"Yes."

"Your last dollar?"

Almendariz nodded. Uncertainty crowded in on him. He
glanced at the woman and accidentally met her eye. Terror
pounded through him, opened up his lungs in a sudden inha-
lation. He tore his gaze away, praying she hadn't recognized
him.

"How you going to get back home, whitebread?"

"I have my bus card."

The man's laughter was a dull rumble deep in his throat.
"Keep your money, man. You're fucking poor. If that coat
wasn't so ugly, maybe I'd tell you I was cold."

With a squeak of worn brakes, the bus came to a stop.

Face burning with embarrassment, Almendariz put the
money back in his pocket. His hand closed around the handle of the shoehorn and he couldn't let it go.

"You don't get out much, do you, whitebread?"

"No."

"Didn't think so. You pretty for a white boy, too. Might
keep that in mind before you go walking down some of
these dark streets. Got some brothers out here that like their
meat white, and don't got no particulars about whether it's a
rooster or a hen."

In his pocket, Almendariz's finger stroked the razored
edge of the shoehorn. A small trickle of warm blood flowed
over his skin.

"You understand what I'm sayin' here, whitebread?"

"Yes."

Breaking into laughter again, the man shook his head in

disbelief and walked toward the front of the bus, past the woman, and out the opened door.

Almendariz watched the man go. His breath fogged the dirty window and his cheek touched the cold glass.

With a jerk and palsied rattle of the engine, the bus was off again.

The street sign was visible for only an instant. They had just passed Wayside. The turn onto South 76th Street was still a few minutes away.

A small man with an eyepatch took the vacated seat, brought the scent of bay rum aftershave with him. Still and silent, he looked out one of the windows, and a lonely tear streamed from his remaining eye. He tried to blink it away harshly, as if he was afraid he would get caught.

Almendariz felt compelled to say something, but he was afraid the man's problems would consume more time than he had to give. He checked for the woman, using the periphery of his vision. She was there.

"Life's just one big toilet bowl," the little man said in a beaten voice. He looked at Almendariz with his tear-reddened eye.

"It can seem that way at times," Almendariz said, "but that's generally when we're more concerned with the questions than the answers."

"I got my answer," the man said. He pointed at the eyepatch. "You know how much you get for an eyeball these days?"

Almendariz noticed the medical bracelet on the man's wrist and knew from the colors that it belonged to one of the licensed organ brokers in the city.

"And I'm talking about a perfectly good eyeball here," the man went on. "Sucker was twenny-twenny. They tested me before they took it."

"No," Almendariz replied. "I'm afraid I don't know."

"Not nearly enough, I'm here to tell you." The man made a show of going through his pockets. "You got any cigarettes?"

"No. Sorry, I don't smoke."

"Ah, what the hell, right? Keep on smoking, I'll be giving up my other eyeball for a lung."

Hastily, Almendariz shifted his attention from the man. Sometimes, if he didn't look at people who wanted to talk to him, they didn't keep trying.

The bus was full. Over fifty people sat in the seats or hung from the straps overhead. Their clothing was patched and worn, creased as much as the faces that had weathered pain, suffering, and loss of hope.

When he glanced at the woman again, Almendariz caught her shifting uncomfortably under the weight of the grocery bag. How could she have ever been mistaken as a madonna?

Ten minutes later, the woman got out at the stop on Avenue N.

Rising from his seat, his hand back in his pocket around the shoehorn, Almendariz followed her. He turned his collar up as he stepped off the bus. Not from the cold, but because he didn't want her to recognize him.

A line of abandoned shops that had once housed cobblers, merchants, and exercise and dance gyms ran the length of the block to his right. Three rusting hulks of broken-down cars sat next to the curb. The wind whipped fast-food cups and papers around in a spiral out on the street. Reflected light from a fire made by one of the homeless people living in the buildings on the other side of the street glazed a shattered bulletproof window that held only naked female mannekins.

The woman's shoes slapped against the broken pavement, louder than the rumble of voices that echoed in the darkness around them.

Almendariz let the distance separating them increase. He didn't want to frighten her. There was no way he could lose her, because he knew where she lived. Silently, he said the Twenty-third Psalm, gathered his strength. His hand closed over the shoehorn, held it loose and ready.

A puff of black exhaust jetted from the bus, covered over the ruby taillights for a moment, then it was gone. Only he and the woman were left on the street.

Almendariz paced her, let the intervening distance continue to build until they reached the corner of Avenue P. She turned west, headed for the cluster of shacks behind the long row of warehouses fronting the Houston Ship Channel turning basin.

A cool wind, thick with the threat of spring rain, blew in from the northeast, across the river's elbow. Feeding from the Gulf of Mexico instead of pouring into it, the sluggish water carried the salty scent of the sea. The odor of diesel fuel from the ships' turbines covered the sickly-sweet fragrance of the dead things that rotted in and around the water. Metallic pinging from the sailboat riggings and cables echoed hollowly onto the street and drummed into the thin wooden walls of the housing area.

Almost at a jog now, he closed in on the woman. Anticipation fired the anger burning low inside him, started a trembling across his chest that was almost painful. She could not take him, use him, as she had, and walk away.

He slipped the shoehorn out of his pocket and carried it close to his side. The stainless steel glinted in the muted moonlight.

The woman sidled through the broken-toothed gap in the board fence closing the alley off from the channel leading down to the turning basin. Her grocery bag caught on one of the broken slats. She turned to free it, slowly, so she wouldn't spill the contents.

It was too late for Almendariz to stop.

She spotted him at once. Fear framed her face and pulled the age lines taut till she almost looked like the young woman she was.

He slammed through the broken fence, knocked more slats free and cracked others. Rusty nails shrieked free of their moorings. Off-balance, he made a wild grab at her and missed. His fingers trailed through her long coat and he fell to the ground.

Her mouth opened and her throat flexed to scream, but a barely audible high-pitched shrill was all that came out. She tried to throw her grocery bag at him. The brown paper tore and scattered a small collection of cans and bags in front of him.

Lunging, he closed his free hand around her ankle. She went down at once. Something snapped in his fist, just under her thin flesh. She kicked at him and caught him in the face with her foot.

Startled and hurt, he released her. Before he could regain his composure, she stood up and tried to run. She hobbled on the leg he had grabbed.

Moving with athletic grace, he rolled to his feet and pursued her. The shoehorn was out beside him. Her voice came back in small, chuffing cries of fright that promised a full-fledged scream at any moment. His foot smashed the bread loaf and popped the plastic bag that encased it. White crumbs scattered across the darkness of the alley.

Holding her hands out before her defensively, she put her back to the wall of the housing unit making up the other side of the alley and turned to face him.

He reached for her with his free hand, avoided her arms, and fisted a handful of hair. He yanked backward roughly, thudded her head from the wall. The shoehorn came around unbidden, drawn by the threat to his safety and well-being the woman represented. The sharp edge, honed so carefully for hours when no one was looking, sliced through one of the woman's wrists.

Blood erupted from an artery, jetted into his face, left the sting of salt in his eyes and the taste of copper in his mouth, and covered him with a syrupy warmth. His tears mixed in with her blood, turning his vision scarlet.

"No!" she begged. She inhaled to scream.

"Harlot!" he yelled at her, wanting to let her know that he recognized her for what she was. "Painted Jezebel!"

Her throat drank in air, looked so white and so vulnerable.

"May you burn forever, whore." Almendariz slashed her throat, cut out the scream that might have alerted the neighborhood. Blood streamed down the front of her clothes.

She coughed. Bright carmine bubbles rimmed the ear-to-ear slit just under her chin. Her hands released him, the one still bleeding, though not nearly so much. She grabbed her neck, tried in vain to stem the blood. Her gaze dulled as she stared at him in silent pleading.

Almendariz watched her eyes closely, moving his face to within inches of hers. Her wet breath sighed against his cheek. His groin tightened, and the rhapsodic exhilaration he knew so well filled him, spilled over him like a spring shower issuing from the core of his being. He shuddered with relief and knew the danger was almost past now.

Though he continued to watch her as the light dimmed in her eyes and she slid to the alley floor, she gave no sign of knowing him for who he was, or knowing that he had avenged himself of the wrong she had planned to do him. It was a trick, though, and it wouldn't work for her, just as it hadn't worked for the others, because he knew it was a trick.

He squatted down beside her as she flailed helplessly. Patiently now, no longer feeling the fear screaming inside him, he waited for her to die.

4

A dead man was holding Bethany Shay's arm. He didn't know he was dead yet, but she did. The bullet had punched through his forehead and come out at an angle above his temple and left the skin on the entry side burned black.

"Stay down, you motherfuckers!" a man's rough voice shouted from inside the main area of the warehouse. "Stay down or you're gonna die tonight!"

Drawn from the hypnotic gaze of the dead man, Shay looked into the casino's pit. Low lighting hung over tables and created green felt islands in the twilight locked up tight in the building. A long bar with a menu and no prices shared an entire wall with a line of cages where cash could be converted into chips. Two of the cages had holes blown through the Plexiglas windows that had to have been done with shotguns at close range. A blood-covered wall was at the other end of one of them.

Shay reached for the dead man's fingers, pried them one by one from her arm, and gently lowered him from his leaning position against a wall under a row of coats hanging on hooks.

Mouthing a quick prayer before she realized it, she used her free hand to close the dead eyes and was relieved when they stayed closed.

Crouching down, Shay moved forward and took cover by the door, carefully staying out of the rectangle of illumination falling inward from the room's scattered lights. She waved Bonner to the other side.

The patrolman fell into position without a sound, the shotgun canted forward.

"No firing," she whispered with an authoritative glance in Bonner's direction, "unless it's by my order."

Bonner nodded.

Accessing the com-chip, Shay pinged for Keever, then moved up to their private channel.

"Go," Keever said quietly when he met her there.

"We have a serious situation here," Shay said without preamble. "I got a dead security guy lying less than a yard from me."

"The people inside?"

"They appear to have been taken hostage. The Scivallys are going for the whole enchilada tonight."

"Dumb bastards," Keever said. "An operation this big, all they needed to know was where the main bank was, hit it, then get the hell out of there. They don't have time for this petty shit."

People lay under the pools of light, arms and legs spread well away from their bodies. From her position Shay wasn't able to see many of them. It wasn't possible to confirm Keever's guess on the number of customers that were inside. Cards, dice, and multicolored chips lay abandoned on the gaming tables.

Backlit by the light below, the ceiling of the warehouse curved into soft darkness. Two black shadows depended from lines of rope, moved quickly between the naked steel beams using their arms like spider monkeys.

"How many with the Scivallys?" Keever asked.

"Two working the upper deck," Shay said. "I count six, maybe seven working the floor."

"Eight, nine guys," Keever mused. "You say there are two upstairs?"

"Not upstairs. They're hanging from suspension belts from the ceiling."

The two men continued moving, working in a circular motion almost twenty feet up.

"Are they on the second story?" Keever asked. "Maybe we can lamp them with the thermal imagers, take them out quick before we move in."

"There's not a second story," Shay reported. "Half the building's been gutted and hollowed out. A catwalk runs around the room, and there's what looks like a small office above us. Otherwise there's only free space."

"Scroggins has plowed some of his profit back into the operation," Keever said. "What about Aaron Scivally and his brother?"

Shay studied the room more closely. "I don't see them."

"Meet me on the tach freq," Keever transmitted.

Shay complied, logged on as Keever explained the situation to the rest of the troops. Nobody had any suggestions.

Mind spinning with the possibilities of the violence waiting to be unleashed in the big room, Shay turned back into the lobby she and Bonner occupied with the corpse.

The foyer was spacious but looked barren. The walls looked plain under the rows of jackets and coats, but bomb-proof shielding was under the spackling texture. Faint traces of pine cleaner lingered in the corners. A chair sat next to the door. Above her, almost covered by the doorframe, was a red plunger mounted on a shiny metal plate.

Shay stood up to make sure it was what she thought it was. Above and below the red plunger on the metal base plate were the letters KIDDE. She disassembled the plunger's safety and accessed the com-chip. "Tully."

"Go."

"I got a fire-extinguishing system here." She studied the thick silver pipes running from the wall into the tiled ceiling. Out of sight of the casino, she moved the chair over by the wall, stepped up on it, and lifted one of the tiles cut out to allow passage for the pipes. A cloud of dust and tile particles spewed into her face. With difficulty, she stifled a sneeze.

"So?" Keever inquired.

"So, I'm thinking that Scroggins wouldn't want to see a fortune go up in flames if this place caught fire. From the looks of things, this may be the mother of all fire-extinguishing systems. Might make a hell of a diversion."

"I like the way you think, kid."

Shay lowered the tile, moved the chair, and took her place beside the door again. Bonner gave her an impressed nod, touched two fingers to his forehead in a small salute. She wiped her hands on her jeans and blinked perspiration from her eyes.

Footsteps thumped overhead.

Tracking the sound, Shay saw Aaron Scivally step into view along the catwalk carrying two duffel bags bulging at the seams. The man was cruelly handsome, blond and built with the hard, angular lines of a natural athlete. When she'd first seen Aaron Scivally's picture, before she knew what he did, Shay had had to admit the man held a certain charismatic charm that would affect a lot of women.

"Hey, motherfuckers!" Scivally shouted from his impromptu stage. He lifted the duffel bags. "Look what I got!"

The hijackers stared up at their leader, then a ragged cheer started, built until it was a roar.

Scivally threw the duffel bags over the catwalk's side. The zipper on one of them burst when it hit the floor, and scattered wads of banded dollars and yen a dozen feet before it.

Grabbing the railing around the catwalk, Scivally threw back his head and laughed in insane glee as some of his men dove for the loose money. He wore street black, with a shirt large enough and loose enough to cover Second Chance armor. An assault rifle was slung over his shoulder. A double shoulder holster rigging hung under his arms with the pistols positioned down for quick release.

"Get that shit cleaned up down there!" Scivally roared as he pushed off the railing, then threw a leg over. "We're gonna blow this pop stand!" Releasing the railing, he dropped to a craps table below the catwalk. Wood splintered under the impact. The table came apart, canted briefly like a sinking ship, then splatted to the floor. Scivally kept his feet under him, agile as a big cat.

"Hey, brother. You forgot one."

Scivally walked away from the broken table and looked up.

Shay saw Larry Scivally saunter up to the railing and throw over a third bag. His brother caught it easily in one hand.

"To the good life," Larry Scivally said as he clambered over the railing and dropped to the floor. Like his older brother, Larry possessed an innate innocence that was completely false. He was blond too, but no longer handsome. Pink scars writhed like worms across his face when he grinned. One pucker almost closed his right eye.

"What do we do with the citizens?" one of the hijackers asked.

Aaron Scivally made a show of walking toward the group of people clustered against the far wall. He scratched his chin thoughtfully as he negotiated the gaming tables. The glare from the different lights wrapped warped shadows over his stubbled face, brought out the icy blue madness trapped in his eyes. "You people look at me and you think, *criminal*. But you got that itch yourselves. Breaking the rules. You know the feeling. Sneak out here, lay down some bucks for illegal gambling. Get your little vicarious thrill about flaunting the system." He laughed, kicked a blackjack table into the middle of the crowd.

A handful of the casino's guests went down under the table's impact before it skidded to a stop.

"You'd like to see me fried on public wallscreen. Make a goddamn picnic of it like all straights do. Watch my brother get fried too if the laws were smart enough to catch us." Scivally spit on the floor. "You're a bunch of fuckin' wimps. And tonight the house wins, 'cause the roll's come up snake eyes." He glanced at his men gathered in a ragged line behind him. "Kill 'em. Kill 'em all." He turned to walk away.

Shay accessed the com-chip. "Tully." The panic was a live thing inside her now, hammering at her temples.

"I copied it," Keever said. "We're at the doors. Do it. *Now!*"

She reached up and slammed a fist into the Kidde plunger, then lifted the CAR-15 to her shoulder. Her finger slid around the trigger.

Inside the casino a blizzard swarmed in from the walls and ceiling. White blobs of fire-retardant foam spewed from the jets. The figures gathered in the center of the big room became a blur, quickly caked by the foam. For one insane moment Scivally and his crew looked like malevolent snowmen sporting automatic weapons.

Startled shouts came from the crowd. Terrified already, they lost the cohesiveness that had held them together. Some ran in any direction that looked available. Others fell to the floor or took shelter under the nearest gaming equipment.

Somebody opened up with an assault rifle. The bull-fiddle moan of the weapon crashed thunder through the casino.

Aaron Scivally winked into Bethany Shay's sights. Just as she was about to put a round into the man's face, one of the casino guests ran in front of him. Shay eased off the trigger.

Unslinging the M-14 from his shoulder, Scivally grabbed the man who'd unwittingly saved his life and shoved him away. He put three bullets into the man as he fell.

Before Shay could drop her weapon into target acquisition again, an explosive shotgun round chewed into the doorframe above her. Splinters, brick, and mortar cascaded down over her head and shoulders. She went to cover instinctively, her hearing ringing with the detonation. Another shotgun round tore a section of the doorframe loose, followed quickly by a third.

Breathing in the dust-filled air clouding the lobby, Shay got to her feet and ran into the casino. Bullets ripped jagged tears in the plush carpet under her shoes and jerked her off-balance. She turned her fall into a roll, then came up behind the solid oak bar lining the wall.

"Beth!" Keever called inside her head.

"Go."

"Where are you?"

Gunfire covered over any noise that might have been made out in the casino area. If it hadn't been for the com-chip, she wouldn't have been able to hear at all. "Behind the bar, at ten o'clock from the main entrance. Bonner's at twelve. Where the hell's the MOP?" She scrambled behind the bar. Bottles, glasses, and decanters blew apart over her head as bullets searched for her. Liquid and glass fragments rained down on her, soaking her and getting caught in her hair and clothes.

"The MOP's unloading outside. They've got six more ground troops coming on the double. Dispatch has pushed this through as a priority operation."

Priority or not, Shay was grimly aware that several long minutes could pass before additional help arrived. Fifteen feet down the bar, she popped up for a quick look, brought the CAR-15 against her shoulder.

Tables had been overturned out on the casino pit, but it was almost impossible to tell who was behind them. The fire-extinguisher system had blown empty, but a layer of white foam coated everything.

A hijacker leaned out from cover for a moment. Shay caught him in the periphery of her vision, registered the muzzle flash from his weapon even as she swung and triggered her own. The hijacker's round caught the edge of the bartop and blew wood chips and glass fragments into her face.

She dropped, barely aware of the sharp stinging beside her left eye. Warm blood slid down her face. Ignoring it, she moved back along the way she'd come, sliding over the slick scum of the fire-retardant foam. She was pretty sure she hadn't hit the man.

Easing to her feet, she raised above the high bar with the assault rifle pulled tight to her shoulder. She swept a three-round burst across the front of the table the hijacker had been hiding behind. It shuddered as the 5.56mm rounds cored through the wood. She didn't see any sign of the man.

Cordite smoke curled up inside the room. Several of the lights had been hit or shorted out by the foam, making it even darker inside the casino. Barely audible over the rapid gunfire, the screams of the wounded and dying echoed within the cavernous room.

Spotting Aaron Scivally standing in the center of the casino, Shay swung her weapon over to the man just as he pressed a button on the small box in his hand.

A series of large explosions wracked the building overhead.

Recovering from the concussion of the blasts, Shay was unprepared for the steel beam that dropped from the ceiling and abruptly landed on her rifle. The immense weight yanked the rifle from her hands with bruising force, then crushed a ten-foot section of the bar before ringing hollowly from the carpeted concrete floor.

A shotgun blast took out a square yard of shelving beside Shay.

She threw herself down and took cover behind part of the bar left standing. Her hand closed around the butt of the Glock 20 and drew it. On her back with both hands wrapped around the 10mm pistol, she saw the huge hole ripped in the casino's ceiling. She accessed the com-chip. "Tully, they had the roof mined." She forced herself to her feet and put aside the pain chewing into her face.

"I see it," Keever said.

"Detective Keever," a man's voice cut into the com-chip conversation, "this is Sergeant Samuelson, of the MOP assigned to your operation. There's an unidentified helo approaching your twenty."

"It's Scivally's," Keever said with conviction. "Put a shot across their bows and warn them off."

"We'll have to hail them first, sir," Samuelson replied. "What with all the private craft the Japanese have, and the craft owned by the media, we can't take the chance that—"

"Dammit, man!" Keever said.

A rocket whooshed outside, filled the air with its crackle and thunder. An explosion erupted a heartbeat later, jarring the street with its ferocity. Orange light washed over the sky.

"Samuelson!" Keever called.

There was no answer.

On the move now, Shay stayed hunkered down and raced for the end of the bar. In motion, senses alert despite the overload going on around her, she saw a woman clinging to the other side of the bar. A hijacker was targeting the woman's back.

Throwing herself in a flying leap over the bar, Shay skidded across the top and collided with the woman. A line of autofire zipped toward them, then abruptly stopped. Air whirled into the casino with hurricane force.

"The MOP's been scrubbed," someone said in a stunned voice over the comnet. "I don't think there are any survivors."

Disentangling herself from the woman she'd saved, Shay came up with the Glock in one hand. The crumpled form of the hijacker lay on the floor, his chest blown open by a load of buckshot.

To her left, Bonner was already in motion.

The woman screamed and tried to hang on to Shay.

Struggling, aware that the helo had settled over the opening blasted through the casino's roof, Shay freed herself from the woman's clutches and got to her feet.

Ropes spilled through the torn roof. The night lights of the helo winked off and on.

Raising the Glock, Shay triggered five rounds at the belly of the craft. Sparks jumped from the bulletproof armor.

A side door slid back and a man popped through in bulky body armor, seated in a cybernetically controlled arm behind a .50-caliber machine gun. Unleashed on full auto, the machine-gun rounds cut a deadly swath through the casino. Wood, glass, and brick chunks flew into the air. Green tracers guided the gunner's aim.

"Get down!" Keever roared over the com-chip. "Get down! The son of a bitch must be wired for infrared or StarTron!"

A line of tracers hosed a uniformed cop twenty feet to Shay's right. The impact of the big bullets picked the man up and smashed him into the bar, then forced him over. Before he fell, Shay saw nothing remained above the man's jawline.

In the casino pit, Aaron Scivally ordered his men into formation and directed them to grab the ropes. As each man locked on, a powerful winch yanked him up through the opening while the machine gunner provided covering fire. Scivally yelled for his brother, out of sight behind the hologram roulette wheel.

Staggering, Larry Scivally ran out of the shadows. He backed toward his brother while holding his pistol to a young man's head. "Don't shoot!" he screamed as he continued backing. "Don't shoot, godammit, or I'm going to waste this fucker!"

The young hostage backed with Larry Scivally, hands clutching at the arm locked around his neck.

Staying in the shadows, moving slowly so the helo gunner might not pick her up, Shay assumed a Weaver stance and dropped the front sight of the Glock 20 over Larry Scivally's face. She took a tense breath, then eased it out as her finger took up the trigger's slack.

The hostage slipped as Larry Scivally tried to take the rope his brother handed him.

Knowing she'd never have a clearer shot, Shay squeezed off a round. The 10mm bullet sank into Larry Scivally's puckered right eye and took out the back of his head. His corpse jerked from the impact and fell away from the hostage, who wasted no time breaking away.

An explosion struck Shay and hurled her backward. It took her a moment to realize she'd been hit by one of the .50-caliber rounds. She struggled to fill her collapsed lungs, felt with her free hand to make sure the bullet hadn't penetrated her protective vest. Her other hand still held the Glock. She tried to raise it but couldn't.

"No!" Aaron Scivally's scream of loss sounded like the howl of a mortally wounded animal. "You goddamn bitch!"

Black spots danced in front of Shay's eyes. She could see them even in the darkness. Her stomach tried to twist and heave but couldn't get past her lungs. On the verge of passing out, she lurched into hiding behind the bar, flopped over on her back, and held her abdomen.

Her first breath wheezed into her. Blinded by the increased pain, she didn't see Aaron Scivally make his escape.

5

Almendariz had both fists knotted at the collar of the woman's coat. Her weight hissed over the wet concrete as he dragged her.

Closer to the dirty water of the turning basin now, the fermented smell of the mud clogged his nose. The concrete drainage ditch sloped gently downward, filled with branches, dead grass, pebbles, and slimy mud slicks. The fence protected him from sight on one side. High weeds sprouted up through the crumbling concrete on the other.

No one could see him. He felt as if he were at the bottom of a well, under no one's eyes but God's.

Tucked into the shadows covering the ditch, he paused to catch his breath. The dead woman's eyes were open, staring up, unmindful of the rain that leaked false tears down her face. Even in the dim light he could see the red-tinted moisture pooling in her open mouth, dappling the long, bloodless slit under her jaw. Her clothes were ripped and torn from the nearly quarter-mile distance he'd been forced to drag her.

"Was there ever an innocence in you?" he demanded.

She didn't answer.

Almendariz knelt next to her and ran his fingers along the smooth skin of her cheek. Her body temperature had already dropped.

Bending over her further, he searched for answers in her face. His breath fogged her eyes, then the dulled sheen faded away. Unable to escape the burning desire coursing through him, he touched his lips to hers, then licked her teeth and tasted her blood. His pants tightened over his groin. He jerked his hips in an unconscious response.

The taste of the raindrops from her cold lips was so sweet he almost passed out in ecstasy. He breathed into her mouth and felt it come blowing back into his own.

He forced himself back and wiped the woman's tainted kiss from his mouth. "Harlot. Even in death you tempt me."

Rain ran down the collar of his coat, chilled him, dissipated the feeling in his groin.

"There is no innocence left in you," he snarled. His hands closed around her collar again. Leaning into the weight, he dragged her after him again. "Maybe you were born innocent. Maybe you knew innocence for a time. But the evil of the temptress has marked you. You would never suckle a true soul of God at your breasts. The only milk you could ever offer a child would be thin, poisonous gruel that held only the promise of pain and misery."

The woman's corpse slid even more quickly when Almendariz reached the mud a dozen feet out from the water's edge. He pulled harder and tried to run with the woman behind him. He had to work at not believing she was rising silently up behind him, ready to rake out with talons that would shred his flesh.

He didn't stop until the basin floor dropped away under his feet. Without warning he slid down into the dark depths of the channel. The icy water closed over his head. He tried to scream, thinking for a moment the dead woman had pulled him under, but his mouth filled and there was no sound.

Pushing away the fear that tried to keep him helpless, he struck out swimming. Coming up out of the water, he sucked in a huge draft of air. Wet hair hung down into his face. The chemicals dockworkers used to keep the basin water clean and cut down on bacteria growth stung his eyes.

The woman's corpse floated facedown in the water only a few feet away.

He swam to her, seized her wrist, and pulled her toward the bank. Standing in waist-deep water, he slid the shoehorn out of his pocket. The razored edge gleamed brightly in the weak moonlight. Dark stains from the woman's blood scarred the stainless steel. Falling rain scattered pockmarks over the surface of the water.

Straining with the effort, Almendariz turned the corpse on her back. Terror continued to thrum inside him, making him realize how close he had come to losing everything.

"Three of you," he told the dead face. "I've tried to be so guarded against you, tried to see you coming before you were there, but, God help me, I'm so weak. So blind. Why do you seek me out? Why? All I want is peace." Warm tears stung his eyes. He gave himself over to the emotion and smothered heaving sobs that left him weak and drained. Minutes passed before he was in control of himself again. "You *won't* get me, though. None of you will. You can't fight His love for me. I will be protected by Him."

The shoehorn's sharp edge sliced through the woman's blouse and bared her white, pallid skin. He refused to see her nudity. Thrusting the shoehorn deep, he slit open the corpse's stomach, reached inside, and spilled the ropy, gray entrails out into the water.

"No child," he whispered. "There will be no godless child from you."

Seeing she no longer had the ability to harm him, he felt safe at last. He put the shoehorn away, then shoved the corpse into deeper water, toward the shelter of the docks where it might not be easily found.

The pallid moon of the woman's face disappeared under the dark water.

Almendariz called after her, the words coming automatically from the Book of Matthew, Chapter Twenty-five, Verse Forty-one. "Then shall God say also unto them on the left hand, Depart from me, ye cursed, into everlasting fire, prepared for the devil and his angels."

His voice carried over the noises of the sleeping port and sounded strong and true in his ears. In the rain-fogged distance, across the turning basin, the neon-stained Himeji Towers gleamed like pillars thrust down from heaven.

"And if there was any goodness in you before," he whispered, "may God show you to the path of your redemption and salvation, and keep you in His mercy."

6

Holding an arm protectively across her bruised rib cage, her other hand still locked around the Glock 20, Bethany Shay stared down at Larry Scivally's ruined face.

The hijacker's remaining eye stared in wide surprise, turned a quarter toward profile.

"You didn't have a choice, kid," Keever's deep voice said quietly. "That hostage was a dead man till you pulled the trigger."

Dryness took away Shay's voice. She shook her head.

Sirens screamed into the building, poured in through the roof with the falling rain. Whirling cherries cast streaks of red and blue light along the walls. The casino looked like a war zone.

"Kid."

She turned toward Keever and holstered her weapon. "Fuck it, Tully. I traded one dead man for another."

Keever looked rumpled and worn. Blood smeared his cheek. He looked down at her as he unwrapped a stick of gum and popped it into his mouth. "I ain't gonna give you no goddam ribbon for capping the bastard, kid, but you did the right thing." He put a hand on her shoulder and squeezed. "You hear me? You did the right thing."

Shay took a deep breath, regretted it instantly when her stomach muscles rebelled at the added stress. It felt like the contractions she'd had right before Keiko had been born.

Uniformed policemen ran into the building and spread out in small squads. Shouted orders from their superiors galvanized them into action. Some worked to secure the area, while others sorted the living from the dead.

Keever took his hand back and shoved it deep in a hip pocket. The .475 Wildey Magnum glinted in its shoulder holster. "Your first one?"

"No." Shay shook her head. "My third. I put two others

down before I took my leave of absence a few years ago."
She wasn't surprised that Keever didn't know. Shootings
weren't something cops talked to other cops about, or anyone else. And they especially didn't talk to the cop who'd
pulled the trigger.

White-suited paramedics filed in after the uniformed cops.
An electric sizzle sparked overhead. Shay thought at first
that it was lightning, then realized someone had hung a
string of high-intensity lights from the steel ceiling beams.
The com-chip buzzed in her head, routing questions and answers from Dispatch to Lieutenant Parker, the on-site officer
who'd relieved Keever of command.

"What about the helo?"

Keever shrugged. "Got away. We didn't have anything in
the air at the time. Dispatch logged on with Hobby Airport,
but the helo stayed below radar range."

"So Aaron Scivally's still running free."

"Can't run much longer. Man's about out of places to
hide. After tonight, his face'll be plastered on every
wallscreen in Houston. And since he whacked Scroggins's
place, the criminal element in this city may be a little more
tolerant of our investigation on Scivally."

News media vehicles had already gathered along the side-
lines on the outside of the yellow police tape. Vidcams
whirred, shot out tunnels of lights that played over the building, the MOP carcass, and the officers assembling the details
and reports. Four bodies, covered with white drop clothes,
lay on stretchers waiting for transportation to the city coroner's office.

Shay tried not to wonder which one was Larry Scivally's,
but couldn't avoid it. Her com-chip pinged, signaling for
their private com-link. She looked at Keever as she made the
adjustment.

The big man shrugged.

"Blue Light Three," a woman's voice said.

"Keever."

"Shay."

"Look, I know you guys are busy," the woman said after
she gave her badge number and identified herself, "but it
looks like that slasher you people have been looking for has
unloaded his latest victim at the Houston Ship Channel turning basin. She doesn't look like she's been in the water long.
Figured you might want to get a look at it while it's fresh."

Keever started walking toward the line of media people. "Seal off the area and call in a full crime scene team. I want a medical examiner standing by. Until I get there to do the screaming myself, use my name and Detective Shay's. A *lot*."

"Yes sir." The policewoman rippled out of the com-link.

Shay's breath caught in her throat when fresh pain slammed into her as she ducked under the yellow POLICE—DO NOT CROSS tape. Reporters repeatedly thrust recorders and microphones in her face, took her picture so much that her night vision was eradicated. When the reporters didn't move out of her way fast enough after she said, "No comment," she stepped heavily on their feet, drew curses and, she hoped, caused more than a little pain.

A third victim had surfaced. Her mind flipped through the possibilities, realizing that if it *was* the Bayou Ripper, the killer's timetable was increasing. It had been a month between the first and second victims. Only eighteen days had elapsed since the last one.

She tried not to think about the fact that the Ripper had taken his third known kill on the same night she'd marked her own.

7

"I didn't touch nothing," Officer Lucita Carina said. "Guy reported the body to nine-one-one, and I come out here to take a look. Went into the water with it to make sure she was dead, but I didn't touch nothing."

Bethany Shay stood at the pier's edge and looked down into the dark water swirling around the pilings. The body floated serenely against the support columns, unmindful of the activity going on around it. A cold breeze followed the ship channel in from the Gulf. She shivered inside her coat, kept her arms wrapped around herself to keep warm, but it didn't really help. "You did the right thing, Luci."

Carina held a thick woolen blanket around her shoulders and gazed out over the turning basin. Water still pooled on the concrete dock from her wet clothes. She was shorter than Shay, with more generous curves even beneath the blanket, and skin so black it looked blue in the morning sunlight breaking through the cloudbank.

A small outboard had been borrowed by Keever and some of the crime lab people. The big detective stood in the water with a flashlight. He restlessly played the yellow beam's tunneled mouth over the floating corpse and the general vicinity.

Shay had opted for a view from the high ground.

A line of police cruisers held back the morning work crews waiting to get into the warehouses and begin their day. Curiosity and frustration echoed in the conversations cycling endlessly from the men and women gathered on the other side of the red-striped police sawhorses. The pressure from the wharf owners was already trickling in through political channels. Despite the fact that a woman had been murdered, there were still businesses to run. The crime scene had to be wrapped as quickly as possible.

Electric flashes rainbowed over the water when a camera-

man took stills of the body. Once he was finished, another
man took over with a camcorder and spilled a waterfall of
incandescent illumination over the pilings. Then the first
photographer turned the corpse over in the water and the
process started again.

Rain continued to fall, soft and almost silent, tainted with
the scent of dust.

As the cameramen worked, one of the woman's breasts
slipped out of her slashed blouse and hung like a small white
moon in the water. Shay felt sorry for the woman and had to
quell an impulse to go down and cover her up. The cynical
side of her told her that the dead woman's privacy had only
begun to be invaded. Once the investigative machine chewed
up her stats, there would be nothing left of the woman's life
that could remain hidden. And the media wolves would only
be a half-step behind.

Shay's com-chip pinged. She glanced down at Keever as
she shifted to their private freq and saw the big man glancing up at her with a look of distaste.

"It's confirmed, kid," Keever stated flatly. "She's gonna
be one of ours. The cuts are in all the same places, and looks
like to me they're made with the same kind of knife."

"Make sure they bag her hands," Shay transmitted in return. "If she got the chance to fight back before she was
killed, we want to make sure those tissue samples are pre-
served."

"These guys know their job," Keever said. "Our best bet
is to stay out of it, let them do it, and take over when it
comes to our part."

Shay broke the connection without saying anything. She
knew he was talking as much for his own benefit as he was
for hers.

"Your guy?" Carina asked.

"Yeah."

Carina stared down at the body. "Media's calling him the
Bayou Ripper."

"I'm not," Shay said more harshly than she'd intended.

"This is the third one, isn't it?" Carina asked quietly.

Shay nodded. Below, the dead woman's clothing had been
tugged away to reveal the vicious slashes that trailed intestines into the water. Shay's stomach heaved reflexively. She
controlled it, helped by the bruised muscles of her abdomen,
glad that she hadn't eaten since late the night before.

Keever pinged for her. "Kid?"

"I see it."

"We may have been wrong thinking the guy favored one spot of the city," Keever said.

"I agree."

The first body had turned up in Little White Oak Bayou near Moody Park when a park ranger had made his rounds. The second had been discovered by a pair of teenage lovers looking for an out-of-the-way spot near White Oak Bayou under the US 90 bridge. While the original spots were close together, this body fanned the area out by another five miles.

"Either that," Keever said in disgust, "or the guy's broadening his hunting grounds to keep us guessing."

The thought settled uneasily into Shay's mind. It was one thing to think of the killer as a rabid animal, and quite another to think of him as a cunning predator calmly choosing his kills.

"She wasn't killed here," Keever said. "Not enough water in her lungs. And the blood was starting to coagulate before she got here. They're using a vacuum to pick up some of the clots from the water to make sure it's all hers. There's ground-in mudstains on her skin and in her clothing. Flesh's pretty abraded, too. Looks like she was dragged from wherever she was murdered."

Shay knew that fit the pattern of the earlier murders. The killer had a fascination with the water, but they didn't know what that fascination was yet. "Is there any ID on the body?"

"No."

It had taken over a week to find out who the first victim was. The delay had set the investigation back light-years. The prime time for fact-gathering was the first twenty-four hours after the homicide, researching the victim's *last* twenty-four hours. But so far no answers had been forthcoming in their investigation of the second victim's last hours either. Answers may have been there, but Shay knew she and Keever didn't know enough about them to know what they were looking at.

The lab techs struggled with the body as they pulled it onto the outboard. The corpse's weight was unevenly distributed and rolled too suddenly from end to end to make the task an easy one. Two men went under the water when their footing gave way.

Wading to the outboard, Keever took up the body like a groom lifting his new bride over the threshold and laid her gently into the bottom of the boat. One of the lab techs unfolded a gray Mylar drop cloth from his back pocket and spread it over the dead woman. One hand, a static cling closure at the wrist holding a plastic bag over it, stuck out over the side of the boat. The man moved it carefully and tucked it under the Mylar. With a chainsawlike burst, the outboard motor chugged to life, then pushed the boat toward shore and the waiting medical examiner's van.

"That's about all we can do here, kid," Keever said over the general freq. He moved under the wharf, caught the rungs of the rickety wooden ladder extending down into the water, and started pulling himself up. "We've got an appointment with the ME later this morning. If we hurry, we can get part of the paperwork done before we break for that. See if we can pass some of the legwork down to the grunts we can get to cover this."

Shay met the big man as he stepped up onto the wharf, water dripping down around him. They were almost back to their car when a uniform on foot patrol in the area broke into the com-link to say he'd found the woman's purse and possibly the actual killing site.

Altering her course to follow the uniformed officer's directions, Shay accessed the com-chip and notifed the crime lab. She prayed this one wouldn't be just another faceless killing zone, that it would help them find the man responsible. But she didn't hold out much hope, because she didn't want to deal with the disappointment. The man had already killed three people and proved himself to be as substantial as a shadow.

8

Felix Carey stood at the floor-to-ceiling windows that made up one whole wall of the huge den and glared in growing irritation at the emerald waters off the coast of Perth, Australia. Sails with multicolored stripes dotted the rolling horizon. Clouds punched white holes in the blue sky. Pearling luggers held sun-bronzed divers who took to the sea with practiced ease and stayed under for incredible lengths of time.

Using an eyeblink of concentration, he increased the window's magnification till it seemed to hang over the water beside the fifty-two-foot yacht that caught his attention. The vessel was called the *Bonny Pleasure*. It was expensively ornate, white, trimmed in mandarin red, and covered with brass.

Once, Carey had owned the yacht. He thought perhaps he still did. To be sure, he'd have to access the assets part of the programming. He elected not to. Trifling with what once-was bothered him more than was comfortable.

Gaining altitude, he continued to gaze through the window. Although the room felt as if it had shifted to a ninety-degree angle over the boat, he no longer suffered the vertigo that had once plagued him. He tried to figure out what had drawn his attention to this particular event out of all the thousands he'd experienced over the years.

People lay in relaxed poses on the teakwood decking. The women outnumbered the men by three to two. It had proved to be an excellent mix, an appetizer to the lucrative business that had been agreed upon that day.

Carey's eyes roved over the occupants of the yacht, taking in the leanly rounded, bikini-clad flesh that he still found maddeningly tempting.

Scanning the length of the boat, he found Kishi at the helm, her mouth open in amusement as she steered the powerful craft. She was Japanese. Her young body was lissome

and muscled, darkly golden against the coral pink of her bikini. Square-cut raven-black hair framed her face, added
depth to the tawny almond-shaped eyes. As usual she had
worn no makeup that day. Surgical cosmetech had inscribed
permanent mascara and a fullness to her tinted lips.

Lust reached out for him beyond all the years that lay between then and now. As he locked into the image, his senses
sharpened to the point that he could smell her musk over the
salt of the sea air.

The sensual effect was blunted when he saw himself
standing beside her. On the yacht he was old, older than he'd
been for over twenty years. He guessed he'd been seventy
then if he was a day. He'd stood straight and tall even then,
but his flesh had begun to loosen. Wrinkles bagged his face,
threatened to hide his china-blue eyes, made his ruddy tan
seem ironed in rather than acquired over an adventurous lifetime. His hair was white, the way it had been since his late
twenties, and was combed straight back. Like an eagle's
beak, his nose thrust out defiantly, led the rest of his sharp-
featured face the same way the yacht's prow led the rest of
the boat. He was not an unhandsome man, then or now, but
his countenance held a muted cruelty that could not be ignored. He'd always thought of it as the face of an aggressive
winner, and he kept it even now when he had a choice of
features.

The only thing he'd changed in his present appearance
was his physical age. He'd rolled the years back, stopped in
his early forties because age was another tool he'd learned
to use in his business. And even though he looked that way,
the weight of those years no longer touched him.

His business was owning things: people, corporations,
material goods. It didn't matter. Whatever possession it
was, he owned it.

That fact was something he would have to teach the man
he waited for now.

Ignoring his past self, his gaze lingered on Kishi. Old
hungers flared anew in him. When he'd first been transferred into the matrix, she was an old dream he'd visited fre-
quently. He couldn't remember how many months and years
had passed since he'd last thought of her. Time no longer
held a meaning for him—except when it came to his agen-
das and timetables.

Carey stretched his arm out, laid the palm of his hand flat

against the glass with his fingers spread. It felt cold to the touch, possessed a citrus chill that bit into his senses. Whispering, he called Kishi's name.

Obediently, she looked up from the helm of the yacht. Her face was still full of laughter.

"Kishi."

Releasing the wheel, she reached up for him.

He seized her fingers through the glass, pulling her to him as though she were weightless. Her body slid free of the window as if emerging from a flat pool of water. There were no ripples. Behind her the windows blanked for an instant. When the image reformed, it showed a view of the actual downtown Houston area where his building really was.

"Felix," Kishi said in that breathless way she'd had. "Darling, I've missed you so very much." She threw her arms around him, curled a leg behind his buttocks, and pulled him firmly against her crotch. Grinding wantonly against him, she glued her lips to his and plundered his mouth with her tongue. Her breath was sweetly alcoholic and warm, filling his lungs with her special ambrosia.

Instinctively, his arms wound around her, feeling the supple curve of muscle under the soft flesh. Her breasts pushed heavily against his chest. Finding the clasp of the bikini top, he released it, then filled his hand with firm, warm flesh that pebbled at his touch. She bit his neck hard enough to hurt but not hard enough to cause injury. He locked a fist in her hair, pulled it as she strained against him and heard her small cry of passion sigh into his ear.

Someone cleared his throat behind Carey.

Whirling around, Carey found Quinn Valente looking up at him, standing between the plush couches facing each other in the sunken center of the den.

"Sorry," Valente said with a smirk. "Don't like to intrude on another man's fantasies."

Accessing the matrix, Carey made the Kishi memory disappear. Even her pink swimsuit top vanished from the carpeted floor. Except for the anger Valente's sudden appearance had started within Carey, it was as if the woman had never been there.

"Must be a hell of a life you have here, Mr. Carey," Valente said. He walked over to the wet bar at one end of the couches and made himself a drink. "Living accommodations that are out of this world—literally—and babes the likes of which this cowboy has seen but seldom."

"You are a crass individual, Valente," Carey said. He remained standing by the windows and accessed the matrix long enough to fade the wall to match the rest of the room's elegant furnishings.

Valente swirled his drink in the thick cut-crystal goblet. "Yeah, well, we all got our foibles to bear."

Linking with the matrix again, Carey turned the projection wall into hundreds of images of clocks. All of them showed 6:17 A.M. "And you're late."

"I tried to explain that over the phone. You wouldn't listen."

Valente looked out of place in the huge room. The man was dressed in casual street clothing, and looked like a leatherboy in his black pants and shirt studded with silver zippers and buttons. The black jacket held pieces of Kevlar armor hidden in its folds. His brown hair hung wildly almost to his shoulders. Mirror sunglasses concealed his eyes. He was thin and wiry, surprisingly in shape for a man in his middle thirties. But Carey supposed the man's profession demanded that kind of physique. Any predator that survived by its own skills stayed lean and hard.

Until it grew too old to hunt.

The thought left a bitter taste in Carey's mouth, took some of the edge off his anger at the other man's lack of respect.

"I don't know if I could get used to a joint like this," Valente said, "but I'd sure as hell like to give it a try someday." He took a seat on one of the couches and deposited his glass on the carved mahogany coffee table, deliberately didn't use the coaster sitting there.

The room was spacious, over seventy feet square. Here in the matrix, square footage was free. But it had been modeled on the room Carey had had in the real world before he'd had to leave physical reality behind. Like the yacht, he supposed it existed somewhere.

Besides the pit area where they conversed now, three more informal gatherings made up of more chairs and sofas were positioned on raised portions of the room to leave the main area dropped four feet in the center. During times of high occupancy, Carey had used the main conversation pit as a forum. The walls had special acoustics that responded to his voice and allowed it, when projected, to flow over his audience. Costly paintings covered the walls, each provided with individual lighting to show it off.

"He has killed again," Carey said without preamble.

"I know that," Valente said. "I listen to police reports too."

Carey left the projection windows and walked down into the pit area. "You make a mistake in thinking of us as equals, Valente."

"You want to tell me how?"

"You want money too much."

Valente tried to settle back into the couch and look nonchalant, but Carey could see through the thin veneer of control. "You don't seem to be turning it away from your door. Word I get on the street is that you may be the richest American left in Houston."

"I am," Carey said with pride and honesty. "And I worked hard to earn it. I don't let petty con artists and grifters hang on to my coattails. Nor do I let them bleed my financial resources without showing my displeasure."

Setting his glass down, Valente stood up. His nostrils flared with his anger. A pinched white dot swelled into view over the nosepiece of his mirrorshades. "Look, if you're unhappy with the present arrangement, maybe we'd both be better off cutting our losses right here."

"I would," Carey said with conviction. "However, I don't know if I can do this without you and your connections. He's killing those women in the underbelly of this city. The access I have to that area is limited. My people could go in there, but their chance of quickly getting the information I need is infinitesimal. Maybe they would find him given time. But I don't want to give time. Every day we can't find him the police—with all their pathetic bumbling around— get one day closer to finding him. I don't want to lose him."

"These people he's offed—they don't connect with you anywhere I've been able to dig up. So why do you want this skel?"

"Because I do. That's all you have to know to do your job." Carey accessed the matrix, tapped a power line surging around him that he knew Valente didn't even know existed. "It's time you learned your place with me." He took a step toward the man.

Lightning reflexes allowed Valente to reach under his jacket and haul out a large automatic pistol between heartbeats. It settled with an easy bounce at the end of his arm. "Stay back, you creepy bastard, or I'm going to splatter your brains for you."

"Not here," Carey said. "Not in this place." The power grid of the matrix flowed into him, made him aware that he was more than human here. He took another step.

Valente squeezed the trigger.

Allowing the pistol to fire, Carey watched the bullet rocket out of the muzzle, and stopped it in midair in less than a nanosecond. It hung, suspended only inches from his left eye, a mushroomed explosion of steel-jacketed lead. His heart rate never elevated.

A wild, trapped look filled Valente's eyes.

Deliberately, Carey flicked the hanging bullet away with a fingertip. The matrix gave the projectile back its inertia and momentum at his direction.

One of the expensive porcelain lamps shattered when the bullet struck it. Jagged pieces spilled over the carpet, table, and couch next to it.

Carey removed the distance separating him from Valente, knotted a fist in the man's shirt, then put his face close to the younger man's. "This is my home, asshole, and everything you do here is only because I choose to allow you to do it."

Valente swung the gun and tried to hit him in the face.

Catching it in his free hand with speed and skill that far surpassed Valente's, Carey closed his palm over the pistol and dissolved it. The matrix left only empty air in Valente's hand.

Struggling to free himself, Valente kicked out at Carey's crotch. His foot didn't even wrinkle the suit's fabric. "You need to be shown how ineffective you are, Valente," he said. He shook the man with one hand. "Your kind always does."

Valente lunged backward in an effort to break the grip on his clothing. His left hand slapped the back of his neck, and he started yelling. "Ren! Goddammit, Ren, get me out of here!"

Accessing the matrix prime flow, Carey opened up a line of communication to the outside world inside his office building. "Welbourne. Valente has an implant. Find it and destroy it."

"Immediately, sir." Welbourne faded out of the net.

Features wracked with pain, his hands holding his temples, Valente started to fade from view, turned translucent, all color gone from him like a man made of glass.

Carey tightened his hand into a claw and refused to let the man slip away. From what he could judge at the moment, Quinn Valente's participation was crucial to his plans. He coiled a knot of power from the matrix inside of him, then exploded it.

The concussion threw them from the den and launched them deep into the black heart of cyperspace. Carey arced like a comet along one of the main gridlines netted over the United States. He gathered speed and momentum as he overrode legal access paths, blurred through Greenwich Data-Main, and bootlegged across Europe, made the jump down to Australia, then followed the transmission lines he owned in Perth up to one of the orbiting space stations he owned.

Though he couldn't see the man, he could feel Valente thrashing in his wake, riding out the rough edges of the circuit. Then they were in true space, bounced off the communications dishes set up on the moon and spread throughout the solar system. Alien life forms hadn't been discovered yet, but the search went on.

Carey came to a stop along a laser-communications transmission beam skirting the asteroid belt. Traffic here was sparse. There was room to maneuver, time that could be his alone. He took a firmer grip in what he could still hold on Valente. It took a moment of concentration to bring a likeness of the physical space into cyberspace.

It was dark everywhere. In the distance the sun was a glowing eye set in a faceless universe. The asteroids tumbling by were highlighted on one side, looked like they were being devoured by black holes on the other.

Carey didn't bother bringing in an atmosphere. He didn't need to breathe, and the sensation of not breathing would unnerve Valente.

Welbourne broke into the comnet. "We've found the implant, Mr. Carey."

Valente felt like fog in Carey's fingers. The man's body looked positively spectral. His escape from the matrix's hold was almost complete.

"Ren!" Valente shrilled. "Get me out of here! Now!"

"Remove the implant," Carey ordered, "and give me an uplink to it. While we still have Valente, place the neural imprint into his system."

"At once, sir."

Phantom arms whipped through Carey's cyberflesh and brought cold breezes that chilled him. Somewhere in the vanishing mist that was Valente, he held on to the man's essence.

The uplink jarred into place. Accessing it quickly, he created a cyberclone with a shared intelligence and sent his second self back to earth. Distance held no meaning in cyberspace because it could be traveled almost instantaneously. He'd chosen to flee because Valente's partner had had to work hard to maintain the tenuous link between them. Now that they were in what was considered to be the DMZ of cyberfields, it was easier to seek the second person out.

The cyberclone zoomed through the gridlines, already locked into target. Carey fed it power directly from the heart of the matrix. The deckjockey sensed him coming, tried to put up defenses, but it was too late.

Carey crashed the Tendrai system with the fury of a lightning bolt. He had a brief impression of the young woman jacked directly into the deck through temple trodes. Then his cyberclone fried her organic neural paths along with the silicon ones. She died even as the clone programming winked out of existence.

The cyberimage of Valente sharpened, became as real as the matrix could interpret the man again. He hung in space awkwardly, reacting to the perceived lack of gravity.

Releasing the man, Carey stepped back, found a hard plane that he could easily stand on, and looked at Valente. He felt the familiar cruel smile twist his lips.

"Ren," Valente said softly.

"She's gone," Carey said without feeling. "I killed her. I do hope she was someone special to you."

"Can't breathe," Valente croaked. His hands slid around his throat.

"That doesn't matter out here," Carey said. "In fact, the only things that do matter in your pitiful excuse for a life are my wants and wishes."

Hovering in the weightlessness, Valente drew up into a fetal position facing Carey.

"I want him found," Carey said. "You are the person I see as being in the best position to accomplish that. You *will* find him for me. There is no other option. Your physical body is even now having a neural imprint layered into your synapses. If you try to talk to anyone about me or about him, your neural passageways will shut down and you will die."

"How am I supposed to find him?" Valente asked.

Accessing the matrix, Carey formed a wallscreen in the middle of space. Finding the files he wanted, he scrolled them across the wallscreen. Two pictures clicked into view. One was of an auburn-haired woman in a windbreaker standing at the edge of a dock. The other was of a big man wading through water near pier pilings with a flashlight in his hand.

"Detective Bethany Shay, and Detective Sergeant Tully Keever," Carey said. "They are the homicide team assigned to his activities. You will be given briefings on them. You will acquire the information they have and add it to your own. And you will keep them under surveillance. If they get too close to him, you will kill them."

The incredulity that filled Valente's face drew him from the fetal crouch. He stood as if on uncertain and treacherous ice. "You expect me to whack a couple of cops?"

"You," Carey said with pointed deliberation, "no longer have choices about the things you do."

9

Leaning back in her chair, Shay stretched carefully, managed to muffle a groan that almost burst through her lips when the pain in her bruised stomach flared to life again. Her eyes felt grainy and dry despite the drops she'd used since returning to the PD.

She scanned the three pictures taped to the wall on her right. Each of them showed a face that had gone down under the Bayou Ripper's blade. Once they'd had pictures of the first two women as they were before the killer had taken their lives. Shay hadn't been comfortable with that. In the "before" pictures, the women had seemed alive and maybe even close to happy. They hadn't been the women she'd been working to avenge, and they'd reminded her too much of the women waiting out there to be next. A week ago she'd taken down those pictures and put up photos of the women as she'd first seen them. Keever had never said a word about it.

A cinder-block wall to her right framed the north side of her work cubicle. Particleboard partitions made the east and west sides, left most of the south side open to the walkway that meandered through the rows of offices in the squad room. Phones rang insistently. Workdeck keys clacked in syncopation. A steady murmur of voices flowed over the room and hung as thick as the blue streams of cigarette, pipe, and cigar smoke rolling across the ceiling. The warm smell of coffee and doughnuts told her the morning shift had come on.

Her desk butted directly into Keever's, so they faced each other when they were seated. Neither of the desks was big enough to hold everything they needed. Keever's was cluttered with files and a clunky workdeck that had a separate monitor. His stained coffee cup that read I'D RATHER BE FISH-ING hung on the empty coat hook behind his swivel chair.

Shay's own desk was neat, held a phone she shared with Keever, and was stacked with in and out trays that already held today's correspondence.

Her eyes flicked to the picture of the blonde with the short-cropped punk hairstyle. Blood pooled beside the woman's left eye, dark in the black-and-white picture, like a blob of mascara. Masking tape held a penciled name below the picture. Mitzi Harrington had been a teacher at Davis High School.

The second picture showed a profile shot (the other side of the woman's face had been badly slashed) of a young brunette with a full-color butterfly tattoo just under the eye that showed. Glitter eyeshadow that had once been powered by her body's electrical field lay dim and inert across her half-closed lid. She had been Aleka, a hooker working the River Oaks district. They still hadn't generated much paper on her.

Shay's eyes were drawn to the latest victim. She stared into the woman's horrified expression. "Who were you?" she asked softly.

"You're too young to be talking to yourself."

Shay rotated her head and found Nate Pascalli leaning into her cubicle.

The detective was in his forties, lean and lantern-jawed. His hair was going thin on top, and he combed it in from the side. His corduroy jacket was slung over his shoulder, a tie tucked into a pocket in case he needed it. "Is Tully still with IA?"

"Yes."

"Shame about Moody turning out that way."

"It happens," Shay said. "Bent cops aren't made, they're just discovered."

"Your old man tell you that one?" Pascalli asked. "Or was it Tully?"

"Maybe both of them. Sometimes it gets hard to remember."

"Well, listen to them. Your old man, he was a good cop in his time. And, hell, when I grow up, I want to be just like Keever. Except for that sorry growth he calls a mustache."

Shay couldn't help grinning despite her present mood. Pascalli had a charm that kept the squad room on an even keel, and helped immensely when he got to play the good cop to someone's bad cop in an interrogation room. "So what can I do for you? I know you're not in the habit of making social calls this early in the morning. Vice pulls some pretty late hours too."

"One of my teams made a bust in the basin area less than an hour after the squeal about your latest body." Pascalli shifted his weight and passed over a Diet Pepsi from a paper bag he held. Then he gave Shay a Styrofoam cup of coffee, and kept one for himself.

"Have a seat." Shay knew from the man's expression that it wasn't all good news.

Pascalli took Keever's chair. "This guy we busted is pretty heavy into red satin and angel dust. Moves a lot of merch for an independent. I've been staking him out for weeks. I put him out of business, I stand a chance to bottle-neck trafficking in that area for three, four months. I've invested a lot of man-hours into taking him off the street." He slid a crooked cigarette from his shirt pocket, smoothed it into a semblance of its former self, and lit it. He blew out a stream of smoke that wreathed his head. "Soon as I get him brought in, he starts wanting to make a deal. What he says is that he knows a guy who saw your freak drag the latest victim's body into the basin."

Anticipation tightened Shay's voice. "Did he say if this guy can identify the killer?"

"No. After that he clammed up, started hollering *deal* at the top of his lungs and hasn't shut up since."

"Do you believe him?"

"I don't know."

"Do I know him?"

"The name Eddie Lupton mean anything to you?"

Shay reviewed her mental files, then shook her head.

"He's been small-time for a couple years," Pascalli said. "Worked his way into Yak territory and started turning bigger numbers. Trouble with being a mover and a shaker outside Yak operations is that he's not covered by their security blanket. And an American guy hanging out with the Yaks is always in dire need of someone who considers him an equal."

"You slipped a narc into Lupton's operation."

"Yeah. And he came across like a champ." Pascalli crushed out his cigarette in the empty coffee cup. It made a tiny hiss. "Lupton's a guy with his ass caught in a crack, and he knows it. He doesn't want to do hard time. We caught him with enough product to send him down for ten, twelve years. He knows it. He also knows if he rolls over on the Yaks, he's a dead man running."

"If he really has the information he says he has," Shay asked, "what are the chances a deal can be made?"

"Very slim," Pascalli replied honestly. "It's an election year for the mayor. Drugs are a major issue. He's cracking down on the DA's office, making sure they prosecute to the fullest anyone we're able to bring in. The diplomatic immunity afforded to the Japanese is deep-sixing sixty, seventy percent of the DA's cases. The Yaks have that much of the drug action in this city sewn up. We're shaving points by taking guys like Eddie Lupton off the streets and making examples of them. Even if he turned state's evidence against the Yaks, they'd only get their hands slapped and be deported. Five years later, maybe less, they're back over here working the same scams."

Shay knew the depression that flickered in Pascalli's eyes. She and Keever had worked homicides that ended in having Yak assassins deported after they'd pinned the murders on them. But it was a hollow victory, and didn't serve as a deterrent at all.

"I'll talk to Andersson in the DA's office," Pascalli offered. "He'll probably be the guy handling this. But I can say right now that he'll more than likely be against any kind of deal involving the release of Lupton."

"I appreciate you trying," Shay said. "So will Tully." Her eyes scanned the wall of dead women again. "Can you arrange a meet between Lupton and us?"

"What for?"

Shay smiled at him. "Maybe we can appeal to his good side, get him to help us take this psychopath off the streets."

Pascalli took his cup as he stood. "Eddie Lupton never had a good side a day in his life. But I'll see what I can do. Don't expect anything quick."

"I won't."

Pascalli walked away.

Returning her attention to the dead woman's purse, Shay opened it.

A faint scent of lilac perfume, baby powder, and cheap plastic puffed out. Taking a deep breath, conscious of her own part in the stripping away of the woman's remaining humanity, she emptied the bag across her desk. She took a microcassette recorder from her desk and started speaking into it to catalog the items she found.

Lipsticks, lip gloss, fingernail polish, carefully folded papers, a comb, a brush, two tampons, loose change in American and Japanese coins, a pocketbook, matches, two necklaces, a card holding six sets of similar but different-colored earrings, a flier from a pizza delivery chain, bobby pins, two pens, three pencils, mascara, a jar of foundation, a tube of toothpaste and accompanying brush, a pack of gum, half a candle, breath freshener, a glasses case holding glasses with a cracked lens, a box of graham crackers, and a small box of Kleenex had been in the purse.

Working slowly, she separated the known from the unknown. The cosmetics and other items were placed in one corner of the desk. She read the name of the manufacturer of the candle, the name of the bar from the book of matches, the name of the place where the earrings had been purchased, and the name of the pizza delivery chain into the recorder. It was possible they would lead her nowhere, but it was also possible they could help her retrace the woman's steps. The papers had to do with data for public records.

She opened the pocketbook and started again. It held dollars and yen, not much of either. The ID pouches held credit cards for Wards, Sears, Hitachi, and Sanyo, a metro bus pass, an unemployment card, an ID for the counseling staff at the state retraining center located downtown, a library card, a phone card, and a card for the state employees' medical plan. There were a half-dozen receipts from grocery stores spanning the last four weeks. Judging from the amounts, the woman hadn't had much to spend and no family to spend it on.

Bringing the lapdeck online, Shay entered the information and started sifting through public records that she could access. While the computer ran the programming, she took a pencil and a piece of masking tape from her drawer. She wrote "Inesita Camejo" on the tape, then pressed it onto the wall below the woman's picture. Knowing her name made the feeling at the pit of Shay's stomach even more sour.

Accessing DataMain, she checked the time. It was 9:32 A.M. A tendril of worry crawled over her mind when she thought of how long Keever had been gone. Even the mention of the internal affairs division sent cold tremors along her spine. It was an ingrained response from the beat cop in her, and she knew it.

Focusing on the lapdeck screen, she recorded the information onto her cassette recorder.

Camejo had been twenty-seven at the time of her death. Fourteen months ago she'd been released from employment at the state retraining center. She'd been a counselor for five years, straight out of college, had helped American workers who'd been replaced by technology or their Japanese competition.

Shay couldn't help wondering if those years of seeing other people go through unemployment had helped Camejo deal with her own.

Her records were clear: no criminal arrests, no traffic violations, no civil court cases logged either by or against her. She took the *Houston Chronicle* on Sundays only. Her utility bills were paid within the grace period, or their penalties were paid with them. None of the credit cards showed charges for the last eleven months, and they were currently paid off. Eight months ago she'd moved into a house owned by Vitoria Camejo. Another couple of moments revealed that Vitoria Camejo was Inesita's mother, and was also a law-abiding citizen living off her dead husband's military pension and social security.

The cursor sat in one spot when it finished transcribing information. It blinked, waited patiently.

Shay was exhausted. Rather than let the cursor silently accuse her of not being able to find the answers she needed, she switched the lapdeck off. The screen blanked. The one interesting thing she'd uncovered had been that Camejo had filed for a marriage license eight months ago but had never used it. Apparently the marriage hadn't ever gone through.

The phone rang.

Grateful for the interruption, she reached for it, noted the light flashed above her extension number. "Shay."

"Detective Shay," an officious and impersonal feminine voice said with the familiar strain of Japanese singsong. "I trust I have not inconvenienced you with this communication."

A tense knot curdled up in Shay's stomach. "No, not at all, Sachi. Is anything wrong with Keiko?"

"No, Detective Shay. Izutsu-san only asked that I call to confirm tonight's appointment."

Breathing a silent sigh of relief, Shay said, "I had not forgotten, Sachi."

"Of course not, but I was asked to perform this duty. Izutsu-san said to tell you he will be there precisely at seven o'clock. His daughter will have already eaten by then."

Unable to stop the anger that boiled from inside her, Shay hardened her voice. "She is *my* daughter too. She is not just another one of Kiyoshi's possessions, dammit." A hand fell on her shoulder and she looked up to find Keever standing at her side. He massaged the back of her neck. "Ah, shit. Just tell Kiyoshi I'll be there. Is there anything else?"

"No."

Even though she'd been ready for the answer, Sachi was still able to disconnect before Shay could. She'd never beaten the woman since this new side of their relationship had begun. She slammed the receiver down again in frustration. "Dammit!"

Keever released her neck, made his way around the desks, and sat down. "The new Mrs. Izutsu?"

"No. I only rate his secretary these days."

Fatigue had settled on Keever's features, turned them pallid. "The visit with Keiko?"

"Is still on, though I'm sure Kiyoshi's not happy about it."

"Good. What's it been? Two weeks?"

"Closer to three. I was supposed to get her last week, but Kiyoshi said she was sick and he didn't want her out in the rainy weather." Shay didn't try to explain how she felt as a mother knowing her child was sick but unable to see her.

"You got a lot of wasted anger there, kid," Keever said. "You might think about taking a more subtle approach for a while. You can catch more flies with honey than you can with vinegar."

Shay couldn't stop the anger roiling around inside her. "Fuck off, Tully. The last thing I need right now is a second-hand Dear Abby. As I recall, you didn't come out of your divorce exactly a champion either." Regretting her words but not knowing how to take them back, she didn't look at Keever as she gathered up her purse strap and strode out of the cubicle.

Heads turned in her direction as she followed the path between cubicles out to the hallway. Whenever she caught someone's eye, he or she looked away immediately. The squad was a lot like an extended family. Everyone knew everyone else's business, but most of them preferred acting like they didn't know.

Shrugging her purse over her shoulder, she walked briskly into the break room. The vending machines stood in rectangular repose, hummed and glowed. A uniform munching on a Twinkie sat at one table, then quickly vacated the room when Shay entered. She ignored the man, fished in her jeans pocket for change, and dropped coins into a soft-drink machine. She punched the button of her selection, heard it whir into motion, then clunk as something inside locked up.

The receiving slot remained empty.

Frustrated, she raised her leg in a side kick that caught the soft-drink machine higher than its center of gravity and bounced it off the wall. Pain rattled through her body and took her breath away. She remained standing through an act of will fired by the anger inside her. When the pain was under control, so was the anger. She breathed easier to hang on to the control. The receiving slot was still empty.

Keever stepped past her, rocked the soft machine with a forearm shiver, then scooped the plastic container of Diet Pepsi out with one big hand.

She accepted it gratefully with a nod, not trusting her voice.

"The ME called," Keever said, sliding his glasses up his nose with a forefinger. "They're ready to do the autopsy on the Camejo woman." He refolded his jacket over his arm and headed for the door.

Shay fell in behind him, wished she didn't feel so damn guilty. "Hey, Tully."

"Yeah."

"I'm sorry."

"For what?"

She also wished he didn't try to make it so easy on her, because it only made her feel more guilty.

10

"No doubt about it," Zachary Fitzgerald said, drawing a forefinger across his neck, "the slash across the throat is what killed the woman. The rest of the cuts were postmortem."

"Just like the other victims?" Shay asked.

Fitzgerald was tall and lean, so black the white lab coat looked stark on him, athletic enough that his soft blue hospital scrubs looked drab on him. His age could have been anywhere from mid-twenties to mid-forties. A gold stud pierced his left ear, echoed the gold gleam on a top front incisor.

"Was it the same weapon?" Keever asked.

"Oh, yeah." Fitzgerald pushed his way through a set of double doors, turned left, and led them into a small room where a sheet-covered figure on a table dominated the available space. "Still haven't figured out what it is, though. Something with a wavy blade, but it ain't nothing like anything I've ever come across before."

Rummaging in her purse, Shay found a bottle of Vicks VapoRub, opened it, stuck her finger in, then rimmed the paste around her nostrils. Finished, she handed it to Keever. The big detective duplicated her action and gave the bottle back. They hadn't talked in the car on the way over. Keever didn't appear to be feeling any of the strain Shay did.

Fitzgerald swept away the white sheet and tossed it into a corner on the counter where stainless steel surgeon's tools lay racked in neat precision. Cabinets covered the wall above it. Two walls held cue cards on postmortem policies and procedures. Someone had taped a child's crayon drawings to the cinder blocks around the cards. Where the cards held only sterile information, the drawings contained stick figures that held life and hope. Purple men in green shirts fed blue squares to a yellow St. Bernard or a shaggy cow. Shay wasn't sure which.

"Jeanie Mitchell's little boy did those," Fitzgerald said when Shay turned back to face him. "After she put the pictures up, Hackabee wanted me to have 'em pulled down. Said they didn't look professional. I told him they reminded me that I was human while I was having to deal with proof that says a lot of us out there aren't even civilized. He grumped. I also told him that the first time one of our guests complained, I'd take them down myself." His smile showed pained humor.

Shay's attention fell unwillingly on Inesita Camejo's body. Her stomach flip-flopped and depression filled her. This part was always easier if she didn't know a name, couldn't think of the particular family who would soon be out there grieving.

Fitzgerald reached up, pulled the swing-arm light down, and flicked it on. The few shadows that had been left in the room fled.

Pale under the high-intensity lighting, the body looked unreal. But the bloodless, meaty gashes across her throat, chest, stomach, and pelvic area took away any dreamlike qualities and left only the stuff of nightmares.

Despite the VapoRub, a faint trickle of the death odor surrounding the body oozed into Shay's nostrils.

Dark blueberry stains from pooled blood showed under the woman's flesh along her back and spilled out into the bowls of her buttocks and thighs. Her toes, cocked out to either side, were pale white with pink-polished nails.

Unwillingly, Shay glanced at the woman's face and had to steel herself when she saw the damage inflicted by dozens of small bites. She shivered.

"The rats got to her first," Fitzgerald said. "They didn't have enough time to do any real damage, but it isn't pretty."

Keever sat his coffee cup next to Shay's and shoved his big hands in his pants pockets. His face was placid, but Shay could see the pain in his eyes. "Was there any sexual contact?"

"No exterior physical evidence," Fitzgerald replied. "No bruising around the vagina that isn't related to the trauma from the cuts. No scratches in the pelvic area. There are a number of bruises in the cranial area, but I believe most of those are from her assailant's efforts to subdue and kill her."

He pulled a computerized recorder from the ceiling and hung it slightly over his head as he worked. Taking the reading wand attached to the compucorder down, he waved its eye over the chip permanently affixed to the nail of the woman's left big toe.

"Identify: Jane Doe, serial number five-five-seven-three-two-one-A-C," the compucorder's stiff voice relayed. "Awaiting instructions."

Fitzgerald slipped the trode free of the compucorder, then clicked it into the trode jack just behind his right ear. It hung down like an electronic umbilical. The medical examiner's movements became more deft, more precise. "Amend programming on Jane Doe," he said. "Keep the same serial number, add file under rightful legal name." He looked up. Ghosts of orange computer circuitry seemed to glow in the pupils of his dark brown eyes.

"Inesita Montoya Camejo," Shay said.

"New file name Camejo comma Inesita Montoya—accepted and catalogued," the mechanical voice said. "Proceed."

"Beginning preliminary autopsy at eleven-oh-three A.M., Friday, April seventh. Dr. Zachary Fitzgerald in charge. I'm looking at the unembalmed body of a Hispanic female, in her late twenties, well developed and well cared for, with bleached-blond hair and brown eyes. She weighs one hundred twelve pounds and measures sixty-eight inches long. Her death was caused by the forced severance of her jugular and trachea by an unidentified knife or edged weapon." The scalpel gleamed in Fitzgerald's hand, then he began his inspection, and the blade turned a ruddy crimson. "The attack still may have been sexual in nature," the ME said to Keever. "You'll have to talk to a psychologist for a more learned opinion, but I'll give you mine for free."

Shay tried to ignore the squirming in her stomach with each new slice the surgeon made. She took short, shallow breaths the way her martial-arts instructor had taught her. It helped a little.

"Whatever kink this guy's got," Fitzgerald said, "you can bet it's sexual in nature to some degree. These cuts scored the sternum, ribs, and pelvic bone. From the depth of the scoring, the guy had to be really trying. And those efforts increased when he reached her vulva."

"What about her fingernails?" Shay asked. "Did she have a chance to fight back?"

"Some of the nails were broken. But the only things we recovered were black cotton fibers."

"What about the possibility of matching the fibers?" Keever asked.

"If you can get me the garment, I can match the broken threads," Fitzgerald said. "But there's nothing about the fibers that's going to set it apart. Strictly off-the-rack material with no special treatment."

"American or Japanese?" Shay asked. Either one would have narrowed the places they could start looking.

"Japanese mass-market stuff, from the looks of it," Fitzgerald replied. "Item."

Shay mentally wrote off that possible avenue of investigation. There were plenty of black garments for sale in the mass market.

The audio receptors of the compucorder whirred to life in response to Fitzgerald's voice.

"Scan and record abdominal cavity." The medical examiner stepped back out of the way. Perspiration beaded his brow.

Tracking along the arm, the compucorder followed directions. The fourth wall of the room drained of color, turned a swirling milky white, then reimaged into a close-up view of the corpse's abdomen. The wounds looked large enough to walk into. Shay turned away from the wallscreen and kept her attention on the table.

"As in both previous cases," Fitzgerald said, "the killer extracted his victim's internal organs after making the slashes, concentrating primarily on the lower abdomen. One of the specific targets appears to have been the uterus."

"Was she pregnant?" Keever asked.

Fitzgerald shook his head. The trode wire jiggled along its length. "The swab from the vaginal canal came back clean. She wasn't raped, and she hadn't recently had sexual intercourse." He walked around the table, intently studying his subject. Computerized surgical programming fed into his brain along with the information from his five senses.

"But you feel the attack was directed at the woman's sex organs?" Keever asked.

"Yeah," Fitzgerald answered. "Just like the cases of the

other two. Not her sexual organs, though. This guy was trashing her reproductive system."

"Yet she wasn't pregnant."

"Maybe he thought she was. Could she be told him she was to scare him or persuade him."

Shay thought back on the unfulfilled marriage certificate in Camejo's personal history, moved it a notch higher in interest value. "If pregnancy was an issue with each of them, that means the guy had to be intimately involved with each of them. I don't see that being the case. We've got a schoolteacher, a hooker, and an unemployed counselor. The first two victims didn't move in the same circles. From what we've found out about this one, her life didn't overlap the other two."

"The hooker had been neutered," Keever said. "And she worked the streets. There's no way the guy could've known he was the one who made her pregnant even if she'd told him that."

"The schoolteacher was married," Shay added. "The follow-up we've done on her background research hasn't revealed any promiscuous liaisons."

"I don't have any answers, people," Fitzgerald said. "I'm just telling you what I see here. The damage to the uterus and the ovaries was deliberate. The guy knew what he was looking for, found it, and destroyed it. End of story. And he's three for three now. Who knows? Maybe number four will prove me wrong."

"It's going to be touchy if we start letting any suppositions like this hit the media," Keever stated. "The schoolteacher was well thought of in the community."

"You don't have to be peddling no warnings to me, Tully Keever," Fitzgerald said. "I got a very politically correct job here. If I ain't politically correct when the shit hits the fan, I ain't got a job."

"I know what you mean."

"I know you do. That's why I'm advancing my opinions to you and Beth. I didn't know you as well as I do, you wouldn't be getting diddly from me except for name, rank, and serial number."

Shay faced her partner. "There's a common denominator in there somewhere, Tully. With three of them now, it's got to be standing out more."

"We'll find it, kid," Keever said. "It's all just a matter of time."

Shay nodded, trying not to think that the time involved might not be time victim number four had. The killer had picked his pace up. It had been less than three weeks since the last murder. It might be only days till the next.

"Hey," Fitzgerald said, "we have something new here."

Not wanting to but drawn just the same, Shay stepped forward, following Keever to the medical examiner's side.

Fitzgerald had the corpse's head twisted back. The mouth gaped obscenely. Tears from tiny teeth showed along the blue lips. Surgical tape held the eyes closed. The medical examiner swabbed her teeth with a sponge-tipped rod.

"What?" Keever asked.

"Came up positive in her mouth." Fitzgerald removed the swab, crossed the room, and held it under a spectrograph tuned for serology.

"For semen?" Shay asked as she trailed the man.

"No." Fitzgerald flicked through the power settings on the spectrograph. "For saliva."

"Saliva?" Keever frowned. "You're sure it's not hers?"

"Oh, yeah. Our boy has just added a new detail to his MO. The saliva belongs to him." Fitzgerald reached into the cabinet, took out a slide, wiped the swab on it, trapped the resultant tissue under another glass slide, and stepped over to a microscope. He turned and pointed to the wallscreen.

A small mass of organic tissue was centered on the screen. Fitzgerald dimmed the room lights vocally through the room's AI.

"What are we looking at?" Shay asked.

"Papillae," Fitzgerald answered. "Taste buds."

"From his tongue?"

"No other place to get them, Beth."

She stared at the wallscreen, hypnotized by the perversity that had taken physical form before her. "He licked her."

"Or kissed her," Keever said. He turned to Fitzgerald. "You're sure nothing like this turned up on the other two?"

"Positive. I checked. I'm good at my job, Tully."

Keever clasped the medical examiner on the shoulder. "I know you are, guy. And I'm good at mine. That's why I asked."

"Have you got enough of a sample here," Shay asked, "to make any kind of DNA search for the killer?"

"Sure." Fitzgerald shut down the projection and brought up the illumination. He unplugged the trode and it slithered back into the compucorder. "Got to remember, though, if the guy doesn't have a record, he may not be on file."

Shay nodded. Most everyone's DNA was on file somewhere. Getting into corporate files meant coming up with a court order, but at least it gave them something physical to work with.

11

Almendariz stood under the hot needle spray of the showerhead and let the water sluice some of the ever-present pain away. He leaned heavily on his arms as they rested against the tiled walls of the shower cubicle. It was a vain attempt to alleviate some of the stress on his lower back.

Near-noon sunlight stained the water-dappled translucent window set into the exterior wall. Outside he heard the sounds of children playing and guessed they were involved in another of the seemingly endless volleyball tournaments.

He took his vial of pain pills from the soap caddy, shook two out into his palm, turned the spray to full cold, and drank them down from the showerhead. They filmed his mouth, and he shuddered. Even after the years of taking them, he had never gotten used to the taste.

He took up a fresh bar of soap and scrubbed his chest, arms, and legs hard enough to leave momentary red welts. He inhaled the soap's fragrance as if it would help purge the dirt on the inside, help wash away the weakness that plagued him. A fine film of perspiration covered him within moments as he continued to scrub. He didn't stop until he was breathing hard and felt physically worn out.

A warm lassitude crept in from the shower water as the pain pills kicked in. Putting the soap bar aside, he sat on the tiled floor of the cubicle and drew his feet up until they touched his buttocks. He wrapped his arms around his knees, hugged them into his chest tightly, and rocked himself, humming a song from his childhood.

A prayer came silently to his lips. He squinted his eyes tightly shut as the water kept falling over him. When he finished the prayer, he dropped his head and rested his chin on his crossed forearms.

Without looking he flailed an arm out and caught up his Bible deck from the hanger on the wall. It felt firm and reassuring in his hands. He drew strength from it, felt His love come pouring out to fill him and drive nightmares and fears away.

Memory of the latest succubus wouldn't leave him. The CNN anchor had mentioned the woman's earthly name, made her resemble a real, live human being even to him. And he knew better. He knew her for the pus and pestilence she really was.

He had taken her life. His fingers trembled as he held the Bible deck. No, he had not taken her *life,* he'd ended the *existence* the miserable demon had engineered inside her body. The woman, the part of her that had once been Inesita Camejo, had been released, had been freed from her spiritual prison to go to God. She could be buried in consecrated ground.

Almendariz truly believed he had done two great rights.

But there was still an atonement to pay. He could have gone to confession, had thought about it after he'd laid the first succubus to rest, but he'd realized any priest who heard his confession would think him mad. God already knew what he'd done, had guided his hand in the doing of it. So the only person Almendariz could confess to was himself. And he decided to set the penance as well.

There would be no Hail Marys or Our Fathers.

His self-inflicted penance was much more severe.

Knowing he could no longer put it off, he plugged the trode into his temple jack. He keyed the deck from memory, bringing the Book of St. Mark, Chapter Six, Verse Seventeen, online. Cyberspace enveloped him, yanked him out of the physical world, and threw him headlong into the programming.

The chains bit deeply into Almendariz's wrists and ankles. Heavy iron links weighed down his flesh even as they confined it. Cold slime dripped down his back from the dungeon's wall. His throat was parched, his stomach a knotted-up thing that lay next to death. A fever burned through his mind, elongated the broad shadows summoned up by the sconces mounted on the walls outside the cell where he was imprisoned.

"Where is this all-powerful god of yours now, John Baptist?" the thief's voice taunted from his right.

Almendariz rolled his head toward the man and felt the

heavy beard of John the Baptist scratch across his bare chest. "It is not for me to understand all of the Lord God's workings, my brother," he said in a weak voice. Fatigue made spots dance in front of his eyes. "I am but a humble student of His teachings."

The thief, bound for only two days now, shook his arm chains in laughter. "They prophesied you as the messiah before the arrival of this man Jesus."

"They were wrong," Almendariz said, giving himself over to the programming. The Bible matrix made everything so alive to his physical senses. If he concentrated, he could still feel the showerhead raining down on him, although it was so far distant that it seemed to be another person entirely. But here he could smell the acrid smoke from the pitch torches, feel the hard knot of hunger in his belly and the cruel kiss of the shackles on his wrists and ankles. The sores underneath them had once again broken loose and were bleeding. His blood was the only warmth he knew. "I showed them who the true son of God was."

"Faugh," the thief snorted. He wore only a loincloth about his manhood, just like Almendariz as John the Baptist. "They say you are a holy man, John Baptist, that you have walked and talked with your god. They say you have worked miracles. Here in this cold and dank dungeon, I see you for what you truly are: a poor, deluded fool blinded by and made a victim of his own insanity."

"I will pray for your soul, my friend," Almendariz said. "For it is well known that King Herod suffers not the preying ministrations of thieves within his land."

A paleness cooled the thief's ardor. "I will be punished, John Baptist, but I will leave with my life. I will bow and scrape before the king, tell him how bad my life has been, how my four children have been starving, and I will live. I do not think any manner of bowing and scraping will save you. You should not have criticized the king's marriage to Herodias. He is much taken with her beauty."

"It is unlawful that they should be wed," Almendariz said. "She was his brother's wife. God will not bless their union."

"You made a powerful enemy, holy man." The thief grinned. "The king fears you, and he fears your god. Herodias is a sly and cunning bitch, and she knows that her husband is reluctant to take your life. But before all is said on the matter, I think she will have your corpse stretched out on her table."

A part of Almendariz shivered at the thief's words. Sick anticipation filled him when he heard the wavering strains of music coming from above.

"It is the king's birthday," the thief said. "In the morning, when I am brought before him, mayhap he will feel more merciful."

"I will pray that God touches Herod's heart and helps him see fit to release you without harming you."

"Better, priest, that you see fit to praying for your own needs. From the looks of you, you will not be long for this world. Your father in heaven had better be getting a room ready."

Almendariz's attention was drawn to the wavering light approaching the cell from the outside corridor. At this point in the verses, John the Baptist had not known what was about to take place. But Almendariz did. His fingers hesitated on the Bible deck.

Programming froze for a moment. The licking tongue of illumination from a torch formed a half-moon on the cell's ceiling as the big man became a flesh-and-blood statue in the doorway.

Wanting only to yank the trode from his temple and be done with it, Almendariz restarted the programming, felt his heart beat rapidly in John the Baptist's skinny chest.

The big man stopped in front of Almendariz and held his torch aloft. Light splashed across the top of the cell three feet above his reach and rained down over the occupants. He looked as if he'd been constructed of oaken logs meant for ship timbers. A double-bladed ax hung from his waist belt. His brown robe was unadorned. A black hood covered his features. The hand that held the torch was big, callused, a workingman's hand.

"John Baptist," he said in a deep and great voice.

"Yes," Almendariz answered.

The hooded behemoth turned his attention to Almendariz and came two steps closer.

Almendariz felt the heat of the torch across his face. Perspiration knotted across his forehead in response to the fever and increased warmth, then dripped down into his eyes. He blinked to relieve the stinging sensation. Inside he trembled as he tried to steel himself for what he knew was coming.

"You are John Baptist?" the hooded man asked.

"Yes."

"I am sent by King Herod."

"He wishes to see me, then?"

"No." The hooded man freed the great ax from his waist, held it in one massive fist. "The daughter of his new wife has danced for him this evening, brought joy into his heart. In return, he asked that he might make a gift unto her. It was a most generous offer. Up to half of his kingdom."

"That is indeed most generous," Almendariz said, following the programming script. His lips quivered in fear. He wanted to shout *no* so badly, wanted to end the sequence of events before they could go any further.

"Salome asked for only one thing."

A gentle smile lifted the corners of John the Baptist's mouth even though Almendariz knew what was coming. "She is not a selfish child, then."

"The thing she asked for, John Baptist, is your head on a platter."

"And King Herod wills this so?"

"He has given his word."

"Then may God have mercy on his soul, and that of the girl and her mother. And you, my brother, know that I forgive you your trespasses against me." A prayer came, strong and practiced, to Almendariz's lips. His eyes were riveted on the keen edge of the ax as the big man drew it back.

The thief whispered into his ear, "Foolish priest. You should curse them all with your dying breath."

Almendariz couldn't shut his eyes even though he wanted to. He was trapped by the programming. Everything slowed down. The crescent-shaped edge of the ax came hurtling at him. Torchlight glinted and emphasized the blade's sharpness.

When it hit, the ax cleaved through his neck less than a handspan above where it joined his shoulders. The dulled sound of the blade biting into the stone wall was louder than the soft meaty noise made by his flesh surrendering to the weapon. He tried to scream as the pain ricocheted off the inside of his skull. With his vocal cords severed and his windpipe no longer intact, he could make no sound.

Almendariz tried to reestablish contact with his physical body back in the safety of the shower cubicle, but couldn't. Death swooped in on him with silent vulture's wings, brushed against his face. For a moment he thought the programming was going to pull him down into real death along with the re-created one. It had been known to happen. This part of the Bible deck was sometimes very uncertain territory depending on the user's strength of will. Most tended to end the experience long before now.

Concentrating, fired by the need to survive, Almendariz exploded back into cyberspace, ran the power circuits and gridlines until the pent-up energy was burned out. He returned to his body.

Crying out as his senses reconnected with his corporeal flesh, Almendariz surged up from the tiled floor. He bounced off the walls, bruised his hip on the soap caddy, and stopped himself short of screaming. He shivered and shook, tried and failed to keep from hypervenilating in the warm mist given off by the shower spray. His imagination, over-stimulated by the Bible deck, made him believe for a moment that the warm water sluicing over him was actually his own blood.

Weak from the adrenaline rush that had accompanied the programming, he leaned against the wall for moment and took inventory of himself till he realized he was truly whole.

He had not died. He had been so close, but God had not allowed him to die. It was proof that God still had great things for him to do, just as Almendariz had been told all his life. Despite the weaknesses of his flesh, the abominable cravings that plagued him, God wanted him here among the mortals. There was still work to be done.

He knew he was forgiven. His penance had been served.

Still trembling, he turned off the water, opened the shower cubicle, and took up his rosary from his clothing stacked neatly by the sink. Dripping wet, he left the shower and knelt on the rug. He touched his head to the floor to show his obedience, then kissed the rosary and began his final prayers of atonement.

12

Vitoria Camejo was a heavy woman who kept her gray hair piled atop her head in a bun and wore a peasant dress that held a multitude of colors but was predominantly turquoise. She did little with her makeup, but Shay knew the woman realized that artificial additions would have detracted from her own beauty. The resemblance between mother and daughter was strong.

The apartment was neat, precise, and had a lived-in air that made it feel like home. It was a subconscious thing that Shay had noticed missing in her own house since Keiko had been taken away four months ago. The walls held pictures of Inesita Camejo at different ages. In some she had gap-toothed grins. Her high school pictures showed the scholar with a hint of mischievousness twinkling in her eyes. Other pictures revealed her with brothers and sisters and more of an extended family, Shay guessed, because the new faces there were rarely shown except at picnics in the park or gathered in apartments that were too small.

"I know no one who would want to harm my baby," Vitoria Camejo said. "No one."

The woman sat and cried quietly on a blanket-covered sofa below a cheap reproduction of *The Last Supper*. She touched the rosary she'd taken from her dress pocket, worried through the beads with trembling hands.

Keever took a handkerchief from his jacket and passed it over. She thanked him and dabbed at her eyes. He switched to Spanish because English appeared to be difficult for her.

Shay didn't understand the language, but she knew the questions by heart. After asking directions to the bathroom, she excused herself and turned down the small hallway. She bypassed the bedroom. Accessing DataMain, she found the time was 11:43 A.M. She set a five-minute alarm to go off inside her head, then slipped through the doorway into the bedroom.

Inesita and Vitoria had shared the room. It was easy to see the demarcation of clothing in the closet, and in the makeup lining the chipped vanity showing dark age spots in the oval mirror. Even the pictures thrust into the framework of the mirror showed separation.

Vitoria's pictures were simple and more numerous. They included all of her family, at various stages in their growth. Inesita had three older sisters and two older brothers.

Shay took a pad and pen from her purse and jotted the names down from pictures Inesita had obviously mailed to her mother during more prosperous times, addresses where she could find them. Grilling the elder Camejo woman wasn't something she or Keever relished doing after delivering news of her daughter's death. But the information-gathering process had to go on to link them as closely to Inesita's murderer as was possible.

Inesita's photographs were more self-centered. They showed her in happier times. One was of her standing in front of her old job. Another showed her with her boss and circle of coworkers. Shay wrote down the names she found on the back. Another showed Inesita standing in front of an apartment door, pointing to it proudly. Underneath was written: *My first home!*

The address was on the back, as well as the date the picture had been taken. Shay copied it down. The makeup looked intact on the vanity. Nothing appeared to be missing. The luggage was scarred and weathered in the closet, but seemed to be a complete set. None of the valises were packed. A plastic-wrapped set of hangers with three business suits hung on the door. A treatment order had been looped around the necks of the hangers. It was dated for today.

The five-minute mark pinged inside Shay's head.

She stood up from her inspection of the carefully ranked footwear on Inesita's side of the closet and took a last look around. Nothing jostled her imagination. An emerald cotton robe hung from a hook beside the door. She ran her fingers through it, picking up the lilac scent she'd smelled on Inesita Camejo's purse. Something hard and rectangular was in one of the pockets. She took it out and looked at it, found out it was a card with WILMOT'S CARPET CLEANING embossed on it. A name and phone number were listed below.

She took the card, then closed the bedroom door behind her.

Vitoria Camejo seemed more in control when Shay returned to the living room. The woman dabbed at her eyes with a handkerchief, then looked up at her and asked in English, "Did you find everything all right?"

"Yes, thank you." Shay felt an immediate twinge of guilt in response to the lie. "Can I get you a drink of water?"

"Forgive me. I have forgotten all my manners this morning. Can I get you a coffee?" She started to stand.

Keever took one of her hands in his. "Please, Señora Camejo, sit. We mean to be no trouble. Detective Shay can get you a glass of water, or make the coffee."

"Very well."

Shay took her cue and walked into the small kitchen. Red-and-gold plaid curtains covered the window looking out over the alley. Though old and stained by time, the kitchen appliances were neatly kept and serviceable. A menu was held by magnets to the refrigerator door, complete with listings of who was to prepare each meal. Not wanting to bring her pad out and chance getting caught with it, she memorized the schedule. It would help cross-reference how Inesita Camejo had spent her last few days.

The metal pot and the coffee were together in the tiny pantry. A blue-tinted wineglass held restaurant-size Sweet'n Low packets. A cracked mug was stuffed with salt and pepper packets. Individual servings of salsa condiments and honey half-filled a Tupperware bowl. Shay wasn't surprised to find the waitress apron folded neatly on one of the shelves.

She put the coffee on, took a moment to rummage through the apron, and found a fistful of paperwork matches with plain white covers and HERMANO'S CANTINA printed on them. Palming a matchbook, she slipped it into her pocket on her way back to the living room.

Keever continued talking in Spanish in low tones. Vitoria Camejo kept nodding or shaking her head in response, then breaking into bits of speech.

When the scent of coffee filled the air, Shay served out. Vitoria thanked her, and laid down her rosary before accepting the cup. Seeing the beads draped across the woman's knees brought a sudden realization to Shay that had started when she'd first seen them.

As Keever continued to speak in Spanish, she assembled her own findings in her mind. The killer was three for three. It had to mean something.

"All three of them were Catholic," Shay said as she pulled through the noontime traffic clustered on Navigation waiting to get onto S/SGT Macario Garcia to Wayside North.

"You know that for a fact?" Keever asked.

Shay released the wheel and reached for the pile of folders in the backseat. By tacit agreement over the years of their partnership, she was in charge of the paperwork floating through the caseloads.

Keever reached across and took control of the car automatically.

Fisting the folders, Shay sorted through them. Traffic ran in long lines beside and behind her. She was sure the accumulation of cars ahead of them still looked the same.

"Brake," Keever called out.

She found the pedal with her toe as she separated Mitzi Harrington's and Aleka's personal files from the compiled data. Inesita Camejo's was on top. She applied pressure to the brake, felt Keever yank it hard right.

"More brake," Keever said.

She put her foot down harder, and groaned inwardly as the pile of folders slid off the seat and cascaded to the floor in a flurry of papers. Swiveling around, she laid the files in Keever's lap and took over the wheel. She glided through the stoplight as it turned yellow, took the northbound lane, and aimed them at US Highway 90.

Keever shuffled through the papers as she drove.

Shay left him alone. When Keever wanted to pursue something mentally, he was usually deaf to the outside world until he'd covered the ground he wanted to.

"So?" Keever slid the folders onto the dashboard.

"Thought you'd want to know. Three for three is unusual."

"Any ideas you want to let me in on?"

"Not yet. I'm not sure it means anything, but I'm not ready to discount it at this point."

Keever lifted the handmike and radioed for dispatch. When he was put through, he asked for the records division, got forwarded, and asked about the religious affiliations of the dead women. "Different churches for Camejo and Harrington," he said when he hung up. "Aleka's still a cipher except for the rosary we found on her body."

"I heard." Shay felt a headache come throbbing up between her eyes. She took a pair of sunglasses from her purse and slipped them on. It blunted the harsh sunlight.

"Maybe it's a coincidence," Keever said. "You and I have both been working homicide long enough to know they do happen."

"Maybe." Shay went under I-10, caught the westbound loop, and accelerated into the traffic drifting across the city. "Inesita was working off the books at a place called Hermano's Cantina. I got an address. It's not far from the apartment."

"The owner's not going to be exactly talkative about the situation," Keever said. "He's got a lot at stake if the Labor Board hears about it."

"We can run the County Health people through there first, buy us some bargaining power when we sit down at the table with the guy."

"It's not like you to play hardball so early," Keever said. "Usually you're holding me back."

"I want this guy, Tully," Shay said as she powered around an eighteen-wheeler hauling parts for a Himeji Electronics outlet. "He's murdered three women that we know of. His MO has changed. He's made the killings more personal. He kissed or licked Camejo's dead body, for Christ's sake. And the deaths are coming closer now. If he's metamorphosing in his mind, it only means the body count is going to escalate, and it's going to make it harder for us to find him." Her hands were white-knuckled on the steering wheel.

"I know, kid." Keever patted her on the shoulder. "But we're going to get him. Don't let yourself doubt that even for a minute. I don't."

Shay's stomach fluttered in nervous anticipation when she pulled the car into the curb in front of the church. It was dark and severe, a worn bastion against the creeping chaos of humanity around it that threatened to swell over its walls. When she'd been a little girl, the Cathedral of Our Lady of Perpetual Help had seemed huge and indominable. Now she could see it for what it was: a building that housed the hopes of a few who wished there were something better in their lives.

The neighborhood had once held professional people, who were lax about tithing and the confession. The families who lived here now were below the poverty level, survived by selling themselves and the few possessions they had on the street and to corporations. Both options tended to use them up, left little that wasn't jaded and uncertain of the fact that a God watched over them at all.

Still, the grounds were kept immaculate year-round. Father Keith wouldn't have allowed anything else. The parking lot was patched with black tar that stood out in sharp relief from the cracked concrete that would continue to erupt in potholes. Only a handful of cars were parked between the faded blue lines.

"I'll be back in just a minute," Shay said.

Keever nodded and turned his attention to the stack of file folders on the dashboard.

Leaving the car running, the air conditioner on, Shay shouldered her purse, made sure her jacket covered her pistol, and got out. The walk to the massive, ornate double doors was long. Flowers blossomed in reds, whites, yellows, and pinks to either side. A stray memory of when her mother had brought her here when she was twelve settled into her mind. She'd worked in the dirt with the other children and planted the flowers Father Keith had given them. When Keiko was still only a baby, she'd thought of bringing her here to plant the flowers too. But that seemed so far away now.

A chill zinged through her when she opened the door and went inside. The last time she'd been at the church had been twenty-one months ago. It had been her mother's funeral. It had been July, so hot that her tears that afternoon had quickly dried.

Stained-glass windows high overhead broke the sunlight into a prism of colors that streaked the interior of the church. Less than a dozen people sat in the wooden seats. Nearly half of them appeared to be homeless. A black-suited priest sat with a young man and woman who held hands the whole time.

Shay knelt on the hardwood floor in the second row, clasped her hands together on the backs of the seats in the first row, and stumbled through a prayer. When she was finished, she went to the right of the altar and stepped into one of the four confessional booths. Drawing the curtain across the plate-glass window that allowed those who wanted it to be seen as well as heard by the priest, she flipped the switch to register her occupancy.

She automatically logged the time through her com-chip. Within three minutes she heard movement on the other side of the dark curtain. She left the light off.

"It's all right," a soft male voice said. "I'm here. You may begin."

Shay took a deep breath, tried to start talking, but couldn't.

"It's okay," the priest said. "We have plenty of time. How long has it been since your last confession?"

"Six years," Shay answered. It had been the same day she'd shot her second man, a twenty-year-old drug pusher named Ramón Farber who'd been stoned on red satin and pulled a pistol on a group of high school students he'd been trying to sell to.

"That is a long time."

"Yes." Her lungs hurt when she spoke.

"What is the nature of your sin?"

"Today," Shay said, sipping a quick gulp of air, "today I killed a man."

13

Almendariz couldn't help staring at the reflection in the mirror. Despite his surname he had thick, wavy blond hair, and cornflower-blue eyes as clear as an uncloudy day. The Hispanic part of his heritage showed in the deep ruddy tan that covered him, in his short stature and wide shoulders. His features were broad and generous. A smattering of freckles trickled across the bridge of his nose. Even a slight smile could dimple his cheeks. He tried it, never failing to be in awe of the image of perfection looking back at him. And in that smile were teeth so white they gleamed. With that smile he could shed at least nine years, look like he was seventeen again. It was a look he'd found could serve him well. He wore only black slacks and was in his stocking feet. His hairless chest and bare arms revealed the build of an athlete. He didn't consciously work at it, but his love of swimming even before his spine had been straightened had prepared the musculature to come forth as it had.

He curled an arm, flexed the biceps. It obeyed like a well-trained animal, bunched into tense roundness.

" 'Only by pride cometh contention: but with the well-advised is wisdom.' "

Almendariz whirled to face the speaker, reaching automatically for the black shirt lying on his bed.

Sean Harper, long and black and gangling, stood inside the doorway of the bedroom. A smile lit up his handsome face. He was so tall he had to stoop to lounge there. A marred orange basketball spun on his forefinger. He wore a maroon sweatsuit, maroon armbands, and a maroon headband, and scarred white Reeboks with maroon striping. "Proverbs, Chapter Thirteen, Verse Ten."

"I know very well where it is," Almendariz said. He slid the black shirt on forcefully, secured the cuffs before buttoning the rest of it. "I also know Matthew, Chapter Seven,

Verse One: 'Judge not, that ye be not judged.' " He added the black vest, dropped the pocketwatch into a pocket, and let the simple black leather fob hang out.

"Ouch," Harper said. "Okay, you got me. I didn't mean to step on your toes. It's just not often I see you preening in front of the mirror." He stopped the basketball's rotation, then came on into the room. "In fact, I don't think I ever have, and I've been your roommate for seven months now."

Conscious of the other man in the room, Almendariz hastily dragged a comb through his hair and dusted it lightly with hair spray. He tucked his shirt into his pants, then took his penny loafers from his side of the closet. The shoes were black as well, glazed with a deep polish that showed his reflection and the work that had gone into them. He used the shoehorn to ease them on, careful of the sharp edge, then tucked it away in a back pocket.

The room was cramped with the two single beds in it. They shared a bureau against the wall opposite the beds. Harper had the top two drawers, and Almendariz had the bottom two. Before his latest roommate had moved in, he'd had the top drawers for five years. But it had meant nothing for him to change the arrangement after Harper had asked. His childhood and training had kept him from being possessive about material things. A nightstand with a lamp was between the beds. As usual, Harper's bedding was hastily assembled, not showing any of the sharp corners Almendariz's own efforts had created. The walls on Harper's side of the room held posters of sports figures. The prizes among them were vintage reprints of Nolan Ryan and Bo Jackson.

A small desk sat beside the room's only window. The sports pages from the morning newspaper were still scattered over it. Almendariz had considered putting the paper away, then realized Harper would only have asked for it later. By leaving the sports pages where they were, he could cut down on the amount of time he'd have to talk to the man.

Harper lay down on his own bed, facing upward. He slapped the basketball a few times, then made it hop from forefinger to forefinger as it continued to spin. "Father Brian wanted me to come check on you. I told him you'd gotten in late last night. Said I'd wake you if you wasn't up."

"I'm awake."

"I see that now. Looks like I wasted a trip up those stairs."

Almendariz put on his black jacket and ran his fingertips over the creases he'd taken pains to put into the material. It was a better-than-average job that even Sister Margaret Mary would have been forced to compliment.

Clapping his hands together, Harper caught the basketball between them and stopped it.

After checking his appearance in the mirror once more, Almendariz removed a piece of lint and dropped it into the wastepaper basket beside the desk.

"So what do you have on tap today?" Harper asked.

"Groundskeeping," Almendariz answered.

"Man," Harper said. "That job sucks. I don't see how you put up with it. There's only so much leaf-pushing and weed-pulling I can handle before I want to puke."

Though he didn't want to know, he asked what Harper was scheduled for that day as well. If he hadn't asked, it would only have taken the man longer to get back to the subject. Once it was dispensed with, conversation between them could grind back to the emptiness Almendariz was most comfortable with.

"Youth services." Harper smiled, set the basketball to twirling again. "Gonna take the message out into the street. Play some roundball with the ghetto kids and see if I can pump them up spiritually. Dink around with them long enough, I can probably get some of them in for church services on Sunday. Maybe save their souls with a little game of twenty-one."

Almendariz took his Bible deck from his bed and slid it into an inner jacket pocket.

"Attendance in the youth groups is up eight percent this quarter," Harper said.

"That's impressive."

Harper twirled the ball again. It floated from the end of his forefinger like a fat orange moon. "I know. Father Brian's not letting on like it's anything spectacular, but it's that damn poker face of his. I think the only thing that would get a smile from him is verification of the Second Coming starting within his lifetime right here at St. Anthony of Padua's."

Concealing the growing irritation that filled him,

Almendariz said, "He's really not that hard-nosed about things. He doesn't like showing emotion. It's just his way."

" 'His way' makes me feel like I'm busting my butt for nothing out there."

"Are you doing this for Father Brian," Almendariz asked, "or are you doing the Lord's work?"

Harper caught the ball again, laughed, and got to his feet. "*Touché.* You never cut a guy any slack, do you?"

Realizing he'd offended the other man by pointing out what should have been obvious, Almendariz tried to soften his words. "Father Brian is impressed with you. If he weren't, someone else would be working those kids today. Before you got here, none of the priests at the rectory could make the strides you've made with them."

Laying an arm across the back of Almendariz's shoulders, Harper guided him to the door. "You know, if you wasn't so tight-assed all the time, you might make a decent human being one of these days."

"I'll keep that in mind," Almendariz said dryly. He slipped from under Harper's arm, snared the clerical collar from the peg on the closet door, and put it on as they headed downstairs.

Warm from the afternoon sun and from his exertions, Almendariz continued raking the front lawn of St. Anthony's. His back was already stiffening from pushing the gasohol mower. Despite the ache, he'd chosen not to use the pain pills because he wanted to keep his head clear. He had eliminated three of the Great Adversary's succubi now. He couldn't believe the events had gone so smoothly.

Words and prayers from the Bible comforted him as he worked and worried. Sister Margaret Mary's prophecy concerning his future seemed to reach from beyond the grave and anoint him anew.

The Lord had special plans for him. He had never doubted that, but he had gotten impatient from time to time for Him to reveal them.

He knelt, took a plastic leaf bag from his back pocket, and scooped the gathered leaves and branches into it. Leaving it sitting and listing slightly in the dry breeze, he moved on to another part of the lawn. In his mind he'd carefully marked off each section of the grounds and worked each in turn.

Sister Margaret Mary had been right. No one could have

suffered through everything he had without some kind of divine intervention. He had been orphaned, born disfigured, with a keen mind within a travesty of a body. Even after the Pope's declaration that physical appearance of priests would meet specific Church standards to satisfy the needs of the general populace, there was a great deal of pain for him to endure.

Most priests only had light cosmetech work done to meet these new standards. Hair and tooth implants were among the most frequent procedures. Weight gain and reduction were most commonly achieved through nutrition and exercise. Only occasionally did the Church surgeons resort to liposuction and stapled stomachs.

He was the most radically altered member of the clergy in the United States, perhaps in all the world. The pain had been a constant companion for a number of years, remained even now, every day of his life. But in the end, he was the most shining success.

True, there were other people whose physical beauty was more striking, but they had begun life with their attributes. He had earned everything he was by retraining cloned and tortured masses of new muscle to do things they had never done before. In the end he had built a physique that was wiry and flexible, that complemented the surgeries done on his warped spinal cord.

But he had found Satan had a hand in the remaking as well.

While the Great Adversary could not undo the gifts the Lord God had visited on Almendariz, Satan could gloss a taint to them. Almendariz had lust in his soul. It was a thing Sister Margaret Mary had helped him strive to conquer from his earliest teenage years. His physical deformities had helped him then. The women he had met had despised him.

The one thing he had never told Sister Margaret Mary of was his only sexual encounter. He had been sixteen. The girl had been one of the Church's wards, like himself. Though she was fat, uninterested in personal hygiene, and bawdy, and had a track record with the other boys at the school, he could not resist her when she came quietly into his room.

Afterward, when he was torn mentally and emotionally with the thing they had done, she had laughed at him. She told him she'd only slept with him on a dare from the other girls. No sane woman, she'd told him, would ever want a hunchbacked gargoyle like him in her bed every night.

The rake handle snapped without warning in Almendariz's grip and broke the seduction of the reverie. He knelt, picked up the bottom half, and trudged toward the shed behind St. Anthony's to repair it.

In the days that followed the night he'd spent with the girl, he was exhausted and unhappy. He'd had no one to talk to. Despite the Sacrament of Reconciliation, he'd felt certain whichever priest he confessed to would tell Sister Margaret Mary. He also worried that the girl would tell. Less than two months after she'd given herself to him and then laughed in his face, she'd tripped down a flight of stairs and broken her neck. No one had even questioned Almendariz about it.

Inside the dark shed, he located a bottle of Elmer's yellow carpentry glue, applied it, fitted the broken handle together, and taped it with masking tape. He hung it from one of the wall pegs to dry more thoroughly. Unwilling to give up the chore, he returned to do it by hand.

He was still picking up accumulated litter, broken branches left by the mower, and pulling weeds when Father Brian found him. He noted the older man's approach but remained hard at work. His heart thumped a little more quickly as the man neared.

"Father Judd," the pastor said. "The grounds are looking as impressive as ever." He was a square and squat man, with a short white beard that matched his head hair. The black suit and clerical collar made him look resplendent.

"Thank you, sir, but the meager work I do only uncovers the beauty that the hand of God has already placed here."

Father Brian beamed proudly. "Ah, you make a fine man of God. Perhaps the best St. Anthony's has ever turned out. And modest, too. You have none of the egotistical crap other young priests seem to find in their bag of tricks when they go out into the world to do Work. And you may tell your roommate I said that, and thought of him in the same breath."

"Yes sir." Almendariz smiled briefly, because he knew it was expected. He rose to his feet. "Is there something I can do for you, Father?"

"An errand, Father Judd. I looked out, saw you working so diligently, and thought you might need a break from the sun and the humidity. Too often I think you forget how rugged the weather can be out here while you toil."

"I need no break. And my work here—"

"—is above even my sometimes harsh expectations," the pastor said. "And even so, the errand is still there and I do not have time to attend to it myself."

"I'll be glad to see to it for you." Almendariz took up his lawn bag and stood in readiness.

"Thank you." Father Brian took the lead back toward the rectory. "There are some books I've borrowed from Father Paul at St. Ursula's. I thought you might be able to return them for me this afternoon."

"Of course, Father." Inwardly Almendariz cringed. St. Ursula's was very near where the first two succubi had been lying in wait for him.

Backpack filled with books and resting over his shoulder with only minor protest coming from his spine, Almendariz waited for the bus at the corner of Cullen and Faulkner. With a hiss of air brakes and a kaboom that belched out a small cloud of noxious gray fumes, the big metro unit stopped only three minute behind schedule.

He waited patiently as five other boarders got on, then climbed the steps and inserted his metro pass into the Tendrai deck scanner mounted by the folding door. It beeped its acceptance and returned the chip.

"Good afternoon, Father," the heavyset black woman behind the steering wheel called out cheerily. Her name badge said "Narrila." Her khaki uniform was white from salt stains under her armpits. She wore a scarf under her hat.

"Good afternoon," Almendariz responded, then carried the backpack to the seat he'd spotted in the rear.

"Hot one today," Narrila said, "and the AC's not working so well." She beeped the horn in warning, then surged out into traffic, moving north on Cullen toward the inner city.

Almendariz took his seat and kept the backpack on his lap as he looked outside the window. When he'd been younger and more naive, he'd lost things in the metro buses. Now he recognized the transit system as an alien landscape with its own rules of behavior and dangers. Over the years he'd become a well-schooled traveler through endured miseries and shrewd observation.

The bus stank of cigarette smoke, reefer, and red stain, all seeping from the bathroom cubicle in the middle of the vehicle. Dirty windows tinted the sun, opaqued the view, and made things look uniformly gray and dismal. The floor vibrated with the transmission. Although she was the usual driver on Bus Route 30, the woman had a tendency to overuse the accelerator and brake, tilting the passengers forward and back as she applied one or the other.

The bus was only a third full. Since it was only a little after three, it wasn't surprising. Most of the passengers appeared to be plant workers going in for evening shifts.

Unexpectedly, he found his gaze locked with that of a young woman sitting slightly ahead of him on the opposite side.

She returned his gaze with frank intensity. Her hair was coal-black, surely dyed, and she had alabaster skin that set off her violet eyes and arched brows. A crimson scarf was tied around her neck. Her lithe, taut body was barely concealed by a short-sleeved crimson midriff blouse that showed plenty of impressive cleavage, and a black spandex skirt that hugged her hips like a second skin and barely crept down her thighs. Her feet were encased in calf-high black boots with stainless-steel spangles worked into a butterfly design. The boots were worn and showed evidence of having been resoled.

When the bus stopped for a light at Griggs, the woman stood up and crossed the aisle to take the seat beside Almendariz. Her perfume smelled of a heady musk he could almost recognize. She crossed her legs. Nylon whispered and caused his groin to tighten immediately in shameless anticipation. He was glad he had the backpack in his lap.

"Hi," she said in a bright voice. "I'm Rawnie."

Not trusting his voice, Almendariz merely nodded and didn't try to speak.

The woman leaned closer, clouding him with her perfumed fragrance. Her body heat thudded into the exposed skin of his hand. She traced a finger delicately along his clerical collar. "Are you really a priest?"

"Yes."

She showed him a smile filled with sharp, carnivorous white teeth. "So that means I should call you 'Father.' "

"If you wish," he said hoarsely. He fumbled for a prayer in his mind but couldn't find one that helped. Beneath his vest and shirt, the St. Christopher medallion on the necklace

Sister Margaret Mary had given him felt cold against his bare chest.

"Father what?"

"Judd. Or Almendariz."

Her finger glided against his neck above the collar. Heat traced her movement. "Father Judd. I like that."

"Thank you." He wanted to stop speaking to her before *it* happened. But he couldn't. Her violet gaze hypnotized him. Already he could sense *it* was on the verge of exploding out of him. He wondered if she was another of the succubi, come to claim his soul and drag him down into the flaming pits. He shuddered inside.

"You're too pretty to be a priest." Her hand trailed up the side of his face. She twisted her fingers in his hair and pulled gently.

He had to quash the impulse to go with her.

She stopped pulling his hair at the point of beginning pain. Her smile turned into a seductive challenge. "Well, Father Judd, what do you do when you're not doing priestly things?"

"I read. I swim. I work in the gardens."

"And that relieves your . . . *frustrations*?"

His groin ached, so close to the edge of releasing *it*. He could feel *it*, buzzing inside him like a swarm of angry bees. With all his willpower, he held *it* back. He managed a smile that felt wan and weak. "I'm not frustrated. The work I do is the Lord's. The rewards I reap are many."

"You're *much* too pretty to be a priest," she repeated. Her hand dropped from his jawline and fell lightly to his leg. Fingers encircling his outer quadriceps, she ran her hand up his thigh, stopping at the edge of the backpack. She licked her lips. "I get off at the next stop. Want to come with me?"

He didn't miss the double entendre. *It* banged away inside him, so near to escaping his control. His groin was swollen, hard, voicing an unspoken demand of its own.

"No," he said. "My stop is farther on."

Brakes shrieked in protest as the bus rolled to a halt.

"Pity," the woman said. Without another word she took her hand back, got up, and walked away with a pronounced roll of her full buttocks.

Almendariz let out a pent-up breath. *It* subsided grudgingly, then surrendered to his will.

"Man alive, I wouldn't want your job."

Almendariz looked over his shoulder at the speaker.

The man was black, bearded, and beefy. He wore a Houston Astros ball cap shoved back over his tangled, kinky hair. "Guy who looks the way you do, I bet you have to beat the ladies off with a two-by-four. And the fact that you're forbidden fruit too, man, that must drive them crazy."

"Not really," Almendariz said, then returned his attention to his window. His hands shook in fear. He had to learn to control *It*. God would have to show him the way.

Because the man's assumption was true. Ever since he'd had the plastic surgeries, women had taken more notice of him. He'd been propositioned in the church, at community functions, and even in the confessional booth. There were propositions at times that had made him blush, and so intrigued him that he hadn't been able to get them out of his head for long, restless nights. But he belonged to God. When no one else would love him, when women had laughed at him or felt only pity for him, God had loved him.

He touched the St. Christopher medallion. He refused to lose God's love, to turn away from whatever plans He had in store for him. No matter what the temptation, no matter the traps Satan put out for him, he would remain true. The razor-edged shoehorn in his pants pocket comforted him and gave his promise tangible proof. Prayer could do only so much, and he was prepared to take matters into his own hands.

He slipped the Bible deck from inside his jacket, freed the trode, and thrust it into his temple jack. Cyberspace fell away under him, drew him into the Word along a blue gridline. His last conscious thought in his physical body was of his selection: Second Samuel, Chapter Eleven, Verse Two.

Almendariz slid into King David's body, locked himself into the programming, and opened his eyes.

All around him lay the opulence of David, son of Jesse, king of all Israel. He walked through the tapestry-covered halls in his robes and felt the despair and loneliness that came with David's command at this time. The Ark had been returned to the Israelites, and wars had been waged and won against the people of Ammon. And still more wars went on.

He rested his hand on the short sword belted at his waist. As David, he felt the toil and turmoil would never end. A hunger for the gentler pleasures of life lay heavy in his heart. His wives and children and concubines were away from him now, visiting with their families while he prepared to march into Rabbah with the rest of his armies.

He did not want to go.

Killing and bloodshed had seemed to follow him for so very long.

But the command of God could not be set aside, only delayed—if even that was dared. He felt empty of life and good things. The fine dinner that had been set at his table had gone largely untouched. The head servant had berated the cook for preparing the dishes badly until David had stopped him.

Even his harp, though it had been his constant companion for years and had cheered him through other bouts of melancholy, could not reach him now.

He had more than a man could ever want, and he knew it. The Lord God had delivered unto him the command of the Israelites after the passage of Saul. The Lord had given him glories in battle, allowed David's army to be the one to recover the sacred Ark of the Covenant. He was a hero.

Inside David's mind, Almendariz felt the loneliness pressing in. His footsteps echoed on the cedarwood floors. The setting sun left enough light inside his house to see, but it wouldn't be long before full dark descended over the city.

At the end of the hallway he opened the door, and took the stairs up to the rooftop. Almendariz knew from his studies that David often came up here to be alone and talk with God. It was his sanctuary, and his place of planning.

He walked to the parapet and peered down over the city. It was arranged neatly in blocks, streets and alleys uniformly regular, created from brick and stone and whatever wood the forests would yield. In some homes cook fires burned, spewed smoke up from chimneys and vented roofs. Children, unaware of the horrors their fathers were even now facing in Rabbah, played in the streets and courtyards. Their shrill voices sounded distant.

A chill hung in the air. Almendariz gathered his robes about him, instinctively wrapped his fingers around the haft of the iron sword at his side. He placed his foot at the edge of the roof and leaned down, drawn by the sound of a melodious voice.

His eyes lighted on a window in the home opposite his

own, and he saw the woman standing in her bathwater scrubbing herself.

She was a thing of beauty, long-limbed, with hair the color of wild honey and strawberries. The thatch between her milk-white thighs was also the same color. Full breasts stood out over a lean stomach that flared out into hips that were rounded and slim. Her areolae were the color of freshly bloomed rosebuds.

Desire filled David as he gazed upon the woman.

Fitted smoothly into the programming through the deck, Almendariz couldn't tell where the king's raging lust ended and his own began. He had visited this part of the Bible many times. It was a favorite of his.

As she spilled a pitcher of water over her hair to rinse the soap away, the woman's eyes met his.

He returned her stare boldly, drawn to the fires that seemed to radiate from her body.

She finished with the pitcher of water, then reached for a towel and dried slowly, tantalizing him with the cloth as she kept first this part of her body covered, then that part. Her eyes remained locked with his while she attended to herself, and she wore a small, secret smile. As she rubbed the coarse material over her breasts, her nipples stood keenly erect. Then in a flurry of bathrobe, she was gone from his sight, leaving him with a need that he could not deny.

Aboard the bus, Almendariz returned to his physical self for only a moment, pushed the programming forward to skip Verse Three, and began where he wished in Verse Four. He tumbled into cyberspace in anticipation.

"Bathsheba," Almendariz said. "It is a beautiful name for a beautiful woman."

She stood uncertainly in the doorway to his private bedchamber. A single brazier mounted on a wall cast flickering shadows around the room, lit up brass accouterments with burnished fire. Dishes of cloves and mints added fragrance to the bedchamber. Curling smoke danced along the ceiling as it wound toward the vent in the corner.

"My king." She performed a small curtsy.

Almendariz got up from the veiled bed and waved her in. "Enter, Bathsheba, that I may get to know you."

She seemed hesitant but did as he bade.

Almendariz directed her toward the banquet he'd instructed the cook to lay out in his quarters prior to sending messengers for the woman. He closed the door behind her, took her elbow, and guided her to the food. He poured her a cup of wine, poured one for himself, and looked upon her.

Almendariz's ardor had not cooled in the intervening time. Neither had David's.

She wore a long dress colored a cool jade that failed to conceal the bounty of her figure. Her hair was pinned up, and golden hoops dangled from each delicate ear. Her neck was long and lean and inviting. For jewelry she wore only a simple copper bracelet and a ring set with a single tourmaline.

"How is it," he asked her as he handed her the cup of wine, "that I have never met you, yet we live so close?"

"You have been busy, my king, conquering opposing armies for the Lord God."

Her fingers, when they touched his, trailed electric fire. Unable to resist the desire that filled him, he set his cup aside and gathered her in his arms, lifted her from the floor. Her body was so hot against his. She smelled fresh-scrubbed. The scent of lilac came from the ivory tops of her breasts.

Almendariz bent close to her, kissed her neck, and heard her gasp of passion in his ear.

Then her hands were on his arms trying to push him back.

"No," she said as she struggled against him. "This is not right, my lord. You are a married man."

Almendariz captured both her wrists in one hand and held her pressed against him with his free arm. Her struggles brought her into active friction against his groin. He moved, let her feel it, and smiled when she guessed what it was and gasped in surprise. She stopped struggling, keeping her face averted from his.

"I will marry you," Almendariz said. "As God is my witness, woman, I have loved you since I first laid eyes on you."

"And I have loved you even longer than that," Bathsheba whispered. She relaxed in his grasp. "I have spent many sleepless nights, my lord, thinking of lying in your arms and listening to you speak words such as these to me. I have heard your voice when you spoke to the people of Israel. I could only imagine what that voice might be like when couched in the whispers of passion." She reached up, held his face between her hands. "But it cannot be, no matter how we might wish it was so."

"Why?" Almendariz placed a hand on her unbound breast, moved under the material, and ran his fingertips over the erect nipple.

She closed her eyes for a moment, lost in her unconscious response. When it passed, she slumped weakly against him, her hands wrapped around his neck. "It cannot be, my lord, because I am a married woman."

"And who is your husband?"

"Uriah. The general who now fights for you at Rabbah."

For a moment David was troubled. Almendariz drifted along impatiently with the programming, knowing what the king's final decision would be before the king himself knew. Uriah had been a brave and loyal commander, and David prized those qualities highly.

Almendariz shook his head. "I cannot deny my feelings for you, Bathsheba, and it would be foolish to think that I could hide them from anyone now that I have discovered them. I have fought the Lord's battles long and hard, found myself empty of caring and saddened by life for too long. You have, in the course of only a few minutes, rekindled the life of a dying man. I shall not deny myself your love, nor allow you to deny yourself mine."

Tears darkened her eyes, but she pressed her lips hotly against his. Her breath was sweet from the wine.

His desire filling him completely, Almendariz pressed Bathsheba against the wall of the bedchamber. His hands worked the fabric of her dress, pulled it up to reveal the long expanse of ivory leg. He leaned against her, felt her teeth sink sharply into his shoulder. Her underclothes tore easily in his hands. He tossed them away, left only naked flesh open for his conquest.

She helped him take his robes off, and he stood naked before her. The firelight from the brazier gave her skin a rosy glow, gleamed from the beads of perspiration dotting her face.

"Take me," she said breathlessly, pulling his body against hers. "Take me, my lord, with force, as you would an opponent in battle."

He filled his hands with her buttocks and lifted her from the floor. Her legs slid around his waist, slick with perspiration. When he entered her, she groaned with pain and pleasure.

Almendariz treasured the heat of her as he drove into her again and again, relished the look of wanton insatiability that crossed her face. The impending climax coiled like a serpent in him, then struck without warning. She cried out, lost in the rapture.

Delirious in the programming, Almendariz wasn't sure if it was David's groans of release he heard or his own.

14

Even in her best evening gown, Bethany Shay felt under-dressed for the restaurant.

The Jeweled Butterfly was a reproduction of the restaurant Madoka Izutsu, Kiyoshi's father, had owned in Tokyo. The elder Izutsu's picture still hung in a place of honor in the foyer.

Shay stared at the picture and saw that it was a new one. This one showed Madoka in a gentler light, one that did not reflect the grim visage he usually displayed to the Western World. She realized that Kiyoshi must have chosen it after his father's death. As always, Madoka was dressed in a simple black business suit, his gray eyes almost buried in the wrinkled pits below his formidable brow. He was clean-shaven, his full head of hair neatly trimmed.

Looking at him now, Shay realized how much she missed the man. They'd been antagonists at first. He had hardly acknowledged her presence at the family dinner table in the beginning, clearly as unhappy about Kiyoshi's marriage to her as her own father was. But Keiko's birth had somehow managed to bring them together and brought a peace that had eased the tension. It hadn't been so with the rest of Kiyoshi's family, but with his father there had been periods of quiet conversation and pleasant warmth spent looking into Keiko's crib as she slept.

"Detective Shay."

She turned and found Hideo standing there.

The man was as grimly impassive as ever. Though he stood barely Shay's own five feet seven, there was not a more dangerous man she had ever known. Hideo's ancestors had spent generations defending the Izutsu family, even died for them when the time came to do that. He was compactly built and appeared ageless. His black hair was cut short and parted neatly. The black suit was tailor-made, but she knew he had made his own modifications to every one he owned. At the slightest need, weapons dropped out of concealed places in the clothing and into Hideo's hands in an eyeblink. She'd never seen him carry a gun.

"Hello, Hideo," she said in fluent Japanese, then bowed.

Though he refrained from personal involvement even more since the divorce, she knew he could not offer discourtesy. He bowed, his eyes never leaving hers. "This way, please," he said in English.

She followed him into the restaurant. They stayed along the wall and bypassed the main dining area. White-jacketed waiters served off folding trays. A line of bonsai trees and bamboo in raised walls formed a circle around the lower section of tables, which in turn made a horseshoe in front of the small stage where performers acted out ancient Japanese kabuki. The baby spotlights enhanced the black-and-white makeup the actors wore.

"They are waiting," Hideo said. He paused at an open doorway and waved her in.

The sound of Keiko's laughter, deep and throaty, reached her first. Tears blurred her vision. Her arms ached to hold her, but first she just wanted to listen. She looked at Hideo. "Just a moment, please."

The man nodded, then fell into his relaxed pose with both hands crossed at his waist. She had seen him stand that way for hours without moving.

Keiko laughed again. Voices, too low to be understood, talked in rapid Japanese.

Emotions back under control, Shay stepped into the room.

Kiyoshi noticed her at once, and straightened up into a more dignified posture in his chair behind the long dining table. Two of Hideo's men stood against the opposite wall, grim-faced youths who took their defense of the Izutsu family seriously or felt Hideo's wrath.

Keiko looked like an elfin princess. Her rapt attention was focused on the puppet theater built into the wall. She wore a white kimono with woven gold trimming. Her sash was tied in a butterfly knot, denoting an unmarried woman. At five years old, she'd lost nearly all her baby fat and was turning long and lean, no longer the dependent child she'd been. So much had seemed to happen in the last year. Though it had been only three weeks since she'd last seen her, Shay thought Keiko had grown.

Her daughter's hair was dark bronze and normally fell halfway down her back, but was now fixed up in a traditional bun style. She had Kiyoshi's black almond-shaped eyes and Shay's fine-boned features.

She giggled in open glee as she watched the puppets. Her chin rested on her palms, her elbows locked on the table.

Lean and broad-shouldered, Kiyoshi was a handsome man who would turn most women's heads for a second look. He had the long-fingered hands of a pianist, and his mother's gift of informal storytelling when he chose to use it, which was seldom since his father's death. Like Hideo and the others, he wore a black business suit. An errant lock of black hair fell across his eyes.

Tamaki, Kiyoshi's wife, sat on his other side. She had an unearthly beauty that Shay still found intimidating. As a onetime geisha, Tamaki had undergone extensive plastic surgery and training that had turned out a nearly perfect woman. Even her name had been carefully chosen. *Tamaki* meant "bracelet," and Tamaki's job had been to be on the arm of whatever corporate exec she'd been assigned to. Kiyoshi's marriage to her after his divorce had caused almost as much of a scandal as his marriage to Shay. A geisha was considered even more as chattel than a respectable woman in Japanese culture, but still above a gaijin woman.

The woman wore a soft blue kimono trimmed in silver, the sash tied in a drum knot. She regarded Shay blankly. In the years since the divorce, Shay had never seen emotion on the woman's face. As a geisha, Tamaki had been trained to keep the mask in place so she couldn't give her employer's strategies away while attending business luncheons or dinners.

Since Kiyoshi had gotten custody of Keiko, Shay hadn't been able to stop wondering what kind of influence the woman had on her daughter, whether Tamaki even knew how to express love for a child.

Kiyoshi got to his feet and called Keiko's name. The lights illuminating the puppet box went out, and the colorful figures dropped from sight.

Shay watched her daughter turn to Kiyoshi and acknowledge his request in Japanese. Kiyoshi nodded in Shay's direction.

Keiko got up, turned to face Shay, and bowed in a much more correct form than Shay remembered.

Shay returned the bow.

Turning away from Shay, Keiko glanced up at her father expectantly and took his hand.

"A moment," Kiyoshi said. "Stay with your mother. Detective Shay and I have some things we need to discuss."

"Of course, Papa-san." Obediently, Keiko bowed her head and sat back down. Her left foot patted the floor in the impatient fidget Shay recognized.

Shay worked hard not to react to her ex-husband's insult about the roles of mothers.

Kiyoshi crossed the floor, waved toward the door with an open palm. He spoke in English. "Please."

Shay walked out before him, promising herself that she would not let him make her lose her temper. Despite the latest murder, everything she could do had been done. Except for a few follow-up calls to uniformed teams working under her and Keever's direction, she had the weekend to herself. She was not going to have it ruined.

Once outside the private dining room, Kiyoshi took the lead and guided them into the spotless kitchen area. Hideo trailed like a shadow.

White-uniformed food-prep staff moved in silent tandem, working efficiently.

Kiyoshi made a show of inspecting the premises, not deigning to look at her as he spoke. "I have heard you experienced some trouble with your job this morning."

"It's nothing that the department can't handle."

"Your department hasn't even managed to locate the Bayou Ripper," Kiyoshi said as he lifted the lid on a pot of steaming vegetables. "There are three women now whose deaths remain unavenged. Do not talk to me about how well the police operate in this city."

Strike two, Shay thought bitterly. First her personal life, and now her profession.

"Aaron Scivally is an unpleasant man," Kiyoshi said, "and he is insane. I have put word out on the street that Keiko is under my protection. He will know not to harm her. However, I take exception with you for perhaps placing my daughter's life in danger."

Shay folded her arms across her breasts defensively. Her jaws ached from being clamped together so hard.

Motioning for the head chef, Kiyoshi said, "You may go now, Detective Shay. I wanted only to voice my displeasure with the way you are running your life. I have already said my goodbyes to my daughter. Please make sure she is brought back to the restaurant at five o'clock Sunday afternoon."

Shay looked at Hideo.

The bodyguard's features were as unfathomable as ever.

Reaching out, she absorbed some of the calm radiating from the man and used it to shore up the weak spots in her own self-control. There was a distance in Hideo's eyes that she'd learned to borrow as her own at times when she'd still lived with Kiyoshi.

She didn't bother to say thank you or goodbye. Even if she'd felt like it, it would have been wasted effort. Kiyoshi was already involved in berating the head chef over the condition of the steamed vegetables.

15

Lying on his back in his bed, naked under the sheets, Almendariz closed his eyes and slowly caressed his body. A familiar yearning filled him, changed pitch as his fingers came in contact with his skin.

Bright light from the wallscreen in front of the beds stained the outside of his eyelids, made moving shadows on the inside. He paid them no mind except to know that they were there. The moviechip was from the rectory's library, an old John Wayne film, *The Searchers*. He'd seen it dozens of times and knew most of the lines by heart. It had been a favorite of Father Chilton, who had been in charge of the boys' wing at the orphanage. Almendariz didn't pay any attention to it now except to know that it was on. The wallscreen was programmed to blank when the door opened. It was a feature Father Brian had insisted on in all the rectory rooms to save power. Almendariz used it now as an alarm. Sean Harper was downstairs playing table tennis with another of the priests. Until Harper returned, Almendariz had full run of the room.

The years had passed for him in the rectory. He'd seen many new priests come and go. Some went on to other churches. Some found that priesthood was not for them. Some found other rooms with more sociable roommates.

Almendariz didn't miss any of them.

Reaching out to the nightstand, he dipped his hand inside the drawer, coated his fingers from the tin of talcum powder he kept there. He rubbed his fingers across his chest, pushed hard against the ridges of his collarbones for a moment, then dragged his middle two fingers down his sternum to his navel.

He opened his mouth when his breath quickened. The scent of the powder coated his tongue.

The sweet, aching tightness filled his groin. He felt his

flesh press against the weight of the sheet. His other hand, still on the outside of the sheet, brushed against his groin for the briefest moment, then moved on.

The contact was exquisite.

A low groan escaped his lips.

The smell of the talcum powder cloyed his nostrils, enhancing the experience. Moving his hand inside the sheet, he placed his palm down, rubbing it over his ribs. He continued to tease his body, sharpening the sensations coursing through him.

Sister Margaret Mary had caught him doing this twice. The first time he'd been eleven. The second time he'd been thirteen. Both times she had yanked him naked from his bed without the pastor knowing, then dragged him down the hall to the community bathroom, where she'd thrown him under a freezing shower. Shivering, scared, and crying, he'd washed himself thoroughly with soap before she would let him out. Then, in the dead of night, she'd lectured him about the sins of the flesh and the evils those desires could work on a man if he ever let them out. The Book of James, Chapter One, Verses Thirteen through Fifteen, was her favorite scripture.

Even now, lying in his bed with her dead and gone these past five years, Almendariz could hear her stern old voice, still feel the freezing drizzle of the shower.

" 'Let no man say when he is tempted, I am tempted of God: for God cannot be tempted with evil, neither tempteth he any man.

" 'But every man is tempted, when he is drawn away of his own lust, and enticed.

" 'Then when lust hath conceived, it bringeth forth sin: and sin, when it is finished, bringeth forth death.' "

Sister Margaret Mary's remembered words added an edge of excitement to the passion. Almendariz gave himself over to it. He dipped his hand back into the drawer, bypassed the talcum powder, and plunged his fingers into the open tub of Vaseline.

Reaching under the sheet again, he anointed his penis with it, feeling the hot glow of the petroleum jelly spread outward along his body. The sensation was almost too much for him. The fragile amount of control he retained was almost not enough to stem the surging tide that threatened to explode out of him.

Pain racked him as he bent his body, his passion, to succumb to his will. Gradually the ebbing tide subsided.

He let out his breath and felt his lungs tight against his ribs. Black spots danced and whirled in his vision. He'd been so close to passing out from the crush of unfulfilled ecstasy. He'd been so close.

Sister Margaret Mary had never understood that he had *not* been giving in to the sins of the flesh. Instead, even at those young ages, he'd been trying to master them. Only by understanding them, by constantly pulling himself back from the verge of being sucked into their maelstrom of confused emotions and passions, could he overcome their hold on his life.

In his earliest teenage years he'd practiced self-flagellation, had left great purple bruises on his body that had turned green and yellow. But after a while those secret sins had gotten the better of him, becoming warped until the punishment he inflicted on himself often triggered the sexual responses he tried to combat.

He'd found his answer in the Bible, where all answers could be found if searched for long enough.

Still spasming from the repressed orgasm, Almendariz took his Bible deck from his drawer, jacked the trode into his temple, and fingered the deck controls.

Cyberspace opened up in his mind like a yawning black crevice. He avoided the gridlines, followed no path but his own. Freezing ebony layered over him and quenched the final remnants of physical desire.

16

Accessing her com-chip as her sister wheeled the rental car into the empty driveway, Bethany Shay pinged the home AI security system.

There was no response.

Automatically her hand dropped into her purse and curled around the butt of the Glock. Despite the warmth of the sun through the car's windows, she was suddenly cold. She reached across her body with her free hand and opened the door. "Get Keiko out of here," she said in a stern voice. She caught Loryn's hand before her sister could switch off the ignition.

"Beth?" A sudden understanding that something was wrong dawned in Loryn's eyes. She was blond and petite, taking more after their mother. She lived in Toronto and wrote children's books; she visited infrequently, coming down to visit Shay and their father.

Keiko hovered expectantly over the seat. "Mama-san?" She was wearing her Little Mermaid shirt and a new pair of black jeans she'd been uncertain about when Shay bought them for her at the mall earlier. Her father, she'd said, didn't approve of women wearing pants.

Shay had remembered that, but had declined to comment on Kiyoshi's sartorial preferences. Instead, she'd pointed out that riding bicycles was much more comfortable in pants.

One leg outside of the car holding the door open, Shay reached back and pushed her daughter down behind the seat. "Stay," she said firmly. "Don't get up until Aunt Loryn or I tell you it's okay."

"Yes, Mama-san." Keiko's eyes were large, and she held her arms across her chest, hands clasping her shoulders.

Loryn's hand closed in the folds of Shay's jacket. "Don't go out there. If something's wrong, let's leave together."

Gently, Shay removed her sister's hand from her clothing.

"Lock the doors," she instructed. "Drive away. Don't stop anywhere you can't see all the way around you. You saw the cruiser on the way in. Find it. Stay with it. I'll be in touch." She slid out.

"Dammit, Beth!"

"Go." Shay flattened up against the garage door with her gun in her purse so Keiko wouldn't see it.

Loryn slammed the door in frustration and drove away quickly but without squealing the tires.

The house suddenly looked different to Shay. It wasn't just home anymore. It was a potential battleground. The failure of the security system to ping back after being programmed to respond had told her the alarms had been voided. There was no doubt that someone had been in the house during the two hours they'd been shopping.

She accessed the com-chip, patched into the 911 emergency cyberlink, routed her query through Dispatch under her code number, and dropped into the freq used by the cover team Espinoza had assigned to protect her till Scivally was caught. "This is Shay."

"Go, Shay," Patrolman Anthony Jenkins said.

She knew Jenkins slightly. He was young, experienced in the redneck slums of the South, had learned that some degree of violence was often necessary in PD work, and had learned when to use it. "My sister and daughter are headed back your way," she said without preamble. "Somebody's forced the security system on my house. I'm going inside. Take care of my family."

"Shay." Jenkins's voice was urgent. "Hey, you can't go into that house by yourself. Espinoza and Keever will have my ass."

"You take care of my daughter and my sister," Shay radioed back. "That's your first priority."

"Let me call it in."

"And if they've got a scanner locked into PD freqs?"

"Shit." Jenkins sounded unhappy. "Shay, don't go into the house."

"It's my house," Shay said, letting some of the anger out. "It's my family they would have endangered if they're still inside. Now get out of my head. I've got work to do." She pressed her thumbprint against the garage ident plate and went inside.

"Shay," Jenkins said. "Your daughter and sister *are* here.

Stebbins has them. He'll stay with them. I'm on my way. Out."

Using a two-handed grip on the Glock, Shay crept into her home. Larry Scivally's memory hovered at the edges of her mind. She worked to keep the pistol from quivering.

At the kitchen door she had to print the ident plate again to bypass the tampered security system. The door hissed sideways into the wall. The lingering smell of baked bread was spread over the room. Nothing except her shadow moved across the tiled floor. She followed it inside, kept pace with it as she checked out the living room and dinette.

She heard a snarled curse at the foot of the stairway. It was a man's voice, guttural and angry. Something thumped onto the carpeted floor of her bedroom.

Easing her weight onto the stairway, avoiding the fifth step because it had a tendency to creak, she went up slowly. The Glock led the way, muzzle locked into the center of the open area. A sharp, electric click ricocheted from the walls. She froze.

"What the hell was that?" a man asked in a tense voice.

"Air conditioner," another man said. "It's been coming on every ten minutes or so. Christ, you're jumpy. Make sure you don't shoot your damn foot off while you're in there."

Two men, Shay realized, armed and separated. They'd been inside the house at least twenty minutes, long enough for the second man to log the air-conditioner cycle. She opted to try for the second man because he seemed more seasoned with breaking and entering. If he was experienced, he'd be less likely to do something stupid that would get someone hurt.

She slid her shield free of her purse, tucked it into the pocket of her chambray shirt, and reached the landing. The door to Keiko's room was open. Bringing the pistol in close beside her face, she flattened against the wall and peered inside.

A man stood with his back to her, sorting through the colorful boxes of games, toys, and puzzles at the top of Keiko's closet. He was thin, dressed in casual clothing that could easily be mistaken for business dress. His jacket lay over the face of the Mickey Mouse doll on the bed. His sleeves were rolled up, showing the latex gloves pulled up almost to his elbows. His back was to her.

Moving inside the room, she aimed the pistol at the thickest part of his chest. "Hey." She made her voice soft so it wouldn't carry more than a few feet.

The man froze for a minute, then lifted his hands. "I'm not armed."

"Quiet," Shay commanded. "Turn. Slowly. Hands where I can see them."

The man complied and came to an uncertain halt standing in the debris scattered over Keiko's room.

For the first time Shay noticed that drawers had been emptied, spilled hastily across the floor. The sheets and comforter had been stripped from the bed and left in a corner. Clothing made indiscriminate piles. The hangers looked naked hanging from the closet rod.

The man glanced nervously from Shay's gun to her face. He turned his hands so his empty palms were presented to her.

Shay tapped her badge. "On your face."

The man dropped slowly to the floor, already locking his hands behind his back.

"One false move," Shay said in a quiet voice, "and I'll shoot you through the head where you lie."

The man nodded, keeping his eyes closed tightly as she approached.

Straddling him, Shay put a knee in the middle of his back but retained her center of gravity so she wouldn't lose her balance if he tried to roll away. She kept the Glock out of his reach. After taking a pair of handcuffs from her purse, she slid the purse under the bed, then cuffed the man and made sure they locked tightly around his wrists.

"Roy," the other man's voice called. "I found it. Files, pictures. Looks like everything. Hell, we ought to get a bonus for this one."

Despite the air conditioning, Shay was covered with perspiration under her shirt and jeans. Her heart sped up when she heard the man's footsteps start toward Keiko's room. Satisfied with the handcuffing job, she recrossed the room, stood by the door, and waited.

"Hey, Roy. Didn't you hear me? I said I found it."

As the second man entered the room, Shay whirled and brought the Glock into target acquisition. The guy was quicker than she'd anticipated, and she found herself unwilling to pull the trigger. She stood locked in place for one frozen moment.

The other man didn't waste a second. She got an impression of medium height, a slender build, T-shirt, sports jacket, and frayed jeans. Then he was gone. She recognized the files he'd been carrying. They were copies of the ones concerning the Ripper murders she had brought home from the PD.

He threw them at her as he backpedaled from the room and reached under his jacket.

The hallway and doorway were suddenly filled with fluttering printouts and 8 × 10, black-and-white and polychromatic contact sheets. The man's shape blurred behind the wall of swirling paper.

Shay tried to pull the trigger but couldn't. Images of Larry Scivally's ruined face were still too vivid. Cursing her own inability, knowing it was because she couldn't focus on what she needed to do, she flung herself at the man.

A silver-barreled pistol arced over her head.

She ducked under it and felt her shoulder impact against the man's stomach as the big gun went off with the sound of a cannon trapped inside the hallway. Her hearing shattered and disappeared. She lost the Glock somewhere on the floor. Still driving her legs, she muscled the man off-balance into her bedroom. Although he outweighed her by thirty or forty pounds, her initial momentum carried her forward.

He flailed, grabbing her shoulder with his free hand.

Reacting immediately, she lifted her head and butted him in the face. Cartilage snapped. His scream of rage and pain lanced through the cotton haze filling her ears. His hand slid away and he spilled across the piles of clothing and books scattered across the room.

Shay caught herself on her hands as she started to fall forward, then shoved herself back to her feet and took a defensive posture.

Blood trickled through the man's mustache. An earpiece had broken off his sunglasses, and they dangled haphazardly from his face. Using one hand to brace himself, he tried to get to his feet and bring the pistol up.

Centered now, her breathing close to normal, Shay let her reflexes take over. She moved as smoothly as if she were on the tatami mats at the dojo where she trained and worked out. She kicked the man's wrist and sent the pistol flying, followed up with a spinning back kick that caught the guy under the chin and popped his head back.

"Fuckin' bitch!" the man yelled. A glob of bloody spittle

trailed down his chin. He crawled toward the nearest wall and used his hands to get to his feet.

Hanging on to her calm, listening to Tarao's rehearsed commands in her head, Shay moved, placing herself between the man and the pistol. She didn't try to reach it yet, because it would have left her off-balance and open to his attack. Time was on her side, and they both knew it.

The man raked a latex-gloved hand across his face and stared down at the crimson sheen that covered it. "Teach you to mess with me, bitch." He shook the fingers of his right hand. Five wafer-thin two-inch daggers slid from under his fingernails and snapped into place through the latex. The sharp edges gleamed. With an inarticulate roar of rage, he hurled himself at her.

The blades caught Shay's full attention and sent cold shivers arcing through her stomach. Her reaction time was off.

Razored metal slashed through the sleeve of her shirt when she parried the swipe aimed for her midsection. She was unable to block the blow completely. The material of the shirt was no defense, and parted easily in shreds, baring her stomach in inches-long rips. Blood trickled warmly across her abdomen, letting her know that the blades had found flesh as well. She waited for the nausea to hit her and wondered if the razors had been tainted with anything toxic.

Stepping inside his personal space, she controlled his arm with one hand and held it trapped against his body so he didn't have the leverage necessary to break her grip. Her other hand seized his belt, then she brought her knee up into his crotch three times in rapid succession.

He staggered, slumped against her, and cried out in pained rage. His breath spilled out wetly against her face, noxious with the smell of days-old alcohol and decay.

Before he could do more than struggle weakly to push her away from him, she grabbed his bio-altered hand in both of hers and slammed the fingertips against the wall. The razors shattered against the plasterboard, leaving gouges in its surface. Blood sprayed from the fingernails and covered the short, jagged stumps of the razors. A mild electric current from the disrupted feedback surged through Shay in tingling waves.

Releasing the man, Shay stepped back, tried to control her own ragged breathing, and carefully measured the space between herself and the swaying burglar. She put all of her weight and remaining strength into a roundhouse kick. It connected at the sweet spot, just as Tarao had taught her. She felt no pain, only the driving force of the kick.

The man went over backward, slamming into the open drawers of her bureau. Wood splintered as he tumbled to the floor. He didn't move.

Forcing herself into motion, Shay took the big silver pistol from the floor, then retreated to the hallway to pick up her Glock. The aftereffects of the adrenaline rush jittered through her body, giving her the shakes. She slumped against the wall inside her bedroom and waited.

"Shay."

The com-chip brushed feathery-light against the inside of her skull. "Here."

"Where?" Jenkins asked.

"Bedroom. Top of the stairs. Door on the right."

"You okay?"

Shay heard the patrolman's heavy tread on the steps. "I'm fine. Thanks."

"I heard gunfire," Jenkins called in an audible voice.

"Two guys," Shay said. "They're both down."

Jenkins entered the room with a sling-mounted Mossberg pump shotgun.

"Guy over there," Shay said, "needs to be cuffed. I've already got the other one."

"You're bleeding," Jenkins said as he took cuffs from his equipment belt and approached the unconscious burglar.

"Scratches." Shay replied. "Guy had a full set of finger razors that were a surprise."

Jenkins cuffed the man and left him lying facedown. "Guy doesn't sound like your typical burglar. Having lethal biotech on a forced entry usually means the DA will go for attempted homicide rather than the B and E."

"I know. He was carrying, too." Shay held the silver pistol up.

"You okay here? I gotta call this in."

Shay nodded. "Phone's in the living room next to the couch."

Jenkins trotted down the steps.

"Beth?"

Peering down the hallway, Shay saw Loryn coming up the stairs holding one of Keiko's hands. "I'm here. Don't let Keiko come any farther. She doesn't need to see this."

"Mama-san?"

"I'm okay, honey. Just stay there a minute and be a good girl."

Keiko nodded, gazing with open fascination at the destruction scattered over the hallway.

"What's going on?" Loryn asked.

"These men were looking for files I kept here," Shay said.

Loryn plucked at the shredded material of Shay's shirt. "You're bleeding."

"It's not bad."

"It's not good either." Loryn headed for the bathroom.

Shay leaned her head against the wall and let her eyelids droop almost closed. Keiko's sudden screams ripped into her, had her moving before she realized what the stimulus had been. She wheeled around the door and saw her daughter standing in the hallway holding one of the polychromatic contact prints.

Keiko held the print up helplessly, large tears running down her face. Her hands shook in fright. "She's dead! She's dead!"

Shay dropped to her knees and tried to soothe her daughter, held Keiko tightly and pulled the contact sheet out of her trembling fists. "It's okay," she whispered into Keiko's ear. "It's okay. Mommy's here. No one's going to hurt you." She turned the picture over after recognizing it as one of the crime-scene photos of Mitzi Harrington's body, then realized the floor was littered with dead faces.

She dropped her gun, pulled Keiko into her, and stood up, carrying her daughter away from the 8 × 10 nightmares. The screaming started again when Keiko realized Shay's blood was on her hands.

17

"What is it you had that drew him to you?"

Felix Carey paced inside his personal matrix and stared at the full-length images of the three dead women that the Ripper had claimed as victims so far. They stood silent, hands at their sides, as they gazed back sightlessly from the wallscreen.

He approached the first one. "Mitzi Harrington," he said to himself.

She was blond, hair too spiky to suit Carey's tastes, and fifteen pounds too heavy. She wore a loose dress, cut to reduce the effect of her generous curves. She looked closer to thirty than twenty, but her personal records indicated she was only twenty-three.

"A schoolteacher and mother of two. Where did you meet him?"

She didn't answer.

Carey moved on to the second woman. "Aleka. Or should I call you Vivian Cates? Valente assures me that was your real name."

The butterfly tattoo on the brunette's left cheek changed colors, flowed from neon pink to indigo blue, then back again. She was dressed in low-cut shorts held up by a wide belt, a studded halter top, and knee-high white boots. Glitter eyeshadow gleamed under her dark bangs. This one was more alluring, but in a crass kind of way, advertising tawdry sex.

"A hooker," Carey said. "Was he cruising the strip bars when he found you? No. Strip bars might still be too upscale for you. A park, then. Did he find you at a park or on a street corner? Was he cruising the ghetto then, looking for a cheap thrill he doesn't find at home?"

The woman didn't move.

"No. I think not. No sex, remember? Your charms didn't

capture his imagination. So what was it about you that lured him on?" Carey moved on to the last woman. "Inesita Camejo."

Like the Harrington woman, Camejo had blond hair, but it had come from a bottle of chemicals. She was a thin, faded woman, tired from fighting life and having her heart broken. Her manner of dress was professional, full skirt and coordinated blouse that allowed no glimpse of cleavage.

"An unemployed counselor," Carey said. He enjoyed the sound of his own voice when he was trying to puzzle problems out. The acoustic structure in the room carried it back to him. "What made him seek you out? Did he receive your professional services at some time? Was he a disgruntled employee who transferred his anger to you rather than some faceless company he could never hope to bring down to his own level of retribution?"

Frustration chafed at Carey as he examined the women again. The answers were there. It was only a matter of finding them in time. He wanted so badly to know the Ripper's identity now. There was so much to do.

He laid his palm against the wallscreen over the Camejo woman's image, willed it through, then took her wrist and pulled her into the room with him. Since she was based on secondary information gleaned from news reports, she lacked personality and a will of her own. And there was a haziness to her that made her look like a colorized holo.

Moving on to the other women, he pulled them into the room as well. They stood looking at him like cattle, ghosts that hadn't been truly laid to rest.

Accessing the matrix, he stripped their clothing from them. They remained standing with no change in their expressions. Keying the matrix again, he blended the women into one combined shape with each woman layered inside it, floated it above the floor, and turned it in all directions, seeking the features the women had in common. There were none.

"Why you?" he demanded. "His attacks against you were passionate."

Using the matrix again, he once more separated the women, added the grisly wounds the Ripper had scored into each of his victims. Blood drained down the pale flesh, followed by the ropy twist of blue-gray intestines slithering free. The eyes turned listless and dull and lost their sheen.

"Something about you turned on a dark passion he tries to hide from the rest of the world. What is it? What does he conceal?"

The bodies turned in unison to his unspoken command, halted together in a staggered triangle at left profile.

"Is it a lust?" Carey asked. "Or an anger? Did someone like you hurt him so that he has found the strength to fight back at that person? No. You don't look similar enough. You don't have the same professional paths. Your backgrounds suggest no ties, no common denominator."

The bodies faced him again. He used the matrix, sucked the wounds from the corpses in the form of designs, coalesced them down to similarities in glistening electric-blue laser lights. He dimmed the room's illumination to bring them more clearly into focus.

"He cuts you," Carey mused. "Again, why? If he wanted merely to kill you, why not use a gun? He's drawn to the water. Why not drown you? He remains hidden from the law enforcement people, chooses not to claim his kills. He doesn't want anyone to know he killed you. Why?"

Taking the resulting analog of the wounds into his control, Carey placed them back onto Aleka, because she was the one who most intrigued him. At once the flesh split and tore, making room for the wounds. Intestines slithered free like snakes, hung down to her knees. Blood followed.

He crossed the room to the woman and inhaled the trace scents from her. She smelled of hair spray, shampoo, perfume, leather, and decay. He touched a pallid cheek and ran his forefinger across her lips.

"He cuts you in all the same ways. It's his pattern. What does it mean to him? What purpose does it serve?" He studied the wounds in the abdomen. "He reaches inside of you, puts his hands into your body, but he doesn't violate you sexually. Penetration means something to him, is very passionate to him, but what is the meaning? Does he find this violation more stimulating than actual rape?"

He turned his attention to the Camejo woman. She stood naked and waiting, eyes forward. There were no wounds on her body.

"He kissed you," Carey said. "Were you a favorite? Were you someone he desired more than the others? Were you the one he was actually after? Or has his passion taken on a new bent?"

Carey leaned forward, took the woman in his arms, and willed her to return his embrace. He kissed her, long and hard and deep, tasted her dead soul and relished the flavor that clung to his lips. Her mouth was cold, taut, because even without the wounds rigor mortis had set in. He ran his hands down her body and caressed her cold flesh.

"Were you someone special?"

She didn't answer.

His breath fogged her glassy-eyed stare. Reluctantly he stepped back from her. Despite the growing need in the pit of his stomach, he could take no passion from her.

Accessing the matrix, he wished them away.

The three women vanished with sharp pops of displaced air.

Feeling the melancholy descend on him, as well as the need for privacy, Carey turned out the lights in the room and summoned up the moonscape view available outside the mining industry he owned on the moon. The stars seemed endless. Harsh, jagged shadows tilted across the gray-white lunar dust.

A beep from the outside communications line hailed him.

He answered it reluctantly.

"Mr. Carey, there is a matter requiring your immediate attention."

"What is it, Welbourne?"

"The men Mr. Valente assigned to the Shay woman's house have been apprehended."

Carey accessed the matrix and shut away the moon. "And the men assigned to Detective Keever's home?"

"They were successful, sir."

Breathing a sigh of relief, Carey said, "Get Dickers out into the field, have him meet with these men and arrange to purchase whatever information they've recovered. I'll attend to Valente myself."

"Yes sir." Welbourne faded from the matrix.

Feeding the file numbers into the matrix, Carey reached for the special gridline connecting him to Valente. He'd hoped that the man would prove more lasting, that some good would come from Valente's efforts. Otherwise Carey would have to content himself with following behind the police investigation for a while longer.

Either way, Valente had become a liability, and that was what Carey had recruited the man to be.

Securely imbedded in the gridline tying him to Valente, Carey eased into the man's consciousness and allowed Valente to become aware of him. He felt the man's horror thrill through him. Then he overloaded the neural imprint and short-circuited Valente's brain, killing the man instantly. Carey stayed with the open gridline long enough to sense Valente's body hitting the floor of the apartment, then retreated back to the matrix.

He almost found the experience satisfying. Almost, and that was the maddening part.

18

"This wasn't connected to Aaron Scivally," Bethany Shay repeated.

Her father, Keever, and Captain Herve Espinoza of homicide stood with her in the backyard. Just beyond them Loryn sat at the picnic table holding Keiko in her lap.

"Then what?" Espinoza asked.

"They wanted the files on the Ripper."

"The files on the Ripper," Espinoza repeated. At five-eleven, he was four inches taller than Shay, but wanted to be over six feet. He always carried himself primly erect, giving the impression that he'd once served in the military. His carefully styled black hair always looked greasy even though it wasn't. Shay knew for a fact that his wife helped him upgrade his clothing by taking off-the-rack suits and tailoring them to her husband's build. The homicide captain smoothed his pencil-thin mustache with his fingers. His dark eyes glittered as he locked gazes with Shay. "Why would they want those?"

"You'd have to ask them, sir." Shay used the respectful term out of context, to let Espinoza know tactfully that she was tired of the continuing round of questions. Her father and Keever had already been through this.

"That'll be hard," Ryan Shay said. He'd been a big man in his prime. He was in his sixties now, and the years had started to pull him down. His hair was rusty silver and cropped close. His face was granite, and the residual fear and anger that had shown earlier was locked inside him. Shay recognized that from the imbedded parentheses the corners of his lips had become. "Both those assholes have been 'printed."

"They worked for somebody," Espinoza said in his deceptively quiet voice. "And they didn't look like the type to be exactly cherry to this kind of thing."

"Working on it," Keever replied. "I've got Napier and Innes pulling jackets on these guys now."

Espinoza touched his chin with a thumb and nodded.

Looking toward her house, Shay found the uniforms still in evidence despite the fact that the two burglars had been removed from the premises almost a half hour ago. A police helo made periodic passes overhead, the .50-caliber chaingun looking stubby and dangerous on its underbelly.

Neighbors gathered at the windows of their homes over the tops of the privacy fence and tried to stare without being caught. A glance through the gate showed the two news vans parked in the street.

Mohammed, one of the junior officers who'd recently made detective third grade, crossed the yard and stopped outside their circle with a notepad in his hand. He was young, up from Trinidad a few years back, and hadn't fully lost his island accent when he was granted citizenship. "Tully."

"Yeah," the big detective said.

"Just confirmed through your landlady that your place was hit too," Mohammed said.

"What? Who told you to check my place?"

"The captain."

Shay looked at Espinoza and realized the man had already been acting under his personal suppositions before she'd given him her own. It wasn't the first time he'd surprised her.

"What was taken?" Espinoza asked without looking at Keever.

"I have a uniform on the scene," Mohammed said. "She tells me that the locks on Detective Keever's filing cabinets were jimmied, and some of the files appear to be missing."

"Files on the Ripper?"

"I had the uniform check for them, but none were there."

"Tully," Espinoza asked, "you had files on the Ripper homicides?"

"Yeah."

Espinoza nodded. "Mohammed, get a crime scene team there now. My authority. No bullshit excuses or I'll have somebody's ass. If those people left any fingerprints, I want them pronto."

"Yes sir." Mohammed stopped himself short of saluting, then turned and left.

Shay heard the detective accessing the com-chip and ringing in for Dispatch, bouncing the signal off the switchblock temporarily set up inside her house. Once Mohammed had the signal lock, they changed to a private freq. She tried to ignore the ache in her body from the bruising she'd received during the fight, and tried not to feel so guilty that it was Loryn holding Keiko and not her.

"This complicates things," Espinoza said. "It could mean that we're no longer looking for one man who could be the Ripper," Espinoza said. "Already we've turned over a small circle of individuals intent on whatever information has come into our possession regarding the Ripper's kills."

"Or it could mean that someone's trying to beat us to the Ripper to take his own vengeance against the man," Keever replied.

Shay was instantly captivated by the line of thinking. "Who?"

"Neither the Harrington woman's nor the Camejo woman's families appear financially able to hire out a contracted skin job," the homicide captain said. "What about Aleka? Do we know anything more about her?"

"She's still a cipher."

Espinoza nodded. "It's something to work on. She worked the streets. You might want to focus your investigation on her for a while. Find out if she was close to anybody with the power and means to do what we're talking about."

Shay excused herself, then walked over to Loryn and Keiko.

"God, she's getting heavy," Loryn said as she passed the sleeping girl over.

Shay sat at the table, tucked her daughter into the crook of her arm and watched her snuggle up to a new position, then fall back into a deep sleep. She ran the back of her free hand down Keiko's cheek, knew she was on the verge of tears, and held them back with effort. There'd be time enough to cry later.

Loryn squeezed her arm. "I'll go get us something to drink. Be right back."

Shay nodded. Eyes still burning, she glanced around her backyard and her house. She felt so invaded, as if her professional life and personal life had overlapped to the point that she had no true life at all left. Part of her had wanted to mother Keiko immediately, wanted to stay with her instead of giving a report to Espinoza. The other part of her realized how important it was that the PD get the information while it was fresh.

Silently, she cursed the Ripper for disrupting her life.

Tires screeched out in the street.

Keiko stirred in Shay's arms.

A concerned voice echoed along the com-chip frequency. "Captain Espinoza?"

"Go." Espinoza turned to face the house like a birddog on point.

"Got a man here named Kiyoshi Izutsu. Says he's here to pick up his daughter. I don't know anything about no daughter."

Espinoza looked at Shay.

A trickle of ice water flooded Shay's veins. She stood up before she realized what she was doing.

"Must have a dozen guys with him, Cap'n, and he don't appear like he's going to take no for an answer."

Shay tried to speak but couldn't. Instinctively she tightened her grip on her daughter. She saw Keever whisper to her father, then Ryan Shay's jaw tightened and he approached her.

"Let the man through," Espinoza said.

"Sir?"

"Let him through."

"Yes sir."

Ryan Shay came to a stop at her side. "Beth?"

She shook her head, unable to make any words come through the painful lump in her throat. It didn't surprise her that Kiyoshi knew, and she had no doubt about how things here would end.

The back door opened and two Japanese men dressed in black suits and turtlenecks came through. Their heads didn't move, but Shay knew the eyes behind the black-lensed sunglasses had already photographed the position of every person in the backyard. They flanked the door, but stayed in place as two more men led the way.

Kiyoshi followed them, lean and unforgiving in his formal attire. The crimson handkerchief in his breast pocket looked like a smear of blood. Sunlight sparkled from his cufflinks and tietack. Without hesitation, he strode briskly toward Shay. The six men trailing him fanned out and visibly took control of the yard's perimeters.

"She's all right," Shay said. "Nothing happened to her." Even though she didn't want to, she opened her arms to reveal Keiko sleeping there. It made her feel unprotected.

Without a word, Kiyoshi reached into her arms and removed Keiko.

"Hey!" Keever bellowed as he started forward.

One of the black-suited guards slipped a short sword from under the back of his tailored jacket. The glittering length of steel arced around and blurred to a stop in front of Keever's throat.

In motion himself, Keever put a hand up defensively, drew his pistol, and pointed it at the swordsman. The guard never wavered.

Beside her, Shay saw her father shift position slightly, saw his hand drop for the pistol he had holstered at his back under his jacket.

"Take it easy, Tully," Ryan Shay said softly. "We don't want anybody getting hurt here."

Kiyoshi remained frozen in place, his features entirely neutral. There were no emotions on the faces of his men.

"Back off, Keever," Espinoza ordered. His voice crackled with authority, but he didn't move. "Mr. Kiyoshi is a member of the Japanese economic community. As such, you know he has diplomatic immunity in this country. If you do anything to precipitate this further, I'll see you up on charges before DataMain rings in the next hour."

Keever remained as he was.

"Tully," Shay said in a thick voice. "Please."

"You're an asshole, Izutsu," Keever said, then snapped the safety back on the Wildey, holstered it, and backed away.

The swordsman turned his head slightly to Kiyoshi.

Shay felt her breath catch in her throat for just a moment as she watched her ex-husband.

Kiyoshi fractionally moved his head from side to side.

With a sudden movement the sword vanished and the man stepped back into place.

"You have endangered my daughter," Kiyoshi said in Japanese. His voice was flat, unyielding. "Do you place such a small value on her life as to involve her in this?"

Shay didn't want to answer in Japanese. It tied her to him on his ground. But she didn't want her personal life aired in front of the departmental people either. "I did not involve her."

"She is here. Those men were here. They tried to kill you. Their bullets just as easily could have found Keiko."

"She was clear of the area."

"And if they had killed you?"

Shay had no answer.

"You do not think your life through," Kiyoshi said. "You enjoy living on the edge too much to be a proper mother. If she was clear of the house, you, too, should have been clear. Did you not think she would be afraid for you, would fear for your safety? Did you even stop to think that the next time she saw you, it could have been when they pulled your body from this house, or when your picture turned up on wallscreen? She knows what you do, and she worries about you. That is no life for a child."

Angry words collided in Shay's brain. "Is that any worse than the life you have chosen for yourself? You're head of Izutsu Corporation. You are the target of assassins' bullets and knives. Your father's first wife, your mother, was killed in an assassination attempt against him in Tokyo." As soon as she said it, she regretted it. He'd never spoken of his mother, nor ever mentioned her death. Shay had discovered it during one of the talks she'd had with Madoka shortly after Keiko's birth.

Spots of color flared on Kiyoshi's face.

"Your presence is just as much of a threat to her as mine."

"Silence!"

Keiko stirred, threw an arm over her father's shoulder.

Kiyoshi started to take a step toward Shay.

Immediately Ryan Shay moved in an interception course between them, and Keever shifted to remind everyone he hadn't faded from the scene.

Kiyoshi pulled back. "You will not speak of my mother, Detective. You are not worthy to mention her name."

His words cut Shay, drew more anger. She recognized the endless circle that had led to the self-destruction of their marriage.

Drawing Keiko in closer to his chest, Kiyoshi said, "Neither will you see my daughter again until you have learned not to act irresponsibly around her."

"Goddammit," Shay said, "you're not going to take her away from me, you son of a bitch. I won't let you do that."

Moving quickly, Ryan Shay caught her around the waist

with one arm. He kept his body between her and Kiyoshi as two of the guards fell into position around her ex-husband.

"You won't have a choice," Kiyoshi said. "I was generous when I allowed you to retain visitation rights after the custody hearing. Today's events have crushed all of that generosity from me. I will no longer be weak. There will be no further mistakes. Keiko will be safe."

Shay struggled to clear her father's restraining arm.

"Ease off," Ryan Shay whispered. "I don't know what the hell you two are saying to each other, but the tone sounds familiar. He's scared. You're scared. Neither one of you is going to be able to talk sensibly to the other right now. Let it lie. There'll be time for discussion later. And Keiko doesn't need this."

Forcing herself, Shay relaxed and moved back away from her father. She wrapped her arms around her upper body in helpless frustration.

Squirming in her father's grasp, Keiko opened her eyes and looked up. "Bad faces, Papa-san," she said in a sleepy voice. "I saw bad faces."

"Shush, little one," Kiyoshi said in a soft voice. "I have you now. No one can hurt you."

Shay watched them go, two men preceding Kiyoshi through the back door of her house while the others brought up the rear. She had the sinking feeling that she'd never see Keiko again. No one understood how unyielding Kiyoshi could be. When her father tried to take her into his arms, she pushed him away and walked into the deepest part of the yard to be alone.

19

The hidden choir sang the hymn beautifully, voices sounding far away and haunting, rolling across the cavernous interior of the old church.

Bethany Shay sat in one of the rear pews by herself and stared at the flower-wreathed casket near the pulpit. For the funeral she'd worn a subtle black dress, tied her hair back in a sedate French braid, and used very little color in her makeup. A small black purse sat next to her. The Glock made it heavy, and didn't leave much room for personal effects.

Nylons rustled when she recrossed her legs. Her need to urinate hadn't passed. She'd started the morning with too much coffee and nothing solid in the way of breakfast. Soon, she knew from experience, her kidneys would start protesting too.

Her eyes ranged over the crowd gathered for the funeral service at St. Gregory's Church, wondered if the Ripper was among them.

Media lenses took in the service with dispassionate views. Emotion would be layered in later. At noon, the wallscreen news reports would be in mourning for a young woman who had died and never had the chance to live to fulfill the promising future she had ahead of her. By five the same footage would be filled with anger and hostility, and reporters would be busy pointing out that Inesita Camejo lost her life because the police were incompetent.

The hymn stopped, faded away as a final singer finished with a solo stanza, holding the high note long enough for Shay to instinctively take a breath for the guy.

The priest stepped up to the pulpit again and went on with another segment of the service. His voice, the words in Latin, droned out over the seated people.

The audience was larger than the one that had attended Aleka's service. Almost two hundred people sat in the pews.

Shay wondered how many of them were actually there to pay their respects and how many were there to see the Ripper's work up close. The church had wanted to limit the attendance to invitation only, but Espinoza had persuaded them to leave it open to the public on the chance that the Ripper might not be someone known to Camejo's mother. The homicide captain could be persuasive when he wanted to be.

A guest book was at the front of the church, provided by the police department, and staffed by a detective assigned there to make sure everyone signed in. Those that refused after being politely asked were supposed to be routed via com-chip to Shay for visual inspection. So far no one had refused to sign.

It still wasn't much, and Shay knew it. Possibly even with the Ripper's real name they wouldn't be able to cross-reference the man to the list of names gleaned from Aleka's funeral. And there was always the chance the man would be smart enough simply to use a false name. People were being asked to sign in, not provide proof of their identity. But it would help build a control group.

The media cameras moved quietly, the photographers having learned a long time ago how to blend into sensitive surroundings. The two that seemed to be the most inept by comparison were the ones assigned by Espinoza. And even they wouldn't be noticed except by the most alert among the audience.

Shay relaxed and let her breath out through her nose in a steady stream designed to release the stress she felt. It did nothing for her sour stomach or her need to go to the bathroom. She crossed her legs again, tried not to think of how Kiyoshi had taken Keiko from her and how she had stood there and let him. There had been no phone calls later, and her own efforts at contact last night and this morning were blocked by the staff at the Izutsu family home.

When she'd called her lawyer that morning and filled him in on yesterday's details, he hadn't offered much in the way of hope. Shay hadn't realized how much she'd been counting on the positive impact of his words till she hadn't gotten them.

She scanned the pews again. Most of the crowd that had

attended Aleka's funeral had been street people like the woman. Instead of grief, the major emotion Shay had noted had been fear. It had hung in the small church, the stench of mortality that most of those street survivors couldn't afford to breathe in and keep their nerve while plying their trade. To the devout believers in St. Gregory's Church, Camejo's untimely death represented the sad letting go of a sister who was going to a better place. The audience at Aleka's funeral had only glimpsed what lay waiting for them if they didn't remain careful.

The choir took up another song when the priest stepped back from the pulpit and crossed himself.

A hand touched Shay's shoulder lightly, and she looked up to find Keever standing there. She was amazed at the sense of sudden alarm that had jangled through her.

Keever was dressed in a fairly presentable sport coat and a tie, but the shirt was one Shay had seen before, usually without the sartorial accouterments. After she scooted over, leaving him the aisle seat, he sat with his hands in his lap and looked at the casket. "Found the guy who handled the bozos who crashed your house," he whispered.

"Who?"

"Guy named Quinn Valente."

The name sounded familiar, but Shay couldn't fit a handle to it. She raised an inquisitive eyebrow.

"Supposed to be a licensed PI operating in Houston. Had an office/residence off Delano and Wheeler."

"Kind of in the middle of the Ripper's action when you look at the map."

Keever nodded.

"So what does Valente have to say?"

"Nothing. He's dead. They've got his body on ice at the coroner's office."

Shay let her silence be her question.

"Somebody burned out his brain through a direct-channel neural imprint."

"So he was somebody else's puppet."

"That's the way it looks." Keever shifted restlessly. "People in records are going through his personal assets. Last couple of weeks, Valente had been showing considerable cash flow."

"Who was paying him?"

"Don't know. The money was electronic transfer, bounced

through the system and buried under a ton of bullshit. Cash would have been easier to trace."

"Was Valente dirty before this?"

Keever nodded. "I don't think for a minute that he was totally coerced into recruiting the guys who hit us. I figure whoever was paying him also had the neural imprint jacked into his system to keep him on the up and up. Valente doesn't exactly enjoy an unsullied reputation on either side of the street. The man was a master at walking that thin line between legal and illegal, and between cross and double-cross."

"What about his files?"

"His office deck was wiped."

"Backup systems?"

"If he had any, we haven't found them yet. It's possible he had the information chipped into his mind. But things are a mess in there, and if anything in the way of evidence is recovered, it's going to be a damn miracle."

Considering that, Shay turned the information over in her mind, looked at it from various angles. "If you were going to hire Valente, and you had money to get someone else to do the job, why would you hire Valente?"

"The man knew the street players," Keever said. "The freaks, the skels, the underground techdocs. And—though it could never be proved—he owned percentages of a number of black markets. If a dollar could be turned anywhere in the inner city, you can bet Quinn Valente had his hands on three cents of it."

"He was pulling down that much?"

"On a safe bet. Not only was he a contact for people who could provide any illegal substances or services anybody could ever want, he also traded off with the PD."

"He was a snitch?"

"Yeah. Used him a few times myself, when I wasn't trying to nail his ass on bunco squad for something I *knew* he had his fingers in."

"If money was no real problem to him," Shay said, "there's only one thing that could have interested him."

Keever nodded. "Big Money."

"Provided he was hired to perform his specialty of turning up people other people were interested in, that points to the Ripper, because of the files."

"That's what I was thinking. Still leaves us guessing who was looking for the Ripper, and why."

"Clues us in to something else too," Shay said. "If Valente was that good, he'd probably have turned the Ripper by now. Proceeding on that, we have two options. Either Valente's client now knows who the Ripper is and silenced Valente because he wasn't trusted, or Valente couldn't find him because the Ripper isn't a street person."

"Leaves us with another problem too," Keever said. "The postmortem puts Valente's death only a few minutes after the call came in to Dispatch about shots fired at your house. Whoever aced Valente must be tied in pretty tightly to the PD."

"Doesn't have to mean a dirty cop," Shay replied. "Could be something in the tech transfers."

"Yeah." Keever rubbed his chin. "If the Ripper isn't a street person, how come he works that territory?"

"Because he knows them best," Shay said. And she knew she was right even though she didn't have any physical evidence.

Vitoria Camejo sat in the front pew dressed in black from head to toe. Clutching a handkerchief in a knobby, blue-veined fist, she sobbed silently and dabbed at her eyes.

Finding herself too easily slipping into an empathetic bond with a mother who'd just lost a daughter, Shay blinked her misting eyes clear and glanced away.

"I do have some good news," Keever said.

"I'm ready for some."

"Espinoza set up a confab with the DA's office early this morning. Looks like he may have set up a deal with Dwain Andersson about cutting us some slack on the pusher Pascalli's people picked up. As Espinoza was quick to point out, even if it means losing pondscum like Eddie Lupton, it'd be worth it to stop the Ripper before he kills again. Even to the DA's office."

"Especially if they get to go to trial with the Ripper," Shay said.

"Don't be surprised if taking the Ripper alive is part of the deal," Keever said seriously.

"Shit," Shay said louder than she'd intended.

A middle-aged woman in front of her turned around to look at her with a chastising expression.

Shay quickly apologized in a contrite voice.

Finished with the eulogy, the priest stepped back and folded his arms into his robe. The choir began to sing again, then altar boys started escorting the family row to view the deceased a final time.

Taking Keever's arm, Shay said, "I'm ready."

Before they made the doors at the end of the cathedral, a blond woman in a black dress that managed to look both funereal and festive at the same time came at them at something less than all-out running. A man with a camcorder perched on his shoulder like some exotic bird followed closely behind her.

"Detectives," the woman said too loudly to go unnoticed in the quiet of the room. "Hey. Wait up a minute."

Shay started to access the com-chip, then felt Keever glide into the freq just ahead of her. She turned to face the woman and cameraman.

"Shay and Keever, right?" The woman automatically checked her appearance with her hands, made sure her hair was in place and her clothes fit correctly. "I'm Corri Bowman, Channel 49 Newsminutes." She held out her hand.

Heads were already turning toward Shay and Keever. More media people abandoned their posts and rallied around them, cutting off their access to the church exit. The mourners turned unwillingly from their goodbyes. Shay had no doubt that by the five-o'clock newsbreak the police department would be responsible for disrupting the funeral service. She ignored Bowman's outstretched hand as the fountain of light from the camcorder spilled over her.

20

"Detective Shay, are you and Detective Keever here because you believe the Bayou Ripper is here also, attending the funeral of his latest victim?"

Almendariz's breath seized in his lungs when he heard the question. Already standing, he turned and placed his hand against the wall beside his seat in the pew to steady himself. The room seemed to spin for a moment, then he looked back over the heads of the perplexed crowd of mourners staring at the scene at the back of the church. He'd seen the media people there earlier and had dismissed them as no threat to him because they had not noticed him at the other two funerals.

Two of the church's younger priests separated from the pulpit and jogged toward the knotted mass of police personnel and media while the senior member tried to regain control of the funeral services.

A cold sweat broke out and chilled the back of Almendariz's neck. He jerked his gaze away from the group of reporters pressing in against the police detectives and studied the twisting path leading to the rear of the church. He'd been there before, on business visits he'd been assigned by Father Brian over the years. Every way out of the building was familiar to him.

His heart thudded inside his chest when he looked back at the detectives trying to extricate themselves from the media. The two young priests only made matters more difficult, and upped the performance value of the news footage. Gesturing and trying to sound angry without sounding loud, dressed in black robes, they became accouterments to the action taking place.

The big detective—Keever, Almendariz remembered— had evidently reached his limit of patience. The man put a wide hand on a camcorder lens and pushed machine and photographer out of the way toward the front doors. A dozen other camcorders swept toward the action. Their incandescent light bounced brilliant hues from the stained-glass windows. The camcorder operator flailed blindly as he tripped backward and went sprawling among his peers. A general clamor of disapproval rippled through the ranks of the reporters.

A hole opened up for a moment, and Keever headed for it by stepping over the body of the downed cameraman, flanked quickly by the female detective.

Almendariz sucked in his breath at the sight of her. *It* shrilled and yelled inside him, demanding release. He'd seen pictures of her on the wallscreen, but she'd never looked anything like this.

She was slightly above average height for a woman, and the long auburn hair was styled in braids that put her femininity in the forefront. The black dress clung to her figure suggestively without revealing everything underneath. Narrow black lines ran up the backs of her calves from her hose.

Before he could stop himself, Almendariz found himself wondering whether Detective Shay wore pantyhose or just stockings. He was at the mercy of *it*, on the verge of allowing *it* to escape. His penis had hardened inside his black pants and he hadn't even noticed. Perspiration trickled down the back of his neck, cold icicles that were blunted and absorbed by his clerical collar. His body trembled from the effort of not giving in to the pleasure that called out so deliciously to him. The first impulse he had was to slam his fist into his body and drown the lust that fired him with pain, to throttle it before it escaped completely. But he was too aware of the woman beside him. Even with everything else going on, she would be sure to notice his action.

A headache sprang to life full-grown and slammed into his temples. He clenched a hand on the back of the pew in front of him. His nails sank into the varnished wood, then tore loose slightly from his fingers. The pain was suddenly incredible. The warmth of blood slowly strained his fingertips and dripped from his little finger.

It subsided within him, fell through his mind and body like the dead calm right after a sudden spring storm.

The media hadn't given ground willingly before the police detectives. They'd rallied behind their braver allies and put up a bold front that stopped Keever and Shay in their tracks.

The two priests pursued them, but stayed well out of the way so that any more violent interruptions wouldn't directly involve them. Media microphones bristled like weapons as the reporters stopped only a few feet short of the main doors in the outer foyer.

Detective Shay halted behind her partner and gazed around the church, seemingly unaffected by all the attention they were getting.

"Do you think the Ripper is here among us?" the female reporter yelled out again. Her question started an undercurrent of inquisitive and demanding tones from the other reporters.

"Do you know who the Ripper is?" another voice called out.

"Why haven't you taken him into custody if you know who he is?" someone else asked.

The mourners stood frozen. Hesitant expressions pulled at their features.

Almendariz turned slightly, taking cover behind the woman standing next to him.

Without warning, the woman turned to Almendariz and gripped the lapels of his jacket. She was an older woman, possibly in her sixties, and wore a black dress with accompanying hat and veil. Her black gloves didn't quite hide the brown liver spots that tracked up her blue-veined arms. "Do you think it could be true, Father? Do you think that killer could be here?"

He murmured something in reply as he returned his attention to the confusion at the door. He almost locked eyes with the woman detective before he realized it. Desire stirred in him, but it was a sluggish thing now.

He was sure he felt Shay's eyes on him, but he didn't chance a look to find out if she was staring at him. He'd viewed her as a potential enemy from the beginning, but he hadn't known she would possess the powers of a succubus too. Still, in a way it wasn't surprising. Why else would a woman be assigned to find him?

More loud voices joined those of the reporters. Uniformed police officers poured into the church despite the protesting clergy members. A wall of policemen bisected the pocket of media members and reached Keever and Shay.

He scarcely believed it when Shay allowed herself to be herded outside under the protection of the uniformed policemen. Keever brought up the rear and freely lashed out at any camcorder operator who was fool enough to get within range.

Sick and shaking from the effects of his fear, Almendariz turned away from them. They could be waiting for him outside. He gazed down at his hand and saw the blood from his torn nails pooling in his palm. Uncurling his fingers, he stared at the blood with renewed interest. Oval in shape, the pool held a sheen that almost captured his reflection. He tried to look deeper, smelling the coppery taste of it now. Saliva trickled over his tongue unexpectedly. He was amazed. He'd only heard about stigmata before, never seen them.

"Are you all right, Father?"

Fingers closed around Almendariz's upper arm. He recognized the thin and bony lengths and who they must belong to before he glanced down at the old woman. Reluctantly he closed his hand, knowing the perfection of the stigmata would be blemished now. He showed the woman a smile when he wanted to reach for the shoehorn. "I'm fine."

"You look ill." She gazed at him speculatively.

"It's the violence," Almendariz said. "I've lived in the church all my life. I'm not used to seeing things like this." He dipped his head slightly, as if embarrassed. "I suppose I should be a stronger priest if I'm expected to deal with the outer world."

"Nonsense." She patted his cheek softly and pressed a tissue into his hand. "You're strong in your faith, Father. Even these old eyes can see that. Don't fault yourself for being human." She smiled, showed ill-fitting dentures seated between crimson lips. "Would you do the honor of walking an old woman through the line to pay her last respects?"

Almendariz was reminded of Sister Margaret Mary. The sister had used her age as an infirmity even though it wasn't.

The line moved slowly.

He stood beside the old woman when they reached the open casket. The woman reached out and patted the dead woman's cheek. Hypnotized by the proximity of the corpse, Almendariz touched the cool forehead. He trembled, stopping himself short of yanking his hand away when he felt hot desire refill him. His mouth went dry. With effort he took his hand from the dead woman and escorted his companion on.

Even in death she had not released her power over him. He hadn't touched the other two, so he hadn't known, hadn't been sheltered against the evil they possessed. He took a deep breath that must have been confused for a broken sob, because the woman looped an arm around his waist and hugged him close.

Shaken from his experience inside the church, Almendariz stood inside the foyer of the rear entrance to the building. He glanced over the rows of carefully trimmed hedges and scanned the streets.

There were no police cars, marked or unmarked, in evidence. They weren't waiting for him as he'd feared.

He barely made the bus stop in time to catch the bus. The other passengers from the funeral had already boarded. The driver was surly and withdrawn. Almendariz whisked his transit pass through the reader and lurched down the aisle to find a seat while the driver pulled into traffic. The mid-morning crowd was light. There were plenty of seats. He found one near the rear and relaxed.

He leaned back in the seat and tried to quell the growing pain swelling across his shoulders and lower back from his spine. The hot flashes felt like electric lines of fire drawn with the blade of a dull knife. He took two pain pills from his backpack and swallowed them dry. He could tell from the agony he was experiencing now that another seizure would leave him just short of crippled for hours. His only release from the pain would be his Bible deck.

He reached into his pocket and touched it. For a moment he considered jacking into it and losing some of the pain for a time. Reluctantly he decided against it.

The bus rolled to a stop at the corner of Cullen and Faulkner with a screeching hiss of air brakes.

Caught unawares, Almendariz started to stand up. Ahead of him, a young woman wearing a black dress got out of her seat long enough to allow the person beside her to get out. She stood in the aisle for a moment, all generous curves on the verge of plumpness. Her brown hair was done in a curly perm that leaked half-moons down over her ears and face. Her nose was too long, but it gave her features a girlish demeanor. Fitting a little snugly, her dress clung to the rounded hips and rode high on her thighs when she stepped back into the seat. A white slip gleamed for just an instant in the split panels of the dress.

By then it was too late for Almendariz to do anything to stop *it*. The orgasm hit him with the fury of a piledriver and flared into a sudden bright spark that washed away all thoughts of his aching spine. His hips moved convulsively twice, three times as he forced his groin against the seat in front of him. The warmth of his seed spilled over his flesh.

Weak from *it*s release and from the depression that was already settling into his mind, he sat back down.

The bus driver glanced at him in the large rectangular mirror bolted over the cab.

Almendariz placed his arms on the seat in front of him and rested his head against them. Hot, salty tears filled his eyes and dripped between his feet to the hard black rubber flooring.

The bus door shushed closed. The transmission whined as the clutch was engaged, then the driver pulled away from the curb.

In control of his emotions again, Almendariz watched the back of the succubus's head. She had her act down perfectly. She had never looked in his direction. Perhaps she'd thought he wouldn't notice what she had done.

Reaching into his back pocket, Almendariz took out the shoehorn and clasped it in his fist. He told himself to bide his time. First he needed to know who she was and where she lived.

A few stops later she got off at Coffee Street and Reed Road.

Almendariz trailed in her wake, his pain and sense of purpose following him like a shadow.

21

"How long has he been gone?" Shay asked as she sifted through the foam fast-food containers and candy-bar wrappers littering the leaning dinette table in the apartment Marty Winston had been leasing.

"A day or two," the super said. "Three at the outside."

"You're not sure?" Keever called from the other side of the apartment. He'd taken the frayed cushions from a badly listing sofa and was going through the cavities and warped springs underneath.

The apartment super was a balding little fat man who sweated a lot in the humid air trapped in the building. His name was Garold Bowlby. He was dressed in green sweatpants and a white T-shirt that had gone gray from perspiration in both armpits. He carried his set of master keys in one pudgy fist. "Look, it's none of my business when these people come and go. As long as they pay me the rent by the first of the month, everything's kosher."

"Do you know what Marty Winston does for a living?" Shay asked. The table had yielded nothing of interest. The cabinets were barren of everything except dust. Winston hadn't eaten at home much.

"I'd have to go punch it up on the office deck," Bowlby said.

"Would it surprise you if I told you Winston was a narcotics trafficker?" Shay asked. Grimacing at the thought of what was next, she took a pair of thin rubber gloves from her purse and pulled them on. Grunting with effort, she picked up the overflowing trash container from the pantry and dumped it into the sink. More wrappers and foam containers toppled to the floor.

"Yeah," Bowlby said defensively. "Yeah, it would surprise me."

"You never suspected anything about the number of people Winston entertained up here?" Shay asked. Maggots writhed in the spoiled foodstuffs, and she had to disassociate herself from the work. Twisting the faucet, she turned on the water and washed the biodegradable refuse away.

"Figured he was just a likable guy," Bowlby said. "Nothing wrong with being likable."

A number of peach and pineapple cans surfaced in the garbage. All of them showed signs of being opened with a knife rather than a can opener. Sometimes plastic spoons with fast-food logos were still stuffed in them.

"He was a quiet guy, you know," Bowlby said. "A pleasant enough sort. Hard to get to know, though."

"You sound like somebody off *Most Wanted*," Keever said.

Out of the corner of her eye, Shay watched the super shift his feet. The man was hiding something, but she wasn't sure what. "Did he have any relatives?"

"None that I knew of. They may have been some of the people who came to see him."

"Any idea of where he might have gone?"

"No."

Keever gave up on the couch and shifted to the plastic crate of wallscreen chips. Their cases rattled as he moved them. "Was Winston's rent paid up?"

"Oh, yeah. He's been really good about that kind of thing."

"That's surprising," Keever said. "When we researched his files, we found three other apartment buildings that had filed eviction notices against him for nonpayment in the last three years."

"Maybe he changed."

"Yeah."

"Uh," Bowlby said, "you people never have said what Marty was wanted for."

Finished with the garbage and having come up empty, Shay said, "No, we haven't."

"Oh." Bowlby shut up.

"The bathroom?" Keever asked.

"It's yours," Shay replied. "I did the garbage." She peeled off the noxious gloves and dropped them on the piles in the double sink.

Keever nodded glumly and went away.

The small bedroom was opposite the bathroom. Shay

walked into it and called for the lights. The apartment AI was slow to respond, but got them switched on. Bowlby was right behind her, looking as if he really didn't want to be.

More litter covered the floor around the bed. Most of it was food packages. At one time a cardboard box had been set up in the corner. Balled-up paper bags with grease stains filled it, and more were tumbled down across the thin carpet. Evidently once Winston had filled the box, he'd lacked the energy or interest to empty it. Shay sectioned the room off in her mind then began her search. The closet revealed nothing except a handful of naked hangers.

"Did you know any of the people Winston saw?" Shay asked.

Bowlby looked away. "No."

Shay knew the man was lying, and was thinking how best to approach the situation when Keever stepped into the room.

"Nothing in the bathroom that isn't gross and disgusting," Keever said. "Nothing informative either. And no sign of a personal stash. He must have taken it with him."

Shay nodded. "Winston knew somebody would come looking for him."

"Mr. Bowlby," Keever said in a pleasant voice.

Shay was so startled by the innocuous tone she looked up from her search between the mattresses.

Bowlby shifted his gaze to Keever expectantly.

"Detective Shay asked you if you knew any of the people who saw Winston on a regular basis."

"Right. I said I didn't know anybody."

"Yet he's lived here for four months."

Bowlby nodded. "About that."

"Let me tell you a few things I've noticed since I've been here," Keever said.

Shay let the top mattress drop back onto the bottom and held her breath till the wave of sour-smelling air stopped swirling around.

"First off," Keever said, "I noticed that the wallscreen reception in this room really sucks." He called for wallscreen. It came on sluggishly, then brightened slightly to a gray sludge of various black-and-white tones. "Like it's being cross-referenced from one of the other rooms rather than receiving its own signal. Then there's the fact that Winston doesn't have a mail drop posted downstairs. And it's interesting to note that a Marty Winston wasn't listed on this building's insurance files." He turned to face Bowlby. "All this adds up to make me believe that you're scabbing off your employer."

The super drew in on himself but lacked the follow-through to stalk out of the room in a huff.

Shay could tell by the man's eyes that Keever had scored.

Walking forward slowly, Keever took away Bowlby's personal space. "Now, I could suppose a couple things out of that arrangement. One, I could suppose that you were helping yourself to a few extra bucks every month without the building's owner knowing by providing Winston a room without the hassle of paperwork. Two, I could suppose that you were working with Winston on his drug business."

Bowlby started to protest.

Placing one hand on the wall, Keever leaned over the man and smiled.

Shay had seen that smile over the years and had still never gotten used to it. It promised to be more corrosive than carbolic acid.

"Personally," Keever said, "I prefer to think that you're just small potatoes looking for a few extra bucks the wife didn't know about. Sandwich and beer money while she was over visiting her mother or the kids. However, I wouldn't want to turn a blind eye to the fact that you could be more than what you seem. Wouldn't be good police work. You understand."

Bowlby's resolve melted.

"Now," Keever said, "if I could find Marty Winston, I bet I could clear you of those nasty suppositions in nothing flat."

"I didn't know any of his friends," Bowlby said in a small voice. "But there was a girl that used to come here a lot."

"You got a name for her?" Keever asked.

"Hoshiko." Bowlby looked at the floor. "She was a working girl."

"You mean a prostitute?"

"Yes sir."

"And where could I find her?"

"The streets, usually. She never—I don't know any address."

Keever took out a pad and made a production of jotting

the name down. "You understand if I have trouble finding this woman I'll be back in touch with you?"

Bowlby nodded.

Finished with her examination of the bedroom and coming up empty-handed, Shay reflected that the extra money the super had been cribbing probably hadn't gone for beer and sandwiches after all.

"There she is."

Seated in the backseat of the unmarked car, Shay followed the line of Asela's gaze. The afternoon traffic on the street was light. Over two dozen females and males worked the corners not far from Winston's apartment building. Every time one series of lights turned red, a group of them tore loose and leaned in through windows of passing cars. Sometimes the drivers thumbed their windows up, but most of them paused to talk. Occasionally one or two of either or both sexes would clamber into a vehicle. The corporate crowd was taking lunch late, or breaking before resuming the late-afternoon shift.

Shay recognized the pattern from her days on loan to vice.

"Hoshiko?" Keever asked.

Asela nodded. She was very tanned and slender, only looking her thirty-plus years in her eyes. Copper-colored hair cascaded down her shoulders and framed a coffee-with-cream face with high cheekbones. She wore pink hot pants, a pink tube top, high heels, and a white jacket that barely reached below her buttocks. Her only jewelry was a small gold chain tight around her neck. "Hoshiko's the one dressed in white. Spandex top, stone-washed jean shorts, and knee-high boots."

"The blonde?" Shay asked.

Making a moue of her lips, Asela said, "It's a wig. Little *puta* doesn't like looking Japanese down here. Too many downhome boys would like to take themselves a little revenge in the name of the Ku Klux Klan or Aryan Guard. Carve their initials on her belly or back. They might be working for Himeji Corporation or one of the others, but their hearts are white."

"Is Hoshiko passing?" Shay asked.

Keever pulled over to the curb and parked. They watched the woman across the street. Hoshiko seemed to be going through the moves but didn't appear too interested in picking up a paying customer.

"Sometimes," Asela said, "she says she's white. Sometimes Latino. I've even been around her when she passed herself off as Amerind. She's got almost as many names as a damn telephone deck."

"You know a guy named Marty Winston?" Shay asked.

"Sure." Asela nodded. "One of Eddie Lupton's pack animals."

"Is he a regular street customer?"

"No. Man's got blow, Beth. Don't need no hard currency for the girls carrying dust monkeys on their backs. And there's a lot of them out there."

Shay knew. Asela was one of the few women she'd met in the life who didn't use chemicals or computer chips to give existence that little extra zing that was missing on the streets. "She's connected to Marty Winston."

"Hoshiko makes drops for Marty. She's dealing now." Asela pointed her chin toward the woman. "Normally she's like an animal out there when she's looking for a john. I've seen her lift her shirt up and flop her bare tits on some guy's windshield when she was really looking to score. She's got no class to work the uptown circuit."

"What's the story on her?" Keever asked.

"She's an ex-geisha," Asela replied. "Got herself a bodytuck a few years back, but she's starting to let it go out here on the streets. Cutting the life expectancy down on her earning power."

"How did she make the street life?" Keever asked.

Asela smiled, and it looked as devoid of humor as a shark's grin. "I got some friends in high places. I've heard that Hoshiko was responsible for some intercorporate trading on techware. Her partners wound up dead. Hoshiko's missing the little finger on her left hand. The corporate people wanted her to be a living lesson to the other geishas."

A dark blue sports car coasted to a stop at the curb. The driver was a young man in a three-piece suit. When the passenger-side window slid down, nearly a dozen women tried to crowd into it.

"That's one of Hoshiko's regulars," Asela said. "If you want to talk to her, you'd better move fast."

"Thanks," Keever said. The unmarked sedan lurched as he dropped the transmission into gear.

Asela slid back and popped the door latch.

Before she could get out, Shay took a hundred dollars in tens out of her pocket and pressed them into the woman's hand.

Unfolding her fingers, Asela looked at the money, then shook her head. "No, Beth. I can't take your money. If it hadn't been for you, I would have died in that alley six years ago."

"Take it," Shay insisted as she curled the woman's fingers back around the bills. "Not for yourself, but for the boys. And give them my love when you see them."

Tears misted in Asela's eyes but remained unshed. She reached out, gave Shay a brief hug and a quick peck on the cheek.

Shay returned the hug.

"Come see us when you can," Asela said after she got out. "They still ask about you and Keiko."

"I will."

Asela closed the door and was gone, long-legged and sure of step till she vanished into the street people.

Shay was sure Hoshiko hadn't seen Asela. She unlimbered the Glock from her shoulder holster and settled against the seat as Keever cut into the flow of traffic. Horns blared as angry drivers made their thoughts known.

"Registration shows the car belonging to Wade Carpenter, a software designer working for HubbleTech, Inc.," Keever said. "Picture matches the guy behind the wheel." The unmarked car shuddered for a moment when he cut the wheels and sent it arcing in front of the blue sports car just now beginning to pull away from the curb with Hoshiko inside. "Guy's got no priors, but watch your ass just the same."

Rubber shrilled when Carpenter hit the brakes and pulled up the nose of the sports car just inches short of the side of the unmarked sedan. Shay clung to the restraining strap and maintained her balance while Keever drove over the curb with the front wheels, then stopped suddenly, leaving the rear quarter panel to block Carpenter's vehicle.

She slid across the seat and out the door and came to her feet with the Glock pointed at the windshield. Her peripheral vision showed her that Keever had slapped the magnetic cherry on top of the car and had the big Wildey in his fist. The flashing red and blue drove the working flesh away from the corner.

Fear distorting his features, Carpenter jammed the sports car into reverse and revved the engine.

Keever loosed a round from the Wildey with it pointed overhead. Trapped between the walls of buildings, the pistol sounded like a small cannon going off.

Carpenter flinched and raised his hands from the steering wheel. The sports car sputtered and died.

Walking around the front of the unmarked sedan with the Wildey held in a steady grip, Keever ordered, "Get out of the car."

Moving in tandem to her partner, Shay circled the rear of the police car and stopped by the driver's side of the sports car. Carpenter got out with his arms stretched straight out over head. "Hands behind your head," Shay said, "and lean over the car."

Carpenter complied.

"You too, sister," Keever said.

A troubled look filled Hoshiko's face.

Shay knew the woman had already scanned them and realized she didn't know either of them.

Leaning over the hood of the sports car, Hoshiko raised one elbow and glared at Keever. "Do you have some ID? You can get one of those lights anywhere. If I don't see a badge real quick, I'm going to ask one of these ladies to call a cop and report you."

Staying out of Keever's field of fire, Shay moved over to the woman and snapped on a pair of handcuffs. When Hoshiko started yelling for someone to call the police, Shay reached into her pocket, opened up her ID case, and flashed her shield. "The next call I make," she said, "is going to be to vice for anyone who wants a trip downtown." The crowd dispersed even faster.

"Oh shit," Carpenter said. "Oh shit."

Keever patted him down, removed his wallet, checked the license, and tossed it on top of the sports car.

After putting her gun away, Shay searched her prisoner. The spandex top and jean shorts didn't leave much in the way of hiding places, and not much to the imagination either. She unzipped one of the knee-high boots, and close to twenty cellophane packets holding white powder trickled onto the street. The other boot yielded even more. A roll of dollars and yen was tucked into a special pocket at the top of the boot.

"Looks like you're in a lot of trouble here," Shay said quietly. "I'd say we have enough to go for an intent-todistribute conviction. If you go down for it, you'll be an old woman by the time you get out."

Carpenter continued to repeat his litany.

Grabbing the short chain between the cuffs, Shay straightened Hoshiko and escorted her to the rear seat of the unmarked sedan.

Keever holstered the Wildey and told Carpenter he could go. The young executive looked as if he couldn't believe what he'd heard, but he didn't waste any time acting on it. The sports car was out of sight by the time Keever fitted himself behind the wheel again.

Hoshiko placed her back against the door opposite Shay.

"If you try to kick me," Shay said in a flat voice, "I'll break your goddam kneecap for you. And if you don't believe me, try me."

Breaking the eye contact first, Hoshiko looked away.

Shay made a production out of gathering the cocaine packets into a plastic bag.

"You guys aren't vice," Hoshiko said.

"No," Shay answered.

Keever powered the car forward again and sliced neatly into the traffic flow.

"If you aren't working narcotics," Hoshiko asked, "what do you want?"

Shay let the last of the cellophane packets drop into the bag, then shook it for effect. "Marty Winston. You know where he is, and we want him."

Hoshiko bit her lip as if torn between loyalties. Shay didn't buy the act. Once Hoshiko knew the scam wasn't going to buy her any time to think, there wasn't any hesitation.

The apartment was six blocks away, a back unit in a building that obviously only generous payoffs to someone in the city housing department could keep from being condemned.

Keever led the way up the creaky steps to Hoshiko's unit. Shay trailed, one hand on the woman's cuff chain as she kept her with them. At the top of the flight of stairs, Keever stepped aside long enough for Shay to press Hoshiko's palm against the ident plate, then went through the open door with the drawn Wildey.

Pushing Hoshiko down on her face in the living-room carpet, Shay silently admonished the woman to stay there, then moved without noise to back up her partner. The hair at the back of her neck prickled under her ponytail. Despite spending years more or less legally invading the premises of others, she'd never become accustomed to the feeling. Every time she went through a door like that, it felt as if she were living on borrowed time.

Her palms perspired. She made herself calmly wipe them one at a time on her shirt, then resecured her hold on the Glock.

Marty Winston was asleep in the bedroom, the sheets twisted around his naked body. He was long and leaned out by constant drug use. Thick, shaggy hair fell in greasy locks down to his shoulders.

Shay could smell the sour scent of the man even through the strong perfume lingering in the room. She couldn't help but think that a good defense attorney would be able to take Winston and his testimony apart on the witness stand. Still, he was all they had for now, and it might be enough to halt the killings.

She stopped inside the doorway where she could maintain watch over the front entrance. Hoshiko stared at her with wide eyes, drawn in on herself as if expecting trouble. Her posture told Shay that Winston probably wasn't unarmed. Turning back to Keever, she saw that it was too late to try to warn him. Despite the silent fears crawling through her mind, she took deliberate aim at Winston.

Quiet as a wraith, Keever had moved to the side of the bed. He tapped a blunt forefinger against Winston's bare shoulder and said, "Hey."

Reacting more quickly than Shay had supposed would be possible, Winston pushed himself to the side away from Keever and came up with a black pistol in one fist from under his body.

Shay's finger tightened on the Glock's trigger as Winston's pistol dropped into firing position.

With an economy of motion, Keever knocked the pistol from Winston's grip, then slapped his open hand against Winston's face. The impact was sharp, meaty, and rolled off the walls inside the room.

Winston collapsed back on the bed, stunned. A trickle of blood flared from his nose and over his lips, staining his teeth.

"Out of the bed," Keever growled. He picked up a

patched pair of jeans, shook out a Buck folding knife from the pockets, and threw them at Winston.

Seemingly unmindful of Shay's presence, Winston clambered out of the bed bare-assed, hopped first on one foot, then on the other as he pulled the pants on. Blood dripped off his chin onto the threadbare carpet.

Shay put her pistol away and leaned against the wall, content to let Keever handle things.

"We've been looking for you most of the morning and this afternoon," Keever said.

"I ain't done nothing," Winston said.

"I wouldn't call pulling a pistol on a cop exactly nothing."

"You didn't say you was no cop."

"Well, now I'm saying it."

Winston brushed the blood from his face. His eyes were dark sullen holes in a too-white face.

Keever took out his handcuffs. "We're taking you in as a material witness. For your own protection."

Looking from Shay to Keever, then back again, Winston said, "Bullshit. What's this really about?"

"Last Friday morning," Keever said as he cuffed Winston. "Early. You were on a rooftop, waiting for Eddie Lupton. While you were there, you got a look at the guy who's been killing women and dragging their bodies into the bayous."

"You talking about the Ripper?"

Keever nodded.

"I didn't see nobody, man," Winston said. He wiped the blood from his face with his cuffed hand. "I wasn't on no rooftop, and I didn't see the Ripper. Whoever told you that sold you a crock of shit."

"That's not how Eddie Lupton tells it," Keever said.

"Lupton?" Winston cackled in disbelief. "Hell, Lupton is the one who saw the Ripper. Said he thought the guy saw him too. So he lit a shuck out of there and told me to grab some empty space for a while. Me, I was booking it when the vice guys dropped the arm on him. I didn't look back. And I didn't see no Ripper either."

"Well, goddammit," Shay said. Turning on her heel, she left Keever to handle Winston, then stopped at the door long enough to gather up Hoshiko.

Shay made the call to the vice division from the pay phone in the apartment's downstairs foyer. A handful of residents walked by, giving her and Hoshiko a wide berth despite the narrow corridor. The prostitute leaned up against the graffiti-covered wall and glared at anyone who met her glance.

A sick feeling twisted through Shay's stomach while she listened to the phone ring. It was answered at the same time Keever hit the second-story landing with his prisoner. Winston was still barefoot and had a T-shirt thrown over one naked shoulder.

"Vice. Berland speaking."

"Mike," Shay said, "let me talk to Pascalli."

"Sure." The phone went dead for a minute as the line was put on hold.

Shay had counted up to thirty-seven before the vice captain picked up.

"Pascalli."

"Nate. It's Beth. Can you tell me the status on Eddie Lupton?"

"With the charges against him reduced, Lupton bonded out an hour ago. Why?"

Shay exhaled and tried to let go of the anger that had blossomed inside her. "Lupton snowed us. It wasn't Winston who saw the Ripper. It was Lupton."

"Son of a bitch," Pascalli said.

"Yeah." Shay shifted, glanced out at the street, and knew she couldn't stand there any longer. "He's going to rabbit, Nate. Can you generate some paper on him, have him picked up if anybody can find him, and hold down the fort till Keever and I get there?"

"Yeah. Goddam, I knew this was too good to be true. The only good thing is that Lupton's too greedy to leave town without his stash. We might stand a chance of catching up to him while he gets it together."

"Tully and I are on our way now."

Pascalli broke the connection.

Shay slammed the receiver into the wall. The black plastic fragments trickled to the floor. The cord remained attached to a small knot of mouthpiece and colored wires. Cracks showed on the plasterboard wall and obscured the dozens of numbers written there in pen and ink. She saw the faces of the three dead women play out over the reflections on the plastic sides of the booth. Even when she closed her eyes really tight, they didn't go away.

22

"Okay, Mr. Almendariz, we're going to break the other arm now."

Almendariz quivered, tried to shout no, and struggled to tell them to leave him alone. But the anesthetic had taken away his power of speech and movement. Even his breathing was done by the heart/lung machine laboring and beeping next to the operating table.

The doctor and the orthopedic assistant calmly positioned Almendariz's right arm on the accessory table they were using.

Almendariz screamed without sound. Fear rattled around in his brain like a bat flying blind. The pressure was intense, building slowly till it reached past the bone's resistance. There was no pain, only the dulled feel of the force being used.

The arm snapped.

"That takes care of the humerus," the doctor said, breathing rapidly from his exertions. "Now to work on the ulna and radius."

They repositioned the arm and began again.

Almendariz clung to consciousness. Perspiration trickled into his eye. Unable to blink by reflex or by choice, he stared at the white-tiled ceiling as part of it slowly went out of focus. The salt sting was a dulled sensation that carried no pain, just a persistence of being.

A nurse, white-masked like the rest of the operating team, stepped forward and mopped his face with a cloth.

His eyes clear, Almendariz concentrated on using his peripheral vision. Despite the mask and cap, he knew she was pretty. Her fingers were slim, delicate, and gave a faint flesh blush encased in the surgical gloves. For a moment he wondered how they might taste if she took one of them out of her glove and put it into his mouth. He thought there might be the tang of soap, maybe a hint of perfume or talcum powder. If he could bite her, break her skin before she could extract the finger, he knew he'd be able to taste the salt of her.

"Hey, Julie," one of the nurses called from the foot of the operating table. "I don't know what you're doing at that end, but you're causing things at this end to work like crazy."

The nurse's face reddened over the mask, and she moved away.

Almendariz couldn't cry or close his eyes. He was ashamed. In desperation he focused on the words of the Lord's Prayer.

"Father Judd."

Blinking his eyes open, Almendariz found himself still locked in the casts. His arms and legs were suspended by traction pulleys. Machinery hummed and blinked in the darkness of the hospital room, monitored his vital signs. He turned his head the small amount he was able, felt it roll heavily on his bare shoulders and chafe his skin. Both eyes were working now. His breath rasped inside the plaster hood over his head.

"Father Judd."

He squinted against the darkness.

Sister Margaret Mary stood beside the bed. Her wrinkled features were stern, almost to the point of being harsh. Her hands, lean and blue-veined, clung to the side rails with skeletal fingers. Wisps of gray hair stuck out from under her hat. "You've been thinking evil thoughts again," she said in a biting whisper that echoed out into the open hallway of the hospital.

Heart racing, Almendariz felt as if he suddenly couldn't get enough air into his lungs. The small hole through the plaster hood centered over his mouth wouldn't let in any more. He thought he was suffocating.

"Don't bother to deny it," Sister Margaret Mary whispered sternly. She leaned closer and stared into the eyeholes of the plaster face cast. "I know all about what happened in the operating room with the nurse."

Trying to shake his head, Almendariz felt the pain in his spine, as if a thousand tiny fishhooks had clawed into his spinal cord and were striving to rip it through his skin.

"The poor girl was probably mortified," Sister Margaret Mary said. "Probably never will be the same."

A choked gasp came out of Almendariz.

"It's because the doctors didn't finish the job." She took a roll of gray duct tape from a pocket inside her habit. "They left ways for evil to get inside you. And in your weakened condition, lying there in your own filth, you're easy prey." She whisked off a section of tape, then flattened it over his left eye. "But I can fix it."

Almendariz wanted to scream at her and tell her she was dead now, that she wasn't around when he started the series of operations that had changed him.

Instead, she continued. Another piece of tape covered his right eye, and he was blind. The pressure on the bottom of his face told him when she covered over the mouth hole. He tried to suck in another breath, but couldn't. He strained against the casts and straps holding him prisoner in the bed. Nothing moved. There was no air left in the plaster hood.

"There," Sister Margaret Mary said. "You're safe now. You can be everything I'd ever planned for you to be."

Almendariz's lips brushed against the plaster wall inside the face mask. He got the taste of chalk, but no air at all.

Leaning on the sink basin in his room at the rectory, he closed his eyes and listened to the running water. It calmed him to an extent. He put more water on his face, sipped sparingly. It had been so long since he had dreamed his memories with such intensity.

This afternoon, however, the dreams had been as vivid as they had ever been.

He was being tested. He knew that at once.

After following the latest succubus to her home, his resolve had weakened. Despite her ability to cause *it* to go out of control and father his baby inside her, he had almost relented.

The dreams and Sister Margaret Mary had served to remind him of all the hardships and sacrifice he'd gone through to build a solid foundation for the future Work he would be called upon to do. Once he understood, he clasped his hands together and prayed for the strength to see it through.

23

Shay fitted herself into her work cubicle and keyed up the deck. She punched in her private filename and started reviewing the latest data entered on the Ripper. A blinking notation told her the video chips from the funeral had been processed by the lab and were ready for review. She booted them up.

Members of the night shift moved through the room but largely ignored her. She'd learned to send out the don't-bother-me vibes when she had something online that required all of her attention. And the other detectives had learned to respect them. She closed her mind to the bits and pieces of conversations taking place around her and briefly scanned the wall of dead faces to her right, gathered her motivation.

The deck cleared, blinked READY, then trailed a notice across the top that her notefile contained two messages. She tapped the appropriate keys to access them.

The first was from Keever: "Beth—Am leaving this message here because you're not at home, so that means you got to be here. If not, I'll tell you in the morning. Figured you couldn't sleep. Me neither. Got a lead on Lupton. Nothing solid, but I didn't want to let it pass by. If it pans out, I'll be in touch. Don't bother me trying to find out. Who knows, if the ass gets bored off me long enough, I may be asleep and I wouldn't want you to wake me up. —Keever."

The second was from her lawyer, asking her to call him.

She lifted the receiver and dialed the number from memory. Troy Pulver answered on the fourth ring in a voice that let her know she hadn't wakened him. She identified herself, tight inside because Pulver was readying the case to ensure she continued to get visitation rights to Keiko.

His tone immediately let her know the news he had wasn't good. "I spent this morning in court, so I didn't see the documentation till early this afternoon. I left messages at your house."

"I haven't been home."

"That's what I assumed after the media started breaking the latest story on the Ripper." Pulver paused. "Beth, I'm not going to play games with you. You and I have put in some hard time fighting Kiyoshi Izutsu for Keiko. The man's beaten us at every turn."

"I'm not giving up on my daughter!" Unable to sit any longer, Shay stood and paced inside the small cubicle. She immediately drew the attention of the other detectives but ignored them.

"I didn't say you had to," Pulver pointed out. "Calm down. I just wanted you to know that we've just entered a new level of nasty in our dealings with Izutsu."

"He's already done something, hasn't he?"

"He's filed a restraining order on you," Pulver said.

"On what grounds?"

"Your job, Beth. Your involvement with the Ripper case and with Scivally. Either or both of those cases have put your life in imminent danger. He has a right to want to protect his daughter."

"She's my daughter too, Troy."

"I know. I know. Hey, I'm not the enemy here. I'm just trying to get you to see this from the judge's perspective."

"What about visitation under monitored conditions?"

"I didn't think you wanted to put up with that."

"I don't."

Pulver cleared his throat. "I don't mean to sound crass, but if we knuckle under too quickly, we may be setting a precedent that Izutsu can use to his advantage later. He could say that this is your admission that you can't take care of Keiko as well as you want the judge to believe."

Shay fought hard to keep her voice from breaking. "I want to see my daughter."

"I know. First I want to fight this thing. Izutsu had already encroached way the hell too far on your right to be Keiko's mother. Even with the pro-Japanese legal decisions being handed down across the board now, I'm hoping to get this case moved to a judge who'll be more neutral about the situation. I've got an assistant working to bar Judge Waring from hearing any further custody suits because of business interests he has in Izutsu Corporation. I think we have a really good shot, but it's going to take some time."

"How much time?"

"I don't know. Depends on how firmly Izutsu is entrenched and how hard-assed he wants to be. I'm figuring he sees this as an opportunity to remove Keiko from you once and for all."

Shay silently agreed.

"Listen, I don't want to put any additional pressure on you, but I'm going to start filing countermotions in the morning. It'll take a few days to reach the judge's court docket. If you could get this Ripper situation closed before then, I'll be able to stand on firmer footing when I take this in."

Shay glanced at the blinking deckscreen.

"If you can't close it," Pulver said, "you might consider stepping down from the Ripper case."

Shay sat down in her chair, not believing what she was hearing.

"Did you hear me?"

"Yes."

"Can you ask for reassignment?"

"That's not what I want to do."

"But *can* you?"

Shay didn't answer.

"Beth, listen, I know how you feel about this. I know you're good at what you do. I know you're involved in this case. But it may come down to a decision between your career and your daughter. I want you to be prepared to make that decision."

Letting out a long breath that barely touched the hard knot of pain nestled under her breastbone, Shay said, "I hear you, Troy."

"Don't give up yet," Pulver said. "I've still got a few tricks up my sleeve. There are people out there in the system who owe me some favors. If I can get Waring off the case, we've made a step in the right direction. Then we can work on gaining back lost ground. I feel good about this, Beth. I really do. I'm not going to let you and Keiko stay apart for long."

"I appreciate your honesty," Shay said. She thanked him, apologized for having called him so late, and broke the connection. She turned her attention back to the deck, trying not to let herself think of how staggering the legal fees were becoming. Pulver had taken the small retainer she'd been able to afford along with the regular but small payments she'd been able to make every month, and he'd never complained. She supplemented the money when she could with earnings from the part-time investigatory deckwork she did for personnel departments in a half-dozen corporations, but with the overtime she'd been pulling on the Ripper and the other caseloads lately, there hadn't been much of it. Some of her regular clients had moved on to other agencies that had proved more dependable. Even when she was able to spend the time on it again, it would take months to rebuild her client list.

She accessed the deck, punched the keys, and had the lists for each of the three funerals cross-referenced through video and ID files. Once the information was assimilated, she directed it to process the names and faces of any male in the audience who'd been at more than one of the funeral services.

The deck whirred and clunked.

When it spat out the list she was amazed at the number of names there were. As she scanned them, she realized she'd forgotten about the media people, the organ jackals, and the crematorium people. With the little they knew about the Ripper, she couldn't rule any of them out.

She took another sip of the soda, blinked the sleep and frustration from her eyes, and knew she was looking at a solid night's work if everything went well.

24

"Shay. Hey, Shay. Wake up."

Vision blurred by fatigue and the need for sleep, Shay opened her eyes and stared at the wall of dead faces. They stared back but didn't seem to notice her with the same intensity she held for them.

"Shay." It was a man's voice.

She recognized it this time. Arnie Birdsong was presently on the day shift at homicide. She wondered what the hell he was doing there so late, then realized the walls were reflecting morning sunshine. When she accessed DataMain she found out it was 6:18 A.M.

"C'mon, Beth. Keever's on line six for you."

"I'm awake." Shay wiped her face and pushed herself up, then regretted it instantly when the sudden headache slammed into her temples.

She wiped sleep from her eyes and gazed at the frozen image on her deckscreen. One side showed the shot as taken at the Camejo funeral, while the other side showed a media license with NO POLICE FILE printed under it. Most of the night had passed in a series of dead ends.

She cradled the phone to her shoulder and said, "Shay."

"Eddie Lupton turned up," Keever said.

Immediately more alert, Shay took a pen and pad from her drawer and asked, "Where?"

"Arboretum Memorial Park. Lupton's dead. Whoever killed him left the body in front of the Aline McAshan Botanical Hall. Do you know where it is?"

"Yes." Shay had taken Keiko to the hall. "I'll be there in a few minutes." She reflected on the area, remembered that there were no waterways in the park. "Was it the Ripper?"

"Don't think so, kid. We definitely got a new wrinkle to consider. We'll talk when you get here."

Shay broke the connection, gathered her things, gave

Birdsong a thin apology, and slowed her rush out of the building long enough to run a comb through her hair, scrub her face, and get a Diet Pepsi for the trip over.

Shay took a final turn around a stand of pine trees and saw the crowd of crime lab people encircling something lying on the ground. The winch cable from the helo hovering overhead was attached to a wire basket sitting nearby on the ground. A line of park employees and gift-shop people stood with their faces pressed up against the windows of buildings just beyond the police group.

Keever looked more drawn and haggard than Shay had seen him appear in months. He was hunched inside a worn and frayed trench coat with at least two buttons missing.

She stood beside him, letting his greater bulk knock the wind off her. "Coffee," she said as she handed the white, chocolate-stained 7-Eleven bag over. "And a danish. I nuked it, but that was almost five minutes ago. It's probably cold again."

Keever mumbled a thanks, fumbled with the coffee lid for a moment before Shay took it away from him, tore open the sip-lock, and gave it back. He sipped cautiously, then took a big drink.

Taking a rubber band from her pocket, Shay gathered her hair, then slid her ponytail down her back under the windbreaker. "You don't think the Ripper did Lupton?"

Keever shook his head, raised a forefinger and touched it between his eyes. "One shot, large-caliber. Powder burns on Lupton's forehead. That sound like the Ripper to you?"

"No, dammit." Shay wrapped her arms around herself, stuck her hands up her sleeves, and held on tightly for warmth. "Means he could have gotten himself killed by anybody for any number of reasons, none of them having to do with the Ripper."

"I think it has everything to do with the Ripper." Keever tore open his danish and took a big bite. Flakes of white glaze stuck to his lips for a moment, then he licked them away. "Before he was executed, Lupton was spiked."

"A mind-wipe?"

"Zack doesn't seem to think so."

"Fitzgerald's here?" Shay craned her neck, then saw the coroner kneeling on the ground beside Lupton's body. She had a brief impression of the carnage done to the back of the drug dealer's head. "So what does he think?"

"He says the spike looks like it was set up to withdraw information rather than supplant it."

Shay looked at her partner. "Fleshes out the theory that somebody besides us is looking for the Ripper."

"And knocks out the possibility that our homes were burglarized to find out what we had in our casefiles so they could start covering up the killer's identity. If somebody just wanted to shut Lupton up, all it would have taken was the bullet. They wouldn't have needed to spike him."

"Whoever it is must not be any closer to uncovering the Ripper's identity than we are."

"Last night might have changed that," Keever pointed out, "if the spike turned up anything."

Shay shook her head. "Whatever they got from the spike, it wasn't enough."

"What makes you say that?" Keever asked.

Over half of the crime scene techs peeled back, leaving four men who folded the corpse's arms in on itself, then lifted it into the basket under the hovering helo. The faces in the windows followed the movements with solemn interest. One enterprising woman had a hand-held camcorder from the gift shop focused on the body.

Shay made a mental note to have a uniform confiscate the camera and film. "If they'd gotten everything they needed, they wouldn't have left Lupton's body out to be found. Killing Lupton and staking the body out like this is too much like making a gift to the Ripper. Letting him know that whatever threat Lupton represented has been nullified. We need to talk to Espinoza, see if we can't play up the spike in the news reports."

"Could be complicated. Once this breaks, a lot of media people are going to be insinuating the police department may have had something to do with it."

"Let them." Shay started forward toward the small knot surrounding the corpse in the basket. "If a rumor like that starts up, maybe it'll take away some of the Ripper's confidence and keep him at home instead of out looking for victims."

"The less he moves," Keever said, "the less likely it is he'll make the mistake that we need to put him down."

"I don't want to see another face on that wall. He's close,

Tully. We're so fucking close to him now that I can almost smell him." Shay accessed her com-chip and had the helo pilot hold his position so she and Keever could view the body.

"You turn up something on the video research?" Keever asked.

"No. That's going to be a dead end unless we can factor in some other information to cut the possibles."

The line of men parted at her approach, and she looked down at Lupton.

The dead man's eyes were open and glazed. Cordite had stained the face blue-gray over the pallid complexion. The eyebrows were singed from the powder burns and curled into tight knots against blistered flesh. The back of Lupton's head was missing.

Glancing back at the scattered bloodstains and chalked outlines of the body on the flattened grass, Shay said, "Lupton wasn't killed here."

Fitzgerald shook his head. "Not enough blood at the scene." He looked tired and rumpled, as if he'd just come from hours of surgery and had been looking forward to bed when he caught the squeal.

"The bullet?"

"It's not inside the body. I put a pencil into the wound and it ran straight through. Wherever the rest of Lupton's brain and skull are, you can bet the bullet—at least what's left of it—is there too."

"What about the spike?" Keever asked.

Fitzgerald grabbed a double handful of Lupton's jacket and pulled at the body. Keever helped, and together they got it flipped over.

The incision ran from the base of Lupton's shattered skull down between his shoulder blades. The jacket had been cut as well. White bone gleamed brightly in the mass of red muscle and blackened blood.

"Messy job," Fitzgerald said. "Could be because whoever did this really didn't care about old Eddie, or could be because he was in a hurry." He pointed a long ebony finger. "Somebody who didn't know what he was looking at might miss this. See the scratches on the insides of the third and fourth disks?"

Shay leaned closer, holding her breath so she wouldn't take in the dead smell, and inspected the vertebrae. The scratches were minute absences of the gleam covering the other bones. Specks of blood dotted the ivory surfaces.

"They weren't gentle about it," Fitzgerald said. "Slipped the neural spike in, married it to the biotrack, and raped his brain."

"What could they have gotten out of it?" Shay asked.

"The Japanese are more adept at that kind of tech than we are. Chances are they know some tricks I don't. Most of the stuff a spike could take are visual impressions, a few auditory and tactile memories. Data's hard to retrieve unless it's in recent memory, and it's filed in a specific place."

Stepping away from the basket, she accessed the com-chip and told the helo pilot she was finished.

The wire basket jerked into motion and sent a ripple of movement through the corpse as it was reeled up to the helo with a whine that sounded like mechanical bees.

Fitzgerald said his goodbyes, then gathered his equipment and walked toward the waiting coroner's van.

Still hugging herself in a failing effort to keep warm, Shay watched the basket pull away till two men inside the helo reached out and swung it aboard. When she turned back to Keever, she saw the thick manila envelope tucked under his arm.

"Lupton's personal effects," Keever said. "We've done all we can here, and the captain's going to want a report pronto."

Shay nodded. "Breakfast is on me."

After they had placed their order with the waitress, Shay poured the contents of the manila envelope onto the table. Keever sat in the booth across from her.

The other patrons of the restaurant were paying attention while trying to appear uninterested.

Shrugging out of her windbreaker because the restaurant was so hot, Shay knew even more attention was on them now that her shoulder holster was in evidence. She ignored it, grabbed the straps of her lapdeck, and pulled it into the seat beside her. Taking it out, she trailed her fingers across the keys and brought it online.

"What are you doing?" Keever asked.

The waitress returned with coffee for Keever and a hot chocolate for Shay. The whipped cream looked incredibly white and homemade. It looked delicious till she remembered it was also the same color as Lupton's spinal column. She took a pair of latex gloves from her purse and snapped them on.

"I'm accessing Lupton's arrest file," Shay said as she began prodding through the assembled articles. "They listed everything Lupton had on him when he was arrested on Friday. It might be interesting to find out what he'd added and lost since then."

She and Keever worked in unconscious tandem. Coins and dollars and yen went into a pile. She recorded the amount on a page of her notepad. There was something over four hundred dollars American. The cash amount Lupton had had on him when he had been arrested was fifty-three dollars. Out only a few hours, and Lupton had managed to better his financial situation.

Keys went into another pile. There were keys to a missing car, to Lupton's apartment, and to three bus lockers. The locker keys hadn't been in Lupton's possession on Friday. When she checked the locker numbers against the bus company's files, she found the keys were registered in three different names. One of the names was female. A brief chip-chase through the deck let her know the names were bogies, clumsily slipped into the system. It didn't take much in the way of ID to secure a bus locker. All three names eventually led back to a dummy cover Lupton used that was listed in the file Nate Pascalli had provided from vice on Monday.

She put the locker keys to one side so she and Keever could check them out later.

The purple rabbit's foot on a gold chain had been noted on the arrest sheet. So had the wallet, the gas card, and two credit cards, which were listed as delinquent for nonpayment. The pack of cinnamon-flavored gum was new, but insignificant. The battered Zippo with the Marine crest had been noted before.

Detaching the electromag reader from the lapdeck, she ran the gas card. Within seconds it told her the last time it had been used had been on Thursday of the previous week.

Frustration chafed at Shay.

Breakfast arrived and she picked at it halfheartedly.

Keever's appetite showed no signs of distress. The big man ate with gusto and obvious enthusiasm and washed his food down with nearly a pot of coffee. He adjusted his glasses and nudged the assorted papers and business cards they'd culled from Lupton's wallet.

Buttering another half-wedge of dry toast, Shay said, "We're drawing a big zero here."

"Better a zero than nothing at all," Keever replied automatically.

Usually the response brought a smile to Shay, but this morning the echo it touched off was false. She stared at the assembled bits of ID scattered across the table between the seasoning shakers and ketchup bottles. A nebulous idea started to take form in the back of her mind. She willed herself to leave it alone until it was ready to come forward on its own.

She scooped up a spoonful of scrambled eggs from Keever's plate, dumped them onto her toast, added apricot jelly, and folded it over. When she bit into it, a pearl of jelly squirted out and dropped onto the metro bus pass at the edge of her plate. A sense of wonderment filled her when she wiped at the bus pass with a napkin. Mind whirling and exploding with ideas now, she washed the toast down with hot chocolate.

"Tully?"

"Yeah?"

"Why would Lupton need a bus pass if he had a car?"

Keever looked up over the rims of his glasses. "To beat the traffic jams. Maybe make some drops. You can bet the narc squad knew what he drove. Mass trans, with all its stops, can be hard to tail."

"That's what I was thinking." Shay picked up the pass, studied it, then looked at her partner. "You know what else the murder victims had in common besides being women and being Catholic?"

"They all had bus passes." Understanding dawned on Keever's face.

Shay smiled. "Bingo. None of them had a driver's license."

"The Ripper's stalking them through the bus system," Keever said picking up her thread. "Not the streets. Not the bars. The goddam metro lines."

Shay used the deck in Espinoza's office to explain the theory she and Keever had spent the last three hours putting together. Her eyes were tired, and her fingertips burned from constant use. Keever had volunteered, but she never could stand to wait through his two-digit approach to a keyboard. The bus locker keys hadn't turned up anything. All of them had been empty.

Sitting at Espinoza's desk, Shay logged onto the deck, then accessed the file she'd created and locked under her and Keever's password.

A map detailing the inner city and a few miles beyond the Loop blinked into being on the deckscreen. Shay tapped more keys and said, "This is the bus route Mitzi Harrington used on her way to and from the the high school where she taught." A crimson dot flared onto the screen, then raced around it, taking abrupt right angles. "Route Seventy-eight."

Espinoza placed a hand on the back of his chair where Shay was sitting and the other hand on his desktop. He leaned in more closely to the deckscreen. "I'm listening."

"Aleka was killed here," Shay said. A drop of sapphire blue hit the screen and jetted through a series of turns and straightaways. "Route Fifty."

"How do you know she used that route often? Way I hear it, the lady was strictly free-lance."

"She was," Keever said. "But vice confirmed that some of her known clientele were in that area. She'd have had reason to take that route with some kind of regularity."

"Okay." Espinoza scratched his chin. "What about the Camejo woman?"

"Route Thirty-seven," Shay answered. An emerald arrow spilled along its prescribed path. "She made regular trips to the employment office."

All three colors sat quietly on the screen and hummed their accusation.

"They intersect," Espinoza said. "But so do a lot of other routes. A regular maze of them cycle this city every day."

"We know," Keever said. "We've done the research."

"Even narrowing down the field this much," the homicide captain said, "you're still looking at the whole city."

"Not really," Shay said.

More detectives moved on the other side of the plate-glass window fronting Espinoza's office. One of them rapped on the thin wooden door. Espinoza waved the man away irritably. Looking annoyed, the detective faded back to his desk.

"The mass trans companies document the usage of their patrons' bus passes for billing purposes," Shay said. "Tully and I have already appropriated their files through civil and economic resources, and we're running a sort program through it."

"Looking for anyone who might have been a passenger on those routes during the times and days those women were murdered." Espinoza straightened up, a hopeful smile twitching under his mustache.

Shay nodded.

"How long before we can expect an answer?" Espinoza asked.

"It's hard to say," Shay replied. She gazed at the incriminating lines on the deckscreen. They continued to spin, triangulating the Bayou Ripper's murderous career. "You've got a lot of people using mass trans. I'd guess hours, days maybe, before we get a final list. And it could be larger than we're thinking now."

"Sure," Espinoza said, "but the odds against being on those same three routes on those same nights as the murders must be astronomical."

"We're hoping so."

"Until then," Keever said, "we may have already gotten lucky. Beth gathered the names of the drivers—"

"At Tully's suggestion."

"—and ran them through the sort program first."

Espinoza tried to cover up his excitement by crossing the room to the Mr. Coffee and filling his cup. "This isn't a magic act. You're detectives. Cut the 'nothing up my sleeve' bullshit."

Shay returned her attention to the keyboard and accessed a new file.

A moon-faced man's front and left profile appeared on the split screen. He was smiling hesitantly, revealing a missing front tooth.

"Who's this?" Espinoza asked.

"Robert Thibodeau," Shay replied. "He's a relief driver for the mass trans system, and regularly drives those routes. He'd know those people."

"So would other drivers," the homicide captain said.

"Yeah," Keever said, "but the other drivers don't have a record for sex crimes."

Shay stroked the keyboard, brought up Thibodeau's record. "Rape and attempted rape. Four counts. The last arrest was eighteen months ago. All of the charges included aggravated battery."

"A preference for knives?" Espinoza asked.

"No weapons," Shay said. "Guy liked to use his hands. He's big. Six-three, three hundred twenty pounds."

"Maybe he's learned something new," Espinoza said.

"That's what we're thinking," Keever said. "Figured it might be enlightening to inquire."

"Don't bring him in yet," Espinoza said. "Play him. If we process him, even just to sweat him, the media will be all over this. I don't want a maybe taken down on circumstantial evidence. I want to put away the real Ripper once and for all, with no chance for a defense attorney to build a case for an unfair trial based on a biased jury." He sipped his coffee. "Get the paperwork started on the QT. Observe this guy, wait for him to make a mistake, then take him. Until you can build a solid case against this guy, I don't want this discussed outside this office. Is that understood?"

Shay and Keever nodded. Inside, Shay was disappointed. Her lawyer's words kept hacking at her stomach like shards of glass. She wanted nothing more at the moment than to bring the Ripper down, but she understood the caution Espinoza advised. She blanked the deck and followed Keever out of the office.

"Did you check Thibodeau's work schedule?" Keever asked as he led the way to the break room.

"Yes."

"When's the next time he's up?"

"Tomorrow afternoon. Route Thirty."

Inside the break area, Keever plugged the soda machine with change. "Then tomorrow afternoon we start surveillance. Feel up to playing bait?"

A cold chill coursed through Shay. "Sure."

"You'll be wired, kid. And I'll be right behind you."

She made her features neutral, tried not to remember the rogue's gallery of the dead hanging on the wall of her cubicle. "I know."

Keever pressed the button for a Diet Pepsi. "Let me buy you a drink," he said with a grin, "before we see about getting you staked out."

25

Paring knife clutched tightly in his hand, Felix Carey cut the woman experimentally, slicing her neatly from throat to crotch while she stood naked before him. Blood poured onto the den's carpet and spattered the furniture around them. He thought he could hear it hiss as it flowed, but that was only his imagination. He'd had such a vivid one for so long.

The woman stared blankly forward when he moved back, unaware of the coiled intestines that dropped and covered the tops of her bare feet. There was no pain in her features.

Carey put the paring knife on the small surgical table at his side. Over a dozen other edged implements lay on the surgical wrapping. Almost half of them were bloody. He inspected the slash that had opened the woman and touched the lips of the wound. He sighed when he checked the results against his memory. The paring knife wasn't the answer either.

He accessed the matrix, wiped away the woman's wound to leave virgin flesh in its place, then picked up a triangular-bladed box knife. A dot of blood appeared at the woman's neck when he pressed the razor edge against her throat. Using the forefinger of his free hand, he traced the blood down between the woman's breasts till the color faded, then followed right behind it with the box knife blade.

Her flesh gave way easily, separating with the sound of a zipper coming unclasped.

In some places the incision wasn't deep enough to completely sever the subcutaneous layers of marbled fat. Without emotion, he stuck his fingers inside the wound and yanked. The fat parted, and the intestines plopped out once more, this time marking the cream-colored suit he wore.

He inspected the flesh again, and was again dissatisfied. He'd found nothing yet that matched the wounds the Ripper left on his victims. His need to know who the man was had reached a frenzied intensity. He was no longer able to even fake the pseudo-sleep the matrix afforded. The endless hours of waking and wondering were taking their toll. The madness was already starting to reach for him again.

He dropped the box knife to the floor and walked up the steps toward the projection wall. Accessing the matrix, he swept the woman, the surgical table, and the blood away. By the time he reached the top step his clothes were once more clean and pressed.

He paused in front of the projection wall. The neural spike had been the best available, but—as usual—the results were less than desired.

The image of the man was blurred, remained indistinct despite the matrix's best efforts at interpretation. It had been blown up, but Lupton's view from the top of the building was unchanged. Even though he was standing beside the man, Carey was looking down on him.

The lightning bolt that had illuminated the Ripper had been frozen in place. It was almost impossible to tell what color things really were. A shocked look creased the Ripper's face.

The Ripper was young, and—in a sense, Carey realized—the man was beautiful. He was sure the man he searched for was no creature of the streets. There was a purity about the man that was almost tangible, but Carey was unable to place it.

Frozen on the projection wall in obvious surprise, the Ripper was larger than life.

A com-link rippled through the matrix. "Mr. Carey?"

Carey forced himself to remain calm. "Yes, Welbourne."

"You requested that I update you on the homicide division's latest suspect."

"Yes."

"He's not the man, Mr. Carey. Our operatives have managed to place him on the night of the first murder. He was nowhere near the site."

"Thank you, Welbourne. Do the police know this?"

"No, sir."

"Stay ahead of them as they check out the mass trans angle," Carey said. He put his hands behind his back and clasped them, then forced himself to breathe out. He was no longer able to handle the tension he felt in this manner, but decades-long habits were hard to break even without the body they'd been forged into. "I believe Shay has something there. She's proving to be a most able young woman."

"Yes sir." The com-link faded.

Crossing the remaining distance to the projection wall, Carey put his hands on the screen, then strove to reach through it and pull the Ripper into the room with him. He couldn't. Sparks of bright color flared flatly across the projected image. He rested his palms against the image, tried to find the heat in it. "I want you," he said in a hoarse voice. "And I *will* have you. Soon."

26

Bethany Shay met the bus driver's quizzical glance in the overhead mirror with a neutral expression.

"You sure you know where you want to go, lady?" Robert Thibodeau asked. While he waited at the traffic light he yawned, then reached under his shirt to scratch his stomach.

"I'm sure," Shay replied.

Thibodeau pushed his hat back on his head, ran his hand through his greasy locks, and shrugged. "Been all through the route now, lady. I'm taking this crate back home for the night. You done seen all the new city lights you're gonna see tonight."

"If I spot someplace along the way that looks interesting, I'll yell," Shay said.

"Whatever you say, lady. But the rules is you gotta be off the bus before I park it."

Shay nodded and settled back more deeply into the seat. The headlights of passing cars looked like a solid river of yellow cutting through the night. The taillights of the cars ahead of the bus seemed like a slow-moving sea of flickering red lanterns.

Despite the protesting squeak of the bus's heaters, the interior of the vehicle was almost cold enough to hang meat. Shay glanced across the empty aisle through the left-hand window and looked without seeing. A weary yawn creaked through her jaw before she could stifle it. Last night she'd checked into a motel and had spent a sleepless six hours on a bed that was too hard. Going home after the burglary—knowing the pictures of Keiko everywhere would drive her crazy, especially now that Loryn had returned to Toronto—had been out of the question. Tonight, after starting her day at five, she thought she'd be able to sleep just fine.

She pulled her coat more tightly around her, but left the way clear to the Glock riding on her hip. She wore mittens because they were easy to get on and off in emergencies, with the fingerless black gloves on underneath them. Even the bulky Kevlar vest concealed by the thick coat didn't provide any extra warmth. Goose bumps rippled along her upper arms.

The com-chip pinged for her attention, and she accessed it.

"Beth?" Keever's voice sounded strained and tired. He'd left the PD after she had, and had met her there this morning, already enmeshed in the planning strategies for keeping surveillance on the bus.

She stopped feeling as sorry for him when she remembered that he was riding in a control van with a thermos of coffee. She felt even worse when she thought of the boxes of doughnuts the surveillance teams had laid in for the night. Her stomach growled. The package of cheese and peanut butter crackers had been finished hours ago. "Go."

"How's it going up there?"

"So far it's boring the ass off me."

"Terrific. The way we got it pegged, we've wasted the whole night."

"How's that?"

"Five minutes ago McCall checked in with a report that cleared Thibodeau of the Harrington murder. He was arrested in a mass booking at the Satin Salamander the night the Ripper hit Harrington. He wasn't processed till the next morning, which is why the date didn't show up to clear him until now."

Shay accessed DataMain and cursed beneath her breath. It was 10:39 P.M. "There's one bright spot. You saved me twenty more minutes of having my kidneys slowly jarred loose."

"I'll buy you a steak at Kip's to help make up for the lousy experience."

"I'm going to hold you to that. How about closing in and picking me up?" Shay broke the connection and reached up for the signal wire to alert Thibodeau, then saw that the driver was already coasting in to pick up another fare at curbside. Grabbing her purse, she slid out into the aisle before the bus came to a complete stop.

"Decided to get off?" Thibodeau asked as he opened the door. He was grinning into the overhead mirror.

The waiting passenger bolted through the door and banged off the broad windshield as he came around.

Shay caught a quick glimpse of a black nylon-covered face and the short, wicked length of a cut-down pump shotgun.

"Drive, fat man," the masked gunman yelled to the driver as he brandished his weapon, "or I'll blow you out of that damn seat!"

Engine growling with torque, the bus lurched into the swamp of nighttime traffic.

Without pausing, Shay raked a stack of printed bus matter from an overhead rack and threw it in the gunman's direction. Sheets of paper fluttered and filled the forward section of the bus. She pulled on a seat to aid her in turning around, then ran full-tilt toward the emergency door.

The shotgun thundered behind her.

Her breath caught in her throat and she squeezed her eyes shut, knowing she was going to feel the impact before the next heartbeat. Then glass fragments flew out of a side window as sparks lit up the metal frame.

Out of her peripheral vision, Shay saw a compact blue pickup truck come sliding into the side of the bus. The bumper struck the bigger vehicle just in front of the rear tires, and locked up. Rubber shrilled as it was dragged sideways by the heavier bus.

Shay lost her footing, and her hip slammed into one of the seats with bruising force. Scrambling for balance, she hit the panic release button on the emergency door and leaned against it as the gunman behind her racked the slide on the pumpgun. Her hand fisted around the Glock.

Hisses erupted from the pressurized canisters inside the emergency exit's frame, and they blew the door clear. It fell backward, bounced and twisted crazily when it hit the street, then skittered to a curb only an instant before a scarred green sedan roared over it with a massive double-basso thump.

Another round from the shotgun punched a hole in the sheet metal by Shay's head. Smoking, torn shrapnel sprouted out like steel leaves. Partially deafened by the gunfire, she managed to access the com-chip. "Tully!"

"Hang on, kid! We're rolling. Just keep your head down until we get there."

The green sedan closed the distance while Shay hung out

the door. The bus swung dizzyingly across the traffic lanes, and another muffled crunch shivered through it, caused it to yaw still wider. Swinging through the passenger window, the man riding beside the driver leveled a pistol at Shay.

Framed above the sights by the passing streetlights, Aaron Scivally grinned obscenely. "Told you I'd get back to you, bitch! Now I'm going to do for you like you done for my brother!"

Shay ducked and hung on.

Bullets from Scivally's pistol hammered into the back of the bus. Glass emptied from the windows in jagged shards. The gunman at the front of the bus screamed obscenities. A sudden screech from the mass transit vehicle's air brakes gave just the barest of warnings before the bus listed out of control for a moment.

The driver of the green sedan was caught unprepared. Already accelerating with less than ten feet separating the car from the bus, the sedan's front end slammed into the rear bumper of the bus.

Aaron Scivally removed a fresh clip from his jacket and never took his eyes from Shay.

With nowhere else to go, aware that the shotgunner was creeping toward her on hands and knees, Shay threw herself out the door. She managed to step on the hood of the sedan, then fell facedown on top of the car. The impact knocked the air from her lungs but didn't injure her because of the bulletproof vest and heavy coat.

"Stop the car! Stop the goddam car!" Scivally yelled.

Holding on to the car with her fingertips, Shay kicked out at Scivally. Her foot hit solidly, and blood spurted from the man's broken nose. Scivally ducked back inside, screaming with rage.

The car slewed, came around in a dizzying ninety-degree arc. Horns honked behind it as other cars passed it by.

Unable to hang on, Shay forced herself to go limp as she spun off the sedan. She hit the street on her side and rolled, lost her gun for a moment. Lungs on fire and feeling as if they'd collapsed, she forced herself to her knees to search for the Glock. The darkness and the spinning black comets whirling before her eyes made it hard to see the black matte finish. She had to concentrate to make her hand work to pick it up when she found it. It was like lifting an anvil. She forced herself to her feet as air filled her lungs.

The sedan had wheeled around in the middle of the street, lost a handful of seconds when it collided with a dairy truck, then shivered free of the crash with a wrenching twist of tormented metal. The right side sagged over a flat tire. Rubber flaps popped and snapped at the wheel well when the driver aimed his vehicle at Shay. One of the headlights had been broken, and bright bits of glass continued to stream from the ruptured chrome socket.

Pushing off with her hands, feeling the road grit sting her unprotected fingers, Shay backpedaled. A muzzle flash flamed from the passenger side of the car. Something jerked at her coat and spat gray filler into the air.

Shay ducked and ran, making for an alley sandwiched between two small shops. Shooting it out with Scivally and the other three men in the car wasn't an option. Her hand slid inside her coat and activated the tracer sewn into her Kevlar vest. She accessed the com-chip. "Tully."

"Go."

"I'm out of the bus. On foot. I hit the tracer."

"We already logged you onscreen."

"It's Aaron Scivally." Shay raised her hands, pushed off the opposite wall, and ran down the alley. She couldn't see the end. "Where are you?"

"Ran into some trouble." Gunfire rolled across the com-link. "Scivally was running a blocker. We'll be there."

Shay rippled out of the connection and turned her thoughts to her own survival. Behind her, the running footsteps of Scivally and his wolfpack closed in. They'd abandoned the sedan, left it bent and broken halfway over the curb.

The alley jogged left. Clutching the Glock tightly, knowing she wouldn't have time to return for it if she lost it, Shay followed the turn and used her free hand to vault over the overturned Dumpster blocking the way. She almost stumbled and fell when she landed on the cracked surface, rebounded off her shoulder from the wall to her right, then picked up speed again.

A familiar *wop-wop-wop* sound came from above.

Shay glanced upward and saw the police helo come screaming down out of the night sky. A FLIR strobe jutted from its belly. Whirling red and blue lights along the landing skids flared to life.

"PUT DOWN YOUR WEAPONS!" an authoritative voice

roared over the loudhailer. "THIS IS THE POLICE! PUT DOWN YOUR WEAPONS AND PLACE YOUR HANDS ON YOUR HEADS!"

Shay ran out of alley without warning. The fifteen-foot wall swelled out of the shadows and became recognizable just in time for her to avoid collision with it. The building to her left presented only a blank concrete wall. A large window gleamed dully under a layer of dust to her right.

One of Scivally's men topped the Dumpster and raised a machine pistol. Muzzle flash from a long burst jetted out a foot from the barrel. Scivally came alongside the man, saw Shay, and dropped to his feet while bringing his pistol up.

A double-tap from a heavy-caliber rifle echoed into the alley. The man wielding the machine pistol pitched over backward, twitched, and lay still.

Before Scivally could fire, Shay lifted the Glock and fired four shots into the window beside her. Webbing surrounded each of the bullet holes. Lifting her coat for protection, she charged at the window, then leaped through it. She felt the glass give way, then come down in pieces around her when she hit the smooth concrete floor. It skittered ahead and behind her as she slid to a stop some feet farther on. The drop had been longer than she'd anticipated. Concentrating on her pistol, she pushed herself up and checked her surroundings.

The huge room was barren and empty, with none of the far perimeters visible. Dust covered the striped floor. Stone pillars reached up to the concrete ceiling. An emergency light tried to flicker to life over the broken window, spurted weak yellow illumination for a moment, then died with a glassy pop. From the way the window was set higher into the wall on this side, Shay knew part of the room had been dug below ground. The yellow lines and directional arrows told her she was in an abandoned parking garage under the condemned office building at the opposite end of the alley.

Pain stitched her right leg. With effort she managed to limp to one of the stone pillars and took up a position behind it, both hands on the pistol.

The com-chip pinged for her attention. "Beth," Keever called.

"Go," Shay answered softly. She glanced around the corner of the pillar, watching the window.

"Are you all right?"

"So far."

"Where are you?"

"In an underground parking garage west of the bus route."

"The helo sniper said he put two men down. There was a third."

"I know."

"He lost the guy in the shadows near your position."

The form that came through the shattered window didn't look human in the dim moonlight sluicing through the opening. It had curled in on itself as it came speeding forward, then spread out as it arced down. The long black duster flapped around it like a bat's wings when it landed. Aaron Scivally's face was white, and the two scratches along his left profile leaked black blood.

An emergency light mounted on the wall thirty feet away fizzled into flickering performance. A white electric glow with a muted stobe effect poured into the room, created a halo of illumination that spread outward from the wall.

Shay blinked. And in that instant Aaron Scivally disappeared. She pressed back tighter against the pillar and listened. The barrel of the Glock lined her face, warm from the shots she'd fired through the window. Only the beating of her own heart, the rotor throb of the distant helo, and the arcing sizzle of the emergency light came to her ears.

"Beth." It was Keever.

"Get out of my head," Shay said. "I lost Scivally. He's somewhere in here with me."

The com-link broke.

Shay wondered how far away Keever and his team were, then realized it was probably too far to do her any good. Under the palms of the black gloves, her hands were wet with perspiration.

A sharp pop echoed in the shadows to her left. She leveled the gun instinctively, then knew it was something that had been thrown to divert her attention when it continued to skip off the concrete.

"Nervous, bitch?" Scivally asked from his hiding place.

Shay tried to pinpoint the man's voice, but the echoes in the enclosed space made it impossible.

"You should be nervous," Scivally said. "In the next few minutes, I'm going to have your guts for garters."

Shifting, Shay peered around first one side of the pillar, then the other. A bullet flamed and spun off the corner only inches from her face. Concrete dust scattered over her eyes and made them tear. A chunk of rock landed at her feet. The gunshot continued to echo in the substrata of her hearing.

"What do you suppose my brother was thinking about when you gunned him down?" Scivally asked.

Hands shaking as she tracked the voice with uncertainty, Shay said, "That I wouldn't shoot him. Do you think he was surprised?"

"Oh, you're a cruel, cruel bitch, aren't you, Shay?"

Backtracking, Shay shifted over the other way, wondered if the echoes and the ringing in her ears were misleading her.

"A regular manhunter," Scivally said. "Word on the street is that before you shot Larry, you'd only capped two guys."

Shay heard the soft scuff of shoe leather, dropped the Glock downward slightly, and committed herself to the direction. Her feet were slightly apart, just as on the firing range.

"Makes you some kind of something on the police force, doesn't it?" Scivally taunted. "Most *guys* never see that kind of action their whole careers, let alone some little whore with a badge and an attitude."

The rotor-throb came close. Shay counted seconds, slower than her heartbeat.

"They won't get here in time," Scivally said. "If that's what you're waiting for. It's just you and me and the dark. After I kill you, there's plenty of ways for me to get out of this building without getting caught."

Shay crept around the pillar, put her back to the emergency light, and tried to keep it between herself and Scivally.

The scuff of shoe leather changed directions, definitely sounded nearer this time.

Easing her free hand back, Shay slid it under her right wrist.

"They say some people never get used to killing," Scivally said from somewhere in front of her. "Me, I've killed seventy-eight people. You're going to be number seventy-nine. Some have said I've got a taste for killing. They're right. But you don't, do you?"

A flicker of darkness moved ahead of Shay. She braced her gun arm against the pillar.

"I like knowing I got that kind of power." Twenty feet away, Scivally stepped out into the open from behind a pillar. The white glow of the emergency light washed over him, painted his face as a pale oval while the smears of blood looked black. His hands were at his sides, hidden in the folds of the duster. He smiled. "It's you and me, bitch, and I'm betting you don't have the balls to pull that trigger." He tapped his empty hand over his chest. "Come on. Go ahead." His voice changed into a hoarse hiss. "Do it!"

Shay let the sight blade of her pistol sit over Scivally's heart. She made the shaking go away. Instead of allowing herself to think of the dead, she thought of Keiko, of how she'd never be able to see her daughter again if Scivally was right. Her finger took up slack on the trigger.

Scivally only smiled bigger.

Eyes locking with Scivally's, Shay realized the duster could be hiding anything, including a Kevlar vest like her own. She shifted her aim.

Instantly Scivally went into motion and brought up his gun.

Shay pulled the trigger and kept both eyes open as she rode out the recoil and stayed with Scivally.

The bullet hit the man in the left biceps and partially spun him around. Scivally screamed curses, lifted his pistol, and jerked off a trio of shots.

One of the bullets struck the pillar beside Shay's head. The others were lost in the darkness. She put her second shot into Scivally's lower face.

Lifted by the impact, Scivally crumpled in on himself and flailed backward. He hit the ground on his back, jerked a couple times, then lay still.

Holding the Glock at the ready, Shay crossed the distance between herself and the man. His sightless eyes stared at the concrete ceiling. The bullet had torn through his chin and ripped most of his throat away.

Shay kicked the gun away from Scivally's hand, covered the dead face with a fold of the duster, and waited for Keever and the others to arrive. Trapped inside the fetid garage, she had to make a lot of effort not to be sick when the smell of Aaron Scivally's death washed over her.

"Somebody sold us out," Shay said.

"Look, Beth," Herve Espinoza said, "I know you're upset, but let's not go jumping to conclusions here."

"Meaning no disrespect, sir," Shay said, "but, bullshit. This operation was wired from the go, and Aaron Scivally knew about it." She led the way through the homicide desks and ignored the stares from the other detectives. At her work space, she lifted her lapdeck and disconnected it, then turned to face her superior. Keever was a silent hulk behind Espinoza. Less than an hour ago, they'd finished wrapping the scene in the underground parking garage, and the emotions were still running high.

"For Christ's sake," Espinoza said, "keep it down."

"I'm right, and you know it."

"I said we'd check it out."

"Let's do it now."

Espinoza met her stare with his own icy gaze, then reached for the phone, punched in an extension number, and held the receiver to his ear. "Get me Foalske."

"I found two monitoring chips," Leon Foalske stated. He telescoped a small metal pointer and used it to indicate positions within the circuit boards of Shay's lapdeck. "Here. And here. Soldered right in." He was a thin, sallow-faced young man who wore his light green lab smock with pride. The creases were perfect, at odds with the holey jeans and tennis shoes.

Shay leaned forward and concentrated to bring her full attention on the lapdeck. It was now after nine o'clock, and the brief catnap she'd managed had been interrupted by Espinoza's summons to his office. The lapdeck lay strewn in components across Espinoza's desk.

The homicide captain was freshly shaven despite having stayed the night as well, and his shirt and tie were pressed and neat. He sat behind the desk and twirled a ballpoint pen between his fingers.

"The bugs were different," Foalske went on. "Both were clever, and were set up to transmit along the interoffice modem line through the PR department's numbers every time you exited the deck."

"So they were getting up-to-the-minute reports whenever she used the deck?" Keever asked from the doorway.

"Exactly." Foalske grinned like a teacher who'd just been surprised by the intuitive leap of logic by a slow student. "But there's no way you could know that from the programming. They were both very subtle."

"You said they were different," Shay reminded as her impatience got the better of her.

"Right. One was definitely street-crafted, and sometimes you won't find a better design on the market. The deckjockeys out there are constantly finding new ways to amaze me."

"And the other?"

"No doubt about it. The second bug was top-of-the-line tech, and must have cost upward of two million yen."

Even doing the current conversion of yen to American dollars, the amount was staggering. Shay didn't like the direction her mind was taking. "Were there any fingerprints?"

"No. Both were clean."

"Do you think either of them knew about the other?"

"Hard to know. But I'd say they didn't. Whoever placed them knew what they were doing. I'd like to think I'd have found them during routine maintenance, but it's possible I wouldn't have."

"Can you trace them?"

Foalske looked at Espinoza. "Captain?"

Espinoza looked at Shay. "We already have. The street bug we followed to a guy named Michael Etami."

"An information broker," Keever said. "Does a lot of hacking for anyone who's interested and can afford him. We've used him a few times."

Espinoza nodded. "We have him in custody now."

"Why weren't we told?" Shay asked.

"Because I didn't want you to be told," Espinoza replied in his soft voice. "Your ass was dragging. You should have went home and got some rest. But I'm not your parent, just your boss. Tompkins and Elverman are still with Etami, but he's already told us he was selling the information to Scivally. Claims he didn't know what Scivally wanted it for. The DA's office is considering charging him with conspiracy to commit murder, but we're still trying to figure out if he's worth more to us out on the street than behind bars. If we let him go, he's in our debt in a big way, and he knows it."

"What about the other one?" Shay asked.

Espinoza tapped the pen against the desktop. "We followed it all the way into the corporate matrix structures, then we lost it." The pen froze, trapped by the homicide captain's fingers. "Personally, I don't think there's anything in the case that would interest the economic sector of this city."

Relaxing back in her chair, Shay understood Espinoza's hidden meaning. If it wasn't the case itself, then what was it? Obviously he'd reached the same conclusion that she did: that Kiyoshi Izutsu had tapped her lapdeck. But even as she thought it, she wanted to reject the idea. Despite all they'd put each other through before, during, and after their divorce, she didn't believe Kiyoshi would do that. Privacy was something her ex-husband expected and respected, except where Keiko was concerned.

Shay wished she had another answer, but there didn't seem to be one.

27

Standing in the shadows reflected in the darkened windows of the line of shops fronting the street, Almendariz watched the woman step off the bus. He knotted his rosary beads up his fist and ceased his prayers.

Dressed in dark clothes, with a hooded rain poncho covering his face, he didn't think Gitana Torres would notice him. He dropped the rosary into his side pocket, opposite the shoehorn.

The Torres succubus went south along Wayside, took a left on Meadowlawn, went down two blocks, then cut across the street and followed North MacGregor to her apartment building on Wildwood Way.

Once he was sure the woman was headed straight home, Almendariz allowed the distance separating them to grow. He kept his pace unhurried, moving it up only during those times she was completely out of his sight. He slowed before he came up on her, able to identify the individual way her shoes spanged against the wet pavement.

Before she reached the apartment building, Almendariz closed the distance. Standing under the eave of a doughnut shop closed for business, he watched her disappear inside. He gave her one slow Our Father, then followed.

The building didn't have an outer security system. He passed through the door and moved for the stairs, disregarding the elevator, where three people with grocery bags and fast-food takeout cartons waited patiently.

Knots of agony connected the vertebrae of his spine, dulled only slightly by the pain pills, as he went up the stairway. The worn carpet barely muffled his footsteps. Wet impressions, oily sheens against the dark brown cut of the carpet, showed that the succubus had taken the stairs as well. He froze when he heard the stair above him creak.

The shoehorn was in his fist, shielded from view by the

poncho. A moment longer, and he went up. He stopped in front of Gitana Torres's apartment.

The door was reinforced plastic and particleboard. He knew he'd be able to force his way through it if he had to. But it would alert everyone in the building. In this part of the city, few would answer the succubus's pleas for help. However, even those that did not come to her aid would be looking for him out of curiosity.

Examining the framework of the door, he found there was no peepchip connected to the wallscreen. He fell in beside the door and pressed flat against the wall. He held the bared shoehorn tightly, then knocked at the door.

The door opened and Gitana Torres poked her head out tentatively.

Whirling around the doorframe as the succubus's gaze turned toward him, Almendariz threw his full weight against the door.

Caught by surprise, the Torres woman went flying backward.

Slamming the door behind him, Almendariz was on her before she could get up from the floor or even attempt a scream. He clapped a hand over her mouth.

Eyes rolling white with terror, she shivered against him, struck out with her fists, and bit his palm.

A choked groan of pain slipped past Almendariz's lips before he could stop it. He knew if he tried to yank his hand from the woman's mouth he would free a chunk of his own flesh. He rolled over on top of her, shaking in agony, and almost plunged the sharpened 'end of the shoehorn into the succubus's throat. Barely in time, he realized that was what she wanted, that she had almost succeeded in deceiving him. If he killed her here he would not be able to attempt to salvage what remained of Gitana Torres's immortal soul. She had been as much of a pawn in her own way as he had.

Instead, he shoved his trapped hand against the succubus's face and thudded her head against the floor with enough force to stun her momentarily and make her jaws relax their hold on him.

Her lips split. Crimson blood spread in spidery webs across her white teeth. She lay there stunned. His own blood splashed garnet drops from his wound across her face. Only then did he notice the deep gash bisecting her left eyebrow where the edge of the door had caught her.

Pocketing the shoehorn, he reached for a dishcloth lying on the coffee table and quickly wrapped it around his injured hand. The binding would serve two purposes: it would stanch his bleeding, and it would keep her from hurting him any further.

She groaned.

Immediately he shoved his wrapped hand over her mouth again. He threw a leg across her body and straddled her to hold her down, managing to pin one arm. As she struggled against him, *it* surged inside him and became a full-fleshed hardness on the verge of release.

"Stop!" he commanded in a hoarse voice.

Her bucking continued, her hips slamming against his, and muffled noises escaped his covering hand.

The orgasm spread warmth across his loins and drained his strength from him. He fell onto her weakly and made himself keep his hand in place while the sinful lusts ebbed from him. He knew that if the succubus became aware of what had just happened, she would only laugh at him.

Something tore at his side, then a harsh stinging pain ripped across his face.

Instinctively, he clasped his free hand over his face, protecting the work it had taken skilled surgeons so many years to craft.

"Damn you, creature!" Almendariz yelled. He peered through his spread fingers at her bloody face. "You want to drag my soul to hell with yours, but you will not have that opportunity!"

More blinding pain wrapped across the back of his neck.

He saw the rosary in her fist when she drew back to strike again. "No!" he cried hoarsely. His hand leaped from his face and caught her arm.

The whirling rosary dashed against the coffee table and came apart, sending black beads spinning in all directions. He pulled her arm under his knee, felt and heard the bone fracture under his weight.

Someone banged against a wall from another apartment and shouted for quiet.

Fumbling in his pocket, Almendariz took out his vial of pain pills. The succubus struggled against him, whipping her head back and forth as she tried to escape. He held her. Uncapping the vial, he tried to pour some of the pills into her throat.

She twisted, caught him off-balance because he was concentrating on her upper body so much, and kneed him in the groin.

Pain paralyzed Almendariz and left him without the strength to even cry out.

Gitana Torres scrambled away from him and got to her feet, heaving for breath and unable to scream. When she turned and tried to run, she slipped on the scattered rosary beads and fell to the floor.

Almendariz grabbed her ankle. She managed two screams while she flailed her arms for anything within reach. A throw rug came up in her hands, and dust went everywhere. Blinking tears from his grit-filled eyes, Almendariz reached forward and drew himself along the woman's back. Her flesh felt smooth and hard beneath his. He ignored the tactile impressions with effort. Even his imminent discovery didn't daunt the feelings *it* caused inside him.

Seizing the woman's hair, he slammed her face into the floor three times. The thuds sounded dull and leaden. She stopped struggling as much.

He climbed on top of her and heard the wet smackings of her throat and lips working. Drenched with perspiration shed from the effort and from the fear, he turned her over and looked into her fear-filled eyes.

She was crying. Tears ran down her grimy, bloodied face. "Please," she said. "Please don't hurt me." One of her front teeth had broken off, and the jagged stump had cut into her lip.

Almendariz wanted to rail at her, let her know the anger he felt. But he knew it would only increase his chances of being caught. He shook some pills from the vial, dumped them into his torn palm, and forced them against the woman's mouth. "Take them," he ordered.

"Please," she mumbled around the pills and her broken mouth. "Please."

"Take them."

She closed her eyes and cried silently, her breath whistled through her nose. Her mouth opened and the pills disappeared inside. He pinched her nostrils closed while he held his palm over her mouth. After a moment he heard her swallow.

Still holding his hand over her mouth, her tears running

over his fingers, he helped her to her feet and shoved her toward the bathroom.

"You people better hold it down in there," a male voice warned through the wall, "or I'm going to call the police. You want to argue, argue. But don't be making anybody else listen to it."

"Sorry," Almendariz called back. "It won't happen again."

"It better not."

Inside the bathroom, he held on to the succubus and turned on the shower. Whatever noise she made now would be partly disguised by the sound of the running water. Pipes groaned and squeaked in the ceiling and wall.

He found a plastic cup by the sink, filled it with warm water, and positioned them so he could see their reflection in the steaming mirror. He was astonished to find her blood spotting his face. He held her from behind. "Drink this."

She accepted the cup, acted as if she were going to drink it, then splashed the contents into his face. She tried to spin out of his grip.

Holding on to her, he used his greater strength and weight to force her into the shower with him. Once under the steady stream of warm water, he held her face up to it. She choked and sputtered, but she swallowed. When he thought she'd had enough, he backed up, clapped a hand over her face, and waited for the medication to hit her system.

It didn't take long.

After he used the broom and dustpan he found in the kitchen closet to gather them, Almendariz counted the rosary beads. Sister Margaret Mary had given the rosary to him when he was a small boy. He knew exactly how many beads there were.

And one was missing.

He spent another frantic twenty minutes searching for it, but was unable to find it. He used the next few minutes to wipe down everything he'd touched inside the apartment.

Then he took Gitana Torres from the couch where she lay in a drugged stupor, pulled her arm across his shoulders, and guided her from the apartment. It was difficult getting down the stairway, but he dared not use the elevator. Her face, though no longer bleeding and as freshly scrubbed as he could manage without opening the cuts, was bruised and swollen and would have attracted immediate attention. He'd found a hooded coat in her closet and put it on over her wet clothes.

Outside, the rain had slowed and the wind came more brisk. A chill tightened his skin under his own wet garments. The succubus mumbled unintelligibly as he guided her down Wildwood Way to North MacGregor, and the words sounded like a litany. He wondered if it was a demon's prayer, spoken in a tongue he didn't understand.

Traffic was light, but the woman's weight and weaving movement made it hard to cross the street. A horn blared at them as yellow headlights blinded Almendariz. Water splashed across the backs of his legs as the vehicle passed.

The remaining distance to Bray's Bayou seemed impossibly long. Once they were past the street the terrain turned to weed-covered mud and clay. His feet sank repeatedly. It wasn't until he reached the water's edge that he realized one of the woman's shoes had come off. Her foot was bare and muddy. He considered going back after it, but realized there was very little chance he could find it in the dark. And he'd already spent far too much time with the woman.

Across the water he saw the wrought-iron fence running around Forest Park Cemetery. He stood for a moment in the quiet and gathered his strength. His spine kept sending explosions of pain rattling through his temples. His jaws were so tightly clenched his molars hurt.

The night air was obviously working to revive Gitana Torres. She raked a handful of nails at his face.

He barely caught her wrist in time to prevent her from injuring him. Grabbing her by the back of her hair, he pulled her down to the muddy ground. The shoehorn gleamed when he retrieved it from his pocket.

Intelligence sparked the woman's eyes as she looked up at him. The succubus spoke through her puffed lips and broken teeth, used the woman's voice to try to break his commitment. "No. Prease," she lisped, "prease, don't hurt me." Tears ran down her face, and her bruised chin quivered.

For a moment, Almendariz hesitated. The three others he'd killed in the heat of the moment, when they'd been able to fight back. There was no contest here. He firmed his resolve and made his voice hard. "Pleading will do you no good, you hellish monster. I know you for what you truly are."

Still, his hand shook as he drove the blade home in her throat. Blood, hot and warm, almost soothing, sprayed across his hand.

When he was finished, he rested for a moment, spent from his exertions. There was blood up to both his elbows. As before, there had been no deformed child's corpse to come spilling from the woman's loins, but those tense, long moments of waiting had nearly undone him. His arms trembled from the amount of work there had been.

When most of the dizziness had passed, he stood and grabbed the collar of the succubus's torn clothes. He pulled her into the water, grateful when the buoyancy took most of her weight.

Out in water that came up to his chest, he turned around, took the woman's head between his hands, and held her face under the water. It was clear enough, and her face pale enough, that he could see her features plainly. The shadows in the water took away some of the harshness of her injuries.

He chose a verse from the Book of James, Chapter One, Verse Fifteen. " 'Then when lust hath conceived, it bringeth forth sin: and sin, when it is finished, bringeth forth death.' "

He released the corpse, and it sank into the water.

" 'And may God forgive you your trespasses, as I forgive you.' "

An hour later, Almendariz was in his room at the rectory. Sean Harper was out. He'd cleaned up and changed clothes at the bus station and thrown the others into the public incinerator, but he didn't feel clean enough. When in the mirror he found the drops of Gitana Torres's blood behind his left ear that he'd missed, he almost panicked.

He immediately stripped and stepped into the shower, turned it on almost too hot to stand. Psalm 86 came to mind as he cleansed himself, and he spoke it out loud, took strength from it.

Finished with the soap and shampoo, he stood under the spray and let it wash over him. Some of the pain faded in his back and shoulders and leg as the minutes passed.

He felt so alone, so powerless to control the destiny that lay before him.

Memory of the woman's death wouldn't leave him alone until he'd done his penance. He reached for the Bible deck, slipped the trode into his temple jack, and accessed the First Book of Kings, Chapter Thirteen, Verse Twenty-four. It was a place he'd never been, and he feared going.

Before he had the chance to change his mind, cyberspace sucked him in, swept him past the warnings and safety designs he'd disconnected in the Bible deck.

No options were presented in the programming. With the safety features out of the way, Almendariz sank immediately into the mind of Silvanus, the prophet charged with the destruction of the altar of Bethel.

The ass moved slowly and steadily beneath him. Both had just finished a large meal at the house of an old prophet, and the day seemed too beautiful to hurry through.

But Almendariz knew the fear that shrilled through Silvanus. The prophet had successfully negotiated the eradication of the altar of Bethel, but he had inadvertently disobeyed the word of God. According to His instructions, Silvanus wasn't supposed to eat or drink in the city, nor was he to retrace any path he'd already taken.

However, Silvanus had been tired from his exhausting trip from Judah, and had been willing to listen to the old prophet's false story concerning the words of God. He had not only retraced his steps, but he had eaten and drunk.

The meal rolled greasily in Silvanus's stomach. Almendariz felt on the verge of losing it, but knew he wouldn't. At this point Silvanus had already tried to ram his fingers down his throat and make it come up. It hadn't, and sat in the pit of his stomach like a cold stone.

The borrowed memories scrolled through Almendariz's mind like an audio sensor across a cracked deck chip. At the end of the meal the real Word of God had entered the old prophet's heart, and he knew exactly how Silvanus had been charged to carry out his task. He'd bidden Silvanus to flee, had had his sons saddle a good ass to carry him.

Silvanus was sure he couldn't outrun God's wrath. When the ass stopped and would go no farther, he knew the time had come.

Almendariz considered running. He knew what was to follow. But he was unable to break the programming.

Gathering his robes around him, Silvanus knotted his fists together before him, dropped to his knees, and bowed as he beseeched God for forgiveness.

A low, coughing growl sounded to Almendariz's right. He looked up slowly, heart thudding in Silvanus's body.

A lion, golden and regal, thick-maned and fierce, eyed him from the dense foliage at the side of the narrow trail he'd been following.

Able to move now, Almendariz got to his feet and ran, arms swinging wildly at his side. In the programming his spine didn't hurt, and the movement wasn't mirrored in explosions of pain the way it would have been in his physical body.

Leaves and branches rippled behind him, and the heavy pad of the lion's paws scraped against the earth.

Its hot breath filled his left ear for one hypnotizing moment, then he saw the flash of white fangs at his shoulder, and paralyzing pain ripped through his arm and back. The lion's weight knocked him from his feet, tangled his legs up with those of the animal. The heavy claws raked at him as he fell on his back and reduced his flesh to bloody ribbons while the animal attacked him from above.

Silvanus renewed his pleas to God, and Almendariz joined him. Fear filled him, and he added his strength to that of the prophet as the lion pushed their body to the ground. He locked his fingers in the lion's muzzle and tried to keep it from him. The big cat's head was a wedge of tawny fur covering steel-spring muscle and hard bone.

Warm slavers dropped over Almendariz's hands, face, and bare chest. He screamed repeatedly, mumbled frantic bits of prayer. He tried to disengage the programming and struggled to retreat from the Bible deck even as Silvanus fought to free himself from the lion.

They both failed.

With another growl, the lion stretched Silvanus out with a single blow from its huge paw. It nuzzled the clothing from his stomach, searched out the soft parts underneath. Trapped in the prophet's unconscious body, still aware of every nuance of the pain, Almendariz screamed soundlessly as the big lion stripped gobbets of flesh away from his body and swallowed them whole.

28

Dawn streaked the eastern skies, turned the cloudbank hanging over Houston the color of bruises. Bethany Shay accessed her com-chip and listened to the running conversations of the investigation teams as she wheeled the nose of the Fiero between three patrol cars, an ambulance, and a fire rescue truck.

She parked the Fiero behind a crime scene van and got out. Taking the knee-length leather coat from the passenger seat, she shrugged into it as she approached the water through the trees, reporters, and uniformed policemen. Her hair was still wet from the shower, tied back in a ponytail that clung to the coat. She wore jeans, tennis shoes, and a Houston Astros sweatshirt that had been in a crumpled heap on her bed.

"Hey," a uniformed officer said, moving from his post to intercept her. "I can't let you go back there, lady."

She flashed her shield and backed the guy off, then fixed it to her coat pocket in plain sight.

Emergency medical techs worked at the side of the coroner's team and the crime lab investigators around a body that flopped helplessly in the water before them.

Despite the efforts of the uniformed police officers to control the site, reporters and curious neighbors and motorists ringed the shore, made occasional forays that required individual attention.

Shay heard her name called out a number of times by the media personnel, but steadfastly ignored it. At the edge of the water, she saw the dark splotches soaked into the ground, and the torn-up earth where a tennis shoe was almost buried. Long, uninterrupted skid marks torn through the dark mud told the silent story that the woman hadn't been alive when she was dragged into the bayou.

The men working the body looked up at her approach,

kept talking in low voices that wouldn't carry to the shotgun mikes some of the reporters doubtlessly had aimed in their direction. Sunlight lanced through the clouds and spilled a golden sheet across the surface of the water.

Doug Chaney waved at her and smiled uncertainly. His partner, Rodney Barker, didn't. Barker was the senior member of the homicide team, was still grooming Chaney through his second year as a full detective. Shay knew the older man had more sense than to try a good-old-boy approach.

Shay slid out of the leather coat, felt the bite of the coasting breeze immediately, and folded the garment before placing it on the dry part of the shoreline. Without hesitation she stepped into the water and waded out toward the body, her skin tightening almost painfully from the cold.

The men parted as she neared, letting her see the dead woman.

She floated in dark, muddy water almost hip-deep to Shay. Her clothing hung in tatters around her, seemed dark because all the blood had been sucked from her body. Intestines spilled like a broken fishing net around her, brushing up against the legs and bodies of the men around her. Leeches clung to her arms, breasts, and face. One of them curled up over her right eyebrow. Jagged pieces were torn from her face.

Quelling the spasms in her empty stomach, Shay took out her bottle of Vicks VapoRub and smeared a little around each nostril. She bent close to examine the marks on the dead woman's face.

"Turtles," one of the emergency rescue people said.

Shay glanced up at him.

He scratched the back of his neck self-consciously, a young blond guy who still hadn't come to terms with the things the job required him to view. "Them marks were made by turtles, ma'am. I've seen them before. They had some time to get at her before the boys found her."

Shay nodded. "Was there any ID on her?"

Dave Webber, the supervisor of the crime lab team, handed her a plastic evidence bag. He was a thick-bodied, gray-haired man with blunt fingers and a blunt personality that masked the care he took with the deceased. "Had a library chip in her pocket under the name of Gitana Torres. I had a guy run the name, and this looks like the woman."

Webber was also careful how he phrased his conclusions at the scene till all the facts were in. "According to records, she lives in the apartment building over there." He pointed.

Shay stared at the building across the open field.

"Rod and I gave it a look-see," Chaney volunteered. "Found some tracks that looked like the Ripper dragged her through the field, then had a fight with her when she got to the bayou. I was thinking maybe he'd knocked her out or drugged her or something."

Shay turned her attention to the detective and gave him a cool glance.

Chaney shut up and found somewhere else to look.

Barker regarded her silently behind heavy-lidded eyes, taking his time lighting a cigar.

"What boys discovered her?" Shay asked the emergency rescue guy.

"Those two right there."

Shay glanced back at the shoreline and saw two boys who looked maybe ten or twelve sitting under an olive-drab blanket by a paunchy uniformed policeman. They acted self-conscious and dropped their heads when she focused on them.

"We're going to take her out of the water now," Webber said, "unless there's anything else you want to see."

"No. I've seen enough." Shay's face was so cold it felt as if it would break if she moved it wrong. "Who's handling the autopsy?"

"Fitzgerald."

"When is he going to start?"

"As soon as we get the body there. They put him on standby when I called it in."

"Okay. Tell him Keever and I will be along."

Webber turned to his crew, and they began the preparations for recovering the body whole from the water.

Shay started for the shoreline. "Barker, you want to give me a minute of your time?" Her legs made slapping noises in the water, but she couldn't feel them very well. The footing was treacherous.

Barker bundled his jacket more tightly and followed. Chaney did too.

"Butt out, Chaney," Shay said. "You weren't invited."

The younger man's face turned hard. "Fuck you, Shay. Since when do I need a goddam invitation to go with my partner? Rod and I have already been taking a look around while you and Keever were catching up on your beauty sleep."

"Butt out, Chaney," Barker said without looking at his partner.

Chaney halted where he was, then kicked at the water in frustration.

On the bank, Shay picked up her long coat and pulled it on, then turned to face Barker. "What are you doing here?"

"We caught the squeal as it came out," Barker said. "Thought we'd stop by and take a peek."

"I don't want to look around and find you sitting on my shoulder," Shay said. "Tully wouldn't appreciate it either." Barker had a reputation for glamorizing cases he was working on and had intentionally worked angles in past investigations that had brought a lot of attention from the media. He'd been upset from the beginning that the Ripper files were assigned to Keever and Shay.

"The wheel's starting to turn, Beth," Barker informed her. He took his cigar out of his mouth, blew on the ash till an orange coal gleamed bright and hot. "It's not going to matter much longer what you and Keever would or wouldn't appreciate. Espinoza can't afford for you guys to waste much more time bringing this guy down."

"Until—and if—Espinoza gets around to making a reassignment like that, stay the fuck out of my way or I'm going to step on you like the shit-sucking toad that you are." She turned on her heel and walked away from the man.

His voice was soft and maybe he didn't think she could hear him when he said, "Sure thing, bitch."

She ignored his words, coiled the anger tightly up inside herself, refused to give the media a sideshow. Keever joined her as she walked to the two boys. He looked half asleep, his short-cropped hair sticking up as if he'd just climbed from bed himself. He handed her a cup of hot chocolate, and she let the aroma breathe life back into her numbed flesh and spirit.

"Found out you were already here when I checked in," Keever said. "When I heard the story break on wallscreen, I took a pass on calling you till I had a look."

"That's what I did too," Shay replied.

"You look?"

"I looked."

"And?"

"She's one of ours."

Keever cursed softly. "What was the deal with Barker?"

"He's wanting to horn in. Said he was sure Espinoza was going to be relieving us of the case before long."

"So what did you tell Barker?"

"That he was a shit-sucking toad."

"Should score a really big one for intradepartmental relations."

"He didn't disagree with the assessment."

"Maybe you moved him up a notch on the evolutionary scale."

"Definitely one of yours," Dr. Zachary Fitzgerald said as he moved around the corpse-laden operating table. His voice was slower than normal because he was jacked into the medical matrix hanging overhead. "Used the same weapon, made the same kind of cuts, serrations look the same."

Shay watched the flash of data, X-rays, and pictures stream in colored and black-and-white blurs across the pathology room's wallscreen. She tried to wait patiently.

"Did you say you can tie this one to one of the other victims?" Fitzgerald asked. He circled the corpse, photographing it from a variety of angles.

"Yeah," Shay replied. "Tully and I ran her back through the sort program we'd set up for the Ripper files. It turns out that Torres was a guest at Inesita Camejo's funeral."

Fitzgerald reached for a scalpel, popped his rubber gloves to make sure they were on snug, and approached the body more deliberately. The bright fluorescent lights splintered from the knife's sharp edge.

When the ME used his hands to open Torres up again, Shay remembered the sharp, splitting sound made by the watermelons her father had sliced open in childhood summers.

"We've got a foreign object here," Fitzgerald said in a distracted voice. "Didn't quite make it to the stomach." He pulled the recording arm of the matrix closer to his lips and made a footnote to the file he'd already opened on the dead woman. "Preliminary CAT scan reveals an oval object approximately one centimeter in diameter at its widest point in Torres subject's esophagus. Preliminary study of the body doesn't show any trauma that would indicate the foreign material was forced into her body. Assumption: Torres subject swallowed this object voluntarily but it didn't have time to move into her stomach before she was killed."

Shay waited, trying not to notice the blood that smeared Fitzgerald's gloved hands.

The man worked slowly, surely, with an economy of motion. He put the scalpel away, took up a small pair of long-handled forceps, and inserted them into the body. A moment later he pulled them out, with a round object locked between their stainless-steel jaws, and walked over to the sink area.

Hypnotized by the process, wondering what it held for her and the investigation, Shay trailed the medical examiner, followed closely by Keever. She stood by the sink and watched him wash the object clean. The water started out red, turned pink, and finally flowed clear and clean.

Fitzgerald snared the attention of the medical matrix's recording apparatus. "As noted, the object is about a centimeter in diameter, made of wood, covered by black paint. Toxicology will follow. A hole is drilled through it at its widest apex, uniformly tubular." He clicked the matrix off, unplugged the trode, and let it snake back up into the computer.

"What the hell is it?" Keever asked. He adjusted his glasses as he bent over more closely.

"May I?" Shay asked, opening her palm.

Fitzgerald dropped it into her hand. "I don't know, Tully. Some kind of bead. Did she have any children?"

"No."

Shay turned the black wooden bead over in her hand. It felt wet, slick, and so familiar. "The sides are smooth, but the ends where the holes are feel rough."

Taking the bead back, Fitzgerald slid it under a microscope, then turned back to face the wallscreen across the corpse. The lights dimmed at his voiced command. "It's worn smooth, not made that way. See the striations? That's from wear. Wherever that bead came from, it's had a lot of use. Chances are it was a part of something until recently, and that's why the rough edges are there. But why would she swallow it?"

"Maybe to tell us something," Keever said.

Shay lifted the bead from the microscope, worked it between her fingers, and felt the polished smoothness of it now that the water was drying.

"It could have been part of a necklace," Fitzgerald said.

"But it would have to have been a very old necklace to account for that much wear."

"I can't see our guy in a necklace," Keever said.

Excitement flared within Shay as she opened her palm in front of the two men and exposed the bead again. "It wasn't a necklace," she said. "And Gitana Torres *was* trying to name her killer for us." She pulled her own rosary from her coat pocket, held it up, beside the bead for a match. "He's a priest, Tully. That's why he didn't show up on the bus records the first time. The goddam son of a bitch is a priest!"

"His name is Judd Almendariz." Shay sat on the corner of Espinoza's desk, too pumped up to sit down.

The homicide captain sat behind his desk with a neutral expression on his face. The room was dark, lit up solely by the wallscreen showing the presentation Shay had arranged and the soft glow of her lapdeck by her side. "*Father* Judd Almendariz," Espinoza said.

"Of St. Anthony of Padua's," Keever said. He sat in a reversed chair in front of the desk, arms folded across the back.

The face was on the wallscreen in full frontal and left profile. The blond hair made a cotton halo around his head, and the blue eyes burned from an inner glow.

"I know that church," Espinoza said. "One of my cousins was married there. Father Brian is the pastor."

"Right," Shay said with a nod. "And Almendariz is a junior priest at that church. In fact, he spent his entire life there. From the state records we have, he was an orphan and was made a ward of the church from the time he was only a few months old."

"He was never adopted?" Espinoza asked. "The church usually has no problems placing babies with foster homes."

"He wasn't just any baby," Keever said.

Shay bumped the lapdeck up in the programming, and the wallscreen melted away to reveal the hideous child that had been Judd Almendariz. The purple birthmarks and cleft palate got larger and larger as the programming cycled through the school pictures culled from the church's electronic yearbooks.

"As you can see," Keever said in a cold voice, "the kid had problems. He was one ugly little fucker, and he was raised in a strict environment that encouraged perfection.

The sister that raised him was noted for being a harsh disciplinarian. We checked the records on her too. Sister Margaret Mary didn't cut no slack."

"There's no way this boy is the same man you showed me at the beginning," Espinoza said.

For once, Shay saw the captain's cultivated neutral expression replaced by revulsion and curiosity. "You're Catholic."

"Yes."

"So you remember the edict handed down by a Pope a few years back regarding clergy. The one about the physical appearance of the priests?"

"The body makeovers the tabloids made such a stink about?" Espinoza asked. "I thought those were just tummy tucks, face lifts, and light cosmetic work."

"It wasn't. Not in Judd Almendariz's case, anyway. Almendariz was the clergy's shining example of what a surgeon's knife could do." Shay launched into a summary of all the medical problems with Almendariz's curved spine, clubfoot, and facial deformities, added the radical procedures that had been used to correct them, emphasized the pain and disorientation that had to have gone into suffering through it, and talked about the probable pain the priest still underwent daily.

"How did you find this out?" Espinoza asked. "Medical records are kept sealed."

"Not in Almendariz's case. There were so many things the plastic surgeons and orthopedic doctors had to learn to fix him that most of those people ended up writing medical papers about their experiences and techniques. It's all logged in at the Library of Congress."

"Almendariz's whole life has been a thing woven together of perfections and obsessions," Keever said. His face looked immobile in the pale light reflected from the wallscreen. "Given that kind of background, he could very easily fit the profile the VICAP people have helped us generate."

"A lot of people could fit that profile," Espinoza pointed out.

"There's more," Shay said. She tapped the keys on the lapdeck, moved the programming along. "Here's a record of the bus routes."

"I thought you'd already come up empty with those," Espinoza said.

"We forgot about the clergy passes on the mass trans routes," Keever said. "They're different from regular bus passes because they go into a different batch file. Most churches get free transportation, or at least a discount, from the different systems."

"How did you get their records?"

"Tax reports," Shay answered. "The mass trans companies write it off at the end of the year. We accessed the batch files, found Almendariz's pass number, and punched it in. He was on the bus with all four of those women the nights of their murders."

"The son of a bitch was also at the funerals of the Camejo woman and Aleka," Keever said.

Shay rolled the video section of the program, froze it both times Almendariz passed in front of the caskets. Everyone remained silent till the file finished running.

Espinoza brought the lights back up with a vocal command, looked hard at Shay and Keever. "Circumstantial evidence," he said in a soft voice.

"Bullshit!" Keever roared. He stood up out of his chair and pushed it into the wall; it crashed and rattled the drawn blinds over the windows. "That son of a bitch has killed four women that we know of, and we've got the goods on him."

Espinoza rose from behind his desk, veins standing out in his neck as he slammed his palms against the desktop and addressed Keever. "Not bullshit, detective. Give me a fucking motive. Give me some fucking proof. You can't take that guy down on the basis of what you're giving me here. He's a priest, for God's sake. Do you know the kind of media coverage this department can expect if you two blow this?"

Shay slid off the desk and moved to a position between the two men in case their flaring tempers got the better of them. She'd seen it happen. Emotions on a case like the Ripper's ran high, and so did the feelings of frustration and helplessness. She was having a difficult time holding her own feelings in check.

"Almendariz is the freak we're looking for," Keever said. "When you cut to the bottom line, that's what you have left."

"You don't have a bottom line in a courtroom," Espinoza said. "You have proof, witnesses, evidence—not a trumped-up fairy tale that sounds like something out of the

Brothers Grimm." The police captain made a visible effort to regroup. "And you can't go charging blindly into a place like St. Anthony's like a bull in a china closet."

"If we pussyfoot around with him," Keever said, "Almendariz is going to get away."

"If he's the guy," Espinoza said, "it's your job to make sure that he doesn't."

Keever growled in disgust, turned, and hammered a big hand against the wall behind him.

Espinoza's voice softened. "If he's the guy, Tully, bring him in. But bring him in clean. If he's dirty, I want him off the streets for good, not just for a two-week vacation after which the DA's office will take a bye on the whole investigation."

Keever remained facing away and kept silent.

Espinoza glanced at Shay for support. "Beth?"

"Almendariz is our guy, Captain, and there's not a doubt in my mind. But if you want him taken down right, we're going to need some additional manpower, and a blanket dropped across this whole operation as of right now."

Espinoza nodded. "You've got it. And if you need me to pull any surveillance shifts, call me."

Shay nodded. "We'll get you a list of the people we'll want on the staff with us. And keep Barker and Chaney the hell away from us till we've wrapped this."

Espinoza didn't like being ordered around, and it showed in his dark eyes.

Shay didn't give a damn. From that moment on, the investigation was totally in her hands and Keever's, and all of them knew it.

29

"A priest?" Felix Carey stared in amused bewilderment at the giant face on the wallscreen of the matrix. His hand relaxed around the brandy snifter he'd been sipping from, allowing the glass to fall, remembering it only in time to blink it out of existence centimeters above the floor. He started up the stairs leading to the wallscreen, drawn by the burning intensity of those incredibly blue eyes. "You're sure, Welbourne?"

"Very sure, sir," Welbourne replied. "Of course, I have an investigative team double-checking those facts now, but I expect them to stand as they are."

"And the police are convinced he is the Ripper?"

"Yes sir."

"Tell me about him."

Welbourne did, beginning with the orphan's delivery to the Church of St. Anthony of Padua, and ending with the latest kill in the Ripper's series.

Carey took his time as he approached the floor-to-ceiling image of Judd Almendariz, listened to every lovely word Welbourne had to utter. He studied each individual line and plane of the young man's face, peeled back the skin and blood and bone until he could see the beginning of the predator underneath. "It is him," he said softly, more to himself than to Welbourne. "I see his hunger burning inside him now. God, I can almost feel it."

And it was true. The passion flared inside him, answering the excited thrum he sensed scratching behind Almendariz's angelic looks. He took a deep breath and savored the feeling. It had been so long since he had felt that way about anything, and he knew this was only the tip of what could be concealed beneath.

"What are the police going to do with him?" Carey asked.

"At this point, sir, there's not much they can do. Keever

and Shay informed their superior less than an hour ago, but they haven't got anything between them to arrest the priest."

"Almendariz," Carey stated.

"Sir?"

"His name. Almendariz. He has a name now. Use it." Using the name made it seem that Carey was that much closer to owning the priest.

"Yes sir."

"Now tell me about the police." Carey ran his hand across the screen, trying to feel the man on the other side of the glass. But since it was programmed information coming into the matrix rather than information originating there, he couldn't. Frustration chafed at him.

"As I was saying, sir, for now the police can't do anything to Almendariz. They have their suspicions of him, but no proof. He is beyond their reach."

"For how long?"

"Until they find something that will tie him to one or all of the murders."

Carey shook his head, and he felt afraid. "That mustn't happen, Welbourne. Whatever is required, take steps to prevent that until I am able to contact Almendariz and win him over to our side."

"Yes sir."

Accessing the matrix, Carey broke the connection to the outside world and closed down everything in the room till it seemed as if he and Almendariz's face were the only two things in existence. They were definitely the only things that mattered. He raised his left hand, placed it over Almendariz's right eye, and let himself sink into those blue depths as far as was possible.

Deep, deep inside, surrounded only by the blueness of that eye, he listened for the predatory drumbeats of the dark passion that throbbed within Almendariz, found them, and slowly linked himself to that passion till it was the only thing in his whole existence. For a time, he almost knew peace.

Shifting uncomfortably in the straight-backed chair, Bethany Shay wiped the perspiration from the lenses of the high-powered binoculars, then returned her attention to the church across the street.

The living room of their rented apartment held four chairs,

the telephone sitting in the middle of the floor, and a trash bag. The accumulated debris caused by six individuals living in the apartment for the last two days had created a loose film of dirt, paper bits, and food stains that had made Shay plan to make a vacuum-cleaner run to her house in the morning.

She and Keever had assigned themselves the evening shift, since most of the Ripper's slayings had taken place at night. But neither of them had been able to really let the day shift go. The apartment they'd rented to base their surveillance in had two bedrooms. Usually one or the other of them used the spare room to catch up on sleep.

So far Almendariz hadn't made a suspicious move.

As a safety valve, Shay had booted a program into all the mass trans systems that ran this part of the city to trip an alarm through police channels that would alert them if Almendariz used his pass on any of their buses.

They had their bases covered.

It boiled down to simply waiting the man out, until whatever dark instinct drove him to kill was in charge again.

Keever brought her a paper plate piled high with pizza slices and salad topped with ranch dressing. They ate in silence and maintained their vigil. Keever drank coffee, and they tanked up on caffeine to help them through the late hours.

Shay logged the call in at 1:21 A.M. automatically.

Keever reached down, scooped the receiver out of the cradle on the third ring, and spoke briefly. When he put it down, he said, "The uniforms have got a corpse one of us needs to go look at."

Shay resented the intrusion. "I thought Espinoza pulled us out of the circuit."

"He did. Everybody in homicide's working something somewhere, and this is a squeal that's got to be covered. Evidently one of the state's upstanding young representatives just shot holes in a Japanese business leader he was supposed to be negotiating with."

"I gather they reached an impasse."

"Till Representative Timmons pulled out his .45 and blew a hole in the guy the uniform told Espinoza you could herd a buffalo through."

"What about Almendariz?"

Keever reached into his pocket and produced a coin. "I'll flip you for it."

"You'll cheat."

"No I won't." Keever held the coin in his closed fist, smiled, then flipped it high into the air.

Shay watched it gleam, felt her heart speed up, knew Keever felt as strongly about the case as she did. "Tails."

Keever caught the coin, slapped it on the back of his hand, then uncovered it. "Heads. You catch the squeal while I stay here."

"You cheated."

"Prove it." Keever's face was impassive as he held out a hand for the binoculars.

Shay passed them over. "Espinoza should know better than to pull one of us out of here. Suppose something goes down tonight?"

"Then I've got the uniformed guys assigned to us to back me up." Keever raised his glasses and adjusted the magnification on the binoculars. "The captain knows what he's doing, kid, and he knows it doesn't take two people to hold a set of binoculars. He's been in a few of these sit-ins himself. The sooner you get on the road, the sooner you'll be back here. With the way the Timmons shooting went down, all you'll need to be there for is window dressing and for a quick look-see."

"Shit," Shay said in disgust. She gathered her coat and headed for the door, trying not to be so mad at Keever. But she was sure he'd manipulated the coin.

Almendariz woke with someone shaking him. He brushed the hands away, disliking being touched in such a familiar fashion. He blinked his eyes open and looked up to find Sean Harper bending down over him.

"Wake up, sleepyhead," Harper said in a soft voice. "You've got a phone call downstairs."

Struggling through the ragged shards of pain that filled his head, Almendariz sat up and glanced at the clock beside his bed. It was 1:49 A.M. He fumbled for the container of pain pills. "Who is it?"

"Didn't say," Harper replied. He stripped out of his sweat suit and dropped onto his own bed. "All the guy told me was that it was personal."

Almendariz pulled on his nightshirt and felt his knees

tremble for just the briefest of moments as disorientation swept through his mind. He swallowed two pain pills, then stepped into his house shoes. "Did the call wake Father Brian?"

"No. I caught it early. I was raiding the kitchen and found those cookies Sophie thought she'd hidden after dinner."

Mumbling thanks, Almendariz went outside and down the stairs, wondering who the caller was. He picked up the phone in the hallway and punched off the hold button. "Hello."

The voice was flat and unknown to him, sounded faintly British or Australian. "The police are watching you," it said. "They know who you are, and they know what you have been doing. There is someone who'd like to help you—"

Panicked, fear slamming around inside him in spite of the two pain pills already starting to work, Almendariz hung up the phone and clung to it for support. He shook his head. His voice came out low and hoarse. "No." His arms quivered, and his legs threatened to buckle as he concentrated on what the voice had said.

The phone vibrated in his knotted fist and almost made him cry out in alarm.

"Hello," he said softly, aware that his voice cracked.

"Ah, Father Almendariz," the man said, "I thought we'd been mistakenly cut—"

Almendariz pressed the disconnect button with his thumb, then left the line open and unplugged the receiver. He couldn't hide in the church anymore.

He fled into his room, rummaged in his closet for his duffel bag there, and packed a handful of garments, adding his Bible deck. The rosary Sister Margaret Mary had given him, restrung now but still missing one bead, went into a pocket. The razor-edged shoehorn went into another.

Once he was finished he took a final look around. A sweet ache filled him as he contemplated that he might not ever be able to return to St. Anthony's. His whole life had been spent here, and the weight of those memories was suddenly a physical force he'd never been aware of before.

He settled the duffel over one shoulder, then let himself out into the hallway. He eased through the living quarters without making a sound.

Outside, he breathed in the cool night air, pulled his black jacket more tightly around himself, and used his intimate knowledge of the landscaping to keep in the shadows. He reached one of the side exits through the brick wall surrounding church grounds and slid on through.

He considered using the mass trans station to make his getaway, then realized he needed the physical exertion of walking to keep himself under control. A block farther on, he reached the alley and broke into a shuffling run that strained his injured leg. His rasping breath burned the back of his throat.

The sound of a motor out on the street drew him up short. He tucked himself into the side of a clothing store and peered around the corner.

There, under the black umbrella of night unbroken by the dysfunctional streetlights, he saw a police cruiser moving slowly through the street. Two men were inside, gazing studiously at the sides of the street. One of them worked a spotlight that examined every nook and cranny of the alleys turning out onto the street.

Knowing they were searching for him, Almendariz flattened against the brick wall of the clothing store and held his breath.

The police cruiser rolled even with his position. The stabbing tongue of illumination from the spotlight raked across the alley where he hid, blinded him for a moment. Then it moved on.

He breathed a sigh of relief and a short prayer of thanks, and resettled the duffel across his back. He started to turn around and saw one of the homicide detectives assigned to the succubus killings enter the alley behind him.

Remaining where he was, masked by the shadows clinging to the clothing store, Almendariz brought out the shoehorn in his hard right hand. Even with the fear clawing through him, he felt calmed by the metal lines and curves. He remembered the detective's name with difficulty. He was Detective Sergeant Keever. For a moment, Almendariz's mind wandered, made him question where the woman detective was.

The voice on the phone had been right. The homicide detectives were on to him and what he was doing. But they would never understand why.

A big pistol rested securely in Keever's hand. The detective moved easily, but a bit heavily. His boots scraped against the uneven alley paving. "Unit four," he said in a low voice that still carried, "report in."

Almendariz shifted as the man, still unaware of him, came closer. As he realized what he had to do, and that the task would be difficult, his heart rate slowed and every nerve in his body tensed for the move he would have to make.

"C'mon, dammit," Keever whispered angrily. "The creepy little bastard couldn't have just dropped off the face of the earth. Find him."

When the detective drew opposite him, took another step forward that put him inches ahead of him, Almendariz uncoiled like a snapped spring. Every movement was instant, instinctive. The razor edge of the shoehorn flicked out, flashed in the uncertain moonlight, and slid greasily through the inner flesh of the big man's right wrist, bouncing off the bones as it skated along.

Blood sprayed the concrete surface of the alley and the brick wall. Keever yelled in pain and surprise, and wrapped his other hand over his wrist as the gun clanked to the ground.

Almendariz was aware of the com-chips inside the heads of policemen and knew Keever was probably calling for help now. He circled to face the big detective, intending to end the fight before it could get started. The shoehorn flicked out again, stabbing for the unprotected throat.

Before it reached its target, Keever lifted an arm and managed to block the thrust. Instead of cleaving his neck, the blade tore into his shoulder, sliced through muscle and tissue, and was almost pulled from Almendariz's grip. He yanked and it came free.

Before he could escape, the back of one huge hand slammed into his temple and rocked his head sideways. Blood flowed inside his mouth from a split lip, tasted salty and unclean. His hand came around low and dragged the rounded razor edge of the shoehorn across Keever's stomach. Crimson stains leaked across his light-colored shirt, spreading downward as gravity took over.

Keever bellowed in fear and rage, took another massive swing that sailed over Almendariz's head.

The priest placed his empty palm against the brick wall of the clothing store and pushed off, evading the detective's grasp. His breath came hard even though he felt calm. With the open alley at his back, he whirled, stepped in close again, and raked the shoehorn cruelly along the side of Keever's face.

The detective brought an uppercut seemingly out of nowhere that exploded against Almendariz's chin. His legs stopped obeying him, went rubbery, and dropped him to the alley floor. He rolled drunkenly, but managed to keep the shoehorn in his fist.

Amazingly, Keever kept his balance and reached down a big hand that closed into a fist holding Almendariz's jacket. The priest swung the curved blade again, feeling his arm go numb when the detective blocked it. When he closed his fingers, he knew he'd lost the shoehorn.

"Son of a bitch," Keever said in a hoarse whisper. Blood dripped across his lips as he spoke and painted them with the life that was leaving him. His free hand, glinting bone, bloody and almost useless, flailed back for the big pistol.

Almendariz struggled, both hands locked savagely on Keever's restraining arm, but he couldn't get away. He watched in sick fascination, yanking at the arm that held him and kicking at the detective's legs, as the bloody fingers wrapped with slow deliberation around the butt of the big pistol.

Metal grated against concrete as Keever dragged the weapon from the ground. The big muzzle focused on Almendariz. Bloody spittle dripped from Keever's mouth when he spoke. "Say good night, you sick psycho son of a bitch."

When Almendariz heard the shots, he thought they'd come from the big gun. He squeezed his eyes shut in panic and waited for the impact of the bullets to rattle through him. He was still praying for forgiveness when he felt Keever's body roll away from him.

Moving on reflex and sheer adrenaline rush, Almendariz pushed himself to his feet in disbelief. His hands trailed across his face and body searching for wounds. He stopped when he saw the two bloody patches high on Keever's chest.

"Hey." The voice came from behind him.

Whirling, already moving away from it, Almendariz saw a shadowy figure dressed in black step out of the alley, a pistol emitting a ruby light in its hand.

"Wait," the figure said.

Almendariz didn't pause. He shucked the duffel and ran as if the hordes of hell were after him.

"I'm here to help you, you idiot!"

The slap of shoes echoed after Almendariz as he ran, and he knew the man was pursuing him. His shoulders hunched painfully as he waited for the bullet to strike his flesh. He reached the end of the alley before he knew it, and saw the police cruiser too late as it glided into position to block the mouth of the alley. He heard the shrill of rubber, then the fender caught him across the thighs, sending him spinning across the hood of the car.

His senses collided. The bright gleam of the windshield came toward his face. Two silhouettes on the other side of it reacted to protect themselves. The metal slammed into his body as the careening motion of his momentum was redirected, and he heard the thud of flesh striking something much more solid.

He was unconscious before he hit the street.

30

Jamming on the brakes, Shay skidded the Fiero to a halt at the side of the street and bounced up over the curb to leave the lane clear for the ambulance already en route. She killed the engine, left the lights on, and hurled herself out of the car. Her hand freed the Glock 20 automatically, thumb poised over the safety release.

Two marked units blocked the entrance to the alley, their cherries whirling blue and red light across the street and building fronts, reflecting from the glass windows. Another one rolled up even as she ran for the alley.

She accessed the com-chip and moved to the Ripper freq monitored by the PD.

"Dispatch," a man's voice said in a mixture of fear and pain, "be advised that we have a confirmed ten-thirteen at the site."

"Roger, Car Fifty-four. Additional help is already on its way. Radio any further needs. Dispatch out."

Shay's heart threatened to explode in her chest as she ran. A code 10–13 meant an officer was down. She ran around the nearest cruiser, barely noticing the cracked windshield as she peered down the alley. At least four figures were aiming flashlights at someone on the ground.

"Shay!" A uniform crossed the alley in an effort to intercept her. His hands locked around her upper body and forced her back against the brick wall.

She recognized the uniform with difficulty. Arnie Golden was an older man with a broad face and silver hair. Tonight he smelled of garlic.

"You don't need to see that," Golden said in a soft voice.

"It's Tully, isn't it?"

"Yeah. Yeah, it is."

"Is he dead?" She hated herself for asking, but knew she had to.

"No." Golden locked her eyes with his, put a rough palm gently against the side of her face. "But it don't look good."

Shay put a hand against the man's chest and pushed in warning. "Get the fuck away from me, Arnie, or so help me God I'm going to hurt you."

"Then you get ahold of yourself, goddammit." Golden stepped back but kept himself in front of her. "You walk up there and let Tully see how bad he's hurt in your eyes, and you're going to cut his chances of making it. The shape he's in, he's gotta *believe* he's gonna pull through."

"By you," Shay said, "or over the top. You pick it."

Golden stepped to one side.

Despite the emotions thrumming inside of her, Shay slowed her gait to a jog. She leathered the Glock at her side, watching the four men around Keever take notice of her and make room. Steeling herself, she looked at her partner as she hunkered down beside him.

The front of Keever's shirt and pants were drenched in blood. The right side of his face was laid open to the bone. His lower right arm and hand were encased in an inflatable pressure bandage that went up to his elbow. He lay on his back, breath coming in slow gurgles that sounded more and more strained. His eyes were closed, and he was as pale as an actor in a black-and-white movie.

"Got as much of the blood stopped as I could, Shay," a young police officer said. Crimson streaks stained his face and hands. His fingers trembled as he adjusted the makeshift bandages covering the big man's body.

"You did good, Robbie," Shay heard herself say, and couldn't believe she sounded so calm.

The *whoop-whoop-whoop* of an ambulance's siren crescendoed in the street, then the vehicle rocked to a stop in front of the ally and disgorged three EMTs in light blue uniforms. Two of them sprinted toward Keever with equipment cases, while the third lagged behind getting a gurney.

The EMTs set up quickly, cleared the other people out of the way. Shay started to move, then felt a hand on her shoulder.

"Stay," Chris Shoemake said. He was thin and rangy, usually slow-talking, always good for a laugh whenever his job field overlapped with Shay's. "You can do us some good by keeping him relaxed and letting us do what we need to." He slipped a com-trode into his temple that would broadcast information back to Texas Medical Center.

Shay remained where she was and tried not to pay attention to Shoemake and the other EMT as they slid the IV needle into Keever's arm and started glucose transfusions.

"The Ripper?" Keever asked.

Shay looked up at the young cop.

"We got him. The guy ran into our car as we were responding to Keever's call. He's alive, maybe got something fractured, but he'll definitely live. He's cuffed and sitting in the back of Golden's car."

"Son of a bitch cut me," Keever said in a hoarse whisper. "Came out of the dark like some fucking shadow. I never even saw him till he cut me."

Shay forced herself to smile even though Keever's eyes were closed and he wouldn't see it. She was sure he'd know. "Getting old for this job, Tully."

A pained grin tugged at the good corner of Keever's mouth. "Shit. Fucker's good, kid. Don't go cutting him any slack."

"Okay," Shoemake said, "we're ready to move him. Texas Med has a team standing by waiting for him. You hear me, Tully? I get you there late, hell, you may miss your turn."

"Wouldn't want that, would we?" Bright crimson foam trickled out the good side of Keever's mouth.

Shay grabbed a double fistful of Keever's blood-slick jacket and nodded to Shoemake.

The EMT glanced at the other three people helping with the big man. "On three, everybody. One. Two. Three."

Grunting with effort, almost losing it to tears of helpless rage, Shay helped lift Keever onto the gurney, then slid her hand back into her partner's. He had no grip now, and very little body heat. Shoemake and one of the EMTs covered him with a blanket, raised the gurney, then carried it instead of rolling it to the waiting ambulance.

Shay crawled in back without being asked. She held Keever's hand and talked to him all the way to the hospital, willing him to live as Shoemake fought to stabilize him.

"Almendariz is going to be okay," Herve Espinoza said. "They X-rayed him, fixed him up with a couple bandages, and checked him out to us."

"Where is he?" Shay asked. They stood in a corner of the waiting room. Keever had been in surgery for forty minutes.

Three young boys, all under the age of ten, kept staring at her from their seats by an artificial tree, openly curious about the gun on her hip and the bloodstains on her clothes.

"At City/County under maximum security," Espinoza said. He'd arrived fifteen minutes ago, his hair and clothing not up to their usual impeccable standards.

"Is he talking?"

"No. He acts like he's catatonic or something. Before we can interrogate him, we've got to wait for his lawyer."

Shay glanced at her superior officer in surprise. "Almendariz has a lawyer already?"

"Yeah. Tyler Grahame."

"*The* Tyler Grahame?"

Espinoza nodded.

"Bullshit," Shay said in a louder voice than she'd intended. The three boys giggled, and their mother, a wan-faced woman with tear-smeared makeup, quieted them sternly. "Grahame's ambulance-chasing."

The homicide captain took Shay by the elbow and walked her into the hallway. Shay glanced pensively through the rectangular window where the doctor would come from Keever's surgery.

"We can't prove it," Espinoza said. "Almendariz won't talk to us, and Grahame's already shoving paperwork at all the right people, threatening to sue if we make a wrong step. He won't be able to bond Almendariz out until at least Monday, but we can't run the risk of blowing the arrest because we violated Almendariz's rights."

"What do you mean, bond out?"

Espinoza held up his empty hands. "We got no case against Almendariz for the Ripper murders. Keever and his team moved in too quick."

"Jesus Christ, Captain, Almendariz was making a run for it."

"That was the assumption Keever made at the scene."

"Because there wasn't another assumption to be made."

"Assumptions, right or wrong, don't make criminal cases in court, Beth," Espinoza said softly.

Shay made herself relax and tried to keep her voice from breaking. "He cut Tully," she said, "the same way he cut those women. Get the knife over to Fitzgerald and you'll have your case."

"There was no knife," Espinoza said. "The officers at that

scene have canvassed the area. There was no knife and no gun."

"What gun?"

Espinoza glanced at her. "Tully was shot, too. Twice. Took both rounds in the chest."

Dim memories of Shoemake's voice in the ambulance trickled through Shay's mind. Maybe the EMT had mentioned something about gunshots. She wasn't sure. She shook her head. "A gun doesn't fit the Ripper's MO."

"I know. But I've had the teams out there searching for both. They've found nothing."

"Somebody else was in that alley," Shay said in a quiet voice. A hospital orderly dressed in whites pushed a cart loaded with linen past them. One of the wheels squealed relentlessly.

"Did Keever tell you that?'

"No."

"Then you don't know that."

But Shay felt that she did. It was the only thing that made sense. Somebody else had shot Keever, because a gun wasn't part of the Ripper's pattern. Almendariz had liked his killing up close and personal. And whoever that third party was had taken the knife away as well.

Shay wrapped her arms around herself and tried to find warmth. Her eyes misted, but she refused to let the tears come. She'd be strong for Keever, keep it together so she could see him when he got out of recovery. She tried to remember what she'd said to Keever in the ambulance, wondered if it was enough and wondered if any of it even made any sense.

Long minutes passed.

She saw the surgeon heading up Keever's surgery push through the door.

Dr. Monroe was a big man with big hands that looked more suited to an anvil than a surgeon's scalpel. He wore a blue hospital smock. His eyes were gray and kind, touched by emotion but holding it back just the same. He looked at Espinoza. "Captain Espinoza?"

Espinoza nodded.

"I'm sorry, but there was nothing we could do. Once we got in there, everything was all torn up. We lost him before we could find and clamp all the severed arteries."

The words hit Shay like hammers and pulverized her into a fragile numbness.

31

"It's a mistake to hang on to the blade, Mr. Carey."

Riding piggy-back on the zombyte chip inside Reazer's head, Felix Carey stared through Reazer's eyes and felt through Reazer's hands as Reazer worked on the pistol he'd used to shoot the detective in the alley. Though no stranger to the seduction of the zombyte chip, Carey was still fascinated with the way the programming could mesh two personalities into one being. The chip was highly illegal. After its introduction on the market for use in helping psychologists work with patients with multiple personalities, the chip found an even larger financial success in the black markets of the world. Despite law enforcement crackdowns, the chip remained available in a few places, though not without considerable cost. Many times the hosts were incompatible and resistant. Most of them died.

Carey felt Reazer's fingertips go through the motions of taking the pistol apart as if they were his own. The metal was hard, certain, and the oily sheen of it clogged his nostrils and coated his fingers.

They were in Reazer's uptown apartment, surrounded by the luxuries the contract killer had afforded himself through his skills. Reazer worked free-lance, for the Japanese, for domestic companies, but mostly for Carey. He sat at the breakfast table, a carefully organized man who looked almost nondescript. His brown hair was medium-length and allowed him to pass for a street animal or a corporate exec with the right clothing. His brown eyes were flat and muddy, never resting too long on anything, nor moving on too quickly. The only outstanding things about him were his hands. They were built like shovels, wide, thick with muscles, the fingers so blunted they were all nearly the same length.

"Did you hear me, Mr. Carey?" Reazer asked.

Carey pulled away from the sensations coming to him through Reazer's fingers. The zombyte chip brought everything so tantalizingly close, brought those delicious feelings so near the surface of his being that he thought he could touch them. But he had never been able to before. Something had always been missing. With Almendariz, though, the possibilities might be endless.

<I heard you,> Carey said inside Reazer's brain. <But I have plans for that weapon. It'll be needed again.>

The pistol came apart in Reazer's hands. He took the barrel tubing and walked into the spacious kitchen with utensils carefully arranged on the walls. Lights gleamed from the copper pots and pans and shone on the stainless steel.

Opening the disposal unit, Reazer dropped the barrel inside, closed it, then thumbed the start button. Ruby illumination flared on the other side of the dark glass as lasers destroyed the barrel, leaving only metallic ash that was sucked into the building's main incinerator units.

Carey knew from experience that Reazer would replace the barrel in the pistol from an assortment he kept stashed in the apartment. Unable to wait any longer, he accessed his home matrix to feed the zombyte chip more power. He felt Reazer's personality go gliding past him, taking the backseat in the body.

Reazer made no complaint.

Carey knew the man was paid too well for that. He crossed the floor, walked through the living room, and stopped in the hallway. In front of the closet, he reached up and thumbprinted the concealed ident plate in the ceiling tile. A small door flipped open and he rummaged inside.

He took down the canvas bag inside, loosened the drawstrings, and spilled the contents into his palm. The shoehorn shone with an inner fire and seemed sharp enough to slice the light as he took it into his hand. With the end curled around his little finger, there was less than a quarter-inch protruding.

<Guy didn't hold it like that,> Reazer said.

"How?"

<The lip goes around from the inside of your middle finger, tucked in close to your palm.>

Carey moved the shoehorn and felt it slide almost naturally into place.

<Now the thumb goes into the depression to stabilize the

blade. Works pretty well, because the rounded edge doesn't allow it to stick or get wedged easily.>

Almost hypnotized by the feelings of power coursing through him, aware that at least four women had had their lives sundered by the blade, Carey locked his hand down on the weapon. "How did you see all this in that alley?"

<Infrared chip hardwired into my optic nerve.>

"And you were never seen?"

<If I had been, I think we'd know about it by now.>

Carey silently agreed. He walked into the bathroom, called for the AI to turn the lights on in Reazer's voice. When they came on, he looked at Reazer in the mirror holding the priest's shoehorn. He made a few passes with it, watched how it splintered the reflected light, thought about how easily it would cleave flesh. He closed his eyes, put himself into Almendariz's mind, and into the passion that he thought must drive the priest. He saw the four women as they had been, resurrected by the matrix for his viewing pleasure. Without warning, Reazer's body got an erection.

Carey sensed the hit man's unease, turned off the lights, and quickly replaced the shoehorn in its hiding place.

<As long as that shoehorn exists,> Reazer said, <they're going to be able to tie those killings to your boy. And maybe that cop's death to me.>

Releasing his hold on the zombyte chip, Carey faded into the background of Reazer's mind. A communications ping came along the gridline connecting him to the matrix in the heart of his building miles from the hit man's residence. He shunted the communications off privately, cut Reazer out of it. <Yes, Welbourne.>

Sorry to interrupt you, sir, but Mr. Grahame has reached the City/County jail. You wanted me to let you know.

<Thank you, Welbourne. I'll be along in a moment.>

Yes sir.

"Are you still there, Mr. Carey?" Reazer asked.

<Yes. Don't worry about the shoehorn. After tomorrow night, it can disappear as well.>

"Yes sir. I just don't like loose ends."

<Tomorrow night we can take care of two loose ends at once.> Carey reached out for the matrix, snared a gridline, and allowed it to sweep him away. He went quickly, excited at the prospect of finally seeing Almendariz in the flesh.

* * *

Felix Carey paced restlessly inside Tyler Grahame's mind as the jailer led them to Almendariz's cell. The sights and smells of the jail were overwhelming. The lawyer took them all in stride.

The jailer was a beefy black man with a thin mustache. He slipped the ident card into the lock, and the bolt whirred back. "Just press the button when you're ready for me to come get you, Counselor."

"Thanks," Grahame said. He stepped inside and the jailer locked the door.

Carey hated the sound of the bolt falling into place. Only the knowledge that he could leave at any time he chose kept him from panicking. He watched through Grahame's eyes as the lawyer made sure the jailer was leaving. <Turn your head, Tyler. Let me see him.>

Grahame turned around and peered into the gloom in the cell that grew darker as it neared the bed chained to the wall. Carey could barely make out the slender figure sitting on the bed. Slatted bars of light barely touched the handsome young face.

"Father Almendariz?" Grahame asked. He stepped forward and offered his hand.

Almendariz remained silent and still, giving no sign that he'd even noticed the other man.

Inside Grahame's head, Carey studied the priest and knew it was important that he be able to establish a line of communication. For the moment he relied on the lawyer's abilities.

But Carey knew firsthand the dark hunger that was leaching into the priest's soul.

Grahame didn't let the silence bother him. He walked across the room, grabbed the straight-backed chair by the wall, placed it in front of Almendariz at a comfortable distance that wouldn't threaten the other man, and sat down. He opened his briefcase on his legs. "My name is Tyler Grahame. I'm an attorney. I want to be your attorney and represent your interests in court. I have some papers I'd like you to sign empowering me to act on your behalf." He held them out.

Almendariz made no move to reach for them.

Carey felt the smile that Grahame gave the priest tighten on his make-believe face in his own matrix and worked to banish it. He studied Almendariz, sorted through everything he knew about him, searched through all that he'd guessed about the hunger that moved Almendariz to kill. For years he had studied men like the priest, serial killers and sociopaths whose own thoughts and motivations seemed to lie in directions normal minds couldn't—or wouldn't—go.

He cleared his mind of meandering thoughts and concentrated on the blue eyes before him. Almendariz had been with the church his entire life, had his mind and his body shaped by those experiences. He remembered the pictures of Almendariz before the surgeries. Assuming there had been no kills taken before the operations, he looked for something that had happened since.

"You need representation, Father," Grahame stressed. "I've looked over most of what the DA's office is getting as evidence, and it's weak. Flimsy. I can turn them away from you. Don't you want that?"

Almendariz didn't answer.

"They tell me you won't talk to them," Grahame said easily. "That's good. You shouldn't talk to them. They'll lie to you and trick you if they can. You need me to protect you."

"The truth will protect me, Mr. Grahame," Almendariz said softly. "You are not needed here."

"The truth is not always a good defense," Grahame said with another quick smile. "I know. I'm a lawyer, and I've seen plenty of times when the truth was not the answer."

"This is God's truth," Almendariz said. "Not the truth of man."

Carey concentrated, accessing the matrix for memories of the murdered women. He saw them, naked and bleeding in his mind, felt Grahame shiver just a moment because the lawyer caught a glimpse of them too. The women were important. He knew that. But he wasn't sure how they were important. The cuts were so ritualistic, followed a set pattern, destroyed the sex organs inside and outside.

"I can help you if you'll let me," Grahame said. "And you're going to need help."

Almendariz closed his eyes. "Go away, Mr. Grahame. There are things here that you don't understand, forces at work that make the promises you're willing to give insignificant."

Moving by instinct, guided by the framework he'd build concerning Almendariz's motivations, Carey yanked Grahame's personality into the rear deck of the lawyer's mind and took over himself.

<Hey, what the hell do you think you're doing?> Grahame bellowed inside his head.

Carey ignored the lawyer and leaned closer to the priest. "I know you killed these women, and I know you killed them because they betrayed you."

Almendariz's head snapped up and swiveled around. His gaze was bright and keen. "How do you know that?"

"Because," Carey said, "God sent me here to help set you free."

<Now we're in the shit,> Grahame said. <You get this guy telling fairy stories, we're going to be here all night and not get anything done. I thought you told me you wanted him off clean, with no psycho billing.>

Almendariz looked doubtful.

Flying blind, Carey elaborated cautiously, working off the mixture of emotions he saw in the priest's dark gaze. "They seduced you, Father Judd," he said. "The things that happened were not your fault." He figured the statement would cover a multitude of sins.

Hands suddenly shaking and eyes brimming with unshed tears, Almendariz said in a hoarse whisper, "You do know."

Masking the euphoria he felt, Carey leaned forward and gripped the younger man's shoulder in reassurance. "I know that much, Father, but I don't know everything. I need to know more."

Almendariz slid the fingers of one hand through his hair and seemed to shrink into himself. He talked in a low voice, speaking of Sister Margaret Mary and the special things she'd always felt were in store for him, moving into the operations that had been so painful, and into the confusion that had filled him when the women of the church suddenly found a new interest in him. Then he talked about the succubi and the way they'd found to steal his soul.

<Son of a bitch,> Grahame said when the priest finished. <You got yourself one grade-A certifiable nutcase here, Mr. Carey. If I get him up on the stand and have him tell this story, document all the pain this guy has been through with those surgeries, let the judge and jury see that Almendariz really believes this crock of shit, we can walk out of that courtroom in a matter of hours—not days. There won't even be a whisper about the death penalty.>

<No,> Carey replied. <There will be no trial, and he will not be found insane.>

<Look,> Grahame said, <I don't know what you want with this guy, but—>

<Nor do you need to know,> Carey replied sharply. <What you need to know is that I want him out of jail, free of charges.>

Grahame fell silent.

Carey returned his attention to the priest. "You can't tell anyone else this story, Father." He made his words heavy, and they seemed to hang in the still air of the jail cell.

"But why?" Almendariz asked. "It is the truth."

"Do you want to die?"

"I'm not afraid of death."

<Of course not,> Grahame said. <This guy's already got a reservation in heaven.>

Carey flailed mentally, looked for a chink in Almendariz's logic that would allow him to yank the man's armor away. Religious matters were not his forte, but there had been a time when he'd been very old and his ID transfer to the matrix hadn't been a sure thing. He sifted through what he remembered and turned up a nugget he hadn't expected. "Telling anyone else about this is suicide," he said. "And you know how the Church feels about that."

Almendariz drew in on himself and looked uncertain. Suicide was the most heinous crime any Catholic could commit. It meant being buried in unhallowed ground and forgotten by God.

A guard passed by outside the cell, shoes shushing softly against the hard concrete. A tuneless whistle followed the man, growing fainter as he walked away.

"Then what do we do?" Almendariz asked. He held his hands pressed together in front of him.

"We're fighting more than the succubi here," Carey said. "We're also fighting Man's basic disbelief in God Himself. We can only hope to dissuade the court from thinking you are the murderer of those women."

"I killed them."

Carey shook his head. "No, Father, you saved those women. You liberated them from a fate far worse than death. If the succubi had continued to stay in their bodies, their flesh would have withered away, left them rotting corpses that would have formed decaying flesh-and-blood graveyards for their very souls. I'm sure that wherever those women are now, they are thankful to you for what you have done."

<Jesus Christ,> Grahame said. <You're making this guy out to be some kind of saint.>

<Maybe he is.> Carey regarded the priest. "Can you trust me to take care of you in this matter?"

"Yes. If He is within you, if He moves you to listen and to believe, I can't turn you away." Almendariz held out his hand, pale and white in the jail cell's shadows. "Will you pray with me, Mr. Grahame?"

And Felix Carey, who hadn't spared a word for God in over five decades, moved from his chair, knelt beside the priest by the bed, and listened to Almendariz's prayers as dark dreams of his own danced in his thoughts.

32

"As you can see, Judge Waring, Kiyoshi Izutsu has every right to be concerned about his daughter's welfare. Ms. Shay is clearly not focused on his daughter's needs."

Bethany Shay sat in her seat beside her attorney and listened to the words of her ex-husband's counsel roll over the nearly empty courtroom. Her stomach felt as if it were overfilled with knotted hands striving to get out.

"Objection, Your Honor," Troy Pulver said. He pushed himself out of the straight-backed chair and stood up. Dressed in a light gray suit with a blue-striped tie, he looked like a workingman who'd girded his loins for a long and difficult day. He was in his late forties and had a shock of unruly black hair that appealed to women jurists.

To Shay, Judge Waring looked like a toad, and it wasn't just because she considered the judge to be another of the enemies she faced in the courtroom. He was a short, gnarled little man with clumsy cosmetech that had taken away his crow's-feet wrinkles and given him a pop-eyed look, and hair that was patchy at best from failed regen treatments. He didn't look impressive even in judge's robes.

"On what grounds, Mr. Pulver?" Waring asked. His tone indicated that he thought the lawyer was only wasting time.

"It's pretty evident to me that counsel is trying to prejudice the court with his constant references to Keiko Izutsu as Mr. Izutsu's daughter. She is also the daughter of Ms. Shay."

Waring looked at the opposing counsel. "You will watch how you refer to the child in the future, Mr. Amaterasu. Although I am not so easily swayed as defense counsel seems to think, he does have a valid point."

"*Hai,* Your Honor." Amaterasu bowed his head in acceptance. He wore a tailored black suit that gleamed with authority along every creased edge.

Shay glanced at the plaintiff's bench and saw her ex-husband sitting there.

Kiyoshi Izutsu wore a dark blue suit and sat in a relaxed pose. Occasionally one of his long-fingered hands would absently reach up to stroke his cheek—a tic that Shay remembered meant Kiyoshi was feeling pressure—then he would catch himself and stop.

The audience was small. Tamaki and Hideo were in attendance, as well as a small group of Japanese whose ties were definitely to Izutsu Corporation. Keiko was not there. Although she didn't want her daughter present, Shay had hoped she might get to see her, even if only for a few minutes.

Most of the usual courtroom spectators had gathered two floors down where Father Judd Almendariz was going through the preliminary hearing. The hearing had been hurriedly scheduled because of all the media and political pressure on the murder investigation. Although defense counsel Tyler Grahame had tried to delay the hearing, he hadn't been able to. After all, the media had been quick to point out, it wasn't as if Almendariz were actually on trial yet; the court and the DA's office were only interested in whether there was a case.

Shay was tired but determined not to let it show. Thinking about Keiko was a double-edged sword. On one hand it calmed her and allowed her to focus her resolve; on the other hand she knew all too well what she was in danger of losing.

"Mr. Almendariz, do you—"

Almendariz leaned into the microphone, still wary of how loud his amplified voice sounded in the cavernous courtroom. "*Father* Almendariz."

District Attorney Dwain Andersson halted in mid-cross-examination, an uncertain look on his face. Tall and thin and tanned, oozing grace and certainty, the man looked at home in the courtroom.

"My correct title is *Father*," Almendariz said. "I'd appreciate your using it when you address me."

The sour look on Andersson's face showed he wasn't pleased with the interruption, nor the correction. It also brought to his attention that at least two dozen priests and nuns were in attendance, their black uniforms and habits making them stand out from the rest of the crowd filling the courtroom.

Cameras moved back and forth from Almendariz to the district attorney.

Unaccustomed to the attention he'd received all morning long, Almendariz tried to conquer his anxieties by comparing the courtroom to the Sunday Mass he gave. Every eye was fixed on him then, and when he delivered his message concerning purgatory in the hereafter, there was just as much fear and confusion in the gazes.

Father Brian sat on the first row, his fingers crossed over his stomach as he studied the events with implaccable features. Almendariz wished he knew what the man was thinking.

"*Father* Almendariz," Andersson said.

"Thank you," Almendariz said.

At the defense table, Tyler Grahame nodded imperceptibly and kept making notes on the mem-o-pad with his electronic stylus. Grahame had coached him on how to handle the district attorney, as well as the other questions the city would be asking.

"How well versed are you in law?" Andersson asked.

"In the canons charged to men by God," Almendariz said, "I count myself as knowledgeable."

"But in the laws of men?"

"I don't drive, and I don't pay taxes," Almendariz replied. "So those are two areas I am definitely underinformed in."

"What about murder?" Andersson asked.

"Objection," Grahame said. "He's badgering the witness, Your Honor. I won't have him painting my client in guilt with his insinuations before we even know we have a case here. Granted, someone killed those four women, but there's been no indication that Father Almendariz was even involved."

"Sustained," Judge Drabeck said. He was a short man with clipped brown hair and features that looked regular and too white. From the witness chair Almendariz had no problem smelling the cologne the man wore. "Mr. Andersson, if you have an agenda here, let's get on with it."

"Yes, Your Honor." Andersson retreated to his table for a moment, checked a memo on his lapdeck, and returned to the witness stand. "Did you know this woman?" He pointed at the vacant area over the holo projection table.

A rainbow sun sizzled into being, gave an audible pop, then became a 3-D likeness of Mitzi Harrington from the neck up. It slowly revolved 360 degrees, then came to a stop facing Almendariz. Camcorders and cameras flashed like night insects.

Almendariz looked at the woman's face, leaned down to the microphone, then said, "No. I didn't." And the answer felt right coming from him. As Grahame had explained, he had known the women only after the succubi had taken over their bodies, so he had never had the chance to get to know the real person.

"Her name was Mitzi Harrington," Andersson said. "She was the first victim. She was a wife, and mother of two small children. She taught at—"

"Objection!" Grahame yelled. He pushed himself to his feet and buttoned his jacket. More cameras flashed in anticipation. "Father Almendariz has already stated that he did not know the woman, Your Honor. What more does the prosecutor want?"

"Move along, Mr. Andersson."

"I did not know her before she was murdered," Almendariz volunteered. "But I prayed for her and her family after I learned of her death."

Andersson didn't appear pleased by the answer.

A wave of murmuring cycled through the crowd.

Slamming his gavel down, Judge Drabeck called for order in the courtroom. "Silence!" he roared. "You people will respect this courtroom and these proceedings that go on here, or I will have it cleared."

Silence immediately descended on the room.

"Go ahead, Mr. Andersson."

"Thank you, Your Honor," Andersson said. He waved to the holo table. "May I have your attention over here again, Father Almendariz."

The image of Mitzi Harrington dissolved, instantly replaced by that of the prostitute Aleka. She looked hard and worn and ill used even before death, that appearance only partially blunted by the glitter makeup.

"Do you know this woman?" Andersson demanded.

"She was the second victim."

"And did you know her before she was murdered?"

"No." Almendariz kept his face calm despite the building inward tension.

"How about this woman?" Andersson asked.

Aleka's features melted into those of Inesita Camejo.

"She was the third victim," Almendariz said. "And no, I did not know her."

"Your Honor," Grahame said from the defense bench, "surely the prosecution has more to offer this court than merely a rogue's gallery of these murdered women. Granted, these were indeed heinous crimes, but let the district attorney trot out evidence that indicates my client should be bound over for trial."

Andersson whirled before Judge Drabeck could make a reply and threw an accusing finger toward Almendariz. "Your Honor, I have evidence in my possession that indicates the defendant not only had the opportunity to know each of these women before they were murdered, but also had the opportunity to murder them."

"Move to strike, Your Honor," Grahame said, getting to his feet. "The prosecutor cannot be permitted to make these unfounded accusations and inflammatory statements."

"Gentlemen," Judge Drabeck said, raising his hands.

Almendariz watched the heated discussion with impassive features. Fear thrilled through him, dulled by the pain pills he'd taken prior to getting into the witness stand. He was still bothered about the swearing in, because he'd been charged with telling the whole truth, and if Grahame had his way, the whole truth would never come out. He slipped his rosary from his pocket and silently prayed.

The rhythmic whir and buzz and click of the media tools formed an audible backdrop to the arguments.

"I need some latitude here, Your Honor," Andersson said. He dropped his hands at his sides in a gesture of helpless submission. "As defense counsel has noted, the murders of these women are heinous crimes, and every effort must be made to discover their murderer."

"Or murderers," Grahame added.

Andersson didn't respond to the man's insertion into the record or the media input.

"I'll grant you some latitude, Mr. Andersson," Judge Drabeck said, "but I want to hear some of your evidence very soon."

"Yes sir. Thank you, Your Honor." Andersson took a step back, appeared to be reflecting, then took two steps toward the witness stand.

Almendariz held the rosary loosely in his hand, all too aware of the missing bead. He recognized the posturing the district attorney was using as a bid for the attention of his audience, the same body language a number of clergy used when wanting to drive home a point. He made himself loosen up, knowing it was hard to hit a target that refused to be touched.

Coming to a stop in front of the witness stand, Andersson locked eyes with Almendariz. "You've stated under oath that you didn't know any of these women."

"Yes."

"You'd never seen them before?"

"I'd seen them a number of times before," Almendariz stated.

Andersson appeared to be confused for a moment. "Would you explain that?"

Almendariz gave him a gentle smile, the same kind of smile he often gave other priests and the nuns who tried to usurp his quiet control of a situation or an event. "It's been hard these past few weeks not to see those women," he said. "They've been in every media outlet I'm aware of."

"Outside of the media, have you seen these women before?"

"No."

"You're sure?"

"Yes."

Andersson returned to the prosecutor's table to retrieve a small plastic package, which he handed to the bailiff. "Your Honor, I give you the prosecutor's exhibit A."

The bailiff handed the package to the judge.

"And what exactly is this, Mr. Anderson?" Drabeck asked.

"A chip copy of mass trans records covering the period of the Bayou Ripper's activities," Andersson said. "When you review those, you'll see not only that Father Almendariz rode the routes with the murdered women a number of times before their deaths, but that he also rode the bus with them the nights of their murders."

"All of which, despite sounding melodramatic, is inconclusive," Grahame said. "Your Honor, what the prosecuting counsel is trying to fob off on you as hard data is purely circumstantial evidence and speculative fiction on the part of the Houston Police Department and the district attorney's office."

"It all goes toward showing means and opportunity, Your Honor," Andersson said. "As you're aware, in serial murder cases, the motive of the killers is often never discovered or, if discovered, never understood. Those bus records are important to our case."

"So noted, Mr. Andersson. Mr. Grahame, you may challenge the presented evidence at a later date. For now, the court accepts it."

Grahame sat.

Andersson turned back to Almendariz. "So, in light of the evidence we have presented—"

"Objection," Grahame said.

Judge Drabeck banged his gavel. "Overruled, Mr. Grahame. And as for you, Mr. Andersson, you'll refrain from making remarks to badger the defense counsel."

"Of course, Your Honor." Andersson nodded.

Almendariz rubbed his palms together and felt the sheen of sweat covering them. He desperately wanted to jack into his Bible deck and erase the accusing faces.

"During the course of your travel along the mass trans routes," Andersson said, "did you ever meet any of the murdered women?"

"No."

"Even though you rode with them?"

"I wasn't aware that we were on the same bus."

"So you didn't know them?"

"No." Almendariz's voice sounded low even in his ears.

"Would you repeat that, Father?"

"No. I didn't know them."

"Did you ever see Mitzi Harrington on the bus?"

"No."

"Did you ever see Aleka on the bus?"

"No."

"Did you ever see Inesita Camejo on the bus?"

"No."

"Did you ever see Gitana Torres?"

As each name was called out, the holo table created the woman's image for the courtroom to see.

"No," Almendariz said. He felt hot, and it was hard to breathe. Repeated denial was so hard, even if it was the truth. He wanted to tell them everything, tell them how he had fought for his life against the succubus-inhabited women so he could remove the doubts and accusations in the eyes that stared at him.

"What did you do on the bus?" Andersson asked.

"I read my Bible, or I took care of paperwork I was assigned to do."

The district attorney nodded. "If you were asked to give me a job description of what it is that you do, Father, how would you answer that?"

"I do as the Lord God would have me do by living my life as an example to others."

"Would God ever ask you to commit murder?"

Almendariz was on the verge of answering when Grahame came up out of his seat like a rocket.

"Your Honor," Grahame said, "you granted Mr. Andersson some latitude. You didn't tell him he could indulge his fantasies."

"Sustained," Judge Drabeck said.

"I withdraw the question," Andersson said.

The general hubbub of shushed comments died down in seconds.

Almendariz waited, tried to lose himself in the numbing waves crashing in from the pain pills. But they seemed so far away.

"Let's move this back into an area where you're more familiar," Andersson said as he hovered like a predator. "In your faith, what would happen to a man who had killed another man?"

"His soul would be forfeit," Almendariz answered in a sure voice.

Father Brian nodded in sage agreement.

"And he would burn in hell forever?" Andersson asked.

"Yes."

"You took an oath to tell the truth when you stepped up into that chair, didn't you, Father?"

"Yes."

Andersson placed his hands on the railing and leaned forward. "By the laws of Man, you would be guilty of perjury for lying on the witness stand. But for lying on the name of God, wouldn't you burn in hell too?"

Grahame erupted as the courtroom crowd became an audible river of mixed emotions.

"So I guess it remains to be seen," Andersson said,

"whether you're more afraid of the laws of Man than you are of the commandments of God."

Grahame and the crowd rose to new heights of vocal support and outrage.

As Almendariz looked into the prosecutor's eyes, he wished he had the razor-edged shoehorn in his fist to cut the man's offending tongue from his head.

"Officer Shay has a very dangerous and stressful job, Your Honor, and no one here is trying to discredit the job that she does," Amaterasu said in a calm, slow voice.

Shay's eyes burned, and she found she couldn't look at the judge, Pulver, or the plaintiff's attorney as he spoke. Twice she was sure she felt Kiyoshi's gaze on her. Both times she ignored those feelings. The hearing seemed to last forever, but when she accessed her com-chip, she found it was only 11:40 A.M.

"But the facts in this case can't be ignored," Amaterasu continued. "Officer Shay is involved in the Bayou Ripper killings, which has already claimed the lives of at least four women. She has been the target of Aaron Scivally—"

"Your Honor," Pulver said. "Whatever menace Aaron Scivally presented has surely ended with his death."

"Perhaps," Amaterasu conceded before Judge Waring could respond, "but what if other members of the Scivally gang decide to wage vengeance for their lost companions?"

"Please, Your Honor," Pulver said, getting up from his chair, "opposing counsel could build a list of what-ifs that could soon include space shuttles falling from the sky. The line needs to be drawn somewhere."

"Agreed," Waring said. He looked at the plaintiff's attorney. "Mr. Amaterasu, you will address yourself to clearly dangerous points and stop borrowing trouble. We all have to deal with contingencies in our lives."

Pulver sat down but didn't look mollified.

Shay felt for the lawyer. It had been an uphill struggle all morning long.

"The bottom line," Amaterasu said, "is that Officer Shay has a very dangerous job. A job that doesn't allow her steady hours or days off, which is why custody was reversed in earlier hearings."

A quiet calm settled over Shay, and she knew she couldn't hang on to the stress any longer. Silently she gave up hope, because it hurt too much and cost too much to hang on. Every word out of Amaterasu's mouth had been damning.

"The very nature of police work is not conducive to a stable home life," Amaterasu said. "I won't trouble the court with facts and figures concerning the divorce and suicide rates for policemen, nor point out they are considerably higher for people who have made detective grade, as Ms. Shay has, because those individuals deal with life and death on a daily basis. Nor will I throw in percentage figures regarding alcoholism and substance abuse by law enforcement personnel. I only ask that the court keep in mind that these things too exist, and they contribute to the fears that Mr. Izutsu has regarding his daughter's visits to Ms. Shay." The attorney sat down.

Pulver stood up and circled around to the front of the table. "Before you make your decision, Your Honor, I want to consider the ramification of that decision. There are hundreds, thousands, of law enforcement people out there who are raising their children in spite of their jobs. Mothers and fathers who put in their shifts fighting to keep whole cities from sinking in the quagmire of crime and sudden death that lies in wait for so many of us. These policemen and policewomen form that thin blue line that struggles selflessly to preserve the rest of us. Those of us who don't want to deal with crime head-to-head. Those of us who are too old, too young, or too weak to fight back against those who would take even our very lives. Your decision here today could affect the police officer's right to have a family. Thank you."

Pulver sat down.

Waring scratched his chin and leaned forward, placing his hands palm to palm before him, managing to look even more like a toad. "Both counsels have made good arguments here today," he said in a slow and ponderous voice.

Pulver knotted his fists and whispered, "Son of a bitch!"

A cube of ice formed at Shay's core and spread out. She wanted desperately to get up and walk out of the courtroom before she heard the words she was so afraid of hearing.

"However, despite Mr. Pulver's impassioned plea that whatever we do here today might set a precedent for other cases, I am dealing only with this one case. With the future of a little girl who never really knew to what extent her life was in danger while she was with her mother a week ago." Waring glanced at Shay. "I'm sorry, Ms. Shay. As a mother

I know this must be very hard for you. But I'm in agreement with Mr. Izutsu's assessment of the current situation, and I'm finding for the plaintiff." He banged the gavel.

"Your Honor," Pulver said quickly.

"Yes, Mr. Pulver?"

"What about supervised visitation, at Mr. Izutsu's convenience?"

"Not for the first sixty days, counselor. I feel that your client needs at least that much time to get her affairs and her priorities in order. Her professional and personal life shouldn't intrude on her daughter's life. At the end of sixty days, make an appointment with me, and I'll reconvene the concerned parties for further discussion on the subject of visitation."

Numbly, Shay stood as the judge left the courtroom.

Pulver tossed his chip-files into his briefcase in open disgust. He turned to her, pain streaking through his eyes. "Beth, I don't know what to say. I'm not giving up, and I'm still working on busting Waring out of this case, but I can't predict how long that's going to take."

Taking a tissue from her purse, Shay dabbed at her eyes and took away the tears. "It's okay, Troy. I appreciate your being here." She hugged him, gave him a quick kiss on the cheek, and walked away by herself.

Kiyoshi was surrounded by the Izutsu employees and his new wife while they celebrated their victory.

Shay met his gaze, but he quickly turned from her. She left and headed for the courtroom where Almendariz was being questioned.

"Is it your opinion then, Dr. Fitzgerald, that Father Almendariz was responsible for the deaths of those four women?"

Almendariz studied the forensics expert on the witness stand. Dr. Zachary Fitzgerald was an imposing figure in his tailored suit as he sat relaxed with one ankle resting on the knee of his other leg. From Almendariz's observation of Grahame, he could tell the lawyer was worried about the medical examiner's testimony.

Fitzgerald smiled brightly. "No, Mr. Grahame, that is not my opinion."

"Then you don't think Father Almendariz committed the murders?"

"It's not my job to guess in these circumstances."

"Or could it be," Grahame rushed on, "that you and your staff simply don't know who the murderer could be?"

"I've verified that all four victims were killed by the same individual with the same weapon. I've verified that the intent as evidenced by the positioning of the wounds—"

Grahame turned to the judge with a look of exasperation. "Your Honor, would you please instruct Dr. Fitzgerald to simply answer the question without all these sidebar details and rhetoric?"

"So ordered. Dr. Fitzgerald, you will answer the defense counsel's questions."

"Yes sir." Fitzgerald didn't appear pleased.

Keeping his head up and his hands resting sedately on the scarred tabletop in front of him, Almendariz watched the people around him as if the events didn't concern him in any way.

"Do you know, Dr. Fitzgerald," Grahame continued, "that Father Almendariz is the man guilty of taking the lives of those women?"

"No."

"Could you speak up, please."

"No."

"You don't know that Father Almendariz is indeed the person referred to in the media as the Bayou Ripper?"

"No."

"Then what are you doing here, up in that witness chair?"

Fitzgerald started to answer.

Grahame held up both hands. "Never mind, Dr. Fitzgerald. I withdraw the question. There's no need to waste any more time here."

The judge nodded. "You may step down, Dr. Fitzgerald."

The medical examiner stepped down, but he didn't look happy about it.

Grahame slid into the chair beside Almendariz and whispered, "I bought us some time, but that's all. I can't dazzle the judge the way I can the media and a jury, and we don't want this to go that far."

Almendariz nodded, because he felt that was what was expected of him. He felt totally lost and helpless, enmeshed in a system he didn't understand.

Judge Drabeck addressed the district attorney's table. "Mr.

Andersson, is there anyone else the prosecution would like to call?"

"No, Your Honor. Detective Bethany Shay is unavailable at this time because she's in Judge Waring's courtroom. We would like to call on her at a later date for testimony."

"Mr. Grahame?"

Grahame stood. "The defense wishes to see all of the prosecution's case, Your Honor. Every hour these proceedings drag on, more irreparable damage is being done to my client's reputation."

Judge Drabeck held up a hand. "Understood, Mr. Grahame, but I'm going to allow the detective's testimony when she is able. I tried to free her up from her other obligations, but her presence there is paramount."

"Surely not more important than a man's life, Your Honor," Grahame said.

A wan smile wrinkled the judge's lips. "No, Mr. Grahame, no, it's not. But it's important just the same. And I don't think her presence here and now would hurry along your game plan at this point."

"Let the record reflect that I'm respectfully not in agreement with this, Your Honor."

"So noted. Have you any witnesses you wish to call for the defense?"

"Yes. The defense calls Father Timothy Brian to the stand."

Voices warbled behind Almendariz, but he refused to turn and look at the crowd. He saw Father Brian out of his peripheral vision as the priest made his way to the witness stand.

As Father Brian was being sworn in, someone pushed through the double doors at the back of the courtroom and yelled, "They've just found another body at Sims Bayou! And this one's still warm!"

There was a confused moment in the courtroom as reporters wavered between loyalties. Then they deserted the courtroom en masse, tripping over each other and shoving their way through regular civilians.

Judge Drabeck banged his gavel loudly. "This court is recessed until tomorrow at ten o'clock."

"Your Honor," Grahame said as he pushed himself to his feet, "in the matter of bail monies. I feel that my client deserves to be released in his own recognizance. His entire life has been spent in and selflessly given to the church. I see no reason for him to have to post anything."

"Your Honor," Andersson protested vigorously. The district attorney was visibly flustered by the turn of events. "We feel that Father Almendariz should not be remanded to his own custody. Despite his long-term relationship with this city—in fact, because of that relationship with this city—we feel he should be kept locked up until such time as the court decides to pursue this case."

"Forget it, Mr. Andersson," Drabeck said. "Due process of law entitles every man to be released on bail if he shows a stable character, as Father Almendariz does. Defense counsel's request is accepted, and in the matter of bail monies, the court sets the amount at ten million dollars American."

A smile settled over Grahame's lips. "The defendant wishes to post bail now, Your Honor." He snapped his fingers.

Almendariz glanced over his shoulder and saw a pair of big men approach the defense council table. Each of them carried two briefcases, but only one briefcase of the four available was given to Grahame.

Setting the case on the table, Grahame opened the locks and revealed stacks of American currency in carefully wrapped bundles.

33

"The Ripper's still loose."

"And a goddam good thing it is. Can you image how much newschip sales would drop if he really turned out to be that priest? We'd have to get out and hustle new copy starting tomorrow."

"Has anyone thought about raiding the priest's quarters at the rectory? I mean, just to cover all the bases."

Still dressed in the skirt and blouse she'd worn to her own hearing, Bethany Shay shoved her way through the reporters already clustered around the yellow tape put up by the police department. Her long coat slapped against her calves with enough force to sting, and the sharp-edged wind made her eyes water. She'd left her pumps in her car and walked in panty-hose-covered feet.

Captain Espinoza was among the fringe group hugging the shore as an emergency rescue team worked with the dead body in water that came up to mid-thigh.

Shay went on, ignoring the cold mud that squelched up between her toes through the holes in the panty hose.

Espinoza turned toward her. "Beth, what are you doing here?"

"I heard about it at the courthouse when the media people made a break for their cars." Shay brushed a lock of hair out of her eyes and watched as two men flipped the body over onto a canvas stretcher. The blood-stained arm flailed limply. The click and whir of cameras and camcorders sounded like the exotic calls of electronic birds behind her.

"How did your hearing go?" Espinoza asked.

"I won't get to see Keiko for the next sixty days." Shay's voice sounded flat even to her, and she knew it would be obvious to anyone who knew her that she was on the edge of losing it.

"I'm sorry."

She nodded and turned the topic away from her family life, because the last thing she wanted right now was people who thought they could understand how she felt. "Who's the woman?"

"Jessica Daniels. According to the personal effects we found on her, she's a dancer at the Glory Hole tavern over on Rook Street at the intersection of Waltrip. A couple of uniforms found her car about ten minutes ago."

"Her car? That's not the Ripper's MO," Shay said. The seed of doubt she'd been nursing on the drive over took root and became conviction. "This isn't the genuine article."

"Maybe it was too soon to think we had the guy's MO," Espinoza said. "And these people change. You can look at recorded histories of serial killers. Sometimes they change for no reason at all."

"It's a setup," Shay insisted. "Somebody's trying to cut Almendariz free."

"The media are going to be speculating about this woman's death enough as it is. I don't want anything that will add to it coming from the mouth of one of my people. Do you understand?"

She made herself nod, her cheeks flaming with anger that didn't come just from Espinoza's words.

When the emergency rescue workers had the body on the stretcher, they covered the woman with a latex blanket that permitted only vague outlines of her to be seen. Four men positioned themselves around the stretcher, settled into their grips, and waded laboriously toward shore.

Hurried footsteps drummed behind Shay and drew her attention.

District Attorney Dwain Andersson jogged to a stop between her and Espinoza and blew into his cupped hands to warm them. He looked like a man witnessing a recurrent bad dream unfolding before his very eyes. "Is it the Ripper?"

Shay took her cue from Espinoza and remained quiet.

"We don't know," the homicide captain said.

"Shit, you don't know," Andersson said in an explosive whisper. "You've got to know, dammit. Grahame is going to fry my ass if the possibility exists that the Ripper is still loose and I'm trying to prosecute the wrong man. The guy's a priest, for God's sake."

The emergency rescue team approached when Espinoza

waved them over. Taking a corner of the latex blanket, Espinoza lifted it up and studied the body.

Shay stepped against Espinoza's side and looked too. Jessica Daniels had been a beautiful woman, with long blond hair now matted with mud and debris, and the long-legged build of a dancer. Her abdomen and pubic area were slashed open as those of the other four women had been. Intestines slithered like jellied snakes across the pale skin that was starting to turn blue. One green eye was open and the other was closed.

Andersson gagged and put a hand to his mouth.

Espinoza released the blanket and waved the emergency rescue team on to the waiting ambulance. "You lose it out here, Counselor, and you're going to be losing it again on the five-, six-, and ten-o'clock news. And maybe catch the morning show tomorrow."

Andersson swallowed and looked even less healthy than before. "I got a phone call from the archdiocese yesterday. The archbishop stopped short of threatening me and the mayor's office with losing the Catholic vote in Houston and the outlying suburbs if I muddied Father Almendariz's name without being able to prove my case. But not much. You and your partner didn't get me much in the way of evidence to begin with, Shay, and if it turns out this murder looks like it was committed by the Ripper while our main suspect was in the slammer, I won't have a pot to piss in as far as trial goes."

"Tully Keever died to get you what we could," Shay said in a hard voice, "and don't you *ever* forget that."

Andersson looked away.

"If you back off this case now, you'll be saying that Tully's death doesn't mean a goddam thing," Shay said. "You just stick to your guns. I'll get you the evidence you need to make the charges stick."

"No you won't," Espinoza said softly.

Shay looked at him.

"You're off the case, Beth," the homicide captain said. "As of now. I'm giving it to Barker and Chaney."

"No," Shay replied. "I'm not. You're not going to pull me off of it. I've got too much time invested."

"Let it go," Espinoza said. "Christ, Beth, your personal life's a mess, and we both know it. There's the thing with the Scivally brothers, and you just lost your partner. And the case you've been building looks like it's just blown up in your face. You need some time off, and I'm giving it to you."

"Captain—"

Espinoza held up a hand to forestall any argument. "Two weeks, or three. Or more. Take whatever time you need and get yourself together, Beth. You can take that as a suggestions, or I can make it an order. However you want it. But if you buck me on this, I'll slap you on a desk job and keep you there for months."

Shay returned Espinoza's gaze full measure, but saw no weakness in the man and knew that his decision was final. She turned her voice hard and sarcastic. "Thanks for the vote of confidence, Captain." She turned and left before he could reply and pushed her way through the aggressive media people.

Shay called for the bedroom light to finish her work as afternoon gave way to evening. After clearing away the legal books that littered her bedroom floor against one wall, she covered the wall with dozens of pictures of the murder sites and victims, securing them with thick strips of masking tape.

The head-and-shoulders pictures of the first four dead women made a clock face around a publicity still of Father Judd Almendariz. The fifth woman was shunted off to the side, lost and on her own.

The house AI kept reminding her of incoming messages from her father, sister, and acquaintances, but she ignored them all. She needed the time alone.

The five-o'clock news had carried the story of the fifth woman's death by the same weapon that had killed the first four. There had even been a brief interview with Fitzgerald. The charges against Father Almendariz had been dropped only minutes after the announcement, and the district attorney's office had already aired a public apology for any inconvenience suffered by Almendariz, the Catholic Church, and its parishioners.

Stepping back from the wall, Shay surveyed her work, felt satisfied, but knew it was far from over.

Returning to the wall, she stared into Almendariz's eyes. "It's you, you son of a bitch. Tully knew it, and I know it. We had you. And don't think you're going to slip away."

* * *

Tully Keever was buried in the rain the next morning.

Dressed in police blues and white gloves, Bethany Shay watched the proceedings from the first row of uniformed policemen who'd turned out for the graveside services. Raindrops spilled from the brim of her hat and pecked little hollow noises on top of her head.

The pastor's voice rolled out over the crowd of people, his words captured forever by the media people in attendance. Though they would have them in computer files, Shay knew the media would forget as soon as that night's news aired. She also knew that she wouldn't.

Rifles cracked in the still air as marksmen fired a salute. Though divorced from Keever for almost nine years, Keever's widow was given the flag from the coffin.

Shay waited her turn, hypnotized by the regularity of the people passing by the coffin to offer their last respects. She spent a moment with the family, mumbled some things she felt weren't worth saying but found herself unable to pass on without saying, and laid the single long-stemmed white rose on the casket.

She said her good-bye quietly, and didn't cry because she had a job to do. And it was a job she knew Tully would want her to finish.

Almendariz sat on the edge of his immaculately made bed in his room at the rectory and stared into the gleam of his polished black shoes. His pocket felt empty where the shoehorn had been, and it was as if a piece of himself were missing. He had had it so long.

"Father, are you all right?"

Startled, Almendariz looked up and found Father Brian standing in the doorway. "What?"

"I asked if you were all right. You don't look well."

"Yes. Really. I'm fine."

"You've been through a lot these past five days," Father Brian said. "Are you sure you feel up to stepping back into your duties at the church now?"

It was Wednesday. The previous two days had passed by in a blur for Almendariz, broken only by the news coverage of the police detective's burial on Tuesday.

Almendariz gave him a small smile, stood, and pocketed the Bible deck. "If—after suffering through all of this, Father Brian—I find that I am unable to continue the Lord's Work in this place, then truly I have lost myself."

Father Brian dropped a heavy hand on Almendariz's shoulder. "That's true, but the Lord also knows we're still fashioned of mortal clay. He would forgive you a few more days' rest."

"There's a passage in the New Testament," Almendariz said. "Second Thessalonians, Chapter Three, Verse Ten: 'For even when we were with you, this we commanded you, that if any would not work, neither should he eat.' I have Work to do, and I can't forsake it."

"Amen," Father Brian said.

Almendariz led the way out of the room. Father Brian followed a half-step behind him.

"You've not talked to anyone at the church of your experiences," Father Brian said.

"I would rather forget them," Almendariz replied as they crossed the living room and moved out into the hallway. "And I have talked to God about them."

"If there ever comes a time you'd like to share your burden with someone, please think of me."

"I will."

"And if working the confessionals becomes too trying for you today, don't hesitate to let me know and I'll have Harper spell you."

"Thank you." Almendariz left the pastor standing at the back entrance to the church and made his way to the confessional booths off to the side of the pews. He stepped inside and took a seat.

The other door to the confessional hissed open and made him gather his thoughts and concentrate on his duties inside the booth.

"You may begin."

Bethany Shay glanced at the dark curtain over the plate-glass window in the confessional booth. She wore a plain black dress that had made her blend with the other parishioners. The voice seemed sedate, secure, held more power now than it ever had on the witness stand. Despite the anger and pain and frustration bottled up in her, she made her words soft. "Forgive me, Father, for I have sinned."

"And what is the nature of your sins, my child?"

The resonance in the voice was perfect, the kind of voice

Shay knew she would have trusted even as a teenager who'd thought everything was a sin in her world. "I have an anger in my soul against a man."

"And you cannot get past this anger?"

"No."

"Can you tell me about it?"

"I can tell you about the man."

"I'm listening."

Shay took a deep breath and steadied her voice. "He's an evil man, and a darkness hovers within him that I don't understand."

"This man has transgressed against you?"

"No. Against others. He has killed four women, and now the court systems have mistakenly set him free so he can kill again."

Only silence came from the other side of the ebony curtain.

"Father?"

"Who are you?" The voice was harsh, demanding, almost insane as it echoed within the confessional.

Shay ignored the question. "There's a passage in the Bible I've memorized, Father Almendariz, and I say it every night now. It's from the Book of Jeremiah, Chapter Eleven, Verse Twenty. 'But, O Lord of hosts, that judgest righteously, that triest the reins and the heart, let me see thy vengeance on them: for unto thee have I revealed my cause.' How long do you think it will be before I have an answer?"

A choked gasp came from the other side of the booth.

When Shay reached up and shoved the curtain back, Almendariz was gone. She relaxed her hold on the Glock 20 inside her purse, shouldered her bag, and walked out of the church.

She pulled her coat tightly about her when she went outside, and smiled when she got into her car, because she figured Tully Keever would have approved of her bearding Almendariz in his den even if Espinoza wouldn't.

34

"You're leaving?"

Almendariz whirled to find Father Brian standing in his bedroom doorway. His heart thumped inside his chest hard enough to make his head hurt even worse than it had been. "Yes," he replied in a dry croak.

"I saw the policewoman leaving the church," Father Brian said. "Did she say or do anything to you?"

"No." He swept an armful of clothes from his closet and tucked them into the plastic bag he'd gotten from Sophie in the kitchen.

"Where will you go?"

Almendariz thought of the lawyer's card in his pants pocket. "There is a place."

"And what will be there for you?"

"Safety."

"You don't feel safe here, at the church?"

"No, Father Brian, I don't." Almendariz gripped the plastic bag and thought of the way the succubus had quoted scripture at him.

Father Brian placed a hand on his shoulder. "Don't leave. Stay here and let's fight this thing together."

Almendariz shook his head. "I can't."

"If you hide the truth in your heart," the pastor said, "it will turn to worms in your silence, and eat you from the inside out."

Trembling with fear and rage, Almendariz passed through the door, moving with quick steps. In the hallway leading out of the building, he broke into a run that left him hurting and panting for his breath by the time he reached the mass trans pickup point.

In his private matrix, Felix Carey leaned on the wallscreen and opened up a recent memory. He fell through cyberspace and landed on his feet in the crowded confines of the Glory Hole tavern in Reazer's body.

He saw the beautiful dancer again as if he were seeing her for the first time. She was lissome, blond, and wore her sexuality like a badge. She danced with a boa constrictor wrapped around her body, the reptile's mind and reflexes wedded to hers by the puppet chips implanted in both of their brains. A sheen of perspiration covered her, accentuated by the body oil on her skin.

The music was loud, raucous, made even more so by the shouts of the bar's clientele as they joined the recordings on the refrains. A blue haze from cigarette, red satin, and marijuana smoke clouded the interior of the club.

In control of Reazer's body, Carey moved through the crowd until he was at the side of the stage looking up at the woman. He felt the hunger on him then, and for the first time in years he allowed it to consume him.

Moving seductively, the woman controlled the snake wrapped around her body, had it move to reveal large brown nipples, first one, then the other. The tail uncoiled from between her legs, oozed through her thighs, and flashed the burnished copper pubic hair clipped so short it was only a triangle of fuzz. But just for a moment, then the snake's tail curled back into place, the tip against the bottom of her spine to separate her ass into generous twin hemispheres. . . .

Carey let the hunger move him and reacted to it as if it were Sunday night all over again. He accessed the main gridline for the matrix and fast-forwarded to the later events.

The woman hadn't been able to outrun Reazer's body when she thought she'd escaped from the car only a few hours later. She'd run, and he'd followed, trusting Reazer's motor skills but maintaining control of the sensations.

Moments later he'd brought her down only a few yards short of Sims Bayou, like a wolf dragging down a doe. The memory clicked into his senses of the present, and he felt her struggling against him.

She fought him, clawing at Reazer's body, but the assassin's trained reflexes fended off every assault. He threw himself on top of her and felt the erection press into her soft, warm flesh even through Reazer's pants. He trembled with excitement, the razor-sharp shoehorn clenched in his fist. He felt on the edge of completion, but knew Reazer's reservations were already pulling him back. If he tried to rape the woman as he wanted to, Reazer's personality would have rebelled and made violent sex a physical impossibility.

Instead, consoling himself with the thought of what would be his once he had the priest in his grasp, he grabbed her hair and exposed her throat.

She looked up at him, lost in fear, both of her hands locked around his restraining arm. Her mouth opened as she got ready to scream. Her vocal cords tightened, and she said, "Father Almendariz is here, Mr. Carey," in Welbourne's cultured voice.

Carey froze the memory, crawled up from the woman's stiff body as it turned two-dimensional, and blanked it all out of existence when he stepped back into the matrix office. "Thank you, Welbourne. Show him in."

Almendariz stared down into the caverns of the city and felt he was on top of the world. His fingers pressed against the thick bulletproof glass of the picture window and could barely sense the chill trapped outside. A cloud cover obscured the tops of the Himeji Twins on the other end of the downtown area, but he knew the penthouse apartment was only slightly dwarfed by the Japanese buildings.

"Father Almendariz."

Almendariz turned to look at the speaker. "Yes."

"Mr. Carey is ready to see you now." The man was young, of Hispanic origins, dressed in a tailored dark suit. He moved effortlessly as he picked up the plastic bag containing Almendariz's clothing. "If you'll follow me, I will take you to him."

"May I ask your name?" Almendariz asked as he followed the young man through the back doorway into a blank, featureless corridor lined with electronic sensors.

"My name is Víctor García," the young man replied. "But Mr. Carey calls me Welbourne, after an associate whom he once had but who—unfortunately—is no longer with us. Welbourne was a friend of Mr. Carey's, someone who helped him become everything he is today."

Evidently García sensed some of the discomfort that touched Almendariz.

"Mr. Carey knows the difference," García said. "It's just that he's accustomed to calling on Welbourne for things, and pays me well enough to respond to that name. I assure you, there are much worse idiosyncrasies out there." He stopped at the end of a corridor, allowed himself to be printed and retina-scanned. The bulkhead became a door that irised open and let them step through.

Almendariz glanced around the room. Totally white walls, echoed by a white stone floor, formed a cube that instinct told him was located somewhere near the heart of the building.

"I see you are altered for direct computer integration," García said as he came to a stop at one of the walls.

The door irised closed again without a sound and left the cube intact.

"Most priests are these days. It allows for a better understanding of the Bible."

"I understand." García pressed his palm against a section of the wall, and a panel dropped away. "You have heard the rumors that not much of Mr. Carey's corporal body remains?"

"Yes." Actually, there were stories that only Carey's brain, heart, and lungs existed in a chem-vat somewhere in the heart of the building. But there were other stories about people who'd actually met the man in the flesh, and rumors that the private matrix Carey maintained to discuss business in with potential partners was only another layer of security.

Small gears meshed and created a shrill whine that was almost inaudible.

"I'm not here to verify nor condemn those rumors," García said as a bank of equipment trundled into the room from a recessed cavity within the wall. "But you will be meeting Mr. Carey in his matrix. Will that be a problem?"

"No."

García pulled out a chair arm from under the bulk of machinery, sat down, and slid a deck keyboard from hiding. He tapped the keys and smiled at his reflection in the glowing screen. "I have to do things the old-fashioned way myself. I've never gone in for the chip augmentation. I still marvel over how surgeons were able to fix my body." He tapped his legs with a knuckled fist. The sound of flesh striking flesh didn't ring quite true, sounded higher-pitched. "Bionics. I was in a car wreck that crushed both of my legs. Mr. Carey paid for all the operations." He tapped a series of keys and another wall opened up. A long, thin bed rolled out on a track that surfaced beneath the floor. García waved to the bed. "Please make yourself comfortable."

Climbing onto the bed, Almendariz lay on his back and stared at the featureless ceiling, realizing only then that the room was illuminated from the outside with a glow that permeated the interior.

García approached him with the trode.

Almendariz accepted it and pushed it into his temple jack.

"Pleasant dreams," García said.

And cyberspace leaped at Almendariz like a thing of wild black, smothered him, and took him down deeper, he was sure, than he'd ever been.

When he opened his eyes, Almendariz was standing in the heart of stone ruins he thought he almost recognized. Night had drawn curtains of shadows over them, blunted the sharp edges, and the sky above was filled with diamond-bright stars. A cool breeze wrapped itself around him, made him realize he was in a robe of animal skins. The musk was thick and heady, but not unpleasant.

"Do you know where you are?" a deep voice asked.

Almendariz looked around at the square buildings built from hand-mortised stone. Smaller squares were constructed on top of others, also of stone. The desert swept away on all sides of the area, littered with scrub bushes, rose in the distance to gentle sloping hills covered with more modern dwelling places.

"Hebron," Almendariz answered. He approached the nearest building, ran his fingers over the stones of the wall, and felt how they had been worn smooth over the passage of thousands of years. "The place of Abraham and Isaac."

"It's only fitting that we should meet here."

"Who are you?" Almendariz glanced around, peering into the darkened shadows inside the stone houses.

"Felix Carey. The man you came to see." A light gray gaseous cloud swirled against the sable night, spiraled down tightly as if trapped by an invisible waterspout six feet off the ground, and became the form of a man effortlessly landing on his feet. His arms were outspread as he landed and became solid. A golden haze might have mimicked wings just above and behind his arms, but never became a definite shape.

Moved by a force he didn't understand, Almendariz wanted to drop to his knees in supplication. His legs trembled with the effort of remaining upright.

Carey was a handsome man, very regal in appearance. He wore a robe similar to the one Almendariz had on. "Have you ever seen Hebron before?"

"Only in the Bible deck," Almendariz said. "It was never in ruins as I see it now."

"This is Hebron as it stands today," Carey said, waving toward the collection of sand-colored buildings. "I wanted you to see it, to know how the roots of your belief have fared." He smiled. "It's amazing to see that things can last so long in this age of disposable products and recyclable materials."

"It is God's Will," Almendariz said.

"Yes." Carey switched subjects as he turned to face him. "Do you know why you are here?"

"To know myself for what I truly am. To know what designs God has written for me, and what I must do to fulfill them."

"First," Carey said, "you must know that you are more than a mere man." He took Almendariz by the elbow and guided him to a well in a crumbling courtyard. Removing the cover, he lowered the bucket into the depths. "And even with that knowledge, the way will not be easy."

Almendariz nodded. That was something he'd already experienced.

The thick rope creaked as it came back up bearing the weight of a full bucket. Carey cranked the handle with both hands. "The succubi are still out there, you know."

"I know."

"We cannot allow them to come after you anymore. Only by tracking them down and destroying them may we get on with your life's Work."

Shaking his head, Almendariz said, "I'm not so sure that is the way. What if we are wrong?"

Carey stopped taking up the rope. "Have you deserted your faith, Father Almendariz?"

"No."

"Then you will be given the strength to do what you must. And I will be there to guide you and help you. I've waited a long, long time for you."

Staring into Carey's eyes, Almendariz sensed that his words were very true.

"I will not let you fail." Reaching out, Carey clasped Almendariz's shoulder in a gesture that was comfortably familiar. He cranked the bucket the rest of the way up, grabbed it in both hands, and tilted it so Almendariz could peer inside.

At first Almendariz thought it was only the moon behind him that created the golden nimbus around his head in the reflection floating on the dark water. Then he saw that it had nothing to do with the moon at all, that the light streamed from within him. When he looked down, he saw that his whole body was glowing.

"Know yourself for the first time, Father Almendariz," Carey said. "And know too that you were not wrong about your purpose in the mortal realm."

Almendariz glanced at the other man and saw that the golden glow emanated from him as well. Overcome with the sudden release of all the doubt that had filled his mind and heart for years, sure he was feeling the first true epiphany of his life, he dropped to his knees by the well of Hebron and started praying.

"Must be quite an experience for him," Felix Carey said as he watched the wallscreen from his personal matrix.

Onscreen Almendariz remained kneeling in prayer beside the well, and a cybernetic clone of Carey knelt beside him.

"I think the subliminals were definitely the right choice," Welbourne replied. "His physical self is resting comfortably now. His heart rate, blood pressure, and respiration are all within the norms. He isn't agitated the way he was when he first showed up at the building."

"How soon will the technicians be able to implant the zombyte chip?"

"Another hour. Perhaps two. No more than that."

"Let me know when it is finished."

"Of course."

"And until then, keep Almendariz recycling through this scene without his knowledge. I want him to believe in me when we go out the first time together to hunt one of these succubi."

"Yes sir."

Carey watched as the wallscreen blurred, went black, then opened back up with Almendariz reappearing at Hebron. "And contact someone to take care of this woman police officer who threatened Almendariz today."

"Yes sir."

Accessing the matrix, Carey closed off communications, blanked the wallscreen, and shifted views. He opened it back up on Perth, Australia, and went in search of a memory that would help him while away the time. He tried to put it into perspective. After waiting decades, two hours should seem like nothing. But here—in the matrix, with the way real time outside often seemed to stand still—two hours was insufferable.

As an added attraction, he also brought in the memory of Almendariz's shoehorn, which had become another thing that didn't exist anymore after Sunday night. He dropped onto the beach barefoot, changed the sand to a temperature he could tolerate, and with the razor-edged shoehorn in a neon orange fanny pack, went hunting through the bikini-clad bodies all around him.

35

"Don't you think you have enough problems now—without compounding them with this?"

Bethany Shay glanced away from the foggy window and the night-darkened streets and looked at her father.

Wearing a plaid dress shirt without the tie, black slacks, and cowboy boots, Ryan Shay fit comfortably into the regular crowd at the Brass Rainbow. It was an Irish pub on South Shepard Drive near where her father had started his first beat. Over the years she had been there for celebrations, business, solitude, and the numerous chewing-outs her father had felt she needed, and—most of the time, she had to admit—she deserved.

They sat at a booth near the back, away from the large knot of men facing the dart board hanging from one of the wooden support posts jutting out from a wall beside the long bar. Sandy O'Darlington, red hair going gray, freckles on his arms and face livid against his pale skin, dropping ash from the ever-present cigar hanging from his mouth, continued to wipe beer mugs with a stained bar towel and berate the players. Several of the bar's patrons joined in the haranguing and hurrahs at conflicting times. The smell of beer and cigarettes hung thick in the still air. Someone cracked a fresh rack of pool balls in one of the back rooms.

"They're after the wrong guy, Dad," Shay said. She glanced away for a moment, then slathered mustard generously on her smoked turkey and rye sandwich. The beer mug holding her Diet Pepsi—kept on hand by Sandy for her infrequent visits—was covered in a cold sweat.

"So what?" Ryan Shay said. "That's their lookout now. Espinoza took you off the case."

Shay toyed with the kosher pickle on the brown plate and choked back her angry retort. "I can't let it go."

"You have to. They're not giving you a choice, and neither is Izutsu." Ryan Shay sipped coffee from the mug Shay had given him on his birthday when she was fourteen. The caption read: WE DON'T NEED NO STINKIN' BODGES.

"Troy's working on that. All I can do is hang on for a while and see what happens."

"Bullshit. You're channeling all the animosity you feel toward your ex-husband into this case with Almendariz."

"Dad, I didn't agree to have dinner with you to listen to this." She crunched off the end of the pickle and winced as the sour taste hit her.

"What if you're wrong? What if Almendariz isn't the Ripper?"

"I can live with that. The thing I can't live with is thinking I'm right and not doing anything about it."

"It's not your responsibility."

"Then whose responsibility is it?"

Ryan Shay sighed in exasperation. "Goddam, but you're hardheaded."

"It's a genetic deficiency."

"Tully wouldn't have wanted you to do this," Ryan Shay said after a few minutes. "You're taking a chance on getting hurt, by whoever the Ripper is, and by the department if Espinoza decides to come down on you for interference."

"It's not just for Tully," Shay said around another bite of her sandwich. She chewed and swallowed, and turned loose some of the frustration filling her. "It's for me too. Dammit, Dad, I have to know I'm right about something. Kiyoshi has managed to take Keiko away from me by getting people to believe I'm a bad mother, Espinoza's blackballed me from the investigation, my work on the case has apparently turned to shit, and I wasn't there when my partner needed me. Bottom line, I need to know I can still cut it at something."

Ryan Shay's voice softened. "Kitten, Ripper or no Ripper, shield or no shield, being a cop is just a job."

"I don't remember you marching gladly for the door when the time came to retire," Shay said. "You put in thirty hard years, and you're still dabbling in the same grimy pool with the detective agency you're running."

"The thing that should be most important to you now is Keiko."

"Nothing I can do there."

"You don't know that. When was the last time you talked to your ex-husband?"

"He doesn't understand me, Dad. And if he does, he doesn't like what he sees there. I wasn't controllable the way a good wife should be, and I'm not controllable now as an ex-wife." A ball of the old pain formed under Shay's ribs. She put the last half of the sandwich down and shoved the plate away. "You and Mother were very happy. You don't know what this is like, then or now."

Something clicked dead in her father's eyes. He glanced out the window for a moment, excused himself briefly, and moved to the bar long enough to bum a cigarette off O'Darlington.

Shay remained quiet when he returned to the table and lit up with his borrowed lighter. She hadn't seen him smoke in ten years at least.

"I'm going to tell you something," he said in a quiet, deadly voice. "Once I'm through, I don't ever want the subject brought up again. Ever. You've got to promise me that. While I talk, you can ask questions and I'll answer them. But once it's over, it's over."

"Okay." Her father's behavior made Shay feel as if she were standing at the edge of a bottomless pit.

Ryan Shay hit the cigarette, let out his breath in a slow stream that eddied around his clasped hands when he rested his elbows on the table. "A few years ago, fourteen, fifteen, I forget, I had an affair."

His words blew her over the precipice into free-fall. "You son of a bitch," Shay said in a low voice.

"Yeah, that's pretty much what Tully said when I told him."

Shay leaned back in the booth, suddenly cold and trembling. She wrapped her arms around herself and tried not to be sick as nausea swirled around the turkey sandwich. "Did Mom know?"

"Not at first. I managed to keep it covered for the first few months." He took another hit off the cigarette. "You're a cop, Beth, you know how you learn not to talk about things to the family, and you know how they learn not to ask. My God, you see a whole world out there every day that's falling apart and devouring its own young and old alike. How can anyone drag that into his home?"

"Who was it?"

He shook his head. "That doesn't matter, and you know it.

Old hurts are like old dogs. They're better if you let them lie."

"Why?"

"Why did I have an affair?" He crushed out his cigarette. "I asked myself that question a lot too. Before, during, and after. Mainly it was because I felt alone, like everything I had to do depended solely on my ability to get it done. Your mother worked, you know that. Hell, she practically raised you kids in her office at home while she worked for that insurance agency. It wasn't the pressure of the family bills, though I felt those on occasion too when I had to moonlight to see us through. But I was just so alone."

"Mom always made time for you. I remember how she'd fall asleep on the couch waiting for you to come home, with dinner keeping in the oven." Unexpectedly, Shay felt tears in her eyes.

"I know that." Her father's voice sounded husky. "But at the time it didn't seem like enough. God, Beth, you've seen what it's like. You roll up on a teenage suicide victim, or a domestic dispute where a husband's crying over the wife he just shot and killed and still doesn't know why, or you have to drag a scared and screaming little kid away from the father who's been sexually abusing him since he was four. There's nothing out there that prepares you for those kinds of experiences day after day. I couldn't tell your mother about them. In the early years I tried to, but she would tell me to quit the force."

Shay listened to her father's painful words and remembered so much that had gone on in her own career and marriage.

"And I couldn't quit being a cop." Tears sparkled in Ryan Shay's eyes again but remained unshed. "It wasn't the shield, or the gun, or the car. It was the damn job that wouldn't let me go. Your mother never understood that."

"The woman you had the affair with was a cop, wasn't she?"

He hesitated for only a moment. "Yeah."

"Was it any better?"

"Honestly, at first it was just being able to talk to her. I never planned on the sex, never even thought about the physical relationship. But you can't get that close to someone of the opposite sex before sex becomes an issue. And

the more I talked to this woman, the less I tried to talk to
your mother. Pretty soon there was no sex at home."

"And it made the other woman even more important."

"Yeah." He cleared his throat.

"Mom found out?"

He nodded. "I couldn't tell her. Some nights I'd lie awake
in our bed and I'd want to tell her so bad I wouldn't get any
sleep at all. Even after she knew but couldn't prove it, I tried
to lie to her. I told myself I was trying to protect her, but it
was me I was trying to protect."

Shay leaned forward and placed a hand on her father's
hand, feeling it shake slightly as he fought for control.

"Your mother was strong, stronger than I've ever been,"
Ryan Shay said. "If the roles had been reversed, I don't
think I could have done what she did. But she looked at it
with the family in mind, for you and your brother and your
sister, and not for herself or her hurt feelings. And she
looked at the situation with me in mind too. She asked me
if I wanted to give up our lives together. I said no. Then she
stood by me while I got my life back on track, figured out
what I really wanted and how to get it. She forced me to talk
about the work, and she acknowledged my need to do the
job I was doing. It wasn't easy, for either of us. And a third
party got hurt in the process."

"I don't know what to say," Shay said.

"There's nothing to say now. Your mother and I said it all
then. It hurt. It wasn't easy. And there are scars, Beth. There
always will be." He paused to clear his throat. "The thing of
it was, your mother sorted it out and found the strength inside herself to put things right for all of us. I couldn't have
done that in a million years. I was too busy being angry and
hurt and prideful to realize anyone else was going to suffer.
And that's the same way you're being now."

"Are you suggesting I go back to Kiyoshi?" Shay pulled
her hand away.

"No. I don't think your marriage would have worked, Kitten." He shook his head. "I don't mean to sound so negative,
but you were wrong for each other. That's part of what held
you together for the time you were married. It was a fight
for both of you. It seemed like a fight against the world, I'm
sure. Kiyoshi had to prove to his father that he was man
enough to stand on his own two feet and defy his father's
authority and wishes. You had your reasons too."

Shay felt a tear trickle down her cheek, and she wiped it away. "We really did love each other."

"I don't doubt it." Ryan Shay gave her a small smile. "You love your sister too, but somehow I can't imagine the two of you living together."

"Neither can I. At least, not without a UN peacekeeping force camped on our doorstep."

"All I'm suggesting is that maybe it's time to try to really talk to Kiyoshi about Keiko. He's got to be hurting too."

"Right now Kiyoshi's holding all the cards."

"You think so?" Ryan Shay challenged her with his eyes. "Right now that man is sitting in his mansion knowing he's keeping his daughter's mother away from her, and knowing that at some point that daughter is going to hate him for it."

Shay wiped her eyes and looked away from her father.

"I just wanted you to think about your priorities," Ryan Shay said. "At this point you have some options. Your life can run a little smoother without the job pressures. Espinoza gave you time off, and you've got back pay coming. Take the time and get right with yourself. Then—if they're still tinkering around with this Ripper thing when you get back— jump in there and give 'em hell."

"Maybe you're right."

"I know I'm right. I'm not always, but I am now." He gave her a lopsided grin, the kind he used to give her when she struck out at softball and tried to mope all the way home.

Shay leaned across the table, grabbed her father's rough-hewn face between her hands, and kissed him on the cheek. Immediately a chorus of catcalls rattled the interior of the Brass Rainbow, followed by shouts of good-natured encouragement and harassment.

Grinning, Shay wiped the unshed tears from her eyes as her father's face turned beet-red, then laughed out loud when he tried to ignore the banter.

Shay returned home just before ten, put the Fiero in the garage, and walked into the kitchen. The house AI registered everything as normal.

Just as she reached for the light switch, someone grabbed her by the arm and clapped a big hand over her mouth. She tried to cross-draw the Glock from her hip.

Her fingertips brushed the slide, then she was whirled

back against the refrigerator with enough force to drive the air from her lungs. A large hand wrapped around her neck and pinned her to the cold metal surface while another hand stripped the pistol from her holster.

Another pair of hands, much smaller than the first attacker's, trailed quickly through Shay's clothing.

"She's clean," a woman's voice said.

Shay tried to kick the man holding her in the groin.

An open-handed slap bounced her head from the refrigerator. "Don't try that again, bitch, or I'll cut your head off."

Tasting blood inside her mouth from her split lip, Shay forced the tension from her body and bided her time, waiting for an opening.

"We're not supposed to hurt her," the woman said.

"I'm not gonna hurt her none. Just gonna have us a little party, that's all." He paused. "Why don't you go check her room, make sure she don't have nothing up there in her deck that we should take with us?"

The smaller shadow drifted away without the sound of a single footfall.

The man's hand fumbled with Shay's pants. His fingers slid inside, then he yanked with enough force to rip out the button and the zipper. "Supposed to give you a warning," he said in a hoarse whisper. "Tell you to mind your own business and stay away from things that don't concern you. Tell you to stay away from the priest."

Her panties were torn away in one short rip. The man tossed them casually into the sink behind him, then reached for his belt buckle. He dropped his pants, held himself in his hand and stroked his erection proudly. "Like what you see, little lady? Meet Ole Stanley."

In the weak moonlight with her night vision uncertain, she saw the tattoo of a black bird over his right pelvic girdle.

The man bent his knees, slipped them between hers to spread her legs as he held her against the refrigerator, and got ready to thrust.

A metallic click froze the man in place.

The silhouette painted in shadows against the moonlight window showed an automatic pistol resting casually against the man's temple.

"Get your pants back up, Romeo," the woman's voice said softly, "or I'm going to paint that wall with your brains."

The man backed slowly away from Shay, fumbled his pants back up around his hips.

Before Shay could move, the woman swung the pistol in her direction and held it inches from her nose. "You got your warning. If you try to find the priest I'll let him have his fun with you, then I'll put a bullet between your eyes to cap off the evening. You got that?"

"Yes."

Without another word the man and woman faded from the kitchen, going out through the door leading to the garage.

As soon as the door clicked shut, Shay forced herself into motion. She breathed in deep, racking gasps as she pulled her coat back on, then ran for the closet, dug out the short-barreled 9mm she sometimes used as a backup, and ran for the front door.

She palmed the entrance open, then went through the doorway with both hands wrapped around the 9mm leveled before her. Tensed, expecting gunfire with every step, she closed on the garage. There wasn't any gunfire. Nor did she find any trace of the man and woman.

She stood there in the night, breathing the cool, crisp air, and waited long minutes till she wasn't afraid of shadows anymore.

36

Moving through the crowd in the priest's body, in control through the zombyte chip hardwired into the priest's brain, Felix Carey locked into the sexual electricity running through the nightclub and moved as surely as a great white shark.

<Are you sure one of them is here?> Almendariz asked from the back of his own mind.

"Yes," Carey replied. He was growing impatient with the priest's doubts and wished there were some way of tuning the man out of his consciousness. He moved across the dance floor, allowing his hands to come in contact with supple bare flesh when the occasion presented itself, passed it off as the result of close quarters and ignored the occasional look of disgust that trailed after him. Most of the women didn't seem to mind. Even the priest didn't suspect him, and he was using Almendariz's hands. "I'm your guide for a time. Let me do the job He has instructed me to do."

Carey took a seat at the bar between an empty stool and a woman with neon-colored blue eyes beneath stainless-steel eyebrows. It was several minutes before one of the three bartenders was able to take his order.

He gazed in the big mirror behind the bar and saw Almendariz sitting there staring back at him. But the smile that twisted the handsome lips was Carey's own, and he recognized it.

<Why are you drinking alcohol?> Almendariz asked.

"To blend in," Carey said. "Every good hunter has to know how to camouflage himself within his quarry's territory."

In the back of the shared brain, Almendariz felt like an uncomfortable wart.

Carey ignored the priest's feelings and sipped from the

glass. The scotch burned his throat in a way it never had in his private matrix.

Ever since his mind had been banished to the matrix after his physical body had failed, he'd believed if he could find someone similar to himself he might be able to experience life again as he wanted to through the zombyte chip.

He had discussed the minds of serial killers with behavioral science experts and with other people he'd hired over the years to act as a buffer for him to keep his identity and his interest secret. Most of the theories advanced had ascribed the murderous fantasies of serial killers to peculiarities within the temporal lobe, limbic region, or hypothalamus.

Carey had never allowed himself to be examined either pre-matrix or post-body. He was certain there were no genetic problems in his own makeup.

But Almendariz's mental dysfunctions permitted the strength of imagery that allowed Carey to cross more completely into the land of the living again. If he'd been wrong in his theories, if Almendariz hadn't been able to afford him a bridge to the sensations he'd missed, he would surely have gone insane knowing he was held captive inside the matrix. It was strange that it took a man with delusions and something missing to make him whole again.

He turned from the bleak thoughts, wondering if the priest might glean something of them as he coasted along in the dark recesses of his own mind.

Taking his refill, he moved away from the bar and back into the outer fringes of the dancers. He noted with satisfaction that the priest's angelic features and the expensive clothes he wore attracted looks from a number of women.

Carey liked this part of the hunt, liked to troll through the unsuspecting and make believe he was one of them. They would look at him, never thinking that he had the power to reach out and crush them, then take what he wanted from their bodies.

"Hey, dreamboat."

Carey turned and saw the woman standing behind him.

She was tall, with dark hair tumbling in a loose fall to her pale, bare shoulders. Her lips were glossy red, her eyes lost in the shadows and in her makeup. Surely no older than her early twenties, she wore a spandex dress that flattered her hourglass figure.

The woman regarded him from under arched brows. "I've seen you walking around by yourself for about half an hour now. Didn't you find anything you like?"

Carey showed her one of Almendariz's best smiles. He'd explored the priest's facial expressions before leaving his building earlier, found the ones he thought suited him best, and memorized them for later use. "Not till now."

The woman came closer and offered her hand. "I'm Holly."

"Joshua," Carey said, and he was sure he'd picked that name up from Almendariz, because he'd never used it as an alias before. He took her hand and kissed it.

"So tell me, Joshua," Holly said as she drew close enough to touch his body with hers, "you want to skip all this getting-to-know-you stuff and come back to my room?" Her breath was sweet and alcoholic in his ear, her words deep and throaty and full of promise.

"Okay," Carey said, and he let her lead him out of the club. His own anticipation overruled the fear radiating from Almendariz, letting him follow the priest's erection after the woman like a compass needle seeking out magnetic north.

Almendariz felt like a spider crouched in a dark corner of his own mind, not trusting the slender cobweb that connected him to his physical body. He wanted to run, to escape, before *it* happened and the woman seized the opportunity to become pregnant with his child and tie his immortal soul to the pits of hell forever.

But Carey seemed determined to step directly into the fire and make Almendariz confront the fears that sent shivers through his psyche. The priest wanted nothing more than to kill the succubus and leave.

They were in the woman's apartment now, and he was unable to focus on her words or Carey's. Though manipulated by Carey's thoughts, he still felt the burning heat of the woman's flesh under his fingers as Carey trailed a hand across the tops of her breasts.

She giggled at him, and Almendariz knew the humor was false. She captured his hand in both of hers and kissed the fingers. Her lips were so wet and so full of dark promise. Inside the recesses of his own mind, Almendariz squirmed in uncomfortable ecstasy.

The apartment was small, dark, overfilled with worn furniture, as if the woman had had to move several times but refused to get rid of any of her possessions. Recycled cardboard boxes peered out from under jackets and other garments in the hallway closet.

She led the way to a small bedroom at the back of the apartment, undressed in the shadow-streaked silver moonlight pouring in through a narrow window.

As he watched, Almendariz couldn't separate his own hunger from Carey's, and the realization that the man lusted after the woman worried him. If Carey fell under the spell of the succubus, perhaps neither of them was safe. He tried to reach for the jackknife Carey had tucked inside his coat before they left the financier's building that evening. But Carey stopped him and changed the motion into an encirclement of the woman's wrist.

When she was naked, she was even more beautiful. High conical breasts gleamed like whipped alabaster topped by cherry kissed nipples. Her rib cage veed down to a narrow waist with a hidden belly button, then flared out again into generous hips. Her pubic area was a carefully shaven dark thatch that jutted out obscenely.

Carey leaned into her, taking the supple body into his arms, and trailed his hands against the goose-bumped flesh of her buttocks. She ground against him, encouraged the erection pressing insistently at her stomach.

Almendariz's control slipped, and he clutched frantically at it. <No!>

"Relax," Carey said. "I'm taking care of it."

The feeling of intense pressure melted away even though the woman pulled them into the bed with her.

Carey controlled their body, shed his clothes quickly.

<What do you think you're doing?>

"Trust me," Carey replied.

The woman smiled up at him, thinking he was speaking to her.

Almendariz felt Carey's smile pull at his lips, felt his right hand close around the jackknife and flip it open with Carey's expert skill. Moonlight kissed the bright blade for a fleeting instant as it swept toward the woman's exposed throat. She never saw it coming till it had cleaved her flesh.

She bucked under them and fought to throw them off. Carey fended away her flailing blows with his elbows and tossed the knife to one side as he used his hands to pin her shoulders against the bloodstained bed. Her attempted screams only showered scarlet mist that smashed warm stickiness against their face.

Horrified, unable to comprehend what was happening, tapped into confusing emotions running rampant through Carey's mind, Almendariz froze in shocked dismay.

Long moments later, the woman shivered out the remnants of her life and lay still, twisted in the bloodied sheets.

Then Carey moved, parted her legs, prepared to thrust home.

Almendariz felt his slim grasp on sanity shred like tissue paper as he frantically clawed for control of his body. His screams bounced off the inside walls of his mind like hailstones from a street surface.

A blinding headache roiled up around Carey before he could penetrate the dead woman. He groaned aloud, felt the room spin around him, and clutched at the side of the bed, only to miss and spill from the bed onto the carpet.

He slapped both hands to his temples and groaned again. For an instant he considered jumping from Almendariz's body and sliding along the nearest gridline back to the matrix in his building. But abandoning the priest to his own devices could cost him the body and the precious ability Almendariz represented.

"Shut up!" he screamed at the priest.

Almendariz's shouts gave way to confused and babbled prayers. He kept railing against the power of Darkness and of Satan's black gifts of falsehoods and betrayals.

Mustering his crumbling self-control, Carey righted himself and came to rest on his knees. He took deep breaths and released them slowly through his nose, trying to get a handle on the hammering pain filling his head. Almendariz wasn't experiencing the same physical pain while lodged in the back of his own brain.

"You lied to me!" Almendariz screamed. It felt as if spittle clouded the back of the shared brain.

"She was a succubus," Carey said. "You saw her with your own senses. She would have stolen your soul."

"Deceiver!"

Carey shoved himself to his feet, stood swaying as the room drifted loosely around him in a slow spiral. He glanced down at the dead woman, staring into her sightless eyes. "She was dangerous to us."

"You lusted after her for your own purposes."

"Not all of that lust was mine." Carey found the jackknife and fitted his fist around it. He crossed the floor, blood still dripping from the wet knife blade. Inside the bathroom, he turned the light on and leaned over the sink basin. Scarlet threads twisted down Almendariz's naked flesh to drip onto the Formica surface. More trickled slowly across the white basin and vanished through the chrome drain. He stared into Almendariz's face, trying to make the priest see himself for what he truly was. "You're no better than me, priest. That lust you're so afraid of has already locked into your soul with claws you'll never pull out. Call it evil if you want to, but you'll only make yourself miserable. These women are sheep. We can take them and have as many as we wish."

"No."

"Yes." Carey held up his fist with the bloody jackknife clenched in it. "And we will take them."

"I won't let you."

"You have no choice." Carey bumped the power coursing through the zombyte chip and bounced Almendariz farther back in his own mind. "I own you now."

Without warning Almendariz retreated. Only occasional words and phrases of prayers and Bible passages slipped through into Carey's mind. The headache faded as well.

Breathing more easily, but feeling detached now because the priest had pulled away, Carey returned to the small bedroom. He left the lights off, preferring security from inquisitive neighbors and the way the shadows dappled the dead woman's body.

He stood at her side, gazed longingly at the pale, fleshy curves, and hoped for some spark of desire that might ignite the repressed passion within him. Mentally he wanted to ravish her body more than anyone else he'd ever desired. Physically, without Almendariz's neural connections, it was impossible.

He cursed in disgust, then reached out and rolled her over. He ran a palm down the smooth skin of her back, feeling it already cool to the touch.

The jackknife blade cut through the woman easily, and he set to his work with grim efficiency.

37

She reached for the phone instinctively and brought it to her mouth. "Shay."

"Beth, it's Asela. I'm returning your call. It sounds like I woke you. Sorry."

"Don't be." Shay heaved herself out of Keiko's bed, brought the 9mm with her, and padded into the bathroom. "I needed to talk now, not later." She used the plastic Mickey Mouse cup beside the sink to drink from, tried to wash the ashen cotton from her mouth. It didn't work. "Somebody attacked me in my house tonight. There were two people." She walked back into the bedroom and peered through the window at the empty street.

"Are you all right?"

"Yeah. I'm bruised, and I'm scared, but I'm handling it."

"Do you need me to come over and sit with you for a while?"

Shay clamped down on the impulse to say yes. What she wanted was for someone to come take care of her worries for a little while, and she knew it. What she needed was work to do to keep her mind off of everything. "No. I just want the bastards who broke into my house." She related the incident, added the details she knew.

"A man and a woman," Asela repeated. "Big guy, tough-talking lady. Obviously paired and have spent some time around each other. Can't be too many like that."

"I figure the guy for a sex skel," Shay said. "I'm going to run him through the sex crimes files in the computer this morning and see what turns up. But I thought you might ask a few of your friends and associates in case he doesn't have a record."

"No prob. Give me fifteen minutes to freshen up, kiss the kids, and make arrangements for baby-sitting and I'll be out on the street."

"Keep a low profile out there. These bastards may be sloppy, but they mean business."

"I will. You just stay chill till I get back to you."

Shay said thanks, and broke the connection. The night closed in around her and she gave up on sleep.

By eight o'clock she was in Tarao's dojo working out her fears and her frustrations. The sensei moved in a position of influence without speaking, turned his morning class over to an advanced pupil, and pushed Shay through her paces. He never spoke to her, never offered encouragement, only challenge. But it was challenge that didn't move her to the breaking point. When she was about to exhaust herself with katas, the heavy bag or the speed bag, he instinctively moved on and she followed.

The leather popped under her gloved hands, and the folds of her gi cracked as she moved with sure balance and speed. Perspiration streamed down her body and soaked her clothing.

She'd noticed the bruises on her forearms in this morning's shower, had watched them turn purple by the time she reached the dojo.

Almost two hours after she'd started, she broke the exercise series, bowed to Tarao, showered, and left. By the time she hit the street, she felt like she was ready for it. The Glock rode in a fanny pack under her short jean jacket.

At 10:10 A.M. she stopped at a drug store and used the phone to dial a downtown law firm she'd done business with. Mason Fletcher was a junior attorney at a prestigious law office, just a couple rungs below achieving a full partnership. She got Fletcher on the line and identified herself.

Normally gregarious and flirting, Fletcher was more somber than usual. "Hey, Beth, what's up?"

An older couple pushed their wobbly shopping cart past the phone while a trio of leatherboys skimmed the aisles tucking items in their pockets under the nose of the store clerk.

"I called to ask a favor."

"If I can."

"I want to know who hired Tyler Grahame to defend Father Judd Almendariz."

Fletcher paused a beat. "That's a tall favor."

"If it was easy, I could do it myself."

"Yeah. According to the court record, Grahame cut himself in as part of the public defense representation he tries to do."

"I'm after the truth," Shay said. "Grahame wouldn't have touched Almendariz's case if he hadn't been well paid to do it. I want to know who hired him."

"You're asking me to put my neck on the chopping block, Beth."

"And I've put mine there for you a few times," Shay replied.

"Are you at home?"

"No." She read him the number from the pay phone.

"It's going to take a little while."

"I'll be here." She broke the connection, opened her purse, and palmed her shield while she stood by the phone. When the leatherboys headed for the door, she slipped a hand inside the fanny pack, took a step toward them to block their way, and held out the shield. "Put it back," she said in a cold voice.

Their eyes drifted down to the gun in her hand. Wordlessly, they moved back through the aisle and put the pilfered items back. While they were doing that, the old couple scurried to the clerk, paid for their items, and left in a hurry. Once everything had been returned to the shelves, she let them go without a word. They paused on the other side of the full-length windows to scream curses at her and make obscene gestures, then ran away.

The clerk appeared shaken by the incident, thanked her, but wasn't so nervous that he forgot to charge her for the double-malted banana shake she had for breakfast and lunch.

Forty-five minutes later the pay phone rang.

She lifted the receiver. "Shay."

"It's me," Mason Fletcher said. "I got a name, but I swear to Christ if you tell anybody you got it from me, I'll deny ever having known you."

Shay waited without commenting.

"Grahame's fee was paid through a subsidiary corporation whose parent company is Carey International, Limited. You've heard of Felix Carey?"

Shay ran the name through her mind. "Whispers. Vague impressions. Nothing really concrete comes to mind. I think he's rumored to be the richest American left in Houston."

"At least Houston," Fletcher said. "Beth, if Carey is involved, you've bumped into somebody who can leverage the whole Houston Police Department with one arm tied behind him. My advice is to just stay the fuck away."

"Why would Carey be interested in Almendariz?"

"I've got no answers for you," Fletcher said. "If I weren't as good as I am about slipping behind the scene on things, you wouldn't have a lead even this tenuous. As it is, I don't know what the hell you hope to do with it."

"I don't know either. But it gives me something to start with."

Fletcher cleared his throat. "You know, for a while, maybe it would be better if you didn't call me." He broke the connection before she could reply.

Shay hung up the phone, not really concerned about Fletcher's withdrawal from her, lost in wondering why Carey would be interested in someone like Almendariz. Rumor also had it that Carey didn't ever involve himself in anything that wasn't going to show a quick profit or some kind of ego gratification. She couldn't begin to imagine what the priest could offer him.

By eleven-thirty she'd reached her office. Someone had stopped by Keever's side of the desk to clear away all the personal effects. It hurt her to see everything so barren and empty, reminding her that he wouldn't be coming along in a few minutes to ask her how everything was going.

She accessed her lapdeck, pulled up files from crime reports and media clips on Felix Carey and Carey International, Ltd. She monitored her time, made sure Espinoza wasn't around, and finished everything up just as the homicide captain entered his office with Chaney and Barker. None of the three men seemed especially pleased with their morning.

Hunched down in her seat, Shay made one last inquiry and found out where the deck bug that had been recovered from her lapdeck had been stored in the evidence room downstairs.

"Hiya, Beth."

"Hey, Benny," Shay said. She leaned over the counter and gave the little florid-faced round man a hug and a quick kiss on the cheek and tried not to feel guilty about what she was going to do.

"I thought you were on vacation," the evidence clerk said.

"I am," Shay replied, "but court cases pick the damnedest times to pop back up."

"Don't I know it." Benny Small was in his late fifties, pushing retirement on a prosthetic lower leg that gave him a limp despite the best medical care the police department could afford in the old days. He moved carefully through the racks and boxes strewn across the floor and shelf space. "So what brings you down to the pit?"

"I need to review the evidence on a case going to trial this week," Shay lied. She moved off through the rows of metal racks covered with stolen auto and deck parts, stolen body organs and bionic replacements, and drugs and cash. "That way when the prosecutor asks me if I remember it, I will."

"A fair and speedy trial," Small said with a chuckle. "They should talk to us guys in the evidence room, find out how slowly these things really do go."

Grunting a quick agreement, Shay wandered down the stacks of metal racks, found the numbered and lettered section she wanted, and turned in. On the second tier up from the floor, sandwiched in between a chip player, an outlaw deck rigged for ripping juice and programming from public outlets, and a prosthetic left hand, she found the monitoring chip Leon Foalske had discovered in her lapdeck a few days ago. It sat under a light layer of dust, kept captive in a sandwich bag tagged with a bar code.

Kneeling, she switched the monitoring chip with the blank one she'd brought with her. She wrapped the original chip in a wad of tissue paper and dropped it into her purse. After uncovering the information on Carey, she'd reconsidered her assumption that the monitoring chip had come from Kiyoshi. Carey could easily have afforded the techware to track the investigation, and that could explain how the man had been able to move on Almendariz so quickly.

"Find it?" Small called out.

"Oh yeah," Shay replied as she stood. "Looks exactly the way I remembered it."

Small laughed quietly.

"Take care of yourself, Benny." Shay headed for the door, avoiding eye contact, because she was afraid Small would see right through her and know what she'd done. She'd never been any good at lying to her friends, not even when she considered that it was for their own good.

"You too, babe."

Randy Minoru twirled the monitoring chip between his fingers. "Something like this," he said in his low voice, "is going to cost." At something over six feet, he looked imposing at a glance. His sunglasses were StarTron-equipped and powered by the same neural circuitry that operated his gene-engineered body armament. His long black hair was pulled back in a samurai-styled ponytail.

"If I don't have it, I'll get it," Shay said.

They sat at a small table in the back of the Torchlight Club, where Minoru worked security. The afternoon crowd was thin, nervously anticipating the evening. Up on the stage the dancer performed with distracted abandon, knowing the real money wouldn't be coming in until after night fell.

Minoru gazed at the chip through the dark lenses of his sunglasses. "Thing could be loaded with all kinds of nasty surprises. Datajackers I've talked to, they might not want to risk riding out a flaming deck to cyberzero."

"If you can help me," Shay said, "let me know. Otherwise I'm still looking." They'd developed a friendship over the years she had been going to the bar infrequently, and Minoru was wired into the street scene. During some joint business in the past, they'd learned to trust each other.

Minoru nodded and sipped hot chocolate. "Where did you get the bruises on your arms?"

Self-consciously she pulled at the jean jacket sleeves and slid them down to her wrists. Without emotion, she told him about the attack in her house the previous night.

"And you think that's connected with this?" Minoru pointed to the chip on the table.

"Yeah."

"Do you know who the people were who broke into your home?"

"No."

"Give me a description."

She did and knew that Minoru was memorizing every word she said to him.

When she finished the security man said, "Maybe I can get you something on that too. In the meantime," he went on, scooping the monitoring chip up and handing it back to her, "I can get you somebody to crack that chip. There's a guy in the biz that owes me a big favor."

"I didn't come here for a handout," Shay said.

"And I'm not giving you one." Minoru swiveled his big head toward her and gave her a brief smile. "One of these days, I'll ask you to do me a favor in return."

"I'm not going to compromise myself or what I believe in."

"And I'm not going to ask you to," Minoru said. "When the time comes, it'll be something you can live with, and something only you can do. Trust me?"

Shay hesitated for only a moment. In all the time that she'd known Minoru, she'd never seen him break his own code or his word. She shook his hand and said okay.

When she tried her answering machine at home from the datajacker's apartment, Shay found there'd been two phone messages. One was from a siding business looking to drum up business, and the other was from a carpet-cleaning company looking to do the same. Evidently Asela hadn't checked in. Although Shay knew the woman had been taking care of herself in a risky business for a lot of years, she was still worried.

"I can tell you right now this ain't gonna be no fucking joyride," Marc Smith said. The datajacker sat in a papasan chair in front of his deck in the dark living room of his small apartment. Marijuana smoke, laced with red satin, swirled in blue layers across the screen. Smith was a short young man with scraggly brown hair and a mustache.

"Can you do it?"

"If it can be done," Smith replied cockily, "I can do it." He reached for the trode, slipped it easily into his temple jack. His eyes glassed over at once, no longer seeing the physical world around him. Another wire was added to the temple jack and snaked a few centimeters inside his head.

Shay stepped forward. "Take me with you."

The datajacker turned toward her blindly, a dull smile twisting up the corners of his mouth. "You ever been inside before?"

"No," Shay replied.

"A lot of people," Smith said, "don't care much for the trip."

"I'm willing to risk that."

Minoru's face was impassive, revealing nothing.

"Are you chipped?" Smith asked.

"Com-chip."

Smith reached up, tugged the trodes from his head, and glanced wildly at Minoru as blurred sight returned to his eyes. "Are you a cop?"

"Yeah."

"Hey, Randy, what the fuck is this?"

"Chill out," Minoru ordered. "Everything we do here is strictly off the record."

"She knows who I am now."

"I don't work deck crimes," Shay said. "You get this done, I forget who you are once I walk through the door."

"And you owe me," Minoru reminded. "That doesn't have anything to do with her."

"Right." Smith didn't look happy about the situation. He reached into a desk compartment and took out a neuro-rig. "You familiar with these?"

"It's a neuro-stimset," Shay answered.

"You ever used one?"

"No."

Smith untangled it till it resembled a carbon-fiber net headdress. "It works off your chip implant, allows you to ride piggyback into cyberspace if you're with someone who can actually jack into a deck." He looked up at her with an expectant grin. "It's dangerous. If I flame out in there, so do you."

Shay gave him a tight nod.

Smith pulled out a small stool, rolled it to a stop beside him, and patted the seat. "Then sit down and let's get this show on the road."

Shay looked into Minoru's eyes as the datajacker worked quickly and efficiently. The neuro-rig was feather-light against her hair. She felt the warning buzz triggered through her com-chip as the stimset was activated. Then suddenly she knew she wasn't in the apartment anymore.

38

Shay felt a world, perhaps worlds, moving around her, but there were no definite signposts to mark her passage. Then a glowing purple line twisted into view before her, writhing like a fat worm at the end of a fishhook.

Her hand closed over the line instinctively, covered almost immediately by Smith's. Despite the feeling, she was sure neither of them had a corporeal body.

"Gridline," Smith's voice whispered into her mind. "If everything works out, it'll provide us with a back door into that monitoring chip and we can trace its transmission paths."

The gridline flew through their fists.

A curving sprawl of multicolored gridlines hove into view above a snarled net of violent reds, then melted quickly away in a rainbow spray.

"The Berkeley logistics matrix," Smith said. They changed the purple gridline for a slender periwinkle thread. "Next stop is Greenwich DataMain, then we try to pop open that chip."

The darkness cleared before Shay, showed her a diamond-hard lance of emerald green slashing through a Valentine-pink pentagon. Black furry shapes endlessly orbited the pentagon, and it took her a few seconds to tentatively identify them as spiders. She moved restlessly.

"Security webs," Smith warned. "Whatever you do, stay the fuck out of my head."

Shay forced herself to remain calm as two of the spider-shapes hovered over her.

When their hands locked around the emerald-green lance, the pentagon began to spin wildly, knocking the spider-things in all directions.

Ruby strands jetted from the cavernous mouths of the spider-things, spiraled out, and snagged the spinning corners of the pentagon. Metal hissing sounds vibrated along the ruby strands, and Shay watched in horror as the spider-things started swooping back toward her. Their legs twitched in anticipation.

Without warning the emerald lance became a two-dimensional pane that possessed gravity. Shay felt herself sucked into a pentagon through the emerald pane as the first of the spider-things scrambled over her body.

The spider-thing vanished, replaced by the interior of a cube filled with glowing white light. A seam closed overhead and shut out the ebony gleam of cyberspace. Shay felt her feet settle on the smooth floor of the cube. Somehow she knew that Smith—still unseen—had taken a step away from her.

At the other end of the cube a middle-aged man with gray-streaked mouse-brown hair and wearing a leather bomber jacket and blue-lensed Ray-Bans came toward them in long strides. "Don't know who you people are," he said, "but you picked the wrong damn matrix for a smash-and-grab invasion." He made a gesture with his left hand.

Abruptly Shay's body became visible, striped vertically in blue and white, and a warm lassitude crept over her. Smith became a Neapolitan confection three steps in front of her. The datajacker's hands filled with gold-flecked sapphire cords.

Smith's hands shook out a noose and fired it from the hip underhanded. It glowed electric gold as it arced toward the guy in Ray-Bans, then trapped the man in quick flips that tied him up tighter than a Christmas package.

"C'mon," Smith ordered. "That tangler weave isn't gonna hold him for-fuckin'-ever." Still striped in Neapolitan, looking runny around the edges, the datajacker plunged over the fallen security guy's body.

At a dead run, not believing her eyes, Shay followed.

Smith paused at a rock the size of a Galapagos tortoise, raised a motorcycle-booted foot, and kicked out hard. A fissure cracked in the middle of the rock, followed by a belch of steam, then a geyser of cool amber liquid spurted toward the white ceiling and spread across it like fog. Stretching forth a hand, the datajacker stuck his finger into the running water.

For the first time Shay noticed Smith's fingers resembled

trodes on the ends, bright and shiny, with multifaceted prongs.

Smith looked at her expectantly. "Does Carey International mean anything to you?"

"Yeah," she said. "It means a lot."

"How much of this do you want?"

"As much as you can get."

At the other end of the white room, the security man struggled with the glowing rope. Scarlet sparks cascaded along the rope, shorted out with the gold color, and loosened the loops.

With a bellowing scream of rage, the security man kicked free of the rope and got to his feet. He broke into a staggering run, planted his feet down solidly, ran up the side of the wall, and fired a blue-tinted crystal lightning bolt at Smith and Shay.

"We're outta here!" Smith said. He reached for Shay's hand and curled talon-hard fingers around it.

The lightning bolt was inches from Shay's face when she felt the chill of cyberspace suck her into its dark depths.

"No connection between Carey and the priest?" They were in Minoru's small office at the back of the Torchlight Club. The bouncer took his seat in a squeaking chair behind the scarred metal desk and levered his feet up on the corner.

"None." Shay leaned back and stretched her cramped shoulder muscles, willing some of the pain away. "From what I've turned up on Carey, the guy's nearly a hundred and twenty years old."

"Matrix extension?"

Shay nodded. "Life-after-life for those who can afford it."

Minoru gave an uncharacteristic shiver. "Not for me. I want to live fast, love hard, die young, and leave a good-looking corpse. Hanging around a matrix extension sounds too much like being a ghost."

Shay considered that, thumbed the lapdeck back to full operation. "And what would a ghost want?"

Shrugging, Minoru said, "To be alive, I guess."

She couldn't come up with a better answer, so she shelved the question for a time. Accessing her com-chip, she found out the time was 5:17 P.M. She reached for the phone, dialed her home number, and punched in the code to play back the messages on her answering machine.

Two were from her lawyer. One was from her father. Another was from Loryn. The fifth was from Asela.

"Beth. It's me. I'm calling at a quarter to five." The woman's voice sounded tired, played out, but there was a spark of enthusiasm not quite buried in her words. "I found the people you're looking for."

The address was off Denham Avenue near Sunset Park in Pasadena, a few miles out of Houston proper.

Shay parked the Fiero six houses away around the incoming curve from Richey Street and got out. At her side, Minoru uncurled from the passenger seat and shut the door behind him. He'd dressed in street leathers before leaving the club, and an interesting array of weapons from the desk had been shoved into hidden pockets lining the jacket and pants.

Shay was glad the big man was along, although she'd halfheartedly tried to talk him out of it. What she was planning on doing scared the hell out of her. But she couldn't have walked away from doing it if she'd wanted to.

The big man's name was Axel Devine. His partner was Yeva Kalinin, a third-generation Soviet immigrant. Asela hadn't been able to find a address on Kalinin. She operated with a lower profile than her partner. Devine was known by several of the prostitutes within Asela's outer circle of acquaintances. Most of them labeled him as bad business, had the scars and nightmares to prove it. Devine had killed two pimps who'd tried to teach him a lesson in humility and sold their bodies to organ jackals. At least, that was the general consensus. Some women that Asela had talked to maintained that Devine had ground up the two men and fed them to his dogs.

Reaching behind the seat, Shay slipped a boken from a cloth scabbard. The dark wood of the practice sword swallowed the moonlight and became a hard length in her hand.

She took the lead, set out at a trot. Minoru followed silently at her heels. She was dressed in black jeans, a dark blue turtleneck, and a black windbreaker. A rubber band held her hair back, fingerless gloves encased her hands, and the Glock rode on her hip.

The house was a small brick two-bedroom with peeling beige paint. The soft glow of wallscreen dappled the stained and dusty windows. Dogs snarled somewhere in back of the house and occasionally broke into angry yaps. The Ford pickup registered to Devine was parked in the garage.

Minoru touched her arm briefly and signed that he was going around back.

Shay nodded, her fist loose and ready around the boken as she watched him melt into the night. She stayed low as she went up on the small porch area, avoiding the loose collection of dishes, glasses, and discarded fast-food sacks trapped between the wooden teeth of the railing.

She moved to the windows and peered in at the empty living room and disheveled bedroom. She was working her way from the condensation-covered bathroom window when Minoru reached for her out of the darkness.

"He's in back."

"Alone?" Shay asked.

"Yeah. He's in the dog run."

Shay followed the big man and noticed for the first time that he'd slipped a black ski mask with stitched, glaring red brows over his face.

The land fell away toward the back of the house, dropped at least two feet so that the kennels butted up against the back-door stairs. Wire mesh gleamed dully, and wicked sharpened Y's of steel crowned the six-foot fence. The back-yard was huge and rambling. Oak trees jutted up from the midst of cages. Barks and rolling canine moans filled the immediate area.

"Feeding time," Minoru said. He passed over a small set of infrared binoculars and pointed.

Shay looked in the indicated direction, saw Devine from the back in the glassy green glare provided by the infrared tech, and knew it was the same guy who'd broken into her house the night before and attacked her. She glanced around and found a flattened cardboard box that had once held dog food squashed beside the fence. "I didn't count on the dogs."

"I'll take care of them." Minoru showed her a small needler. "Tranks. It'll put them down without hurting them."

"Leave Devine alone," Shay said as she slid the cardboard over the top of the fence.

"He's yours."

Once the cardboard was in place, Shay tucked the boken through her gunbelt and pulled herself up the wire mesh. Her heart hammered inside her chest as she went over the top, eyes locked on Devine's dark shadow, expecting the man to turn around and catch her before she could clear. Memory of the man's rough hands sliding around her unprotected body invaded her conscious mind, made her stumble when her feet hit the ground. She drew the practice sword and started moving for the man, her breathing light, coming from the pit of her stomach as Tarao had taught her.

With less than fifteen feet between them, Devine turned suddenly, and his eyes—bloodshot and filmed yellow— widened in shocked surprise. His palm slapped against an electronic pad on the cages in front of him.

"Kill!" Devine roared as he shoved himself to one side.

Four dogs launched themselves from their cages as the electronic doors slid away.

Shay backpedaled, brought the boken up before her, and tried to watch Devine in case the man went for a firearm.

Moonlight gleamed on slaver-covered ivory teeth. Two of the animals were German shepherds. A third was some kind of dark mongrel with huge jaws and mottled fur. The last one was a red-eyed rottweiler foaming at the mouth in anticipation.

"Move!" Minoru shouted.

Diving to one side, Shay came up with the boken at the ready. Behind her, the needler spat mosquito-whines in rapid succession.

One of the German shepherds crumpled to the ground in a flailing tangle of legs and tail. The needler continued to whine as Minoru became a part of Shay's periphery.

Devine was moving quickly through the cages, alternating looks forward with looks back over his shoulder. Something metallic glinted in his hand.

Reacting to the threat of the rottweiler, Shay swung a short stroke that caught the big dog between the ears. The skull popped hollowly and the jaws snapped shut, biting off strands of silvery saliva.

The dog tried to plant itself, scrambled in the loose dirt of the kennel run, and struggled to launch itself at her. The needler whined in increased fury. Without a sound, the rottweiler collapsed and rolled over.

Checking on Minoru, Shay found the big man kicking the dark mongrel away while reloading the needler.

"Go," Minoru said. "I've got this." The second German shepherd lay at his feet.

Shay nodded, then took out in pursuit of Devine through the maze of dog runs.

The rear wall of fence had blocked Devine's escape. He pawed at the electronic release on the other side of the gate, but couldn't reach it.

Shay came to a stop on the balls of her feet ten feet away and took the boken in a measured grip in front of her.

The big man whirled to face her. A saw-toothed blade flashed in front of him. He sprang for her without warning. The blade licked at her face.

Shay riposted, blocked the knife, felt it slice splinters from the boken and hang for just a moment before freeing itself. Devine tried to hit her with his body weight, using a forearm shiver. She went with the force, slipped to the side, and fired an elbow into Devine's exposed temple. The blow rocked his head and staggered him. Using his free hand to maintain his balance, Devine tried to rush past Shay. Sidestepping, Shay thrust the sword between his legs, tangled them.

Devine fell, struggled immediately to face her and get to a standing position.

As he came up, Shay whirled, light on her feet, came around, and smashed a boot into his face.

Devine went backward, rebounding from the wire mesh of the cage behind him. Blood trickled from his nose in a dark streamer. He tried to focus on the knife.

Shay rapped the boken across the back of Devine's hand, spilled the blade onto the ground, and stepped close enough to kick it away.

Roaring in unrestrained rage, Devine came at her.

Giving ground before the attack, Shay chose her moment, stepped in quickly, and brought the butt of the sword around in a powerful arc. Devine's nose broke in a scarlet, explosive spray. As he put his hands to his face and tried to stumble away, she concentrated on her next swing, put all of her weight and muscle into it, and aimed at the side of his left knee.

Bones broke with hollow pops. Devine went down immediately, his shouts mingling with the general furor of the dogs.

Breathing hard, shaking from the emotions coursing through her, Shay held the boken in one hand and drew the

Glock with the other. She squatted down beside him, out of his reach.

Devine lay on his back, rocking, clutching his shattered knee.

She let him see the Glock and watched his eyes get wide in pools of blood from his nose. The pistol didn't waver from Devine's head. "That was to get your attention," she said. "Now we're going to talk."

Devine tried to push himself into a sitting position.

"No," Shay said. "You lie there, or I do the other knee." Devine lay back.

"Who hired you to come looking for me?" Shay asked.

"Fuck you."

Shay moved the Glock, fired a round into the ground between Devine's legs that was only inches from the man's groin.

One of Devine's hands slipped between his legs to reassure himself everything was okay. "Kalinin worked the deal. She cut herself a deal for some stock in Debbsun Corporation. Worked it through a third party so it never touched a database in her name."

Shay stood up and kept the Glock leveled on Devine. "You live. But if you ever come around me again, I'll kill you."

Minoru moved forward, letting Devine stare at his ski-masked face. "And if anything questionable happens to her, *I'll* kill you. Understand?"

Devine nodded.

Before the man could move to protect himself, Shay swung the boken in a vicious arc, slamming it into his groin. He gasped with pain and started retching immediately. "And keep Ole Stanley out of my sight too," she said softly.

Shay accessed the lapdeck at the first red light.

Minoru's ski mask had disappeared into a pocket. He drummed his fingers in time to the music coming from the chip player. "You would have been better off killing him," he said.

"I couldn't," Shay said as she punched the keys.

The traffic light turned green, and a car honked behind them as the lapdeck churned through the information Shay had stored on the Felix Carey database. She shifted into gear, handed Minoru the lapdeck, and put her foot on the accelerator.

"Got an answer," Minoru said. He held the lapdeck so she could read the screen.

Glowing orange letters said: CONFIRMED. DEBBSUN CORPORATION IS A SUBSIDIARY OWNED EXCLUSIVELY BY CAREY INTERNATIONAL, LTD.

"All roads lead to Carey," she said softly, and wondered what she would find at the end of them.

"Yeah," Minoru said. He closed the lapdeck and put it away.

"About today and tonight . . ." Shay said.

Minoru held up a hand. "Nothing's free in this life, Beth. The moment comes, you'll do time for me too." He gave her a grin. "It doesn't hurt to have a stand-up person at your back when things look bad, and I don't exactly work in a world of pretty sunsets. There's not many people like us left."

"How do you mean?"

"People who know themselves. People who know what they want out of life, what they'll do when the chips are down, what they can do if they have to. And what they *won't* do if it comes down to that." He paused. "We're different, you and I, see the world in different terms, and different challenges, but we meet it on our own terms."

She laughed uncomfortably. "I don't see myself that way at all."

Minoru hesitated. "It's this thing with your daughter. Once you get that cleared up, get some time in behind you, you'll understand yourself again. You're somebody other people can rely on, and that's saying a lot in this world."

Shay checked the mirror again more to break the honest eye contact than to see if someone was following them.

Then the chip player broke for a news announcement. In a ten-second bite, Shay found out about the dead woman who some thought was another victim of the Bayou Ripper even though the police department denied it.

39

"The deceased's name," Fitzgerald said as he whipped the sheet off the body in the morgue vault, "is Constance Hardy. She was local talent at a nearby bar. Worked under a handful of names. A dozen people identified her by the picture Chaney and Barker circulated. None of them had her real name until they printed her."

Scanning the body, struggling to remain impersonal, Shay nodded. "I got all that off the reports Chaney, Barker, and the uniforms filed."

"You read the police reports?" Fitzgerald knew she'd been pulled from the case. The visit was off the record.

"Yeah. I raided them last night and this morning. But it was mainly B-sheet stuff. Nothing pertinent to the condition her body was in." She looked at Fitzgerald. "The throat wound was the cause of death?"

"Yeah. Figure she was lying on her back. She drowned in her own blood before she had the chance to bleed to death."

"She's not cut up the way the other women were."

"No."

"What did Espinoza say about it?"

"He didn't."

"Chaney and Barker?"

"They figure a jealous boyfriend, the pimp, or a sex skel with a violence jones."

"Strictly file-it-and-forget-it stuff."

"That's how they're treating it. But Espinoza told them to keep their asses glued to it anyway."

"Where did you find the DNA match?"

"Fingernails."

"She tried to fight him off?" Shay looked but she couldn't find bruises, scratches, or any other signs of struggle.

"I don't think so. I think the guy was close to her, slipped her the knife before she saw it coming. Maybe even while they were having intercourse."

"They had sex?"

"There were secretions indicating coitus shortly before she died. And some vaginal bleeding from torn and bruised tissues. The guy was playing rough. No semen was found on or in the body."

The information sounded false to Shay, didn't feel right, but in a weird way it connected with what she'd been thinking. From the psych profile they'd generated from Quantico's FBI Behavioral Science Unit, there was no reason for the Ripper to change his MO. So someone had changed it for him. Looking at it that way, the new fact fit the puzzle. "Where else did he cut her?"

"Help me roll her over."

Shay grabbed the woman's shoulders, suddenly glad of the fingerless gloves she was wearing because they cut down on the amount of skin-to-skin contact with the corpse, and pulled the slack weight toward her.

The body rolled, and Fitzgerald pointed to the neat lines of the incision across the corpse's lower back. "You have to look close to see it for what it is."

Arms trembling with the dead weight, Shay peered closely. "A rose?"

"Near as I could figure it," Fitzgerald said.

The carving was rough, with sections of skin filleted out to make pink meat petals. The thorns were hard sections of black and twisted skin that had been pried free and left sticking straight out.

"Have you got any pictures of this?"

"In the office."

Shay nodded, and together they lowered the body back to the table and recovered it with the sheet. "I'll want a couple."

Sitting on the floor of the bedroom at home under the rows of dead faces, Shay stroked the keyboard, opened a window in the center of the flashing data from FBI VICAP files strung across the screen, and punched up the digitized picture of the bloody rose that had been carved into Constance Hardy's back. It scrolled into place, then suddenly shrank inward as it meshed with the files.

It clunked as it cycled, and files flashed in heartbeats across the screen. Pictures of serial killers appeared before the official reports, media footage, and news hardcopy that detailed their careers. Several of them had no names and no pictures, and only a handful didn't even have representations created by police artists.

The Bleeding Rose Butcher was one of those.

The file photograph of his handiwork, though, was an almost exact duplicate of the rose that had been cut into the dead woman.

A moment of elation touched Shay, then a glance at the file squelched that. The latest entry into the Bleeding Rose Butcher's file was over forty years old.

She accessed the file and waited as it came up.

Twenty-two rape-murders in and around Houston had been attributed to the Bleeding Rose Butcher over a thirty-year period. The last one had been a woman who'd been picked up in a singles bar forty-three years ago. All of them had had the significant rose carved across their backs.

The file was thin on any other information regarding the serial killer. Apparently the carvings had been performed with a variety of sharp instruments, and the quality of the work had remained constant over the decades.

No suspects were listed by name, but there were a handful of added files concerning interrogations of known sexual offenders. No mention whatsoever was made of Felix Carey.

She stroked the keyboard again and got the names of the chief investigators of the Bleeding Rose Butcher's homicides. There were six of them. Four of them were dead. The remaining two were still alive, living on pensions in and around the city. Robert Ames was seventy-eight, living in Rolling Meadows Senior Citizens' Home, and had been logged onto the Butcher case more times than any of the other chief detectives.

She copied Ames's address onto her notepad, closed up the lapdeck, and left.

"The Bleeding Rose Butcher," Ames said with a persimmony twist to his wrinkled lips. They looked blue in the sunlight slicing through the trees overhead. He scratched his iron-gray hair, smoothed it toward his balding crown, and leaned back in the lawn chair. He was reed-thin, of medium height, and wore a trench coat over his pajamas. "Ain't heard about him in a long, long time."

"I know," Shay said. She passed over a copy of the photograph Fitzgerald had given her.

Ames took it in a shaking hand, smoothed it against his lap, and studied the scene through thick-lensed glasses. Then he turned it over, pulled a crumpled pack of cigarettes from his coat, shook one out, and thrust it between his lips. Waving the curling wreath of smoke out of his face, Ames said, "Sadistic son of a bitch. Got close to him, almost caught him a time or two. Then he'd up and vanish like fog."

"Who was he?" Shay asked.

Ames gave her a hard squint. "I know you got the ID and all, but you look kind of young for the homicide game, sweet cheeks."

Shay bit her tongue and smiled instead. "According to the files, you weren't any older than I am when you took your first crack at the Butcher."

"You that old?"

"Yeah."

He laughed for a moment, then it turned into a barking cough that almost shook the cigarette from his hand. "I know a lot of women who wouldn't want their age to be known."

"Yeah, well, they're not carrying my caseload. I don't have room for vanity right now."

"You working the Butcher files as a hobby case?" Ames asked.

Shay shook her head. "Officially I'm assigned to the Bayou Ripper."

"Why are you interested in the Butcher?"

"That picture I gave you isn't from the Butcher file. That tattoo turned up on the back of a woman murdered the day before yesterday."

"Son of a bitch." Ames took his glasses off, held them over the picture, and studied the details through one lens.

"Is that his work?"

"Looks like. But my eyesight ain't what it used to be. Still, I'd never be able to forget that goddam brand of his."

"I've read the file," Shay said. "Says there that the Butcher was believed to be an older man, but there wasn't a name."

"Damn straight there wasn't a name." Ames shifted uneasily in the lawn chair. "You wearing a wire?"

"No."

"Got anybody listening in over your com-chip?"

"No."

The old man scanned the parking lot on the other side of the black wrought-iron fence walling the south side of the rest home. "Anybody with you?"

"No."

"You got a partner?"

Shay felt the icy loss run through her. "No. He's dead. He got killed trying to stop the Ripper."

"Sorry," Ames said in a soft voice. "Know how that one feels."

Shay gave him a tight nod.

"Is that why you're working this case even though you've been unofficially pulled off it?"

Shay gazed at the man silently.

He showed her his empty palms in a wry grin. "Comes with the territory, lady. Once a cop, always a cop. I never go to a sit-down with anybody unless I know answers to most of those questions. I made a few phone calls after you set up this little meet."

"I think they're backing off the right guy," Shay said.

"You figure the priest for the Ripper?"

"To the last decimal point."

"Then why the interest in the Butcher? That priest is a kid. Way the hell too young to have been the Butcher. Unless you're thinking reincarnation or something."

"With the techware possible these days," Shay replied honestly, "reincarnation's not something you can rule out."

"So why the Butcher?"

"That picture you're holding," Shay said, "makes the tie. The bleeding rose tattoo says Butcher, but the DNA found on the scene points back to the Ripper."

"And nobody's stopped to ask why he's changed his MO?"

"Just me."

"What do you know about the Bleeding Rose Butcher?"

"Only what I found in the files."

Ames tapped the picture thoughtfully. He dropped his cigarette to the yard and stomped it out with a slippered foot. "This case, there was a lot of pressure on it from the git-go. Everybody wanted it solved, but the brass got skittish about where the trail was leading."

"I've been there," Shay said. She throttled her own need to push the man.

"Everybody figured a street guy for the kills," Ames said. "That's who he picked as his victims. People living in the streets. Had an affinity for them, we figured. So when we started getting cross-wired on information we got back from the field, we had to rethink things. Witnesses described the Butcher as best they could. Guy wasn't street material. Maybe he was at one time, but not any more. He had money, enjoyed flashing it around at first, then wised up, I guess, because he suddenly realized that having it set him apart. A couple times his car was spotted as he took his victims to motels or their homes. The guy never used the same car, and he never used the same hotel."

"That indicates a certain financial latitude too."

"Yep." Ames nodded. "So we started checking out rich guys with kinks. We checked with vice, put people out on the street, and started catching nine kinds of hell from the top brass. You see, we were ruffling the feathers of some of the socially elite of this city. Suddenly the funding for the Butcher investigation started getting whacked. We couldn't get results, see?"

Shay nodded.

"So they penalized the task force. Took away man-hours, started leaning on the top field cops, gave them case overloads. A month after we started looking in the right direction, we no longer had a task force."

"But the Butcher kept killing?"

"Oh hell yes. He slowed down for a while, but he didn't go away. I suspect there's a few bodies we never uncovered."

Shay waited, then said, "You didn't back off, did you?"

"Not completely. Not at first. Then the captain found out I was still working the case on my off-hours and made sure I had too much to do to put in any free time. The Butcher case was reassigned to a young guy, a hot dog. To bring in new blood, I was told."

"You found a name, though, didn't you?"

Ames looked at her, his hooded gaze filled with decades of pain and suspicion. His voice was hoarse when he spoke. "Yeah, I found a name." He shifted in the lawn chair and pulled his robe a little tighter across his bowed shoulders. "Started checking the hotel rooms, got a guy to cut through the protective bullshit strung up by the hotel people and the Butcher's private defenses. Took me some time, and cost me some heavy favors. Each one of the rooms where the Butcher left his victims was registered to a different name that turned up as a false identity. They were paid for by credit card, but when we tracked them back they never connected. The companies they were assigned from told us the names on the cards weren't employees."

Tense with expectation, sure she knew what Ames was leading up to but not wanting to overplay her own need, Shay said, "You shifted focus from the fictitious employees to the companies themselves."

"Yeah. It seemed like a natural move."

"A lot of people wouldn't have thought of it."

Ames shrugged. "I was deep in that case, detective. I would have moved heaven and hell if I could have reached them."

"You found a connection?"

"Yeah. All the companies involved were owned by one conglomerate."

"Who?"

Ames shifted his gaze away from her.

"That name," Ames said, "can get you killed." He waved at the grounds of the retirement center. "The life I got, it ain't much, but it's all I got. My years on the force, spent carrying that gold shield and seeing things no human being should be asked to see, they don't mean nothing. I lost a good marriage, lost my kids, ended up with ashes of an existence spent working against the grain. I'm the only one who gives a shit about me. You understand that?"

"Yeah," Shay said in a soft voice. "Yeah, I do."

Ames fell silent and turned his attention to the traffic out on the street.

Shay sorted through her options, knew she couldn't force the information from the old man, and didn't look forward to the opportunity to unleash a guilt trip on the guy. And she knew guilt would have worked. Ames had been a homicide cop who cared about the job he'd done. Guilt was a part of the job, because a homicide cop lived with the fact that he or she got there too late to help the victim.

"What have you got?" Ames asked quietly.

"I think I've got the Butcher," Shay said, "and I think I've got the Ripper too."

"How?"

"It gets complicated."

"I can see how it would. Especially since the Butcher should be a dead man."

"Let me give you a name," Shay suggested. "If it fits the Butcher, you let me know and I'll go away."

"Just like that?"

"Yeah. Just like that."

"You going to try to sell this to your captain? That a dead man is going around murdering these women?" Ames tapped the photograph.

"It's the truth as I see it."

"He's not going to believe you."

"That's the risk I have to take."

"And you'll keep me out of it?"

"Yeah. All I've got are the files. Anything you could say would be hearsay, not admissible in court."

Ames appeared to consider that.

"If we let him go," Shay said, "more women are going to end up dead."

"I tried everything I could to stop the guy. They wouldn't let me pursue the investigation any further. Made everybody too nervous. And I could have been wrong." He dropped the cigarette and crushed it underfoot. "Dammit. You sound too sure of yourself."

"I am. If I wasn't, I wouldn't be here."

"So give me the name of the Butcher," Ames said, and leaned forward.

"Felix Carey," Shay said.

Ames nodded. "That's the name."

Shay used the video uplink on the telephone when she made the call to the Dallas Police Department, and asked for vice. Normally she didn't like using the feature except with close family. For one thing it cost more, and for another it forced a feeling of intimacy with the other person she usually wasn't comfortable with. But she wanted to see the person she was calling, wanted to understand past the words he would be able to give her.

Abruptly the screen cleared from the image of the Dallas PD's protect-and-serve logo. A head-and-shoulders shot of the man was framed in the viewer. Behind him were the cramped walls of a departmental office painted an obviously unplanned two-tone beige.

"Detective Mick Traven?" Shay asked.

"Yeah." Traven regarded her coolly. He was not a handsome man, but neither was he plain. The street had stamped its brand on him, made him hard and cautious, tempered it with an ability to make a quick decision and stick to it. Shay had seen the same kind of look in the faces of the narco cops she'd worked with. A scar sliced through his features, and pink skin testified that cosmetech surgeries had been unable to eradicate the disfigurement completely. Personally, Shay thought the scar gave the man character. His dark, unruly hair, beard stubble, and dark blue eyes fit the battered black duster he wore over a chambray work shirt.

"I'm Detective Bethany Shay," she said, adding her badge ID number, "of the Houston PD."

"What can I do for you?"

"You handled the Mr. Nobody case in Dallas last year," Shay said.

Traven's blue eyes narrowed and dark glints floated almost hidden in them. He nodded.

"I'd like to ask you some questions."

"The report's been filed," he said. "I can get you a copy sent over today." He gave her a facetious grin. "Or you can wait another few weeks and catch the book when it comes out. Reporter named Robin Benedict covered it, and did a good job from what I hear."

"I've looked through the files," Shay replied. The stacks of paper sat beside the recliner.

"So how can I help you?"

"I need to know something that wasn't in those reports."

"Everything was in those reports."

"Not everything," Shay said. "I need to know what it was like to go inside Brandstetter's mind."

For a moment he just stared at her, his face lean and fox-like. Then his finger stabbed out for the disconnect button. "Look, lady, I've got a busy schedule, and that's not a subject I particularly care to talk about."

Shay had known that going in. From the rumors she'd heard in the last few months, she knew Traven was still dealing with backlash from his experiences. The scars on his face weren't the only ones, and the psychological ones would take even longer to heal. "Don't," she said.

Traven's hand froze. "Why?"

"Because," Shay said, "I think I'm dealing with something similar down here. And I need your help because the department doesn't want to back me."

Traven's hand dropped back as she began to explain about the Bayou Ripper and the Bleeding Rose Butcher.

40

Adjusting the metronomic slap of the wiper blades, Felix Carey drove the luxury car mechanically and worked to force the repressed rage out of his system. Rain continued to pelt the windshield, made the night a total black that hovered threateningly above the city and seemed on the verge of sucking buildings, streets, and citizens into a lightless void.

Accessing the matrix feed, he tried to connect with the priest again, tried to force the union of awareness. He felt Almendariz there in the back of his own mind, but he couldn't get the man to open up to him.

He cursed and retired from his efforts at communication. He swept the street with his eyes.

With the hard rain coming down and flooding the city, there weren't many prostitutes working the streets. The boys and women huddled in the recesses of buildings and shops, talking and sharing cigarettes. Glowing orange dots illuminated hard-featured faces and drug-dulled eyes briefly.

He came to a stop in front of a boot shop with a green-and-white-striped awning. Eight people, nearly evenly divided between male and female, milled about underneath it. They looked at him in open speculation.

Carey singled out the woman of his choice, wished that the decision wasn't so businesslike and that he could be pulled to her by lust instead of simple expediency. She was a few inches over five feet in height, and five more pounds would have changed her from well-endowed to plump. Long brunette hair spilled across her shoulders, and her eyes were dark pools set into a face that seemed to challenge and mock at the same time. She wore jeans and a simple white T-shirt with a current movie poster printed on it.

He killed the wiper blades, shut off the radio, and left the engine running. Taking the wallet containing tonight's false ID from inside his jacket, he thumbed out three hundred-dollar bills, then fanned them across the passenger-side window so they could be seen even in the weak streetlight.

The money removed all hesitation and the crowd surged forward, moved in hopeful, hopping skips as they held paper bags and their hands above their heads.

Carey thumbed the window down, listening to the quick pitches from males and females alike as they attempted to crowd into the car. He didn't release the door lock, and he kept his hand on the window control ready to close it.

"You," he said, and pointed to the brunette.

A pleased smile with all the real emotion of a shark's grin twisted her lips. The rest of the prostitutes quickly drew back to the shelter of the awning, grumbling and cursing their luck.

Carey allowed her to open the door, and she slid in.

"Thanks, mister," she said. "You won't be sorry. Damn, it's a cold night. I was afraid I was going to be standing out there for hours."

Carey drove unhurriedly, marked the streets and his passage against the mental map he'd drawn. Occasionally he reached for Almendariz but was unable to find the man. But he knew the priest was there somewhere, and he knew he could get him when he needed to. He smiled, felt warm at the thought.

"Hey," the woman said brightly, "you got a nice smile there."

He looked at her and said thanks.

Unable to access his Bible deck directly, Almendariz retreated to his memories of the Book of Exodus. He closed his eyes inside his own mind and built up the reality around him.

When he opened his eyes again, the desert was harsh around him, the glare from the sun blinding. Yellow sand spilled in three directions, blocked away in the fourth by the immense pyramid being constructed before him. Beads of perspiration ran down his nearly naked body, and the burn of the sun moved restlessly under his skin. His hands and feet were caked with sores and cracked open to release infections when he moved. His throat was parched and swollen from dehydration.

A leather harness chaffed under his arms and down his back. He tested the weight with a bleeding fist, turned to see what he was pulling.

At the other end of the leather strands was a woven net latched securely behind a huge squared-off block. The block trundled along over wooden poles carefully placed by other men dressed as he was.

"Back to work, slave. They're waiting for you."

Almendariz turned toward the voice automatically. Without warning a length of braided leather uncoiled toward him and caught him on his bare shoulder. Pain flared through his synapses, almost caused him to stumble and fall. A ribbon of bright blood spilled down his arm, twisted around the stringy muscles.

He moaned as he struggled with the leather straps and leaned his weight into them. The block moved more surely across the wooden poles, pressing them deeply into the shifting sands trickling between his bare toes.

A final flick of the whip wrote fiery pain across his neck.

For a moment he considered backing out of the mental world he'd created for himself. There were other memories he could channel from the Bible deck, ones that were much more pleasant. Except that he didn't feel that he deserved them.

The block followed behind him as he pulled with the other slaves. The sour smell of the sweat and dirt caked on them moved sluggishly around him, and he knew some of it was coming from the body he now inhabited. Placing his foot on the incline of the pyramid, he took the first step on the arduous task of hauling the stone into place above him. One of his feet split open and bled.

He deserved to suffer, he told himself. Carey had fooled him, had perverted his faith and used it against him.

Abruptly his bleeding foot betrayed him, slipping out behind him. Before the other slaves could regain the momentum, the block's weight dragged them helter-skelter back down the side of the structure.

For a moment he was dazed. Then the overseer's whip smashed into his face again and again, drawing blood. He held his hands up before him to protect himself. His palms and fingers were flayed to the bone in seconds. Blood streamed down his wrists to his elbows and dripped into the baked sand to be greedily sucked away.

Blinded by the pain and the terror that filled the slave, Almendariz almost flipped out of the experience.

Then, like sound torn away in gale-force winds, he heard

Carey calling for him, demanding he come back into his own mind.

Shivering, Almendariz forced himself to endure the pain and scramble to his feet again. He took up the straps and pulled himself up the side of the pyramid as quickly as possible.

Inside the motel room, a white robe with the motel's insignia on it covering his nakedness, Carey stared down at the battered hooker tied to the round bed. Her head still swung back and forth occasionally as she struggled to scream against the gag in her mouth. Streams of spittle ran down her cheeks and stained the chartreuse satin sheets.

Carey delighted in the absolute terror that shone in her eyes. He placed a hand on her breast, rubbed the fear-hardened nipple with his palm, and stroked the emotion to new heights. But the delight he felt wasn't strong enough to enthuse the priest's libido. The borrowed genitalia hung there flaccid and unmoving.

"Just hang in there, bitch," he said with a smile. "It's going to get better. Trust me."

She closed her eyes and tried to scream again. Only a choked, gasping cry came from her straining throat.

Reaching into the jacket draped across the chair near the bed, Carey took out the small techbox Welbourne had given him earlier. He'd known after the first woman that he would have problems getting Almendariz to come around to his way of thinking, and the techbox was supposed to be the answer.

It was squared, slightly less than four inches to a side and just over a quarter inch thick. Black plastic encased a complicated chip infrastructure he'd been briefed on. Pushing gently with a forefinger, he uncovered the trode wire and slipped it out. He jacked it into the priest's head, annoyed at the small pang of nausea that twisted his stomach. It reminded him of how little was actually left of him outside the matrix.

"I'll be back," Carey promised as he sat up straight, "and I'm bringing a friend." He hit the button and activated the canned programming.

Cyberspace slammed into him like a big black wave and swept him away in the undertow. He went with it readily.

Almendariz was curled into a fetal ball in the back of the mind they shared.

Carey called the priest's name but got no answer. He accessed the techbox and upped the power, felt his mind forcibly meld with Almendariz's, overlaid it like the peel covering the pulp of an orange. He had a brief impression of a desert and a pyramid, thought he identified it as Egypt, then the scene was blown away in a hurricane of sand as the imagery disrupted.

"What are you doing here?" Almendariz demanded as he got to his feet and stood in the emptiness of black space. As always now, he wore his priest's clothing in the matrix, the collar of his shirt a brilliant white.

Reflexively Carey established a half-dozen points of light—distant suns he didn't even bother to name—to give himself a sense of direction. "I came for you."

"No," Almendariz said. "You will stay away from me. You are a *thing*, accursed by God. You can't hold me in your power forever."

Carey channeled his anger and used it to ignite his own weak passions. "God has nothing to do with this."

"You lie. You are an abomination."

"Am I?" Carey stepped forward, smiled slightly when Almendariz flinched back. "Do you know why you are afraid of me? You're afraid of me because you see yourself in me and you don't want to admit it." He accessed the matrix, reformed his cyberself into an exact mirror image of Almendariz, and dropped into the same pose as the priest's. "If I'm accursed, then so are you," he said in the priest's voice.

"No."

"Yes," Carey said, and he showed Almendariz one of his own smiles. "You're so in love with the idea of someone else taking responsibility for your actions and passions that you don't want to face them within yourself."

"Liar!"

"Truth!" Carey shouted. "If you are good and righteous, you credit your God with your behavior. If you see yourself as evil, you blame it on the taint in your soul. And you have an out if you fail to live up to your expectations because you know you were born with sin. I don't remember where the Bible says that, but I know that it does."

"What do you want here?" Almendariz demanded. "You have my body. Isn't that enough?"

"No," Carey replied. "And I wish that it was. But it's not. I have to possess that craving that lies at the heart of you as well."

"It's no craving. You make it sound dirty. It was a Gift, from God, something to be revered."

"It's an appetite. Nothing more. But it is special. Not everybody can do or experience the things and emotions that you and I do. We share a taste for exquisite pleasures in the physical life that most other men can't dream of." Carey accessed the matrix, opened a window into his own mind, and gave it physical representation. A flat projection flared into view like a wallscreen, slightly above and to one side of them. When the gray clouds on the screen pulled away, it revealed the prostitute lying bound and gagged on the motel-room bed. "She's ours," he said in a seductive whisper. "All ours. We only have to reach out and take her."

Almendariz tried to keep from looking at the window. Carey saw the physical struggle inside the priest, saw the sheer effort it took for the man to try to fight his own desires. At length, Almendariz's eyes were drawn to the helpless naked flesh stretched across the bed, and he was captivated by the scene. He lifted his hands to touch the window, then recoiled when his fingers passed through.

"No!" the priest shouted.

The image shuddered at his touch, rippled like the reflection on a stirred lake surface.

"I won't have any part of this."

"You already have a part of it, fool," Carey snarled. "Just open up to it and let it breathe."

"No. I will not serve Him this way."

Carey resumed his own form. "You and your God." He spat. "Don't you realize this is what life is all about? The sheer carnality of it all? The world is full of takers and givers. You're a wolf in a world of sheep, and you don't even want to face the greatness that is within you. You will see yourself for what you are, priest," He snared a gridline and accessed the matrix, then exploded the world he'd created.

In the motel room again, Carey slid on top of the prostitute, feeling her warmth against the priest's body. His back and arms held him above her despite the aches and pains from Almendariz's past surgeries. Staring into her eyes, seeing the priest's face reflected back at him, he tapped the techbox and jacked back into cyberspace.

Thunder cracked, and silvered ball lightning chain-flashed throughout cyberspace.

Carey accessed the Bible files from the matrix, brought a borrowed reality into existence, and plugged himself and Almendariz into it. When he opened his eyes he stood on a hill in front of a cross where a man was spiked to the wood through his wrists and feet, and tied with ropes as well. Blood had almost stopped leaking from the wounds at his extremities, and from the scratches and holes made by the crown of thorns on his head.

"Almendariz," Carey called, and reached for the priest. When he had the man, he forced Almendariz's consciousness into the body of the man hanging from the cross.

The figure on the cross changed and became the priest. The hair became blond and the pain-filled eyes turned blue. "No," Almendariz screamed into the dark skies overhead. He struggled briefly against the spikes and the ropes.

Carey glanced down at himself and noted that he was dressed in leather armor and sandals that had seen better days. A short spear leaned against the rocks an arm's reach away.

Two other men hung on either side of the priest, but their slumped posture and the incessant buzzing of flies landing on their open eyes and parted lips gave testimony that they were long dead. Down the hill a crowd of spectators were kept in peaceful formation by more men dressed in uniforms similar to Carey's.

"Calvary," Almendariz whispered through cracked and bleeding lips.

Taking up the short spear, Carey stepped in front of the priest and looked up at him. "Isn't this what you wanted?"

Almendariz stared down at him. His eyes held suffering and fear and a glint of madness. "What are you doing?"

"Helping you realize your dreams."

"You're insane. You don't know what you're doing."

"You wanted to be a fucking martyr," Carey yelled above the swirling winds. "I'm just here to help you out, let you try the role on for size."

Turning his face toward the black heavens, Almendariz

drew a ragged breath and cried out, "O my Father, why hast Thou forsaken me?"

"Because," Carey said as he took up the spear, "He doesn't give a shit about you." He thrust the spear into Almendariz's side with all the strength the Roman soldier possessed, drove the iron tip toward the man's beating heart.

Almendariz screamed as the spear transfixed him, then shuddered and lay still against the cross.

Carey drew the spear out, accessed the matrix, and restarted the programmed events a handful of seconds before he'd stabbed Almendariz. Reality wavered. He stared again into the priest's astonished and pain-racked face. "It's not over," he said. He thrust home again, accessed the matrix, and restarted the programming. Reality waved once more.

Almendariz was on the cross again, the flesh of his side unblemished.

"I can keep this up for a very long time," Carey promised. "It doesn't matter to me." He watched the spear go sliding skillfully under the priest's last rib. Accessing the matrix, he began again. Reality stuttered, then started over.

"No," Almendariz cried out weakly.

"Yes," Carey grunted as he shoved the spear into Almendariz's side. "This is what you fucking well wanted, priest. Now take it." He accessed the matrix and reality blinked back to the beginning.

"Stop," Almendariz begged. Tears gleamed in his eyes, and the madness trapped in them shone like a beacon.

"No," Carey said. "You've been wanting all your fucking life to climb up on that damned cross. Now you're going to learn the truth of what it really means." He thrust again, feeling the warmth of fluids and blood drench his hands and the wooden haft of his weapon. He used the matrix to begin again. The wood became dry.

"Stop!"

Carey thrust again, absorbed the fear he felt inside Almendariz, and wedded it to the passion he'd already managed to stoke to life. When he checked the gridline holding him to the physical world inside the motel room, he found his physical body was responding. He stepped back into the room for a moment, found the skinning knife in his clothing, and held it tightly in his fist.

"No more," Almendariz croaked helplessly.

Ignoring the plea, Carey rammed the spear home as hard

as he could. It plowed through the priest's cyberflesh and ripped through his heart, and the iron point jutted suddenly from the base of his throat. Blood flew from the wounds and from his open mouth.

When he accessed the matrix this time, Carey reached out for Almendariz, sucked him into the body of the Roman soldier with him. The form on the cross became that of Jesus. Controlling the soldier's body, aware that Almendariz's presence had been grafted onto his, Carey stepped forward and thrust the spear vigorously.

Flesh gave way before the iron head.

Carey held the spear in place as the body on the cross kicked out its last few moments of life. He felt as if he could hear the priest's warm breath in his ear. Accessing the matrix, he repeated the murder three more times, eased out of control by degrees until the final blow was struck by Almendariz without any coaxing.

"Now," Carey said, "considering that life is much like that spear you're holding, which end of it do you want to be on?"

As if suddenly realizing what he had done, Almendariz threw the spear away and collapsed into a sobbing heap at the base of the cross. Blinded by tears, he reached up to hug the corpse's ankles to his face and chest.

Riding high on the rampant emotions released by the priest, Carey accessed the matrix and erased the spikes and ropes holding the body to the cross. In the slow motion it came tumbling down, wrapped its flailing dead arms around Almendariz, and smeared his face with its bloody features.

Almendariz screamed in horror.

Coiled up within the excess passion, Carey snared a gridline and shot back into the motel room.

He was hard now, and he bucked his hips forward to take the woman. Her flesh gave way before him, parted easily, and he glided into her. The skinning knife's blade sparked once as it sliced through her exposed throat. Her lips moved but no sound came out. Blood cascaded over her naked breasts.

Carey lunged on to completion, screaming in savage exultation when he hit his peak inside the dead woman. There *was* a god in his world, and he was it. And Almendariz was that much closer to realizing it too.

41

"What the fuck are you doing here?" Doug Chaney demanded.

Shrugging through the packed doorway into the hotel room, Bethany Shay ignored the young detective, briefly noted that he lacked his usual refreshed appearance; he looked frayed and worn this morning. A quick glance around the room showed her that Espinoza had engineered a meet with the head of the crime scene team in the corner near the couch area behind the small wet bar.

"Hey," Chaney said, "I asked you a question, Shay." He started for her.

Shay used a forensic member videotaping the blood-spattered body lying in the twisted sheets as a blocker, made headway into the room before Chaney could intercept her.

A newscopter juked back and forth in front of the balcony windows like a hovering dragonfly before the crime scene chief noticed it and bellowed orders to a subordinate. The drapes were quickly drawn.

"Who the fuck let her into the building?" Chaney asked the uniform standing guard at the door.

Lansdale was a seasoned street cop Shay had known for years, and she'd never known him to take anything off anyone that he didn't have coming. He came erect from his slouched posture beside the door, adjusted his equipment belt with both hands, and repeatedly poked Chaney in the chest with a forefinger, driving the man back out of his face. "Listen, junior, you wanna get me a goddam guest list together, I'll start paying attention. For right now she's got a detective's shield same as you, and I figure that's invite enough."

"Ah, batshit," Chaney said as he dropped the argument and started for Shay again.

Ron Barker stood beside the bed taking notes. He glanced

up from his battered notepad long enough to favor Shay with a scowl. It was a close race between his hair and his sports coat as to which was more rumpled.

"Shay," Chaney called, dodging technicians who grumbled in his wake.

Swallowing a yawn, eyes still burning from the long hours she'd pulled the previous night putting all the facts and suppositions together on the case, Shay made for Espinoza.

Espinoza, not a hair out of place even at 6:37 A.M., saw her as Chaney dropped a hand on her shoulder.

Slowing for just an instant, Shay reached up and caught Chaney's hand in hers. She caught the pressure points in his hand with ease, applied the force, and dropped the detective to his knees. "Don't," she said without turning around, "*ever* make the mistake of putting your hands on me again."

Chaney mewled in pain as she released his hand.

Work in the room came to a momentary halt as Chaney scrambled back to his feet and tried to appear graceful and unperturbed about it. When no one laughed it got a little easier.

"We need to talk," Shay said to Espinoza as she came to a halt in front of the homicide captain.

Espinoza glanced at Chaney, then back at her. "At least about a couple things. Come on." He dismissed the crime scene chief and led her to a back door, opened it, and went through into another bedroom.

"He did her in there?" Shay asked.

"Yeah."

"What did he use?"

"A skinning knife. We got the possible blade in an evidence bag."

"He left it here?"

"If it's the one that was used."

Shay looked at her boss, saw the relaxed stance he was in, and knew he was just waiting for her to wind down before he unloaded. Letting her run out of questions and confidence was his way of making sure she listened when he chose to speak. She didn't figure on slowing down until she was finished with what she'd come to say. The police scanner she'd kept by her bed had been sparing with details, but she'd figured the new homicide as the Ripper's. "Any DNA samples?"

"Semen," Espinoza said.

"On the body?"

"And in it."

"He raped her."

"We think so."

A knock sounded at the door, and Chaney stuck his head inside. "Captain—"

"Out," Espinoza growled.

"But, sir—"

Espinoza pinned him with his full attention. "Now, Chaney."

"Yes sir." The door closed a little louder than necessary.

"The DNA's going to match the Ripper," Shay said.

"You think so?" Espinoza seemed only mildly interested.

"Yeah. Same way the last murder matched the Ripper's."

"You've been talking to Fitzgerald."

Shay felt a flush of guilt when she realized she'd given up her friend's confidence and knew she was more tired than she was willing to believe. "Not really. I accessed some of his files."

The look Espinoza gave her clearly showed he didn't believe her.

Unlimbering the lapdeck from under her arm, Shay flipped it open and placed it on the desk against the wall. She stroked the keys and brought her personal files up. The screen rainbowed with colors, settled into a picture of the bleeding-rose tattoo favored by the other serial killer she believed they were chasing. "Recognize this?"

Espinoza nodded.

Shay knew the man was only giving her enough rope to hang herself. She took a deep breath and rushed on. "Is it on the woman in there?"

"Yeah." Espinoza rubbed his smooth cheeks with a forefinger and clenched his jaw muscles. "I guess Fitzgerald's files aren't the only ones you've made available to yourself lately."

"This isn't from the Constance Hardy case," Shay said. She pointed to the reference file number and date in the lower-left-hand corner.

"Forty-seven years ago?" Espinoza asked.

"Yeah," Shay replied. Her fingers hit the keyboard again, jumped through the file photos. "And that's not the only one." She verbally outlined the Bleeding Rose Butcher serial murders, pointing out the obvious similarities to the new homicides besides the tattoo.

"Where are you trying to take this?" Espinoza asked, obviously interested in spite of himself.

"I'm trying to help you understand," Shay answered. "We're not after one killer. We're after two. Almendariz is the Ripper."

"Chaney and Barker don't agree with you. Neither does the DA's office."

"Do you know where Almendariz is?"

Espinoza shook his head. "Not since he left the church." His accusation was no less sharp for not being voiced.

Shay pushed her guilt to one side, concentrated on the issues she'd outlined for herself. "That puts Almendariz with Felix Carey."

"Felix Carey," Espinoza repeated. "As in Carey International, Limited?"

"Yeah." Shay punched the keyboard, brought up the decades-old files. "I'm convinced that Carey was the Bleeding Rose Butcher."

Stepping in front of the lapdeck screen, Espinoza said, "Convince me."

Carefully, threading together the physical evidence from the old cases with the creative leaps she'd taken, she took him through her hypothesis. "Two killers," she repeated when she'd finished, "one body between them. You're familiar with zombyte chips?"

Espinoza nodded.

"I believe Carey interfered with the Ripper case enough to set Almendariz free, got him legal counsel, then took him when he hit the streets."

"And used a zombyte chip to crawl inside his mind?"

Shay recognized the undercurrent of doubt in the homicide captain's words. "Yes."

"No."

"Captain, you've got to listen to me. Almendariz *is* the Ripper, and Carey is using him."

"To go out and murder women?" Incredulity showed in his features.

"Yes."

"Like Almendariz was some kind of exosuit?"

Shay knew she was losing him. "I don't know exactly

how it works. If it were that easy, Carey could have used anyone. Maybe he has before."

"It would be stupid for Carey to go after Almendariz when the guy was running such a high profile."

"Unless he needs Almendariz that bad to do what he wants to do."

"You don't know that."

Shay squeezed out a short breath and took the plunge. "That tracer chip Foley found on my office lapdeck?"

Espinoza regarded her in stony silence.

"I swiped it from the evidence room and had it traced. It led back to Carey International."

"And you compromised the evidence. Dammit, Beth, you're no rookie. You know better than that."

"Fuck it, Captain. That chip was sitting there, nobody doing anything with it. I took it and got some results."

"Results we can't use."

"We know where to look."

"Maybe." Espinoza rubbed his hands together in front of him and stared at the floor.

"What do you mean, 'maybe'?"

"You know the kind of people you're talking about here?" Espinoza demanded. "Carey's got money and influence up the ass. With him in the picture—if it's true—it's no wonder Homicide's been feeling the pressure it has to back down off Almendariz. And it's no wonder the DA's office has backed off either."

"Curled up and died, you mean." She met his glare unflinchingly, let her own anger show through and keep her strong. "You can't ignore this."

"I'm not going to," Espinoza replied.

"Then let me follow it up."

"No." His denial was flat and low in the room.

"That bastard is responsible for Tully getting killed. We had Almendariz pegged, and Carey killed Tully to keep the son of a bitch free."

"I want you to stay away from this."

"I'm not going to make you any promises." Shay tried to keep the emotional side of things out of it, but it was too hard.

"Then I want your shield and gun," Espinoza said. He held out his hand. "You're suspended until further notice."

Shay stood without moving for a long, silent moment, ignored the hand stretched out to her. "If we don't lock this thing down fast, more people are going to die. I have to ask myself how big the body count has to get before somebody's willing to take the risk to stop Carey and Almendariz. You want my shield, then you take it away from me. I earned it, and I gave up a lot to get it, because I believe in what it stands for: to serve and to protect. And I'm not going to just walk away from that."

Espinoza let his hand drop to his side. "I'll have charges drawn up against you within the hour."

"Fine. That just means I'll get my day in court. And if I'm wrong, I'll say that I'm wrong." She stared into his eyes, realized he wasn't going to say anything else, then turned around and left.

Shay held her detective's shield in her hand, turned so the noonday light glanced off it. The weight seemed both reassuring and confining.

Ryan Shay approached the corner booth in the Brass Rainbow carrying a wooden platter covered with two submarine sandwiches, a foaming bear mug, and a Diet Pepsi in a frosted glass. Two small packages of potato chips sat in a round wicker basket. He deposited the tray in the center of the table and sat. His thick, blunt fingers tore open one of the potato chip bags. "You look like somebody with something on her mind," he said without preamble. "Sounded like it on the phone, too. Now I see you staring at that shield like it's some kind of crystal ball."

"Sometimes," Shay replied, "I've thought it was."

"Carrying a shield doesn't mean you know everything there is to know about right and wrong either."

"Dad, I've got a handle on this case. I just can't get hold of it."

"Espinoza won't back you?"

"No. And in a way I can't blame him. I really can't. His position is politically correct. And even if he did back the play I want to make, chances are departmental involvement might blow it."

"You're working somebody with heavy influence?"

"Yes."

"Is there anything I can do?"

"Just believe in me, Dad, and tell me that you love me,

because I'm scared to do anything, and I'm scared that if I don't, I won't be able to live with myself."

Ryan Shay reached across the table and took her hand. "Don't do anything foolish, Kitten," he said in a low voice filled with concern.

When she said "I won't," she knew she was lying.

Kiyoshi agreed to meet her in the private conference room of the corporate building, and then kept her waiting almost a half hour. Keeping her waiting was meant to be an insult, and an opening bid in whatever conversation they had.

Shay tried not to let it bother her much. That Kiyoshi had agreed to the unannounced meeting at all was several points in her favor. She kept her focus on that, and on what she might be able to gain from her ex-husband if she handled things correctly.

The conference room didn't look any different. A long oval table crafted of inlaid dark woods sat in the center of the room under a ceiling that had to be at least twelve feet high. Furnishings were Spartan, consisted of a few serving tables against the walls, pots containing twisted and sculpted bonsai trees and flowering plants. The wall overlooking the street ninety-seven stories below was tuned to an aquarium scene. Darting flashes of golds, silvers, blacks, crimsons, and blues threaded through an underwater seascape that filled the entire wall.

Twenty-seven minutes after her arrival—Shay had automatically logged the time because of her training—Kiyoshi entered the room.

He walked to the head of the table without looking at her. As usual, he looked every inch the corporate head in his black suit with the crisp white collar and cuffs showing. "Please," he said, waving to a chair at the table, "have a seat."

"I'd rather stand," Shay replied. She saw in his eyes that he'd immediately taken her answer as a hostile one. "How is Keiko?"

"She is fine." He sat.

She could tell by the tension in his back and shoulders that he was fully prepared to be challenged on his ability to care for their daughter by himself. "I knew she would be, but it's nice to hear it."

He relaxed a little, and the corner of his left eye tightened the way it always did when events perplexed him.

A side door opened and a geisha came in bearing a tray with coffee and a soft drink. She served them out, Kiyoshi first, politely and silently, then disappeared again.

The woman's beauty hurt Shay and dredged up memories she didn't want to remember around Kiyoshi. In her mind she could see Kiyoshi and Tamaki again as she'd found them shortly before her marriage had ended. She'd known even then that Kiyoshi had intended her to find them, in order to put an end to the lie they were both struggling to cling to. Amazingly, she still recalled the scent of the woman's perfume.

"I do not mean to rush you," he said, "but there are many things I must still do today."

"Of course." She pulled the tab on the soft drink to buy herself some time. It hissed, helped push the pain and the memory back into the niche it had crawled from.

"I've been told your lawyer is preparing an appeal regarding your rights to see my daughter."

"Yes." Shay bit off her immediate retort, thought of the regrets and truths her father had shared with her.

"Of course, you know that my counsel will attempt to quash any such claim."

"Yes." She cleared her throat, tried to make her voice calm. "Our daughter is not some prize to be won, Kiyoshi, nor is she a goal this corporation should actively seek."

"I *am* this corporation now," he said in open rebuke. "And Keiko is my daughter. My father always believed in the sanctity of family. I do nothing now that would offer his memory disgrace or dishonor."

"No, and I didn't meant to imply that you were. If that was your impression, then I offer my apologies."

"They are accepted."

Shay waited, not knowing how to go on, suddenly on the verge of tears for no reason that she could name.

Kiyoshi shifted in his chair, leaned forward, and placed his elbows on the tabletop and his palms together. "This is not like you. Since we have been apart, we have been nothing but the bitterest of enemies."

"Only because we couldn't find a way to follow our separate lives. Keiko binds us."

He nodded.

"If I could," Shay said, "I would let you go. But I can't seem to be able to do that without losing my daughter in the process."

"As I feel." Kiyoshi paused. "Do you think that we might be able to work out an arrangement between us that our lawyers and the judges have not? And how would you expect me to give up everything I have won? At present you have no control over Keiko. I am dealing from the position of power."

"She still knows I am her mother," Shay said in a hoarse voice, "and she knows you are keeping her from me. Do you ever consider how she might come to feel about you as she matures?"

"So you've come to play on my sympathies and fears of the future."

Shay shook her head. "No. I had not come to talk about Keiko at all, other than to find out how she was. There's too much hurt between us to talk about her without making things worse."

"So it would seem."

"I also came to apologize."

He regarded her with ill-concealed surprise.

"My father talked to me a few days ago," Shay said. "He helped me put a few things into perspective."

"Your father has never cared for me."

"My father is what he is."

"Yes." Kiyoshi nodded. "And that is one thing that I have admired about him. In an American world filled with inconsistencies, he is a constant."

"There was a time when I loved you so very much," Shay said in a soft voice. It amazed her how strong that feeling was still within her. She thought they'd killed it so very long ago. "You were everything I believed I ever wanted in my life. I didn't hold anything back from you, gave you everything I had inside. And I truly believe you did the same for me."

Kiyoshi didn't reply.

"The problem was," Shay went on, "it wasn't enough. We couldn't grow together, couldn't find a cornerstone for our dreams. After your father died, you had no choice about assuming leadership of the corporation. I didn't understand that. I'd been raised believing we have choices in our lives, that we didn't have to take responsibility for some things if

we didn't want to. I felt that we could choose our own lives.
I was wrong about some of that."

"Are you speaking about your own career?"

"Yes."

He gave her a sad smile. "You walk in your father's
shoes. You are not trapped."

"As you are?"

He didn't respond.

"Tell me," she said, "truthfully. If you could get out of
this building, away from this life, would you?"

Leaning back, he let the chair swallow him, stared with
unseeing eyes at the tropical fish swimming across the wall.

"Kiyoshi, the truth. We always had that between us when
we had nothing else. If we can't have that now, then I can't
talk to you."

"No," he replied softly.

"Why?"

"Because I can't."

"Because of the responsibility inherent in this position?"

He regarded her fiercely. "Hai. At times, when I am
alone, when I am faced with a decision that I alone must
make, that will possibly affect the life of every person connected with this corporation, I understand what drove my father to be the very best that he could be at this. It was not
greed that drove him, nor do I find that to be what motivates
my own career now. I have to perform my functions at the
peak of my abilities for the people depending on me."

"That's how I feel when I'm doing my job," Shay said.
"People depend on me to do the best that I can, or more of
them die. I can't walk away from that, because I'm damn
good at what I do."

"What you do is dangerous," Kiyoshi said. "You must
work the streets of this city, take chances where no one can
protect you and killers may freely take your life. They killed
your partner, Beth. It could just as easily have been you."

The emotion evident in his voice quieted her.

"Do you even think about that?" he asked.

"Not often. I can't think about that and do my job."

"I don't want my daughter growing up with the knowledge that her mother was killed on these city streets. I would
rather she lose you now, get over her loss now, than have to
see your corpse at some funeral. You live by your gun,
Beth."

"It's not like that," she said. "Not all the time."

"All it takes is once."

"You talk about the choices that I have open to me," she said. "But it's not as easy as you think. Could you get security to send my lapdeck up?"

Kiyoshi touched the table deck and issued the order.

Within seconds the geisha reentered the room, carrying the lapdeck.

Shay slipped the trode into the walljack and accessed her files. The aquarium scene blinked out of existence, and a series of dead faces paraded across the wallscreen. "Do you know these women?" she asked.

"Hai. They are the victims of the serial killer you've been pursuing."

"Yes." Shay moved through the file. "Once they were little girls much like Keiko. They were young, innocent, and their parents loved them. At least I know this to be true for most of them."

"These things happen. Murder in these streets has become a way of life for some people."

"True. And the organ jackals stand in line for dibs on the bodies before they even cool." She moved on, flicked through actual video footage of the bodies being removed from the water at different sites. "And if one of these women was Keiko twenty years from now?"

"The man who did it would be a corpse himself." Kiyoshi's voice was tight with emotion.

"Why?"

"That requires no explanation."

"Would you wait for the police to catch him?"

"No."

"Because you've got men like Hideo to take revenge for you."

Kiyoshi remained silent.

Shay turned to face him. "The parents of these women aren't so fortunate," she said softly. "They've got me, and other detectives like me. If I get assigned to the case and I don't give a damn, who's going to care about them?"

"That's not an issue to me."

"But it is to me. I don't just look for a killer for vengeance for the dead person," Shay said. "That doesn't do any good. When I go after someone like the Bayou Ripper, I look at my job as preventive maintenance. I don't think about how many lives I can avenge. I think about how many lives I can save. So you see, like you, I'm trapped by my position too. I'm good at what I do, Kiyoshi, and not that many people can handle what I do."

Kiyoshi's coffee had grown cold, and he made no move to touch it. "Why have you come here?"

"They won't let me do my job," she said flatly. "I was pulled off the case after the DA's office cleared Almendariz."

"They think you and your partner made a mistake."

"Yes. But they're wrong. And I found out there's been some political pressure put on the investigation. Someone with enough power to turn the mayor's office and the police commissioner's office inside out." With the aid of the lapdeck files, Shay quickly outlined her theories about Carey being the Bleeding Rose Butcher and wanting Almendariz's body for his own.

"What do you want from me?" Kiyoshi asked when she finished. It was obvious from his expression that he was having trouble accepting everything she'd said.

Shay hesitated only for an instant. "I want to get inside Carey's building and try to get proof that this is what's really going on."

Kiyoshi shook his head. "That is out of the question."

"You have people who can help me get in. I'm not asking for any assistance once I get inside. Just a door."

"I won't be part of the suicide pact you have drawn for yourself."

"What do you mean, 'suicide'?"

Kiyoshi spread his hands across the table. "If you are caught, you will be killed by Carey if he is guilty. At the very least, you will be committing political suicide, and possibly even draw a criminal sentence."

"There's no other way to stop them."

"The police department will find a way."

"No one will listen," Shay said.

"They will. In time. You will make them."

"And how many more women will have to die before they do?"

"I don't know."

Shay returned his level gaze full measure for a moment. "If you won't help me, I'll find someone else. And I don't fool myself for a moment that I know anyone else as good as Hideo and his people."

"And if you are caught?" Kiyoshi asked. "What will Keiko be left to think?"

"I can only hope that she understands eventually, and that she's proud of me."

Kiyoshi slapped the tabletop with an open palm. He wasn't given to frequent physical displays of emotion.

Shay stood her ground, waited.

"You are so damn stubborn," he said in a tight voice.

"Yes."

"I will not be a part of this no matter what you threaten me with." Kiyoshi turned, started to walk away.

"There is something I have to offer," Shay said. She trembled inside, hated the words she had to say, but knew she no longer had a choice.

Kiyoshi halted with a hand on the doorknob.

"I won't walk away from Keiko," Shay said. "I'll fight you tooth and nail for the rest of my life over her if I have to. I want you to understand that."

Kiyoshi didn't move.

"But if you help me with this," she went on, "no matter which way it goes, I'll resign from the police department. That's the only deal I have to make, and the only thing I can offer you. And you've got my word on it."

Without turning around, Kiyoshi said, "Go home and wait for my call. I will think about it." Then he was through the side door and gone.

Shay stood for a moment, lost in her feelings of helplessness and self-betrayal. The burbling of the wallscreen aquarium projection filled the large room. With shaking hands, still not knowing if she was doing the right thing and wasn't compromising too much of herself, she gathered the lapdeck and exited through the main door. By the time she hit the corridor she had squared her shoulders and locked her doubts inside herself.

Shay worked her backyard on her hands and knees, wore thin pliant gloves to protect her hands from the sharp blades of the weeds. The sun had almost faded from the sky, left a worn-out rainbow smudge of colors plastered along the western horizon, broken by the neon-dotted black fingers of sparse buildings. The eight stone lanterns shaped from Japanese mythology sat in ashen silence around the yard. Hardened candle wax clung to their exotic features.

As she pulled the weeds and stuffed them in the plastic trash bag at her waist, she recalled the last time Keiko had been with her. She'd envied her sister as she played with her daughter. Loryn had always been so attuned to the emotional needs of children. Keiko's remembered laughter pealed around her, lost her so deeply in it that for a moment she didn't realize the cordless phone was ringing for her attention.

She reached for it, scooped it up, punched it into operation, held it to her ear, and said, "Hello."

"Your offer is accepted." She recognized Hideo's voice instantly.

"Okay." Shay felt as if a concrete block had been dropped into her stomach. She'd known when she went to see Kiyoshi what it might cost her to get his help, but it was another to think of it as a done deal.

Hideo gave her an address that she recognized as only a few blocks from Carey International's home offices. "Be there at ten o'clock," the Izutsu family bodyguard said. "Come alone."

The phone clicked dead.

Shay punched it off, took a few deep breaths to unwind the sudden onslaught of knots in her stomach, then forced herself to her feet. She shifted the Glock from its position at her back, trying to make it ride more comfortably. A stress headache flared up from her back and shoulders.

Inside the house she took three analgesics, washed her face, and started making preparations for the night. However it turned out, she'd already put the thing in motion, and she wasn't about to back away from it.

42

Almendariz crossed his arms over his chest, closed his eyes, and held his breath as John the Baptist took him in his fierce grip. The murmur of voices along the riverbank grew louder as the prophet continued his message of repentance. Almendariz had never heard John the Baptist in finer glory, counting even those times when he'd jacked into the Bible deck and been the prophet himself.

"Are you ready then, son?" John the Baptist asked in a whisper, turning his attention back to Almendariz. They stood off the riverbank in the slow-moving water, soaked up to their waists. The odor of wet animals clung to the prophet from the hair shirt he wore. Fat droplets of water hung like glass beads from his honey-covered hair and beard. He looked more like a madman than a vessel of God. Almendariz didn't check his own reflection in the water.

"Yes," Almendariz replied.

Without further warning, the prophet dunked him. The cold, sand-colored waters closed over him. Sound went away except for the damp thud of his own heartbeat. It thudded in metronome, in stereo, till he felt as if it filled him. Just when he thought he could hold his breath no longer, he was pulled to the surface.

"May the peace of God be with you," John the Baptist said, "and be assured that your soul will know eternity." He slapped him on the back.

Almendariz coughed up water and rubbed grains of sand from his eyes. When he scanned the people lining the riverbank, he saw Jesus waiting among them, and was reminded instantly of how He looked hanging from the crucifix with the bloody wound in his side. Almendariz's hands could almost still feel the blood-slick spear.

Something white fluttered in the sky and heeled in Almendariz's direction unexpectedly. He pursued it with his gaze, aided by the dozens of arms pointing at the ivory heartbeat of motion.

The dove spread its wings at the last moment, dropped its feet, and came to a rest with its claws hooked securely in Almendariz's hair. Despite the sharp bite of the talons, he let the bird rest there, knowing what it represented and taking pride in what was to come.

The voice of the Lord pealed over the huddled masses. "Know you that I am the Lord, the Father of Jacob and Abraham. And know too that you are in the presence of My Son."

Almendariz wrapped himself in the love he felt pouring from the heavens. Carey, the succubi, his own flight from the police, that was part of some monstrous nightmare he was only now awakening from. He held his arms out as John the Baptist stepped back and bowed.

The hundreds of people lining the riverbank kneeled and dropped their heads.

Only Jesus remained standing. Then He stepped forward, walked on the water with one hand outstretched to Almendariz. He smiled, said, "Welcome, brother, We have waited so very long for you. Our House has been so empty without you."

The dove launched itself into the air. "Bullshit," it cried in a harsh screech.

Almendariz turned to face it as it flew in circles around him, his heart cold and heavy in his chest. He had to squint to make it out.

"Drivel," the dove screamed as it swooped toward his head.

As it neared, Almendariz made out the blasphemous changes that the bird had undergone. Instead of a smooth, sleek head, it wore the face of Felix Carey, only slightly larger than his thumb. Feathers grew in the place of Carey's hair, and formed a peaked white beard that poured down his chest. Carey's arms were barely defined, merged with the wings with only hints of fingers protruding.

"You fill your life with wishful fantasy, priest," Carey called out. He spiraled against the sun, became a black silhouette against the glare. "If your God cares anything for you, where is He?"

Tears leaked from Almendariz's eyes, and he shaded them

with one hand. "No," he yelled in frustrated anger. "Go away."

"Accept yourself for what you are," Carey said, revolving in a small, tight circle overhead.

"You can't turn me away from God."

"I haven't turned you away from God," Carey said. "He turned away from you. You just haven't realized that yet. Your answers are in the passions that drive you, not this false piety you struggle so fiercely to maintain."

Almendariz tried to wade out of the river. Muddy arms reached up from the bottom, curled around his legs, and held him fast.

"You can't run from what you are," Carey said. His laughter sounded more birdlike than human and sent shivers down Almendariz's spine. "You're only fooling yourself."

Wings flickered, then the dove with Carey's face blurred into motion, streaked for Jesus standing in bemused puzzlement on top of the river water.

"Don't!" Almendariz yelled. He tried to throw himself forward, but the muddy arms held him tight.

"Illusions," Carey crowed in delight. Just before he reached Jesus, the water opened up and swallowed Him. Jesus vanished without a trace, but Almendariz saw something dark and sinister moving in the dust cloud that erupted from the bottom. Blood spread over the surface. "You blind yourself to the truth, priest."

Almendariz wanted to collapse, but the arms held him upright.

"And you can't continue to be blind and be of any use to me." Carey flapped his wings, sped toward Almendariz with bared talons.

Reacting instinctively, Almendariz raised his arms to protect himself. He covered his eyes, wrapped his head as best as he could.

No one else moved.

Instead of the razored claws, warm blobs spread across Almendariz's head and shoulders. A foul odor became a heavy fog that rolled over him. When he glanced fearfully between his fingers, he saw that he was covered in green-and-white fecal matter.

The Carey dove soared toward the sun, laughing madly.

"No," Almendariz said hoarsely as he gazed at his stained hands. He screamed up at the retreating dove. "Stay away from me! Leave me alone!" He jacked out of the Bible-deck-inspired dream, launched himself deeper into his own mind, and tried to find a place where Carey couldn't reach him.

Standing in the real world, at the wall-sized window that overlooked downtown Houston from the actual room his personal matrix had made the center of his existence, Felix Carey grinned and took another sip of the excellent port Welbourne had located for him. He swirled the liquid through his teeth, relishing the sharp bite of taste. The matrix had been able to compensate for so many of his missing senses, but being locked in the priest's body gave him unique sensory access to things he had already experienced.

He put his hands to the glass, found it cold, and accessed the matrix to warm it. Immediately heat pulsed through the glass and leveled off at a comfortable temperature.

"Mr. Carey."

Carey turned and found Welbourne standing in the doorway. For so long Welbourne had been just a voice over the matrix gridline. He still wasn't used to looking at this incarnation of Welbourne. Even though he'd picked the man to replace Welbourne's last successor, it jarred him to see a stranger wearing the name of his old friend.

"The woman is ready, sir."

"Thank you, Welbourne." Carey tried to make the wineglass fade from his hand, then realized the matrix held no real power here. He sat it on a nearby table. Before, his trips from the matrix in the bodies of others had been limited. Now that he had found Almendariz, he rarely left the physical world.

Welbourne bowed and left. The door hissed closed.

Carey walked to the wall on his right, pressed his palm against it. Already recoded to accept Almendariz's print, the hidden door irised open and revealed a hidden elevator. He stepped inside, pressed the lighted control panel as the door closed. There was a brief drop that gave him a sense of disorientation.

When the door opened again, he walked out into the hallway to the room at the end. Specially soundproofed, the room was lost in the building's design, invisible.

He slid the panel back on the door and watched as the fluorescent lighting automatically came on.

The woman inside was little more than a girl, lean and

blond, with pale skin, big brown eyes, and a dimple in her chin. Carey didn't even know her name. He'd picked her up in a bar little more than two hours previously, offering to pay her for her time. She hadn't hesitated.

Carey felt a tremor of desire thrill through him, reached for it, only to have it vanish like a wisp of smoke. He searched for the priest inside his mind, had to access the zombyte chip to find the man at all. Almendariz was almost beaten. He had to be. The priest simply couldn't hold out much longer.

And to become what he had once been himself, Carey needed Almendariz to accept himself for what he was. He felt the priest cowering in the back of their shared mind like a rodent trapped in a sudden bright light. Carey passed through the alleys of Almendariz's religious conditioning, doubts, and crumbling beliefs. He swept in on the priest before the man was truly aware of him.

The wilderness rolled in broken mountains and barren rock in all four directions around Almendariz. Small and twisted berry bushes and plants hunkered like crippled dwarves in occasional sand pits scattered across the lifeless land. Trees were sparse, bent and dying like weeds.

He stood, wavering and uncertain, in a narrow defile with high, sharply angled rock slopes on either side of him. His sandpapery tongue traced the cracked and swollen surfaces of his lips. He couldn't remember the last time he'd tasted water. When he looked up at the hot sun overhead, he saw the elongated shadows of vultures and other carrion birds circling high overhead.

Curious, wondering why he couldn't remember how long he'd been there, he ran his hands over his face. The features were similar, nerve-dead in some spots from the surgeons' scalpels, and smooth-shaven. He wasn't Jesus. He was himself.

Lowering his head, knowing it was useless to empty the sand from his sandals, he went on. Before he had gone ten feet a howling wind roared into his face and physically pushed him back.

"Almendariz!" Carey's voice bellowed.

"I will not come with you again. You want to corrupt me. You want me to lose my soul too." He pushed himself to his feet, felt the razor-sharp sand flay his face, and ran.

"You can't hide from me," Carey said, "and you can't hide from yourself. You want what I have to give you."

"No." Almendariz tripped over a stone, sprawled full-length on the ground. About a dozen fist-sized stones lay before him, baked dull and hard by the merciless sun.

"You have a hunger," Carey said. "A very special hunger. I know all about it. Why stay here and starve yourself when you can come with me and feast?"

The stones wavered in Almendariz's sight. He blinked, but they continued to appear insubstantial. Abruptly the stones exploded outward, like taffy being pulled. The dull gray-white color gave way to pinks and browns. By the time Almendariz got to his feet again, he was facing a dozen naked women of Caucasian, Oriental, Amerind, and African extractions.

They held their arms out to him in open supplication.

"You can have them," Carey whispered from the center of the storm. "You can have all of them and more. All you have to do is let me lead you out of this."

"This," Almendariz said in a quavering voice, "will not feed my soul."

"Idiot!" Carey snarled.

Without warning the windstorm wrapped around Almendariz and lifted him into the sky, tossing him end over end. He closed his eyes against the sudden nausea that filled him. Only when his feet settled on a solid surface did he dare look.

He was on top of a gold-domed temple. Reflex made him reach out for the iron cross jutting from the apex of the dome well within his reach. Jerusalem was spread out around him in its walled glory. No one seemed to notice him standing there.

"You believe in your religion so much," Carey said. "Throw yourself off this building. See how fast your God comes to your aid. If any such Being truly existed, would He have let you go through all the hell you have endured? That's not a benevolent god by my definition."

"He has a special purpose in mind for me," Almendariz howled at the heavens. "I must be tested by Him. I must be found worthy."

"If so, you'll be found both wanting and lacking. You're a killer, and you can't get around the mountain of lust that resides inside you. Give in to it and you may still find you have a life."

"No."

"Stupid bastard."

The wind rose again, slammed into Almendariz with enough force to rip him from the roof of the temple. He tumbled through the air and held his breath, expecting the ground to hammer the life from him.

Instead he came to a gentle stop on his feet. He blinked his eyes open regretfully, found he was standing in the office in Carey's building where he'd first met Welbourne. He faced the wall-sized window overlooking Houston.

Night had descended over the city, becoming a backdrop to the neon advertising that scaled the buildings. Traffic was rivers of light in between the concrete canyons.

Carey popped into existence beside him, resplendent in a carefully tailored suit and styled hair. He waved to the metropolitan area below. "All of this could be yours," he said seductively. "I have money. Power. No one could touch us. We could sate our passion unfettered, never know a moment when police could come near us."

"You're a deceiver," Almendariz said in a quavering voice. He faced Carey, realized how afraid he was of the man. "Your words are sharper than a serpent's tooth, and filled with poison."

"You've lost yourself," Carey said. "The madness that's inside you is consuming you, and you don't even know it. I'm offering you a hell of a deal, because I can help keep you sane if you'll just let me." He stretched out his hand.

Recoiling instantly, Almendariz said, "The Lord is my shepherd. I shall not want." Wheeling quickly, he ran and threw himself toward the window. His arms smashed into it, followed by the driving hard weight of his body. Glass broke, rained down in big chunks, and he was through. Wind slapped at him immediately as he floundered in the air ninety stories above sea level.

"It's not that easy," Carey screamed down at him. The man stood in the yawning cavity of the smashed window.

Bands of force closed around Almendariz before he'd plummeted thirty floors, halted him, and set him on his feet in midair. He hung, suspended, trapped like a fly in amber.

Carey stepped from the gaping mouth of the building and walked through the air toward Almendariz with steps that covered a floor or more of descent with each stride. Behind him pieces of glass sparkled in the moonlight as the window reformed and sealed over. "You damned fool," he roared when he came to a stop in front of Almendariz, slightly elevated. "If this hadn't been inside a matrix, you'd be dead now. And suicide would damn your soul to hell for eternity."

"Maybe," Almendariz said with conviction so cold he scared himself, "it already has been."

"Get away from me," Carey said.

The wind from his words slammed into Almendariz and sent him spinning into another pseudo-reality.

When Almendariz opened his eyes again, nausea swelling inside his stomach, he saw that he was back in the wilderness. He pushed himself to his feet, stared helplessly at the gray sliver of sky revealed between the rocky walls of the defile. "Why?" he screamed.

His voice echoed around him, trailed away down both sides of the defile.

"Because," a voice said behind him.

He turned quickly, wondering what new threat was about to be unveiled.

The man leaning against the rocky wall behind him was old and withered, face sunburned to a leathery texture, gray hair and beard matted by the elements and time. He held a chipped and dulled staff in his scarred, gnarled hands.

Almendariz recognized the man at once as the Bible-deck representation of Moses, who had led the Israelites from Egypt to the Promised Land, but hadn't been able to enter himself. "What?" he asked.

"It's our pride," Moses said in a whiskey-roughened voice. "We've been guilty of taking for granted God's love for us. My pride kept me from the Promised Land, and I wandered all those years desperately seeking it only to be denied. And yours, Father Judd? I don't know what your pride will cost you."

Sweat trickled into Almendariz's eyes and made him blink. When he looked for Moses again, the man was gone. He was unsure if Carey had put Moses there or not.

Overwhelmed by his fears of what might come to pass—knowing that Carey would eventually be able to encourage that tainted part of his soul into power—he sat down to rest, pulled his robe over his face, and tried to ignore the bite of the flying sand as it continued to pound him.

43

Leaving the Fiero parked in front of a closed leather shop a dozen blocks from the Carey International building, Bethany Shay got out, locked up, and walked. She wore new black jeans, cut for martial-arts maneuverability, that weren't faded from washing so they would blend with the night. A black turtleneck, dark British Knights, and a black wind-breaker completed the ensemble. The Glock 20 rode her hip. Two extra clips were on the belt, and a handful more were in the pockets of the windbreaker. The Semmerling .45 derringer was in an ankle holster at the bottom of her right leg. She was conscious of the extra weight but worked at not compensating for it so her movements were natural.

Traffic was sparse. She crossed at the corner without being noticed. Her shield and ID were in a hip pocket of the jeans. The disposable plastic container with the wafer chip she'd gotten from Smith by way of Minoru earlier was in her windbreaker pocket. She touched it when she made the opposite corner and turned her steps toward the skyscraper.

Three blocks from the Carey building, Hideo stepped out of the shadows and took her by the arm.

Shay checked an instinctive blow designed to free herself when she recognized the man. His hiss of warning sounded flat and sibilant, like a viper in prestrike mode. He pulled her into the shadows and led her down a narrow alley lined with trash receptacles that had long ago overflowed. Rats and bugs scurried through the debris with shuttling and scraping noises.

Hideo was dressed in black ninja clothing complete with a hood equipped with an infrared visor. A short sword was sheathed across his back, the handle near his right hip, positioned for a quick draw. The hidden pockets inside the loose-fitting suit would be filled with an assortment of deadly devices. The fingers of his left hand tapped against his jawbone, paused, then tapped again. Without warning almost a dozen other shapes separated from the dark alley walls and formed a troop. They'd been there the whole time, but their clothing and training had kept Shay from seeing them. They were faceless, indistinguishable from each other.

Reaching into her windbreaker pocket, Shay took out a rubber band, pulled her hair back, then slipped on a pair of black gloves—complete with fingers—that felt like another layer of skin.

Hideo led the way, twisting through a labyrinth of alleys. "Sensors are scattered around the building," he said in a voice that didn't carry more than a few feet. "An earlier team knocked some of them out and gave us access to the building, but we couldn't take a straight approach to it. Any kind of linear movement within this distance would be perceived as a threat by the Building AI."

She followed Hideo, tried to be as silent as he was, yet was all too aware that she was the clumsiest of the group.

They circled the Carey building three and a half times and zigzagged in as they followed the predetermined course Hideo had laid out. He waved, and the ninjas melted into the shadows lining the spacious and clean alley behind the building.

Perspiration covered Shay under her clothing.

"My orders," Hideo said as he reached inside his blouse and took out a compact remote control device, "are to get you inside the building, provide you with blueprints, and get you as close to the nerve network of the corporate matrix as I can without sacrificing my team or myself."

Shay nodded, wished she could take her gloves off long enough to wipe her sweating palms.

Hideo touched one of the remote control's buttons. Two small explosions sounded overhead, *bamf, bamf.*

Shay glanced upward and saw the locked access panel of the building's incinerator unit on the second floor tumble gracefully out of its recessed port, trailing thin streamers of gray smoke that curled toward the sky. For a moment she thought it was going to fall on her and Hideo. The Izutsu bodyguard watched it without flinching.

Then the thin-corded mesh of a net appeared against the dull gray exterior of the access panel and halted its downward motion only a few feet overhead. Three ninjas stepped forward at once. The lead man's matte-black blade flashed easily through the cords, and the access panel dropped into the hands of the two men waiting below. They handled its weight with difficulty but without noise and tucked it behind a Dumpster.

Hideo gestured with a curt wave.

Another ninja ran forward and braced himself face forward against the wall of the building with his arms outspread. Less than a heartbeat after he'd settled into position, another man ran lithely up his back, put his feet on the first man's shoulders, and pressed himself against the building also. The third man scampered up the first two with acrobatic grace, swept his sword from its sheath on his back, then rolled into the yawning cavity of the recessed port.

"Put this on," Hideo instructed.

Shay took the ninja hood, hesitated for just a moment, then slipped it over her head. Cloudy shadows appeared through the visor.

Hideo reached out and tapped her temple lightly. "On," he said, as greenish figures were revealed by the infrared function, "and off." He tapped again. "Simple, hai?"

"Yes," Shay replied. She tapped the side of her head and the infrared winked back into operation.

Touching the beaded knot along her left jawline, Hideo said, "Radio. On and off." He pressed to demonstrate. A low buzz crackled in her ear when it flared to life. "Small-frequency broadcast. The structure of the building may be enough to block clear communications. I have preset signals which I use here." He pressed at the side of his face.

Metallic clicks sounded in the earpiece set above and behind Shay's left ear.

"Code," Hideo explained. "My team knows it. You don't. So don't worry about it."

"Okay."

"Any verbal broadcast on your part," Hideo went on, "that is not asked for, will result in the automatic exfiltration of this unit. You will be left on your own."

"I understand."

"The communications network is for our use. But you can benefit from it as long as you don't compromise us."

Shay nodded. "I won't."

Hideo's blank visored gaze studied her. "Hai."

A coil of black leather strands slithered from the recessed

port and dropped to the alley floor. One of the ninjas at the bottom shook it, revealing a woven ladder.

"Quickly," Hideo said, and took off up the ladder.

With only a moment of hesitation, Shay trailed after the man. Two ninjas braced the ladder at the bottom and pulled it taut. Hideo went up the ladder like a spider climbing its web. Shay slipped twice. The second time the man below her had to grab her foot to keep her from falling.

Arms trembling from the combined effects of exertion and excitement at breaching the building's security, Shay pulled herself into the recessed incinerator port. Warm air, tainted with the odors of chemicals and burned materials, pushed around her and leaked out into the night.

Hideo handed her a deck viewer handset. "It's programmed with the building's blueprints," he whispered.

Two ninjas, lit up a glowing green in the infrared, slipped suction pads on their knees and hands and started up the narrow tower of the incinerator shaft. Their movements were muffled, becoming undetectable against the background of grinding and hissing put out by the incinerator unit.

"Are you familiar with it?" Hideo asked.

"Yes." Shay worked through the simple controls. "It focuses on me, on my present location, and reproduces schematics that I ask for." A dozen diagrams of the inner skeleton of the building floated through the small screen. A lambent blue pinprick indicated her position on every one. When she punched it up, it showed that she was standing in the mouth of the incinerator tubing. "How accurate are the details?"

"Very," Hideo replied. "Izutsu-san paid a lot of yen for the information. When you get to Carey's private quarters, however, you will find the accuracy is reduced because of the small amount of information we were able to obtain."

Shay slipped the deck viewer into the windbreaker and snapped the pocket shut.

Another braided leather ladder dropped from the incinerator tubing. Hideo took the lead. Shay followed and hoped she wasn't in for ninety more floors of climbing. Kiyoshi's people might make it, but she had serious doubts about herself. The tubing was small and they had to crawl in single file.

On the fifth floor the tubing made a right angle and opened to form a small platform where a broad blade set into the back wall would scrape collected debris toward its final destination. The two lead ninjas cut through a steel wall with hand lasers and revealed a dark cavity that spilled cool air into the incinerator shaft. The jagged edges of the cut steel glowed cherry-red with the heat retained in them. The stink of burning metal filled the tubing with claustrophobic intensity.

Shay's throat felt raw and parched from the smoke.

"Supply tubing," Hideo said. "It goes all the way to Carey's private floors." He took out the remote control and punched it again. Immediately the well-oiled vibration of hydraulic equipment hummed through the supply tubing and into the incinerator. The supply tubing bullet whisked to a stop slightly below the level of the incinerator.

Through the greenish cast provided by the infrared, Shay figured it was big enough to hold several people at a time if they didn't mind being cramped.

After they put the hand lasers away, the two ninjas unrolled rectangles of fire- and heat-resistant fabric and blotted out the cherry-red glow at the bottom of the opening. Once it was in place, they opened the access plate and quickly slipped into the supply tubing bullet.

At Hideo's urging, Shay went next, followed by the corporate bodyguard. She stood squeezed in among them.

The supply tubing bullet took off with enough speed to buckle her knees. She had to put out a hand to catch her balance and was embarrassed because the only thing she had to grab was Hideo's uniform. The bodyguard acted as if he hadn't noticed. Vertigo whirled around her when the bullet suddenly slowed down, then came to an abrupt stop.

Hideo opened the access plate from inside and pushed it up and out of the way.

A blank metal wall filled the opening.

Without hesitation, Hideo took a hand laser from one of his men, slashed a rectangle from the wall, then folded his leg in toward his chest and kicked out with explosive power. The metal clanged dully and gave reluctantly. The panel popped out and fell with a muffled thud.

"Carpeted floor," Hideo explained. "We knew it was there. There was no way to circumvent the security on the supply tubing doors farther up." He grabbed the handle of his short sword and stepped through. Inside the room, the blade flashed briefly as it came free in his hands.

Shay went next. The Glock came loose in her hand, and with it came the weight of the responsibility for the building's invasion. She'd bent rules before and explored possibilities sometimes better left undisturbed until legal jurisdiction had been established. But she'd never broken the law so blatantly. She forced herself to remember the faces pasted to her bedroom wall.

The two ninjas secured the perimeters of the room.

Hideo used the remote control.

With a pop of compressed air, the supply tubing bullet dropped from sight.

In the garish greens of the infrared, Shay easily identified the area as a conference room. The furniture was ornate and functional, forming a subconscious arrow that pointed at the head of the table. A blanked wallscreen was to one side, overlooking the street—unless she had gotten her sense of direction screwed up, which she admitted was entirely possible. There was no decor. The room was sterile and empty.

She accessed the com-chip and reached out for DataMain. It was 1:13 A.M. It took under two minutes for Hideo to assemble his men inside the room. By that time one of the ninjas had forced the electronic lock on the door.

Hideo waved two of them out into the hallway, then quickly followed.

Shay put herself a step behind him, the Glock heavy in her hand.

Halfway down the empty corridor, Hideo stopped and gestured at the tiled ceiling. One of the men got down on his hands and knees and let another man stand on his back. The acoustic tiles were removed in short order, and white specks of the material rained down over the carpet. A hand laser sliced through the aluminum skeleton framing the tiles till there was space big enough for a person to fit through. The hand laser flared again—blue light this time instead of ruby—and bit through the concrete floor overhead.

The flooring came down in cubes as big as two fists placed together. Other members of Hideo's team caught the concrete cubes as they tumbled free, handling them quickly with protective gloves. None of them hit the floor, and they were stacked inside the conference room they'd entered the building through.

The hand laser winked out, and the first man padded the

edges with the heat-resistant matting and slithered through. The second man formed a stirrup with his hands.

Hideo placed his foot in the man's laced hands and vaulted upward.

Shay was next, and didn't make the moves nearly as fluidly. She holstered the Glock. On her way up she reluctantly let go of the man's shoulders, and was afraid her head would strike the concrete in passing. The ninja propelled her upward as her knees straightened to take her weight. Her hands hit the edges of the hole and guided her through. Before she could attempt to take her own weight, two sets of hands grabbed her arms and pulled her through in a blinding rush that almost took her breath away. Her next impression was the jar of her feet against the floor. As she turned, Hideo and the other man pulled the next ninja through the hole.

When the last man had taken his place, Hideo fell in beside Shay and guided her to a locked room. "The computer's beyond," he said in a terse voice. "We get you through this, you're on your own."

"All right." She touched the wafer chip in her pocket to reassure herself.

With short, quick movements, Hideo yanked the cover off the lock and dumped pieces of the mechanism across the floor. He pulled it open slowly.

Shay waited until she was motioned forward, then stepped to Hideo's side and peered into the room. The floor held a polished sheen even in infrared. Static curtains fluttered in the breeze, not quite making contact with the floor. The walls were covered by banks of computer hardware that hummed and clicked almost noiselessly. Lights of various hues flickered through operational sequences across the faces of the hardware. Four small tables held Tendrai deck systems facing each other in pairs. The screens were blank.

The ninjas had pooled together in a silent group of inky black at the rear of the hallway.

Taking a fresh grip on the 10mm, Shay started to enter the room, pulled by the excitement of being so close to her goal.

"Wait," Hideo said. His arm blocked her from entering the room. Then he flicked his fingers and a number of pellets bounced into the room. Tiny pops punctuated the computer hum. White smoke billowed up from each pellet, joined together to make a single cloud that filled the room. There, in the rolling layers of smoke, translucent beams of neon pinks and blues appeared and stabbed from wall to wall and from floor to ceiling till a three-dimensional checkerboard was created in the swirling air.

"There is room to negotiate if you are careful." Hideo dropped to his stomach and crawled under the first sensor beam. It swirled in the smoke scarcely two inches above his back.

Shay was smaller, but she didn't feel as confident as the man acted. She crawled through on her stomach, following Hideo's lead. Monitoring the slow passage of time in her head via the com-chip, she continued across the room. Eight minutes later, sweat dripping from every pore and muscles aching in her arms and legs, she got to her feet and stepped over the last of the sensor beams.

Hideo pointed to one of the Tendrai decks, said, "There," and took another for himself.

Shay sat, took off her gloves because she planned to destroy the keyboard when she was finished and didn't want to mis-strike keys any more than she had to, and set to work booting up the unit. "Will anyone be alerted to our using these?"

"No," Hideo said, as he continued working at his own board. "Security access to this room concerning the computers was rerouted. As long as no one attempts to integrate these systems with an outside deck."

Shay nodded. She hadn't intended to raid the Carey matrix and push it out of the building. That was what the wafer chip was for. Once she had the information she needed copied onto the wafer chip—provided it existed within the matrix—she could force people to listen to her, even if they were legally hamstrung for a time.

If she made it out of the building alive.

Despite the perspiration staining her neck, the thought ghosted a cold chill down her skin. She yanked the ninja hood off and took measured breaths as she worked the board.

Once it was set, she took the wafer chip from her pocket, peeled the adhesive backing from it, brushed her hair back behind her left ear, and laid the wafer over the com-chip so the gel slicked and sealed, cold against her skin. She pressed the enact-tab, only imagined that she felt the minute trodes snake into her com-chip linkage. Her skin pebbled into goose bumps. She slipped the trode free of the Tendrai, flipped the connection over, and merged it with the wafer chip. "I'm going inside for a while," she told Hideo. Only then did she notice that the sensor beams filling the open space of the room had disappeared.

Hideo nodded.

Shay felt her body relax, peel away from her like the skin unraveling around an orange. Her vision clouded, and she flipped into cyberspace with the sudden suction of a clogged drain opening under pressure.

The feeling was different at this time. Marc Smith had explained that to her. With the wafer chip she shouldn't be able to achieve a true entry into cyberspace. But she could pass along the outer fringes of the construct.

Shay had figured that would suit her needs.

She felt as if she were in a fishbowl looking out at the world, thought she knew what a guppy felt like as it peered through the glass at a cat watching it hungrily.

Entry into the Carey matrix was violent. She felt as if she were sinking through layers of increasing densities, and as soon as the thought hit her, playing cards the size of trampolines materialized in the endless black below her. She burst through the eight of diamonds, queen of clubs, and deuce of spades in quick succession. Smith had told her the wafer chip was programmed to feed off her subconscious mind to build a comfortable framework that would allow her conscious mind to collate data.

She slammed through the nine of clubs and the ace of diamonds, came to a halt on the jack of hearts. The card rocked underfoot, but held her weight easily.

In the back of her mind she was dimly aware of the physical world, sensed the cool roll of sweat leaking from her hair down the back of her neck, the keys hot under her hands. Somewhere, Hideo had stood up and was surveying the security monitors against one wall. Then her attention slipped from that world back to the field of cyberspace.

She accessed the wafer chip, pulsed her inquiry at the matrix.

An explosion of color filled the ebony space in front of her, swirled around like rainbow-inspired comets, coalesced into a manlike form. It stood on nothing, feet together, arms spread out to its side, naked. Immediately it reminded Shay of the puppets her father had bought her when she was a child. The only thing missing was the strings. And if that came from her subconscious, she didn't even want to think about the possible significance.

It also struck her that the pose reminded her of the Church.

Almendariz's features—carved without any emotion at all—stretched across the mannequin's face. The cyber-creature remained translucent, shadowy, and inconsistent. <Query> it prompted in a scratchy mechanical voice.

"Personal files," Shay said. "Subject: Felix Carey."

<Affirmative. Do you have access codes?>

"Access codes as follows." Shay manipulated her connection to the wafer chip, locked onto the code-breaker sequence Smith had set up. Once she'd gotten close enough to the main neural network, the man had assured her, the codes would work. When she finished and waited for it to process, her chest was tight with anxiety.

<Code accepted. Further query permitted.>

"Subfile, personal," Shay said.

<Continue.>

"Subfile subject: Father Judd Almendariz."

<File accessed: Almendariz, Judd. Subclassification, priest. Title, Father. Continue.>

"Display," Shay instructed.

The cyber-creature made a throwaway gesture with its left hand. Gold-colored dust flew outward, formed an inverted tornado that upended with the mouth facing Shay. The interior of the cone blurred, turned gray, then filled with color. <Display activated. Continue.>

"Access the video and audio files concerning subfile subject Almendariz."

<Affirmative.>

A heartbeat later, images and garbled voices threaded through the flickering screen trapped inside the glowing cone.

<Is display satisfactory?>

"Yes," Shay replied. "Cut audio and video modes to files created within the Carey International building only." The display blinked, and old footage of the priest dropped away. It was passing her by so quickly she couldn't get a good grasp on everything, but she had the impression that the files held what she needed. She felt the pulse of the wafer chip as it sucked up the files and stored them inside her own brain for later retrieval.

Faces flashed onto the screen as well. Shay recognized them from the bodies she had seen, from the bloody collage staining her bedroom wall.

Without warning the cone emptied, became a flat gray screen.

"Continue display," Shay instructed. "Access other files relating to present subject." Maybe she had enough, but at this point she wanted everything she could get.

The cone vanished.

The cyber-creature's face pulped, writhed like a volcanic mass. Then, like ocean flooring pulling loose and rising to the surface to form island chains, flesh tones and human emotion filled the face. Genitals formed on the crystal-smooth body. The outline became ridged with real muscle, heavy with real bone. The blond hair was bedraggled and mussed. The blue eyes held pain and terror.

"You've got to help me," Father Judd Almendariz said. He stepped down onto the playing card with her. It rocked with his weight.

Shay felt for the Glock at her hip, found it hadn't made the jump into cyberspace with her, realized it wouldn't have done any good anyway.

Almendariz came closer. Blood suddenly covered his hands, dripped onto the cards. He stumbled to a stop and looked at his hands. Tears filled his eyes, ran down his cheeks, and splashed onto his palms. "My God," he said in a hoarse whisper. "What has been done to me?"

Shay accessed the safety line to the wafer chip, drew it taut, ready to flip out in an instant.

"Help me," Almendariz repeated. "He's stealing my soul, tying it to his. If I can't get free of him, I'm lost. I'll burn forever."

Fighting the fear that rose in her like waves spurred on by a hurricane, Shay said, "Where are you?"

"Lost," Almendariz answered. "He has my body. He wants my soul."

"How can I help you?"

"Find me. Take him out of my head. Make him leave me alone."

"Carey?" Shay asked, wanting to get his statement on the wafer chip.

"Yes."

"Carey is making you kill those women?"

"Now he is." Almendariz stopped his approach, as if realizing that he was scaring her away from him.

"And before?"

"Before?" He looked puzzled, like a little boy.

"What made you kill the women before?"

"They were temptations," Almendariz said. "Satan knew I had been given the Gift. He wanted *it* to be my downfall, wanted to use *it* to pull me from the arms of God. He wanted to prove that I was unworthy of God's love. Those women were soulless creatures who only wanted my destruction. I couldn't let them taint me."

"Why did Carey want you?"

"Not me. My body. He wanted my body to live out his own sick perversions."

"Isn't that a case of the pot calling the kettle black?" a loud voice rolled out of nowhere.

"Carey," Almendariz whispered, glancing over his shoulder. "He's found us."

Green laser lights rocketed across the black heavens, carved Felix Carey's perfect face against the ebony, lit the torches of his burning eyes. The mouth moved when he spoke. "Judge not," he intoned, "lest ye be judged. Isn't that right, priest? People who live in glass houses shouldn't throw rocks."

Shay took a fresh grip on the cyberlink tying her to the wafer chip.

Almendariz whipped around to face her. "Don't leave me. For God's sake, don't leave me." He put out a hand to stop her.

Shay hesitated, knew Carey must have already alerted the building security teams. She thought she heard Hideo calling her name, maybe even felt his hand on her shoulder, shaking her.

"If not for me," Almendariz implored, "then you have to stay for the girl. He's going to kill her if you don't."

An image rattled into Shay's mind, showed the hidden room on the ninety-ninth floor, revealed the frightened face of the girl curled into a fetal ball on the small bed. The drain in the center of the floor was full of ominous portent.

"He'll use me to do it," Almendariz said. He stepped

closer, reaching for her with bloody hands. "You can't let him kill her."

"You'll have to forgive the father," Carey said. "He hasn't learned how to enjoy the special aspects of himself yet. But give him time. He'll develop the taste he needs."

"Stay back," Shay ordered Almendariz.

The priest froze in place, his shoulders slumped with helplessness.

Shay saw the same madness lurking in Almendariz's blue eyes that she found in the laser representations of Carey's.

Shay. It was Hideo's voice, sounding as if it came from a galaxy away.

"You surprise me, priest," Carey said. "The whole time I was claiming more and more ground into your mind, I didn't know you were worming your way into my personal matrix."

Almendariz ignored the laser image, locked his gaze on Shay. "Please," he said.

"She can't help you," Carey said with conviction. "She's dead. She just doesn't know it yet."

Behind Almendariz, Shay saw the jack of hearts pull free of the playing card, stand twelve feet tall, and limber his sword. When she looked over her own shoulder, she saw the jack's twin behind her.

"Don't leave," Almendariz said, starting for her.

At the same time the playing card thudded with the running footsteps of the giant jacks as they raised their swords. The green laser lights played on the keen blades.

As the swords swept toward her, Shay accessed the cyberlink to the wafer chip and flipped out.

44

"Son of a bitch," Shay said as she yanked her hands back from the deck's keyboard. She took a deep breath and tried to exhale the chill trapped inside her lungs.

"Come on," Hideo said.

Klaxons screamed throughout the length of the building, and security lights beamed brightly, painting garish shadows on the walls. The sensor beams were gone.

"Now," Hideo ordered. He wrapped a hand around her upper arm and dragged her to her feet.

Shay. It was Almendariz's voice, sounding like it was coming from the bottom of a well. **She'll die . . . her blood will be on your hands. And mine. You can't leave her to him.**

Shay destroyed the keyboard underfoot and moved instinctively, trailing the Izutsu security officer to the door and pulling her hood back on. Hideo held her at the corner and peered around cautiously.

Autofire raked the corridor. Bullets tore chunks from the plaster wall, scattering white dust that became a roiling backdrop and made the ninjas visible. The gunfire, trapped in the narrow confines of the hallway, sounded like explosions.

The Glock came away in her hand and she snicked the safety off. She glanced around the corner.

The ninjas scattered like bugs caught in a spotlight. At the other end of the hallway three men stood partly concealed behind the buttressing architecture of the corridor. Machine pistols flamed steady bursts in their fists.

"Take them down," Hideo said over the hood radio, and called out numbers.

Immediately two ninjas peeled away from the walls and moved for the center of the hallway. Short bows snapped into locked positions in their hands, and arrows were nocked. Whatever sound they made was masked by the thunderous roar of the machine pistols. The arrows sped true, pierced the eyes and throats of their targets. The three building security people went down with blood streaming from their wounds, hands wrapped around the fletched shafts that drank the life from them.

One of the ninjas went spinning away, hit by one of the last frantic bursts the security people had gotten off. When he came out of his recovery roll, he brushed the torn cloth over his chest that revealed the Kevlar vest beneath.

"Come," Hideo said. He tugged at her wrist.

Shay twisted her arm and used her other forearm to knock his grip free. The image of the trapped girl wouldn't leave her mind. She kept seeing Tully all bloody and torn in the alley. "No," she said in a hoarse voice. "No. It stops here. There won't be another one."

Before Hideo could react, she wheeled around the corner and sprinted down the hallway, vaulting over the spilled corpses of the security people. She knew it was possible that Kiyoshi had given Hideo orders that she was to be taken out of the building at any cost regardless of her own wishes.

Feeling the pulse of the Carey matrix around her, she accessed the wafer chip and went looking for the priest. "Almendariz."

"I'm here," the priest replied. His voice sounded stronger now, no longer strained by making the one-sided contact.

Shay slammed a hand against a corridor wall at a four-way intersection and slowed her stride only long enough to change directions, going with her instinctive sense of direction. The hood jarred as her feet pounded against the carpet, making the infrared images blur ahead of her. The walls on either side of her were unbroken and unmarked except by a few doors placed some distance apart. A quick glance over her shoulder showed that two of Hideo's men were in pursuit. She lifted the 10mm and fired two warning shots over their heads.

An unlit fluorescent track light exploded and cascaded down in glittering pieces. The ninjas went to ground as if operated by a single mind.

"Where is she?" Shay demanded.

"One floor up. I'll direct you. You're coming up on an elevator. Use it. The emergency exits are guarded."

Another four-way intersection suddenly loomed ahead of

her. Shay ducked around a corner, peered in all directions, and saw only corridors. The muffled thud of running feet sounded in the hallway she'd just quit, but the noise was covered by the shrill scream of more klaxons going off and the sudden eruption of autofire in other areas. "Which way?"

"Left," Almendariz said in her mind.

She raced across the intersection and barely caught the lunge of the ninja as the man reached for her leg. Breaking stride, she came to a stop with him at her right side. She knew she had an advantage because Hideo would have given them orders not to injure her. Whirling, she came through with a roundhouse kick that caught the ninja on the side of the head and bounced him off the wall behind him. Before the other man could get by his partner, she was moving at full speed again.

"Here," Almendariz called out.

Shay came to a stop in front of two elevators. The Glock weighed heavily in her hand. Glancing at the control panel between the two sets of doors, she felt her hopes sink. "It's got a palm-plate."

"Put your hand on it," Almendariz said. "I'll get you past it."

Without hesitation she transferred the Glock to her other hand and did it. Despite everything she knew about Almendariz and the women he'd killed, she believed he really was trying to save the girl.

Clothing rustled behind her.

She turned and saw the ninjas gathering, their blades gleaming in their black-gloved fists.

With a shushed hiss, the elevator doors opened.

Shay threw herself inside, rebounded from the opposite wall, and started for the control pad.

"I have it," Almendariz said.

The doors closed just as the ninjas sprang for the opening. Their bodies thudded against the doors, and there was a muffled curse in Japanese.

The cage bobbled, then started up fluidly.

A matte-black edge shot through the slit formed by the closed doors. The sword grated as the cage moved up, scraping with nail-biting intensity as it slid along the metal. Sparks showered down. The blade twisted, tried to force the doors apart, but never succeeded in gaining more than a couple inches. The end of the sword snapped off with a twang.

"He's found us," Almendariz said with a quaver in his voice.

Shay didn't have to ask who.

"He's coming for you. He knows where you are."

Without warning, the elevator cage rocked to a sudden stop and the emergency light flaring down from a corner of the ceiling winked out. Terror slithered up Shay's spine. She put her face in her hands, accessed a RAM file she'd had programmed into the wafer chip. "Almendariz."

"You've got to get out of there." For a moment the bleed-over from the matrix spurring into the wafer chip was so intense that she could *see* the priest's face—wild-eyed in fear—against the dark interior of the elevator cage.

"Almendariz." She felt Carey's thoughts invading hers, confusing her, twisting her attempts at linear concentration.

"What?" the priest asked.

"Take him away from here."

"How?"

Shay reached up, removed the emergency exit panel from the ceiling of the elevator, and sneezed when the accumulated dust hit her. "I have a file in the chip I'm wearing." She guided him to it.

"I have it," Almendariz said. He paused.

Grabbing the edges of the emergency exit, Shay heaved herself through the opening. The air inside the elevator shaft was dry and heavy.

"It's from the Bible," Almendariz said.

"Yes," Shay replied. The closed doors of the next level were well within her reach. She used the Fiero's keys to make room for her fingers, then pried them apart. "Where's the girl?"

A map etched itself inside her mind.

One elbow braced in the elevator doors, she fumbled for the deck viewer, activated it, and found the schematic that most closely resembled the blueprints the priest gave her.

"It won't do you any good," Carey said. "You'll never get out of this building alive."

Shay finished programming her chosen route, hung the deck viewer from her belt, and scrambled through the elevator door. She pushed herself to her feet and staggered into a run through the darkness of the interior of the building.

Almendariz's presence hovered for a moment inside her

head, then evaporated like smoke sucked through an exhaust duct.

Shay felt the RAM file open in her head and was pulled in. Reality altered around her, but she forced herself to focus on what had to be done, and went on.

Almendariz wept as he embraced the file the detective had given him. It was from the Book of Genesis, Chapter Four, Verse Three. He gathered his strength and knew that part of the trial God had ordained him to face lay before him. He vowed to be up to the task.

Reaching out a cybernetic tendril to Carey, he caught the man unaware and held him fast as he jacked into the RAM file.

He spilled over into nothingness and fell to the hard earth with a bone-jarring thump. Forcing himself to his hands and knees, he coughed air back into his bruised lungs.

Farm fields surrounded him on all sides, well lit by the noonday sun burning down overhead. He was dressed in animal skins, wore a knotty beard and long hair. Taking a deep breath, he shouted out his brother's name. "CAAIIIN!"

Nothing moved within the tilled fields. Oxen stood in nearby pens, their leather harnesses draped over the timber fencing.

"He's coming."

Whirling, Almendariz faced the speaker and experienced for a moment what he was certain was rapture.

She was as tall as he remembered from his early years, no longer stooped with age. Her nun's habit fluttered around her sock-encased ankles. A polished sheen showed on the toes of her plain black shoes. Her gaze was lifted skyward expectantly. Her eyes looked like gleaming agate.

"Sister Margaret Mary," Almendariz said with reverence. He dropped to one knee before her to show his respect.

"Arise," she said in that impatient tone of hers. She crossed the distance between them in brisk strides, placing her hands on his shoulders with a touch that still felt so very cold. "You know what you have to do." Her stern gaze never left his eyes. "Do not falter now."

"Of course not," he said automatically. For an instant he thought her features wavered, believed for a nanosecond that they belonged to the woman detective, Bethany Shay. But then he saw that he was wrong, that they were Sister Margaret Mary's own.

"There," she said, pointing. "He's coming."

Almendariz turned and tried to master the primeval fear that stirred in the bottom of his belly.

A small comet hurtled to earth only a few meters away, plopping to the ground with a rainbow-colored pyrotechnic display. Flames laved the tilled rows. Felix Carey strode out of them untouched, curled his right hand into a fist, and shook it at the azure sky. "Bitch!" he screamed, and his voice echoed over the pastoral lands. "This isn't going to do anything but buy you a little time. And I promise you I'm going to take my time before I let death release you from the pain and suffering you're going to experience."

Able to "feel" Shay somewhere outside the current programming, Almendariz knew the woman didn't bother to make a reply. Her thoughts were too intent and focused on what she was trying to do.

"Now, Cain," the priest said in a strained voice, "now this ends between us. You won't use me anymore."

"You're insane, you pathetic bastard!" Carey roared.

"Strike," Sister Margaret Mary commanded, pointing at the industrialist imperiously. "Do not hesitate. He is the evil you've warred against your whole life."

"Bullshit," Carey said. Before Almendariz could move, he stepped forward and backhanded the nun with his fist.

Blood sprayed as her face crumpled under the blow. She left her feet and flipped backward through the air. Still tumbling, she winked out of existence like a black rose dying and caving in on itself.

"Goddam harpy," Carey said as he turned to face Almendariz. "Don't listen to her. If we don't find that detective, she's going to be the death of us both."

"No!" Almendariz roared. He stooped, scooped a smooth stone as big as his fist from a tilled furrow. With a scream of rage and fear, he launched himself at Carey. "No more killing!"

Shay pulled herself up from the elevator shaft, pulled her feet under her, and got her bearings in the darkness. Taking the deck viewer from her windbreaker, she flipped it on and called up the schematic Almendariz had altered in the files. The bright blue blip told her where she was in relation to her goal. She plotted the quickest course, memorized it, and tucked the deck viewer away.

Keeping the Glock loose and ready before her, she moved at a cautious trot down the corridor. She sensed Almendariz in the back of her mind and knew the events taking place between him and Carey were chaotic and violent. The special file in the wafer chip had been an option. It hadn't taken much consideration to realize that Carey's "working" relationship with Almendariz wasn't based on a joint desire. The verse from the Old Testament had suggested itself to her, as did the programmed presence of Sister Margaret Mary, and provided a diversion. How lasting it would prove she didn't know.

The corridor opened up into an atrium. Benches and chairs formed a half-dozen conversation areas around a sculpted landscape of growing plants and dwarf trees in the center of the room. Water splashed down over rocks near the top, creating a happy burbling that didn't fit the background erratically lighted by the security lamps.

Distant barks of gunfire and the keening whines of klaxons punctuated the vibrating hum of the building and let Shay know the clock was ticking.

She swept the walls, caught the movement of the security camera as it swiveled through its prescribed course. Lifting the Glock, she took careful aim and squeezed the trigger. The 10mm round cored through the plastic housing of the camera and spilled its mechanical guts over the floor of the atrium. Sparks flashed in the wiring and started a fire that jetted up from the mounting hanging crookedly from the wall.

Shay went on, alert for movement ahead of her.

She took two lefts as the corridor spiked out, ended up at a door on the right side of the hallway three rooms up along the arm she was currently following. She knew it even without the brass plate screwed into place on the door.

When she tried the door, she found it locked. Stepping back, she raised the Glock and triggered three rounds into the lock. Metal screamed. Then she was deafened by the rolling thunder trapped in the corridor. Sparks flared out like novas, most of them dying before they struck the floor. The locking mechanism came apart and trickled across the carpet.

Shay lifted her foot and drove it hard against the door.

The wood shivered under the impact, then reluctantly gave way with a screech that rattled through the dulled cotton filling her ears. She went through with the Glock in both hands, sweeping it across the darkened interior of the room.

Copy machines and fax machines sat against one wall and formed islands in the middle of the room. The other walls were filled with built-in shelves holding bulk office supplies. The stench of harsh chemicals burned Shay's nostrils.

There wasn't a door where she thought there would be one.

After making sure no one else was in the room, she grabbed a straight-backed chair from a workstation and secured it under the door handle. Satisfied, she pulled the hood off and tucked it into the pocket of her windbreaker. She kept the 10mm in her hand. According to the information Almendariz had given her, the secret room was on the other side of the wall behind the copy machines and fax machines.

She wished she'd thought to protect her hearing when she blew the lock on the door. She got her weight behind the first copy machine and muscled it into the center of the room. The fax machine went easily, followed by the last copy machine with more difficulty. Once it started rolling, though, it went quickly. She lost control of it and it smashed into a workstation, which collapsed under the impact. Papers, pens, and paper clips spilled out over the tiled floor.

Using her free hand, she inspected the wall by touch, but felt nothing that indicated the room beyond. She tapped with her gunbutt. There was nothing hollow about the wall.

She stepped back from the wall, frustrated. Accessing the com-chip, she slid into the wafer programming and checked on Almendariz. It still took too much concentration to figure out the events taking place in the makeshift reality. Backing out of the wafer, she accessed the police bands and monitored the service calls. Nothing was on any of the frequencies regarding the Carey International building. Evidently Carey intended his private security staff to take care of everything without interference from the police.

"Dammit," Shay whispered angrily.

Without warning the chair holding the door shut splintered. Wooden shards scattered across the floor. The door flew open.

Immediately Shay raised the Glock in a two-handed grip and dropped into a Weaver stance. She aimed instinctively, lining the barrel up on the ninja's chest as he stepped into the room. "Stop right there," she said.

His head turned while the rest of his body remained motionless. Shay thought he looked like a human owl. He held the naked sword easily in his fist. Gunfire and screams sounded from outside, cutting through the steady whine of the warning klaxons.

"Put the sword down," she ordered. "Slowly."

The point drifted down and came to rest an inch from the floor between his tabii. "I am not here to harm you," he said in Japanese.

"What are you doing here?"

"Following orders," he replied. Although muffled by the hood, his voice sounded vaguely familiar.

"Your orders were to get me inside the building. That's all. Once the security net was tripped, you people were supposed to evacuate."

The ninja shrugged. "So you were told."

"By whose command?"

"Hideo-san."

"And on whose orders is he acting?"

"I do not know. The only orders I acknowledged are those he gives."

"What are his orders?"

"To save you," the ninja said, "in spite of yourself." His tone bordered on disrespect.

Shay knew that wasn't acceptable behavior. Of all the employees associated with Izutsu Corporation, Hideo's people were the most trustworthy and respectful. The voice sounded so tantalizingly familiar. "And who ordered that?"

"I do not know."

"Where is Hideo?"

"I cannot say."

"You mean you won't." Shay had heard the clickings of the coded transmissions along the com-net, but couldn't guess what they might mean.

The ninja shrugged again. "It is the same thing."

Shay tightened her grip on the Glock. "I'm not leaving. There's a woman on the other side of this wall who will be killed if I do. I'm not going to abandon her."

"You may forfeit your own life."

"I'm not going to walk away and let her die."

"Even if it means your own life?"

"Yes."

The ninja studied the wall. "You're sure she is there?"

"Yes."

"There is no door."

"No."

He rested the pommel of his blade in one hand. "Permit me. I have a laser in my equipment."

"Slowly," Shay cautioned.

He nodded, reached carefully inside his uniform, and brought out a hand laser. After he sheathed the sword he activated the laser, adjusted the blue beam, and approached the wall. "How thick?"

"No more than a foot." Shay stepped to one side, out of the way.

With concise movements, the ninja cut a four-foot-by-two-foot rectangle into the wall. Smoke curled up from the razored slices. The heavy smell of burning metal, brick, and plastic clogged Shay's lungs, making it hard to breathe. She held her free arm across her nose and mouth, trying to filter the air. Her eyes watered.

When the last line had been cut, the ninja pulled the laser back and switched it off. The inches-long blue beam disappeared with a liquid pop. He put the tool away, then hooked a pair of steel-taloned climbing claws into the wall and pulled. The wall groaned but refused to move.

Knowing time was running out and that Carey knew where she was, Shay joined the ninja at the wall, taking one of the climbing claws and adding her strength to his. He counted to three in Japanese. They pulled together.

The wall creaked, gave way suddenly, and fell out. Sections of brick, metal, and plastic smashed across the floor. Dust swirled in the sudden bright release of yellow light that ripped outward from the room.

The ninja ripped his sword from its sheath.

Shay raised her pistol as a shadow filled the opening, then backed off when she realized it was the woman Almendariz had shown her. The ninja threw a heat-resistant pad over the heated wall.

"Help me," the woman cried out. She tried to scramble over the lip of the lasered portal.

The ninja reached for her to steady her.

The door slammed open behind Shay. She turned to see

two men in Carey building security uniforms enter the room with assault pistols in their hands.

"We're made!" she yelled to the ninja.

Without hesitation, the ninja shoved the woman back inside the room they'd worked to free her from.

Shay fired point-blank at the men to cover the retreat and didn't stop firing until the slide locked back empty. She was unsure if her bullets had hit anything.

Autofire raked the wall beside her, sending bottles of correction fluid and copier chemicals squirting over the room in a sudden snowstorm of paper confetti. The bullets stopped in mid-burst.

"You damn fool," one of the guards snarled. "Carey wants that bitch alive."

"Come on!" the ninja yelled from inside the room. The wicked snout of a mini-Uzi materialized in his gloved hands. Hideo preferred the old weapons in his craft, but he wasn't averse to his people using modern technology. The silencer muffled the three-round bursts as the ninja chased the guards to cover.

Gathering her feet under her, Shay ran for the wall and heaved herself through the portal. A hand grabbed her windbreaker and pulled her roughly into the room. She landed in a sprawling heap, managed to keep the Glock in her fist. Bracing her back against the wall, she forced herself to her feet, dropped the empty magazine from the 10mm and shoved a fresh one in, and released the slide. It snapped back into place.

The woman had crawled onto the narrow bed and covered her head with her hands. She was crying hysterically, curling into a fetal position.

"We cannot stay here," the ninja said as he stabbed another clip into the mini-Uzi.

Shay tried the door but couldn't open it. Standing on tiptoe, she reached up and batted the light out with the barrel of the 10mm. Glass fragments rained down around her in the sudden darkness.

"There are more of them," the ninja whispered.

Carey was unable to avoid the priest's charge completely. He focused on the rock in Almendariz's hand, kept it deflected from his face, but couldn't remain standing. They tumbled into the loose earth of the tilled field.

Almendariz strained to bite him, frothing at the mouth like a rabid dog.

Evading the priest's attempts, Carey elbowed him in the mouth but felt the sharp teeth slip into his flesh anyway. Warm blood trickled along his arm.

Howling with pain, Almendariz released his grip on Carey's animal skins and reeled backward. The stone dropped as he lifted his hand to his bleeding mouth.

"Stop it," Carey commanded. He struggled to get up, his fingers sinking into the loose earth.

Almendariz reached for him with a blood-and-dirt-encrusted hand while his other hand searched for the dropped rock. A mad gleam lit his blue eyes. "You're a tool to the Deceiver. And like any tool, you *can* be broken." Shattered teeth clung to the rictus grin painted on his bloody lips.

Carey tried to access the matrix and pull out of the contraband programming but couldn't. The priest held him there.

Broadcasting his blow, Almendariz swung the rock.

Carey ducked easily and gave ground, to wanting to hurt the man. Still accessing the matrix, he analyzed the programming through the deck and tried to figure a way through. It was tight, allowing no slack for loopholes. Whoever had designed it had known what he was doing.

Almendariz swung again.

Partially distracted from the events going on in the constructed reality, Carey was unable to move in time. The rock exploded pain beneath his chin, almost succeeding in unhinging his jaw. His vision wavered. He came off his feet in a crashing heap with Almendariz on top of him.

The priest moved around, straddled his waist between his legs, and took up the rock in both hands. "Die, monster!" He brought the rock plummeting down.

Desperately, Carey reached up for the priest's arms and barely caught them as they came down. For a moment he felt certain his thumbs were going to snap off. Fear gave him the strength he needed to stop the rock's descent.

"No!" Almendariz screamed.

"*Don't* fight me," Carey ordered. "You won't win." He shifted under Almendariz, spilling the priest over.

Unable to keep his balance, Almendariz went over.

Before the priest could regain his position, Carey dug into

the dirt, kicked out with his feet, and threw himself on Almendariz's back. Holding the priest pinned beneath him, he grabbed a double fistful of Almendariz's hair and shoved his face into the loose black earth.

Almendariz struggled against him.

"You're a damned fool, priest," Carey shouted. "She was using you. That's all these damned women are good for. They use you, get whatever they can from you, then they leave you. They're parasites, don't even know a moment of loyalty." He leaned his weight harder on the back of the priest's head and forced his face more deeply into the loose earth. Dirt puffed out on both sides.

It took Carey a moment to realize the priest was no longer offering any resistance. When he released his hold on the priest's hair, Almendariz still didn't move. Carey pushed himself to his feet, conscious of the quiet that had fallen over the land. He nudged the priest with a foot and felt only slack flesh. "No," he said hoarsely. He knelt, grabbed the back of the priest's head, and lifted. "No, you son of a bitch. You can't be dead. I won't let you be."

Almendariz's eyes were wide and staring, clotted with black dirt tears that had turned to mud. Some of the blood vessels in the whites had ruptured and spiderwebbed across his eyes. His nostrils and mouth were packed with dirt, and his cheeks were rouged with it.

Reaching into the priest's mouth, Carey removed the packed earth with a curled forefinger. He worked in fearful desperation. Teeth came out with the saliva-covered mud. "No, damn you. You're not going to die on me. Not now. Not after I've waited so long to find someone like you."

He leaned down, sealed Almendariz's lips with his, and tried to blow life back into him. All he succeeded in doing was sucking dirt into his own lungs. After a time he rocked back on his heels as a coughing fit left him weak and gasping for his own breath. He tasted the death that had filled the priest.

Accessing the matrix, he searched for anything that might be left of Almendariz. He found nothing. There was no trace of the man's conscious mind either in the construct or in the body. The only satisfaction he found was that the body still lived.

Unrestrained fury raged in him as he pushed himself to his feet. Almendariz stared up at him with unseeing eyes.

Shay was responsible for the priest's death. She had given Almendariz the means to end both of them. But what she hadn't known was that Almendariz would fail.

Accessing the gridlines, he hurled himself free of the construct, zipped along the matrix, and came alive in Almendariz's brain. When he did, he was intensely aware that he was alone. He paused for a moment, still linked with the matrix, as he searched the security files and found the detective. Then he moved into pursuit.

45

Almendariz was gone.

Shay knew that from the empty feel of the programming in the wafer chip. She wanted to feel sorry for the man but couldn't. Memories of his victims would live with her for a long time, and she knew it. The wafer chip was cold and unclean against her bare skin, tainted with her own guilt from using Almendariz. She reached up and peeled it away, then dropped it to the floor.

The ninja whispered another nearly silent burst from the mini-Uzi. "They're not going to wait," he said grimly.

"Can you do anything about that lock?" she asked.

"Yes."

"Then get it done. Wherever that door leads, they probably know it too. If we don't get out of here soon, we're just going to run into the second team."

"Here." The ninja tossed her the machine pistol.

She caught it, bobbled it for a moment, then secured a grip on the butt. She exchanged places with him and got into position in time to squeeze off a three-round burst that cut the legs out from under a security officer.

A fresh salvo of bullets chipped steel and stone splinters from the wall and drove them at her. The splinters stung and cut. She blinked her eyes to make sure they were clear, wiped at her face with her hand, and saw streaks of blood that swept across her palm.

"Down," the ninja called in warning.

Shay ducked.

White phosphorus ignited around the lock and burned a molten hole through the metal. Dancing shadows wavered on the walls, and the hard lenses of the ninja's mask gleamed. The climbing claw on his left hand flicked out and speared the lock. The door came open when he drew it back.

"Go," he said.

Shay tossed him in the mini-Uzi, grabbed the woman's wrist as she rounded the bed, and dragged her to her feet. "Come on," she said harshly. "Lie there and you're going to die." She propelled the woman toward the corridor on the other side of the door, using a lock-step grip that she knew had to be painful, but she had no time to waste being gentle.

"Don't hurt me," the woman said in a small voice.

"I'm not going to hurt you," Shay said. "I'm with the Houston Police Department. I'm here to get you out." She glanced over her shoulder, saw the ninja reach into his pocket and scatter a handful of objects over the floor. Then he lobbed a smoke grenade into the room. Inky black smoke filled the closed quarters. "Run," Shay ordered.

The woman ran blindly, bouncing off the walls in her haste to escape.

Shay paused in front of the small elevator, punched the control panel and hoped it wasn't coded. The cage clunked smoothly into motion. While she waited, she checked the direction deck, but found no schematics for the top floor or the elevator. "What's your name?" she asked the woman as she shoved her into the open elevator.

"Kris," she said, hiccuping in fear. "Kris Tackett."

"Listen to me, Kris," Shay said with as much authority as she could. "Listen to me and do what I tell you to, and we're going to get you out of this alive."

Garbled, angry voices came from the hidden room, punctuated suddenly by yells of pain as men screamed about their feet.

Instantly Shay knew what the ninja had thrown on the floor had been the spiked balls designed for disabling an enemy. Maybe Carey's security force wore bulletproof armor, but their shoe soles didn't have the same defense. It had bought them a little more time.

She nodded at the ninja and saw him working the special code button sewn into his hood. When she glanced at the control panel, she saw there was only one button. She punched it, and the doors closed as the first bullets slammed into the walls from the sluggish security team. "Doesn't go anywhere but up," she said. She didn't think that was a good sign.

The ninja didn't comment, just kept his sword loose in his hand. Kris slumped against the back wall of the cage, tears running down her face.

"I have no idea what's waiting for us up there," Shay said. The ninja gave her a silent nod.

With a quiet hiss, the elevator came to a stop and the doors swished open.

The room was huge, sunk in the middle around a conversation group. Three other conversation areas were staggered around the tiers. Paintings adorned three of the walls. To her left, the fourth wall was clear and opened up on a magnificent view overlooking Houston.

Nothing moved inside.

"There's a door," the ninja whispered.

Shay saw it, barely recessed into the wall across the den. All it represented was another possibility, no promise of safety. She held the Glock in her fist and used her arm to block the door open and keep it from closing. She could tell from the frequent attempts it made to shut that the group below were trying to call the cage down again.

"Staying here isn't an option," the ninja pointed out.

"I know," Shay said irritably. She stepped into the den and pulled Kris behind her. The woman didn't come easily or willingly.

The ninja followed, pausing long enough to jam a throwing knife into the elevator doors so they couldn't close and allow the cage the lower.

In motion now, Shay picked up the pace. Kris stumbled and almost fell as she dragged the woman along. They skirted the outer edge of the central den area, staying along the upper perimeters and circling toward the door. Shay accessed the com-chip, giving up all hope of escaping quietly in the chaos to fight again. She tried a police emergency band and received a painful squelch that reverberated inside her skull. She was unable to transmit beyond the building.

The door was unlocked when she reached it. The hallway beyond was cloaked in shadows, unlit even by emergency lights.

Shay took the lead. Kris followed more closely now, obviously encouraged by the possibility she recognized for escape. A shadow stepped out from the others and moved into the periphery of Shay's vision. "Look out!" she yelled. She whirled, pushed Kris to the floor, and tried to bring the 10mm into target acquisition.

Hissing ruby-and-gold electricity slashed from a disruptor,

sizzled into the Glock, and sent it spinning out of her numbed hands.

"Beth!" the ninja said. His concern was evident.

Dazed, Shay sank to her knees, tried to will feeling back into her hands. The Glock was canted against the wall to her left, just beyond arm's reach.

Backlit from the moonlight spilling into the den at the other end of the hall, the figure stepped out into the open in a martial arts crouch. It wasn't Almendariz. It took Shay a second glance to recognize the man as Víctor García, Carey's majordomo. The file had even contained Carey's quirk of calling each successive majordomo Welbourne, after the first man to occupy that post.

"You will stay," García said. "Mr. Carey wants very much to see you."

With an economy of motion, the ninja whipped his sword out and struck for the man's leg as he stood in the hallway.

García didn't move.

The blade clanged when it struck the leg. It lodged, held fast.

The ninja released it and stepped back.

García gave them a very white grin. "Bionics." He flexed the leg, knocked the sword away with his hand. "Impressive, yes?" Before anyone could move, he set himself and spun, swinging the leg out in a roundhouse kick.

The ninja blocked it with an upraised arm, unable to defend himself any other way. The forearm splintered with audible cracking.

García moved in for the kill.

Shay forced herself into movement, reaching for the Glock with unfeeling fingers and closing them around the gunbutt. She spun, put her shoulder to the wall, and fumbled for the trigger.

Before she could get off a shot, the ninja's uninjured arm flicked out. A pair of spikes flitted from the ends of his fingers and imbedded deeply in García's forehead.

Trickles of blood dripped down into García's eyebrows. He gasped in surprise, then died on his feet, fell to the floor in sections on his face, slamming the spikes even more deeply into his brain.

Shay glanced at the ninja's arm. The way it hung at his side showed that it had a compound fracture that would require surgical expertise to reassemble. Blood gleamed wetly on the black material.

"Get on your feet," she told the woman. She aided her clumsily, still unable to feel her hands. She looked at the ninja. "Do you need help?"

"No. I can manage. Are you all right?"

"Yes." Shay's attention was taken away by a movement at the opposite end of the corridor. A half-dozen security guards poured into the hallway. She turned, shoving Kris ahead of her. "Back," she ordered. "We're blocked."

Staggering but stubbornly holding on to his sword, the ninja let them go by, taking up rear guard.

Shay's mind raced, turning over options. Going down in the elevator was out, but she had to wonder if there was a way to get on top of the roof. She didn't know where they'd go from there, but at least it gave them more running room. She shoved Kris ahead of her as they ran back into the den, totally locked on the elevator. The noise behind her didn't register until it was too late.

Pneumatic hisses ripped through the echoing noise streaming from the hallway they'd just left.

Shay flung her free arm out to wrap around the woman, stuck out a foot and tripped her, made her go down instantly on the carpet. Kris screamed in pain. Continuing her movement, Shay struggled to make her numbed hand obey and bring the Glock on line.

A glance showed her the steel door that had dropped into place and shut the hallway off. Then thunder rolled and a foot-long muzzle flash licked out at the ninja as he turned to face the man waiting beside the door.

Propelled with deadly force, the ninja came up off his feet as at least three bullets struck him. He tumbled over and came to a flailing halt facedown on the carpet.

Almendariz stepped into the pool of light seeping through the window wall. Smoke curled from the barrel of the big pistol he held centered on Shay's chest. It didn't waver. "Put the gun down, bitch."

Shay froze. The gun in her hand felt as if it were a million miles away. "Carey?" she asked.

The mocking smile that played on Almendariz's perfect lips had never belonged to the priest, nor did the excited sheen that filled the blue eyes. "Put the gun down *now*. Or make your play and see if you're fast enough. I'm betting you're not."

Relaxing her hold on the Glock, Shay started to pitch it to the side.

"Here," Carey ordered, indicating the floor in front of him. "Slowly."

Kris was blubbering in big, racking sobs that shook her whole body. She sat on her folded knees, wrapping her arms around herself.

Underhanded, Shay tossed the 10mm to the floor. It thumped to a stop inches from his feet.

"Almendariz is gone," Carey stated. "He fought me, and I lost him somewhere out there." He waved into the air. "He may even be dead. If he's not, it'll be a very long time before I can find him and bring him back to me."

Shay held her arms at her sides and tried to concentrate on her breathing, forcing the air out and inhaling naturally. The Semmerling derringer holstered on her right ankle was a comfortable weight, but it was too far away to do any good if Carey chose to use the gun.

Someone beat on the door, tried to force it.

Shay felt the buzz of com-chip accession inside her head, listened to the noise on the other side of the door fade away, and knew that Carey had communicated with his people.

Carey knelt and picked up the Glock. Crossing the room, he dropped it into an incinerator shaft built into the wall. The pistol banged and rattled as it disappeared down the chute.

Shay turned slowly, staying with the man. The elevator cage was still open, jammed by the throwing knife. She knew there must be another way into the room. It was possible that she could make it to the cage and rip the knife out, maybe even close the doors before Carey shot her. But it would mean leaving the woman and Hideo's man with Carey. She had no doubts what Carey would do to them. And the floor below might offer no escape either.

"You know what I feel, don't you?" Carey asked. There was more of an edge to his voice now. "The thrill of the hunt. Knowing you've got your prey in your sights. That's what drew you here tonight, isn't it?"

"I was doing my job," Shay replied.

Carey grinned with Almendariz's lips, but Shay was sure

it was a smile that had never been seen on the priest's face. "Lies. I know that you were taken off the Ripper case by your captain. I've been watching you, Detective Shay, watching as you and your partner helped me find him. I'd planned on staying ahead of you, counted on the bureaucratic bullshit of the police department to give me the time I needed to acquire him. Instead, you very nearly took him from me."

"You had Keever killed that night," Shay said.

"Yes. And I was on hand for the experience."

"You son of a bitch."

Carey cocked a blond eyebrow at her, looked like a smirking angel in Almendariz's body. "See? Add a little anger, something you can use as justification, and the predator comes out in you too."

Shay forced herself to remain silent. She accessed the com-chip, pulsed a steady broadcast on the police emergency band, but knew it went no further than the dampening field surrounding the building.

"You may not admit it to yourself," Carey said, "but you like the scent of blood. It calls out to you the same way it calls out to me, and the way it called out to the priest. You hold yours in check. Almendariz let his desire hold him in thrall, found religious reasonings that allowed him to explain away his behavior. But me . . ." He grinned. "As for me, I enjoy the killing. There's nothing like it." He reached into his pocket and took out a lock-back hunting knife. With practiced ease, he flipped it open with one hand. The blade was wicked, sharp and thick and unrelenting, bathed to a crisp sheen by the moonlight streaming through the window wallscreen. "And I especially enjoy it close up, when I can take my time."

Maneuvering for room, still holding her hands out before her in a nonthreatening gesture, Shay walked away from the crumpled, sobbing heap that was Kris Tackett. She was conscious of the lip of the den less than a foot behind her. One misstep would send her tumbling down the incline.

"But you took that away from me tonight," Carey said. "I waited for years for someone like Almendariz. Do you know what it's like to be a ghost?"

"No," Shay said, stalling for time.

"I do," Carey said softly. "I've spent decades trapped in that matrix, wired into my memories, unable to really experience life the way I wanted to. Almendariz provided a conduit back into that existence. He allowed me to know the passion again. Now you've taken him away." He lowered the pistol, dropped it to the ground behind him, and took up the knife in his other hand. "You're going to die very slowly for that, whether I enjoy it or not."

Seizing her chance, Shay dropped to one knee, lifted her pants leg, and tried for the Semmerling. The restraining strap held it fast, and her fingers were too clumsy to remove it.

Without a sound, Carey took two running steps and launched himself at her.

Abandoning the gun for the moment, Shay tried to avoid the man but couldn't. His arms closed around her, followed by the sudden impact of his full weight. Her breath coughed from her lungs. A low-slung sofa caught her across her lower thighs and they toppled over together.

They landed on a real wood coffee table that smashed beneath their combined weight.

Shay muffled a cry of pain, thought she felt a couple of ribs go, and wondered if her lungs had been punctured. Instinctively she closed a hand around Carey's knife wrist. The man was stronger than she was, but she used leverage to twist the knife away for the moment and remove the threat.

They rolled in the wreckage of the coffee table, then slid over another edge.

Taking advantage of the battering as it loosened Carey's hold on her, Shay drew a leg up between them and kicked out. It didn't cause much damage, but it did allow her to get free. She continued rolling, unable to keep from crying out as the successive drops further injured her side.

She scrambled, aware that Carey had stopped. She pushed herself to her feet at the bottom of the den with difficulty. Letting her training take over, she dropped into a defensive posture, assuming a side stance with her open hands up and her knees slightly bent. She knew she didn't have time to go for the hideaway gun again.

Carey took a moment to steady himself on a plush chair. Blood from his torn lip dripped onto the expensive fabric. Unconsciously he ripped the hunting blade into the chair's back, shredding stuffing out onto the floor. "Do you feel it?" he asked. "I see by the way you're standing. You think you can take me whether I have the knife or not. But don't fool yourself. You have to think that way now. You have no choice." He took a slow step down. "But I know better. You're dead. You just haven't realized it yet."

Shay tried to make her voice sound confident and harder. "Then come and get me, you psycho bastard."

"Trying to anger me?" Carey asked good-naturedly. "It's a good tactic. But it won't work. Anger, like lust and other predatory instincts, requires passion. Since you took Almendariz out of the picture, I don't have that." He stopped in front of her and lifted the knife so the moonlight glinted off it.

Shay uncoiled like a snapped spring and threw a roundhouse kick at Carey's head. He partly blocked the blow with his shoulder. She whirled and kicked again, landing once more. But neither attack had the effect that she was expecting.

Carey was bleeding from an ear. Crimson stained his teeth when he leered at her. "Not my body," he said. "Makes it easy for me to pull back and shut the pain down. You're going to have to cripple me to stop me."

Feinting with her hands, Shay kicked out again, aiming at Carey's face.

His free hand closed around her foot with crushing force. Effortlessly he jerked her off her feet and pushed her onto her back. Before she could attempt to get up, he was on top of her. The knife blade halted a half inch from her bared throat. His breath was warm against her face. She smelled the coppery blood on his breath. "Do you feel it?" he asked. "How very close you are to death right now?"

Shay started to move.

"No," Carey admonished. "Don't do that." The naked blade kissed the skin of her throat with enough force to spill warm blood across her neck.

Trembling, Shay forced her hands to uncurl from his clothing.

"You're on the edge of death," Carey said reverently, "about to go tumbling over the precipice into free-fall. How does it feel?"

"Go fuck yourself," Shay said.

"Defiance," Carey said. "Another trait of a good predator. You can't know when to give up. If you learned that, you wouldn't be the hunter that you are. And you're good. I have to admire that in you." He moved the point of the knife blade, traced the soft underside of her chin. "You have so many admirable points."

Her stomach twisted suddenly when she felt the blunt outline of his erection against her leg.

Bending his head down, Carey kissed her, his lips burning hot against the blood staining her neck. "Maybe," he whispered, "maybe the priest isn't so very far from us now." He kissed her again, sucking on her flesh till it hurt. "And since it was your doing, maybe it's only right that you *should* be the one to bring him back."

On the verge of retching, Shay swept her hand up, her first and second fingers twisted together, and thrust it into Carey's eye socket. The organ pulped under the sudden pressure and splattered across her face. Penetration wasn't complete. She held her breath, tense and ready, expecting the knife blade to rake across her throat.

Instead, Carey reeled back and clapped his hand to his ruined eye. Blood ran down his face. "You bitch!" he roared.

While he was off-balance, Shay twisted and leveraged his weight off her. Before she could get to her feet, her breath burning her lungs like a bellows pump, Carey came at her with wild swings of the knife.

The blade caught the sleeve of her windbreaker, slit it and cut the skin beneath.

Carey took his hand away from his face. Streamers of blood ran down his face and neck and dripped onto his shoulder. He smiled. "It doesn't hurt if I don't want it to. And I don't want it to. Eyes can be replaced."

Shay dodged back, barely able to avoid the knife as it slashed at her midsection. She fell up the incline leading to the wallscreen.

"Don't run," Carey said. "We're just getting started." He moved after her rapidly, jumped over fallen and broken furniture littering the tiers.

Her breath broken and harsh in her ears, Shay paused at the top of the pit and knelt, trying for the Semmerling again. Her fingers felt better, not quite as numb.

Like a ghost, Carey flitted through the wreckage strewn along the sides of the den's incline. The hunting blade was the only bright part of him.

The derringer came free in Shay's hands. She took a tight grip, rested the butt on her left hand, raked the safety off with her thumb, and took up the trigger slack. "Stop!" she commanded. The barrel barely protruded past her curled knuckle, but she knew Carey would see the yawning mouth.

An uncertain look quivered into place into Carey's borrowed features. He slowed to a stop almost eight feet from Shay. The hunting knife danced erratically in his fist at his waist. His good eye bored into hers. "Can you do it?" he asked in a dry whisper. "Can you shoot me?"

Shay lifted the Semmerling with menacing authority and got to her feet. She wished her knees didn't tremble. "If I have to. That's your call."

"Is it?" Carey laughed. "You forget: I've researched you. You're a natural predator, Detective. You love the thrill of the hunt, love the chase. But you don't have a taste for killing, do you?"

Shay held the Semmerling centered on Carey's chest.

"You and the priest are alike in that respect," Carey said. He took a step forward.

Shay fired, putting the round between Carey's feet. It gouged the carpet.

Carey stopped. "You should kill me."

"Not unless I have to."

"You're afraid of it, aren't you?" Carey asked. His smile mocked her. "You're afraid you'll learn to like it. You've killed four men, Shay. How many more is it going to take before you realize your own appetite?"

Shay's elbows felt weak. It took everything she had to keep the derringer from shaking. Perspiration leaked into her eyes and made them sting.

"You can't stop me," Carey said.

"Yes, I will. I have."

"Have you?" He slid his foot forward, prepared to take another step.

"Everyone's going to know about you. People are already starting to look."

"That can be taken care of. They couldn't catch me all those years ago. They won't catch me now. And even if they did, this city needs me and my financial influence to survive the Japanese economic invasion." Carey put his weight on his forward foot and took another step. "There's only one way you can stop me."

Shay took a step back and felt her grip on the Semmerling weaken in spite of herself. Four people were dead by her hand now. Maybe five if Almendariz was truly lost. A dark part of her wanted to pull the trigger and shoot Carey, and that part scared the hell out of her. An unexplained buzzing tickle flared to life in her com-chip.

"Too late," Carey said softly.

A bomb blast seemed to go off inside Shay's head. She felt it jet free of the com-chip and go ricocheting across the inside of her skull. Nausea swelled up inside her, violently twisting her stomach. Double vision made it hard to track Carey as he went into motion. She fired, but knew instantly that she'd missed the man. There were three shots left in the clip, and it would take too long to get the spare magazine strapped to her ankle.

You should have killed me. Carey's voice echoed inside her head, amplified by the com-chip.

Pain quaked throughout Shay's head and down her spine. She circled to her left, away from Carey and felt like she was moving in molasses. He was no longer afraid of the gun. The knife gleamed brightly.

You're a sheep, Carey taunted, **playing at being a lion. You should have given yourself over to your instincts.**

Thoughts flooded Shay's mind.

Behind the dark silhouette that was Felix Carey, the wallscreen changed, became a collage of the four men she'd killed in her years on the police department. The Scivally brothers figured prominently. Aaron Scivally was depicted in frozen rage as he pointed his gun at her in the deserted parking garage that night.

I can know you, Carey said. **Know you in ways that you don't even know yourself. And I know that you're afraid. More afraid of yourself than you are of me.**

Other images flickered through her brain, revealing pieces of things Shay was sure Carey would have wanted to remain unknown. She was deluged by images of the women he'd killed over the years, watched the work of the knife as he carved the bleeding rose into their skin and experienced his need to find Almendariz before anyone knew for sure who the priest was. However Carey had arranged the cybernetic hookup through the building's matrix via the com-chip in her head, it wasn't a one-way circuit.

She also learned about the false wall in the den.

**You have to ask yourself if I'm going to be the one

that's going to change you into something like me,** Carey said. **You're going to die never knowing.**

He came at her, letting the knife lead him, the light from the wallscreen reflecting liquidly in his empty eye socket.

Shay moved in response. Rather than depending totally on her blurred vision, she gave herself over to her martial-arts training. Her empty hand closed on Carey's sleeve and she shifted weight instantly, guiding him over her outstretched leg.

The knife scored a shallow furrow along her ribs and brought an electric jolt of pain with it.

Then Carey was going past her, propelled by the force of her throw to impact heavily against the wallscreen. He cried out in unexpected pain and slid down briefly before he caught himself.

The fuzzy vision cleared and the headache went away as Shay raised the Semmerling. "You're wrong," she said, more for herself than for Carey. "You hunt because you want to. I hunt because I can, because sometimes it's a necessary thing. Not because I like it."

Carey launched himself from the wallscreen, knife held high as he charged her.

Shay stood her ground, no longer doubting, no longer afraid of herself. There was no confusion about what she had to do. She fired the remaining three rounds in the Semmerling's clip.

All three .45 rounds caught the man in the chest, hurling him back into the wallscreen. A shocked look froze on his ruined features. He sank to the floor and left three bloody blossoms spreading on the cracked surface of the wallscreen across the still of Aaron Scivally.

Grimly, Shay ejected the spent clip and retrieved the spare from her ankle holster. It clicked into place. She crossed the floor to Amendariz's body, held the pistol on it, and checked for a pulse. There wasn't one. She stood and looked at the wall on the other side of the den. "Do you hear me, Carey?"

The silence of the room echoed around her.

She walked along the outer perimeters of the den, staying with the top level. Blood trickled under her shirt and warmed her side.

At the opposite wall, she reached for the hidden button and pressed it. A section of the wall slid away, revealing the gleaming machinery beyond. Tanks of nutrient fluids swirled in the tangle of life-support systems and hoses. Something dark and visceral floated in the tanks.

"Carey," Shay called.

The thumping at the steel door was resumed.

"Can you hear me, you son of a bitch?" she asked as she raised the Semmerling.

To her right a small monitor flicked to life. Felix Carey's face looked out at her. He no longer looked confident. "What are you doing?"

"I wanted you to know I hadn't forgotten about you," Shay said. "The *real* you. That tangle of dying brain cells and spinal cord tucked away in those chemical vats." She aimed the derringer at the main vat and thought she could see an eyeball floating somewhere in the witch's brew.

"You can't do anything to me!" Carey screamed. "I'm helpless in there!"

Shay shook her head. "I don't think so."

"Shay—"

"How does it feel being the prey for a change?" Shay asked.

"You'll be committing murder!"

"No. Actually you've been dead for a very long time. You just haven't admitted it." Shay pulled the trigger and emptied the clip in a string of explosions.

Fluids gushed from the shattered vat tanks and ran across the floor, splashing over Shay's shoes. Something plopped on the floor with a meaty smack.

"Welcome to the real world, asshole," she said harshly. The Semmerling hung hard and heavy at her side. She turned as the steel door came tumbling down, expecting to see Carey's private security force. She was surprised to see Hideo and his team instead.

Hideo ran to the fallen ninja already in the room, knelt beside him, and gently lifted his head into his lap.

"How is he?" Shay asked, staying away, knowing Hideo's people wouldn't let her near the man.

"Alive," Hideo replied.

"He was shot."

"His vest protected him." Hideo waved at his men, and they started to retreat.

"Be careful of his arm," Shay said. "It's broken pretty badly."

"Hai." Hideo gathered the man into his arms as a father would a child, then stood up easily in spite of the weight.

"Take care of him," Shay said.

"Hai." Hideo carried the ninja out, surrounded by his black-clad shock troops.

After they were gone, Shay pocketed the derringer and walked over to where Kris Tackett lay on the floor. She sat down beside the woman, drew her into her arms, and tried to calm her. Shay had no doubt that Carey's security teams had been routed by the ninjas. She had no trouble accessing her com-chip and broadcasting to the police dispatch. She asked that Espinoza be on hand when the investigators arrived on the scene. She clicked out of the band before the dispatch officer could ask many questions. They'd be asked later, and she didn't have all of the answers. She rocked Kris as if she were Keiko suffering through a night terror.

"Is it over?" Kris asked in a broken voice.

Shay glanced at the dark hollow in the den wall, saw the reflections on the pools of nutrient fluids on the floor and in the carpet. "Yes," she said. "It's over now." She distanced herself from the whirl of emotions inside her and waited. It seemed as if it took a very long time for Espinoza to get there, but it really wasn't.

46

"So internal affairs isn't bringing any charges against you for breaking and entering," Ryan Shay asked, "even though they know that's what you did?"

Taking another handful of popcorn from the bag on the park bench beside her, Bethany Shay said, "Right." She flung the popcorn out before her, scattering it across the placid surface of the pond only a few feet away. The motion stung for a moment, pulling at the cut on her side.

The fluffy kernels struck the water and floated. At least two dozen ducks of various colors attacked them with angry swishings of beaks and quacks of frustrated rebuke.

"But Espinoza knows you went in there on your own?" her father asked.

"Yeah." Shay sat back against the bench and tried to relax. The afternoon sun warmed her and countered the chill of the memories of that night in Felix Carey's building. That had been four very busy days ago. The hours had seemed compressed into each other, till they'd passed in a bone-weary blur. Today was the first day she'd really had to spend free of the job.

The excited voices of children floated across the flat water. Running feet slapped against the concrete path. After last night's rain, the playground toys looked bright and new again. The air smelled fresh, clean.

If she hadn't felt so empty and drained, she realized, she'd probably be enjoying herself. Maybe it would have been better if she'd stayed home, but she hadn't cleared the faces of the dead women from the walls yet. It was just that the park reminded her so damn much of Keiko it hurt.

"Espinoza knows the real story," she said as she threw more popcorn. "So do the DA's people and most of the top brass."

"But they're not going to touch the truth?" her father asked.

"No. Not as long as this story holds together and the witness stays firm about contacting me with information about Carey's involvement with Almendariz. The board of directors managing Carey's assets aren't too keen on Carey International's being dragged through the media any more than it has to be. This way it looks like a loyal employee concerned only about the welfare of the corporation stepped forward and brought in police intervention."

"And you never knew this guy who claimed he gave you the lowdown on Carey and Almendariz?"

"No. He came forward that same night, but I didn't meet him for the first time until two days later. He already had my schedule, knew when I was alone these last few weeks, so the times and dates he gave Espinoza and the others didn't conflict with anything they knew or could be found out."

"Guy was well informed."

Shay nodded. She threw another handful of popcorn, watched the ducks paddle furiously in pursuit.

"And everyone bought it?"

"The people that don't know what really happened? Oh, yeah. Once the police department and the DA's office got their PR machine behind the guy's story, it *became* the truth."

Ryan Shay shifted, squinted his eyes against the sun. "Do they know about Kiyoshi's involvement, or the involvement of his people?"

"No."

"But you think Kiyoshi was responsible for the witness coming forward?"

"Yes."

"Why?"

"I don't know." She shrugged. "I guess it just feels right. I also heard that Izutsu made hostile-takeover noises at Carey International behind the scenes and pulled those people into line."

"What does Kiyoshi want?"

"I haven't a clue," Shay admitted. "I've already laid everything on the table that I had to offer." The missing weight of the shield in her pocket bothered her. It sat at home in the manila envelope with her letter of resignation. She intended to deliver both to Espinoza on Monday.

"With all the pushing he's been doing," Ryan Shay said, "the guy's got to want something."

Shay gave her father a small grin. "From the way I hear it, Kiyoshi hasn't been alone in pressing for my exoneration. I've been told that a certain ex-cop has been bending the ear of every media person he could, and threatening a few highly placed political and police officials with hints of blackmail if charges were leveled against me."

"Rumors," Ryan Shay said with a straight face. "Nasty, vicious things. You should never pay attention to them."

"So I've been told."

Ryan Shay laced his fingers and dropped them in his lap. "You did a good job. You figured this thing out, and you stuck to it until you saw it through. I'm proud of you. On the other hand, part of me would like to bend you over my knee for taking so damn many chances."

Shay nodded. "I know. But it was worth it, Dad."

He reached over, took her hand, and squeezed it. "The things worth doing usually are."

She tried to take solace in her father's words, but so much had been lost. She still woke up some mornings thinking she could go talk everything over with Keever, then remembered he was dead.

"Looks like the other shoe's about to drop," Ryan Shay said.

Shay looked away from the ducks and saw the black limousine approaching on the side road. It stopped at the curbside fifty yards away. The driver got out and trotted to the back door, sharp-looking in his black livery, unmistakably Japanese. "Kiyoshi," she said. She folded the popcorn bag closed and stood up, not really knowing how she was supposed to feel.

Kiyoshi stepped out of the rear. He was dressed in a dark business suit and sunglasses. He looked immaculate, except for the dark sling supporting his right arm. Reaching back into the limousine, he took Keiko by the hand and helped her out. He paused to point Shay out.

"His arm," Ryan Shay said.

"Broken," Shay replied in a hoarse whisper. She stared at her daughter, so pretty and clean in her pink short set, so very innocent.

Keiko waved excitedly.

Shay waved back, couldn't hold in the tears, felt them go sliding down her face.

Kneeling, Kiyoshi spoke briefly with his daughter, eyes at the same level as hers, then hugged her tight and stood up. They bowed to each other, then Keiko was running for Shay as fast as her little legs would carry her.

Unable to hold back, Shay dropped the popcorn and ran for her daughter, swept her up in her arms, and held her tight. Her hair smelled of herbs. The tears came freely now, but she couldn't help but laugh at the same time. She looked past Keiko's shoulder and saw Kiyoshi getting back into the limousine.

"Mama-san," Keiko said, "I have a message from Papa-san, but I am not sure what it means."

Shay looked into her daughter's eyes. "Okay, little one."

"He made me learn this."

"Yes."

"Papa-san says you should do what your heart tells you to in your work. He says that he was wrong about your reasons. He told me that he thinks you are a samurai, and that you know only honor. You are free of your promise to him."

Shay glanced back at the limousine, but it was already disappearing into the traffic.

"What does it mean?" Keiko asked.

"It means," Shay said as she hugged her daughter, "that I'm going to get to see you more. And right now, that's all I really care to think about."

If you and/or a friend would like to receive the *ROC Advance*, a bimonthly newsletter featuring all the newest and hottest ROC books and authors, on a complimentary basis, please fill out this form and return it to:

ROC Books/Penguin USA
375 Hudson Street
New York, NY 10014

Your Address

Name _____

Street _____ Apt. # _____

City _____ State _____ Zip _____

Friend's Address

Name _____

Street _____ Apt. # _____

City _____ State _____ Zip _____